ENEMIES

"You may call me Lucius."

Lucius. It fit him. A bold name, but not a rough one. Rhiannon was drawn to the sound of it in spite of a fierce wish to snap the thread of fate that joined her soul to his. She shifted backward on the bed, away from him. No matter what he was called, no matter what connection his kinsman's blood had forged between them, he was her enemy.

The heat in his gaze told Rhiannon that he desired her and the knowledge of it filled her with dread. Her captor was above all a man, and like all men, he would take what he wanted. But she would not yield easily.

She kept her expression neutral. "How is your arse, *Lucius,* where it was struck by my arrow?"

CELTIC FIRE

JOY NASH

LOVE SPELL NEW YORK CITY

To my mother, who first showed me the stars.
And to my husband, who believes I can reach them.

LOVE SPELL®

June 2005

Published by

Dorchester Publishing Co., Inc.
200 Madison Avenue
New York, NY 10016

ISBN 0-505-52639-5

The name "Love Spell" and its logo are trademarks of Dorchester Publishing Co., Inc.

Printed in the United States of America.

Visit us on the web at www.dorchesterpub.com.

CELTIC
FIRE

Prologue

Northern Britannia, 116 A.D.

The Roman refused to die.

His screams spiked through the clearing, but any who might have come to his aid were beyond the echoes of his cries. He spun, staggering, his fingers clenched on the iron blade jutting from his belly. The sword's hilt protruded from his back.

He reeled toward Rhiannon, then away, his bare feet slapping the ground. His naked torso jerked and shuddered. Blood trickled down his chin. Gurgled words followed.

Curse or prayer?

Rhiannon drew her cloak tightly about her shoulders. She understood the harsh language of the conquerors, but could make no sense of the man's garbled speech. Whatever his entreaty, it went unanswered. Jupiter, mightiest of the Roman gods, had forgotten his son this day.

The doomed man tottered forward, one hand extended. Rhiannon wrenched her gaze away and sought peace in the cool mist of the forest. Soft tufts of mistletoe clung to the autumn branches of the sacred oaks, but by

1

the light of the setting sun the crimson foliage reminded her of nothing so much as blood.

If only the prisoner did not have to die . . .

A futile wish. The man was a Roman wolf—his life was forfeit to Kernunnos, the Horned God. She'd come with the whole of her clan to witness her enemy's death. Yet if the choice had been hers to make, she would have set him free.

As if sensing her compassion, his soul tangled with hers, desperate, pleading. Her heart cleaved in two. Because Rhiannon had a healer's skill, her spirit often intertwined with those in pain. This Roman's touch was something more. Something she couldn't name.

Her heart broke as he loosed another keening cry. The wail shriveled to a groan, then a whisper. His body swayed. Shouts rose as Rhiannon's kin pressed forward, eager to witness death's victory. Would the enemy die looking at the sky, calling vengeance down upon his tormentors? Or would his mouth fill with dirt, foretelling the triumph of the clan?

Madog stepped to the fore, his pale cloak washed red in the glow of the sunset. Rhiannon had begged the Druid master to excuse her from the Rite of the Old Ones, but he'd refused. The freedom of the Brigantes hinged on his interpretation of the Roman commander's death dance. Rhiannon was the tribe's rightful queen. Her presence lent power to the augury.

The Roman sank to his knees. Madog circled behind, his gaze intent. The doomed man pitched forward and clutched Rhiannon's hem. She gasped and yanked at her skirt, but the Roman's fingers entwined in the wool and would not be dislodged.

"Tell him," he whispered on a groan; then his body went limp and he spoke no more.

Madog grasped the hilt of the killing sword with both hands. With a strength that belied his age, he heaved it overhead. Blood trickled down his bare arms.

"Kernunnos, the Horned One, is well pleased with his prize."

Chapter One

Assyria, Kalends of Januarius, 117 A.D.

"A real ghost wouldn't have to piss."

Lucius Ulpius Aquila skimmed a glance over the apparition hovering near his left elbow. The specter dropped the hem of its tunic, an apologetic smile playing about its pallid lips. Executing a graceful turn, it glided to a nearby boulder where an ethereal white mantle lay neatly folded. The transparent linen rippled in the desert air, passing under the figure's right arm and over its left shoulder. Pale fingers adjusted the garment's creases with utmost delicacy.

"And a real ghost certainly would not concern itself with the drape of its toga," Lucius observed.

The specter's shoulders lifted in a familiar, self-deprecating shrug. Lucius's chest tightened. The hallucination had been a faceless phantom when it first appeared two months before, but with each passing day its features and mannerisms grew more recognizable. Yet even if Lucius believed souls could drift out of Hades, Aulus could hardly come to haunt him.

Aulus was alive.

3

"You are a product of the desert sun," Lucius said, forcing a conversational tone. "Or perhaps the result of some Assyrian spice. A few more days and you'll be gone."

The apparition shook its head. It waved one hand toward Lucius, then gestured to the northwest. Aulus commanded a small frontier fort countless miles away in that precise direction.

"You wish me to journey north?"

The ghost nodded vigorously.

Lucius steeled himself. "To Britannia?"

The specter extended its right arm, fist clenched, thumb raised.

A chill raced up Lucius's spine. He closed his eyes and willed the apparition to vanish, but when he dared another look, it remained, regarding him with an expectant expression.

By Pollux. Was he losing his mind?

He wheeled about and strode toward the camp. Twilight had taken over the Assyrian desert with merciful swiftness, bringing blessed relief from the blistering heat. But far away, winter ice encased the forests of Britannia. When the ghost drifted closer, the chill of the northlands seeped into Lucius's bones.

He nodded to the sentry as he entered the encampment. Off-duty soldiers fell silent at his approach, resuming the throw of dice only after he'd passed. One man spiked two fingers in his direction—a sign against evil. Lucius scowled at the ghost. By the gods! Why could he not control the compulsion to converse with his damned hallucination?

"Move aside," he told it, and ducked into his tent.

An oil lamp flickered on the center table. Lucius took a steadying breath and lifted a bronze pitcher from the edge of a map detailing Emperor Trajan's invasion of the East. The papyrus curled back on itself.

He poured wine into a goblet and drank, his parched tongue barely tasting the fragrant liquid. He made a short circuit of his empty cell. No doubt his secretary would soon return from the cooking fires bearing a meal that would go uneaten.

The ghost lounged on a cot, inspecting its fingernails.

Lucius gripped the cup until his knuckles turned white. " 'There is no case in which the soul can act without involving the body,' " he quoted, but the words gave scant comfort. Aristotle, it was to be assumed, had not been prone to delirium.

The tent flap lifted, admitting Candidus and the aroma of roasted meat. The stone-faced, balding secretary set the tray on the table midway between the curled map and the pitcher. He nodded at a flat wooden box partially hidden by a round loaf.

"The post courier brought a message, my lord."

The ghost rose and drifted toward the table.

Lucius frowned and set his cup aside. "From Rome?"

"No, my lord." Candidus peered at the label on the sealbox. "From Britannia."

Every muscle in Lucius's body tensed.

Candidus lifted the sealbox lid, revealing a shallow compartment flooded with wax. The ghost bent its head over the impression left by the seal of the sender and went very still.

"From Tribune Quintus Vetus," Candidus said.

Lucius's breathing ran shallow. He slid his dagger from its sheath, sliced the wax from the edges of the box, and extracted the thin wooden tablet underneath. Tilting it into the lamplight, he read the concise message once, twice, and then a third time.

"Distressing news, my lord?"

He looked up, disoriented.

"My lord?" In an unprecedented display of familiarity, the older man touched Lucius's arm. Lucius dropped the tablet onto the tray. He gripped the edge of the table, fighting nausea more fiercely than he had ever fought a barbarian sword.

When at last he spoke, his voice held steady. "A report from the frontier fort Vindolanda. Aulus has been . . ."

He broke off, inhaled, and began again.

"Tribune Vetus sends notice. My brother is dead."

Full Moon of Cutios, 117 A.D.

"Does the pain bother ye still?"

Rhiannon pressed her palm to her brother's chest. Owein's cheeks were no longer flushed. His breath came steady, with no hint of the rasp that had struck terror into her heart the night before. She searched for the pulse at his neck. It was slow, steady, and his skin was cool. That was good.

He shook off her hand. "The sickness be gone, little mama. Dinna worry so. I drank the potion ye brewed and your magick worked, as it always does."

"The magick is nay my own. It belongs to Briga."

"The Great Mother smiles on ye then, for when I woke my breath came easily." He leaned forward and kissed her cheek.

Rhiannon's heart melted as it had when she'd first held Owein in her arms fifteen winters past. She'd been a girl of nine and grieving for her mother, but the tiny babe had sparked a flame of joy. Russet curls so like her own clung to her brother's neck, but his eyes were his own: bluer than the sky and sparkling with mischief.

She ruffled his hair.

"Nay, stop," he protested, but his lips curved in a grin.

Rhiannon smiled back. Owein might have grown tall and muscular, with a man's beard sprouting on his chin, but the lad who had hidden his face in her skirts was not yet completely gone. "How is the ache in that thick head of yours?"

Owein's expression sobered. His gaze roamed the round-house, touching the center hearth and the high peak of the sloping roof timbers before he returned his attention to Rhiannon. "Tolerable enough," he said with a shrug.

His seeming lack of concern did nothing to allay Rhian-

6

non's anxiety. "The night vision returned despite my spell," she guessed. It was not a question.

"Aye. The same. Pain, then the dream. A raven in flight. Blood."

A chill hand gripped Rhiannon's heart. "An omen of death."

"Perhaps not. It might just as easily be a prophecy of power."

"Ye must tell Madog."

"I'm afeared to," Owein said. "He's not been . . ."

"Not been what?"

"Not . . . right, somehow. He schools me in the wisdom of the Old Ones as always, but I sense . . . I dinna know. A wrongness." He shoved his blanket aside. "Surely ye have felt it."

"Aye," she said. "I have." For nearly two seasons, since the Roman commander's death. She shivered, though the fire was warm. "I hoped the chill would fade with time."

"It grows stronger." Owein lowered his voice. "Madog visits the stones day and night. He talks to the skull."

An icy finger clawed Rhiannon's heart. She'd not been to the sacred circle since Samhain, when the Druid master had set the Roman's dripping skull atop a spike within the ring of stones.

" 'Tis not right," she said, gripping Owein's arm. "No soul should be imprisoned. Not even a Roman's."

" 'Twill be worth my own soul if the Rite of the Old Ones brings Kernunnos to aid our warriors," Owein replied grimly.

"Nay, do not speak so! Kernunnos is a dangerous ally. We are the Brigantes, the children of Briga. Madog would do better to seek the favor of the Great Mother. Not the dark powers of the Horned God."

As if summoned by her words, Madog's voice, strident but unintelligible, sounded from the yard beyond the hut's doorway.

Edmyg's booming speech answered. "—'tis nay my fault."

Owein scowled. "Nay, it never is. How can ye think to join with that hulking animal, Rhiannon? The entire clan knows Glynis is about to birth his bastard."

Rhiannon's hand stole to her flat stomach. "He seeks a son. I will not give him one."

"If Edmyg wants a son, he shouldna take ye as his mate. But he will, because his lust to be king is far greater than his honor."

"Madog blessed the match. Edmyg is the Brigantes' greatest warrior."

"Aye, and the tribe's greatest brute as well." The flash of a man's anger showed in Owein's young eyes. "You are queen, Rhiannon. He is nay fit to carry your cloak."

"The clan chieftains have put aside their differences to follow him."

"They'll follow another just as well."

"Nay. Niall has been dead less than a twelvemonth, but his memory is far from cold. If I do not accept my husband's brother as my new consort, the chieftains will be at each other's throats within a fortnight." She shook her head. " 'Twould be the greatest service to Rome I could perform. I canna risk it."

Owein opened his mouth to reply, then fell silent as the hut's wooden door scraped a path over the dirt floor. The spring wind sent a swirl of dust into the air.

Madog entered with Edmyg dogging his heels. "The clans must gather today, not on the morrow," the Druid muttered.

"Kynan's dun alone answers my call, and reluctantly at that," Edmyg replied, scowling. "The other chieftains will nay come while the moon of Cutios shines. They await the fires of Beltane."

"They be fools, then," replied Madog. "Cormac's message was clear. The new Roman commander arrives on the morrow afore the sun sets. Once he disappears behind the high walls of Vindolanda, we'll not be easily drawing him out again."

"He'll nay reach the fort," said Edmyg. "We'll attack on the road with the Horned God at our backs."

Madog stroked his white beard. "Kernunnos or no, we'll have need of every man in Kynan's dun and our own."

"We will have them." Edmyg's gaze lit on Owein. "The lad will come as well. 'Tis past time for his weaning."

Rhiannon sprang to her feet and drew herself up to her full height, which, to her misfortune, barely reached Edmyg's shoulder. "Owein cannot join ye. He's weak still."

"He'll ne'er be strong if ye persist in coddling him," Edmyg retorted. He took a step toward her.

Owein jerked to his feet and stepped between them, the sudden movement causing him to sway. Rhiannon put out her hand to steady him, but he brushed it off and looked at Edmyg. "My sister is forgetting I am a man grown. I'll accompany ye."

"Ye serve her well in this, lad," Madog said. "We'll be driving the Romans south afore the next snow." He lowered himself to a stool by the fire and nodded for Edmyg to do the same. Owein took a third seat.

"Rhiannon will sit the throne of her grandmother," the Druid continued. "Ye'll erase the memory of her shame, lass, once the Romans are gone."

"Aye," Rhiannon said. She'd been weaned on tales of redeeming Cartimandua's folly. Two generations past, the great queen of the Brigantes had spurned one king in favor of a less popular consort, plunging the clans into civil war. In the end, only the Romans had benefited. Another reason why Rhiannon could not spurn Edmyg, despite his perfidy. She would not repeat her grandmother's selfish mistake.

Now a new war approached, one in which the clans would unite against the conquerors. Bloodshed was as certain as the sun's rising. The thought of the Brigantes' crossing swords with the formidable Roman army left Rhiannon sick with dread. How many of her kin would perish?

"Now then, have ye food and *cervesia* for an old man?"

Rhiannon nodded, not trusting herself to speak. She took the flask of barley beer from its hook and filled three mugs. She set them on the low table, then moved to the cauldron and ladled the remains of the past evening's stew into wooden bowls. Taking up her own portion, she joined the men by the fire.

Edmyg used a barley bannock to retrieve a hunk of meat from his bowl. "We'll take the Romans where the road crosses the fens," he said, chewing around a large mouthful. He washed the stew down with a swig of *cervesia*, straining the liquid through his blond moustache. A portion dribbled onto the braids in his beard. "The forest is dark there even at midday."

Rhiannon put her meal aside, her meager appetite now completely gone. The fens were a day's journey to the south. If Edmyg meant to be in the marshes tomorrow, he would have to travel through the night. Owein's breathing had eased, but his strength was still fragile. The journey, coupled with a battle, would surely bring on a relapse.

But Edmyg's will was set, as was Owein's, who was determined to prove himself more than a lad. And the Great Mother knew a woman had little hope of shoveling sense into a man's head when it was filled with thoughts of war.

As the sun rose into a line of clouds, the clan gathered in the muddy yard to prepare for the raid. The honing wheel turned, scattering sparks from iron blades. Above, the pointed roofs of the roundhouses scratched the gray sky. A wall of logs ringed the huts, capping the crest of a steep hill. The palisade would protect the women while their men fought.

A raven sailed into view overhead, then disappeared just as quickly. Rhiannon shivered. The creature of Owein's vision. Did it foretell victory or death?

She plunged her frayed willow twig into a wooden bowl and mixed the woad and water with savage strokes. Her hand painted blue swirls on Edmyg's face and chest. When his protection was complete, she turned to Owein, murmuring a fervent prayer with each pass of her brush. She rubbed a mixture of lime and clay in his hair and drew the curls into spikes.

The warriors gathered outside the palisade, spears and shields ready. Edmyg slung his battle horn onto his saddle and mounted his war pony. Though the men numbered no more than twenty, they were fierce, and—with the exception of Owein and one or two other lads—well honed for battle.

Edmyg raised his sword. "Death to Rome!"

He kicked his pony into a gallop. Madog, Owein and a handful of others followed on their own mounts, but the greater number ran afoot. They vanished into the forest in a heartbeat, leaving only a spatter of mud and the stale reek of hatred. Rhiannon hugged her arms to her chest as she walked back to the village with the women. The men of Kynan's dun would more than double the band. Would it be enough?

She bit back the taste of bile. Madog wanted the new Roman commander taken alive. If her kinsmen managed that feat, the Druid master would repeat the Rite of the Old Ones. A second Roman skull would overlook the ancient stone circle.

And Rhiannon's nightmares would begin anew.

Lucius pulled back on his stallion's reins and allowed his escort to advance on the road. The tattoo beat of the soldiers' footfalls didn't falter. The auxiliary unit marched in two columns, eight deep, with their centurion at the fore. An equal number brought up the rear. In the center, the remaining soldiers flanked a boy and an old man on horseback.

The road threaded a narrow valley crowded on either side by dense woods. An idyllic scene, but Lucius would have gladly traded it for the wind-scoured moorland he'd traversed the day before. Far better to freeze his ass in the open than to present an easy target in comfort.

He shot a glance to his left, where his younger brother rode in ghostly majesty, the hem of his toga trailing over the flank of an invisible mount. The specter had dogged Lucius's every step for near half a year, driving his well-ordered life into chaos.

Aulus hadn't been this annoying since childhood.

"Britannia leaves much to be desired," Lucius said. "I cannot fathom why you preferred this wild country to Rome."

Aulus looked away into the shadowed forest. Lucius's gaze followed. He detected no hint of movement, but he was not yet delusional enough to believe his passage went unnoticed. It was said the *Brittunculi* sprang as if from the earth. The half-naked, blue-painted wildmen struck like lightning, spewed death, then vanished into the mists like wraiths bound for Hades. Aulus had written of Britannia's beauty, but gazing into the depths of the ancient forest, Lucius sensed only malevolence.

His fingers tightened on the reins. The official report stated that A. Ulpius Aquila, commanding officer of the frontier fort Vindolanda, had died in a hunting accident. A plausible scenario, but Lucius was certain it was a lie. His younger brother had been no huntsman. His eyesight lacked a proper perception of depth, a handicap he'd kept secret since boyhood. Indeed, Aulus would have eschewed military service entirely if such an option had been possible for a senator's son. A strong suspicion of foul play, coupled with insistent prodding from his brother's ghost, had propelled Lucius north to investigate.

Aulus floated closer until he rode less than an arm's length away. A frigid aura rode with him.

"At the least, you could put on your uniform," Lucius said irritably. "Who in his right mind would ride all this way wearing a toga?"

Aulus shrugged.

"I suppose I should be grateful I haven't conjured a voice for you. I—"

"Father! Who are you talking to?"

Lucius turned to the small stranger who was his son. At ten years of age, Marcus sat his horse well and had been allowed to ride in the fore rather than with the wagons. He should have stayed in Rome, of course, but the boy had begged to come north, and with Julia so recently dead, Lucius hadn't had the heart to refuse. To Marcus's credit, he'd offered few complaints during the six weeks of hard travel.

Just endless questions.

"Who—"

"No one, Marcus."

"But I heard you."

"To myself, then." By the gods, the boy never let go of an inquiry without an answer. Lucius sent an annoyed glance past his son to Demetrius, but the old Greek physician who had been Lucius's own tutor merely raised his gaze to the sky.

"How much longer to the fort?" Marcus asked.

"We'll reach Vindolanda by nightfall."

Demetrius gathered his saffron mantle about his rigid shoulders. "Not a moment too soon, if you request my counsel on the matter."

"I don't remember asking for it," Lucius said.

"You should not have split the century," Demetrius continued, unperturbed. "We will be fortunate to escape with our hides when the barbarians fall on us."

"Forty men is a sufficient escort, my friend. The Celts rarely travel in large numbers. Besides, the repairs to the supply wagon will take only a few hours. The rear company will soon catch up with us."

"Let us hope they find us alive when they do."

Marcus stirred, his eyes shining with excitement. "What will we do if the blue warriors attack?"

"If Mars sends a battle, we will fight," Lucius replied.

"Even against the women?"

Lucius shook his head. To be sure, he'd heard tales of

13

Britannia's females taking to the battlefield with their men, but he could hardly believe such an arrangement was common. Did the wretched Celts not protect their women? He tried to imagine Julia fighting at his side, but the vision was too ludicrous to contemplate. A woman would be a deadly burden in battle.

"Be prepared for anything, Marcus," he said. "A Roman meets his fate with strength and fights with honor."

Marcus gripped the hilt of his small sword. "I'm ready."

Lucius hoped it would not come to that. The boy was a miserable swordsman.

The road dipped into mist-shrouded marshlands. Vapor rose from the black water to entangle the booted feet of the soldiers. The scent of decay clung to Lucius's nostrils. Willows nudged the oaks aside as the forest drew close to the road.

Too close. Unease clawed at his nape and his hand drifted to his sword hilt. Behind, the road curved to the right and disappeared. The damaged axle was taking longer to repair than anticipated. Could barbarians have attacked the rear company?

Lucius let his mount drift closer to Marcus and Demetrius. The road curved, bringing the Tyne into view. The swollen river had overflowed its bank and crept onto the paving stones.

When the spear sliced out of the shadows, it came so silently Lucius thought at first he had imagined it. Then a soldier lurched to one side, blood spurting from his neck. Aulus gestured like a madman toward the forest.

The blast of a battle horn rent the air, loosing a flood of shrieking barbarians. Lucius wrenched his sword from its sheath as the enemy poured from the trees like a raging river. One blue-faced demon lunged for Lucius's reins. He skewered the apparition and it fell, howling.

"Orbis!" he shouted.

The soldiers fell into a circle around the horses, shields

14

raised in a tight wall. Leaning, Lucius caught Marcus by the arm and hauled him off his mount. He dropped the boy on the road beside Demetrius, who had already flung himself to the ground. "Keep the beasts steady," he commanded.

Marcus clung to his mare's reins, for once without question.

Demetrius glowered his outrage. "I told you—"

"Later," Lucius replied, dodging a spear. Mounted, he made a fine target, but he took a moment to gauge the enemy force before snatching his shield from its saddle hook and swinging from his stallion's back. The Celts numbered, incredibly, more than fifty men. His best tactic was to stand firm and hack them to pieces, one body at a time.

He muscled into the orb formation between the centurion and one of the foot soldiers. The officer shot him a startled look. "Commander! You cannot risk yourself on the line."

"I don't mean to cower with an old man and a boy," Lucius replied, thrusting his sword at a spike-haired wild man. Behind him, Demetrius rattled off supplications to an impressive list of gods and goddesses, both Greek and Roman.

Aulus floated above the melee, wringing his hands.

Barbarian shrieks mingled with curses and grunts as the battle wore on. Another Roman fell and the orb tightened. By Pollux! What the Celts lacked in armor, they made up for in fury. Lucius's men were holding, but it was clear they couldn't stand against the barbarians much longer.

The horses shied, causing Marcus and Demetrius to struggle with the reins. Worse, the orb was being forced toward a thatch of willows. The circle would break. Lucius swore under his breath and fought with renewed energy, the scent of blood in his nostrils and the sting of sweat in his eyes.

He ignored the ghost hovering above his left shoulder.

A Roman shout went up. Lucius swiveled his head and was

15

greeted by the sight of Roman helmets at the bend in the road. Swords raised, the rear company charged into the fray.

"Break!" Lucius shouted. His men separated. Half joined the reinforcements in surrounding the largest group of barbarians, while the rest rushed the remaining wild men into the swamp. Lucius angled Marcus and Demetrius into a tight copse.

"It will soon be over," he told the terrified boy.

Marcus looked up at him and nodded. Then his shoulders stiffened and his eyes grew wide, fixed on a point above Lucius's head. A choking sound emerged from his throat. Too late, Lucius looked up to see a barbarian poised on the branch above.

He managed to deflect the Celt's sword, though he staggered under the impact of the attacker's leap. He tossed the man onto his back in the mud. He was a mere youth, with wild red hair and a beard not yet fully grown. Lucius lifted his sword, prepared to dispatch the young warrior to whatever barbarian god he held sacred.

Pain erupted in his hand, causing the sword to spin out of his grasp. By Pollux! An arrow had bitten the flesh between his thumb and forefinger. Where in Hades had it come from?

He had no time to speculate, for the young Celt had used the distraction to regain his feet. The Celt's sword glanced off the edge of Lucius's curved shield. Lucius slammed the shield down on the barbarian, groping for his battle dagger with his free hand.

A second arrow whizzed by his right ear. He stumbled. The Celt youth danced away. The unseen archer's third projectile struck Lucius on the back and glanced off his armor. The next grazed his forearm, drawing blood. Lucius uttered an oath as his dagger slipped from his grasp. The youth leveled his sword at Lucius's bare legs. Lucius parried the blade with his shield and lunged for his fallen sword.

A dart hit his right buttock, sending him face-first into the mud. *Merda!* He recovered quickly, jerking the arrow from his flesh. At the corner of his vision, a flash of color disappeared behind the silver-green curtain of a willow frond.

The barbarian war horn shrilled. The signal must have been a retreat, for after a moment's hesitation, the Celt warrior raced for cover. Lucius barely noticed the youth's departure. Sparing a glance toward Marcus and Demetrius, he snatched up his sword and plunged into the forest, vowing to take down the hidden archer.

He paused in the shadows, listening. Long moments passed, measured by the angry rush of blood in his ears. At last the archer showed himself, scrambling toward a tree to his right. Lucius lunged toward the movement and swung. His blade glanced off the tree's trunk, jerked, and hit flesh. The archer went down with a cry. Lucius raised his weapon for the killing blow.

The barbarian twisted to one side and stared up at him, eyes wide. Lucius's arm wavered. This enemy was even younger than the last, not yet old enough for battle paint. Dirt smeared his face and checkered tunic. His hands clutched his wounded leg.

The boy's soft cries brought to mind a kitten, not a warrior.

Lucius sheathed his sword and propped his shield against a gnarled trunk. The young Celt had showed courage and a steady hand on the bow. If the gash on his leg was not deep, he could be sold as a slave, perhaps to be trained as a gladiator. He dragged the boy into a shaft of sunlight and knelt to inspect the wound.

His gaze caught instead on the archer's face. Thick, coppery lashes fringed golden eyes, flecked with blue. Wisps of russet hair framed a delicate sweep of cheekbones and a perfectly formed nose. Lucius's gaze drifted lower, taking in moist red lips and a firm pointed chin.

The boy's chest heaved.

Lucius drew in a sharp breath. *By Jupiter's mighty rod . . .*

He grasped the neckline of the barbarian's tunic and

17

ripped the garment apart, exposing bare flesh. His hand closed on one small, pink-tipped breast.

He swore.

A girl. He'd been shot in the ass by a girl.

She barked a word and bucked, knocking his arm away. In the brief moment before he gathered his wits, she scrambled backward, clutching the edges of her torn tunic with one hand.

Lucius sat back on his heels, stunned. The girl snarled another imprecation and this time the words she hurled at him were in his own language.

"Roman dog! Pig! Defiler!" She jumped to her feet, golden eyes savage, a doe facing the wolf's teeth. A thick coppery braid fell over one shoulder.

Lucius rose slowly, his gaze never wavering from the incredible vision before him. Had he believed in such creatures, he would have thought the Celt girl a forest nymph.

His loins tightened.

He moved closer. The nymph sprang back, her full weight coming down on her wounded leg. She cried out as she crumpled to the ground.

Lucius darted forward. Never before had he lifted a sword against a woman, but now a dark trail of the barbarian archer's blood stained the forest floor. The wound needed tending, and quickly. He scooped her into his arms. Her small fists pummeled his breastplate.

"*Quies,*" he said. "Quiet, little one. I'm not going to hurt you." She struck one more time; then her eyes rolled upward and she went limp.

He emerged from the forest into a scene of carnage punctuated by soft moans and angry curses. Too many Romans lay sprawled in the dirt. Others crouched by the road, cradling their wounds. Demetrius knelt beside one soldier, binding his arm. Marcus hunkered at the physician's side, pale but steady, assisting as well as he could. The supply wagons, which had avoided the worst of the battle, creaked to a halt on the road.

Out of habit, Lucius's gaze sought Aulus, but his ghostly brother was nowhere to be seen. He came to an abrupt halt, wrenched his head around, and looked to the rear. Nothing. By the gods! The specter had haunted Lucius night and day for more than half a year.

Now, inexplicably, it was gone.

He frowned. At what point in the battle had the ghost disappeared? Lucius couldn't say.

The centurion, bloodied but unhurt, hailed him. Lucius strode toward the officer. The man dropped a startled glance at the woman in his commander's arms.

"Losses?" Lucius asked.

The centurion recovered his composure quickly. "Fifteen dead, sir, or nearly so. Twenty-two injured."

"Unload the foodstuffs onto the road and gather the wounded into the wagons. The slave price of any Celt you salvage is yours." His gaze dropped. Even unconscious, the barbarian archer looked more alive than Lucius had felt in a very long while. His arms tightened on his prize.

"This one is mine."

Chapter Two

Tendrils of warmth caressed Rhiannon's body, stroking her limbs with the tenderness of a mother comforting her new babe. Had summer come so soon? She snuggled deeper into her blanket and grasped at a dream, but the pleasant fragments scattered, laying wide a path for the pain. The sensation drove forward like a sliver of winter ice, growing sharper the nearer it came. It sliced into her leg.

Her spine arched. A strong hand pushed her back into soft cushions. Not her own straw pallet. Where, then?

A low, rich voice spoke a single word. *"Quies."*

She opened her eyes. A face wavered in the dim light. She blinked and the vision stilled.

A man with features that surely belonged to some dark god. A wide brow, harsh cheekbones, and somber eyes. Streaks of grime marred his bronze skin. A proud nose crooked to the side—had it once been broken? Black curls clung to a high forehead. Full, sensual lips pursed in a grim line.

The strong angle of his jaw fascinated Rhiannon most.

She had never known a grown man to be beardless. Hesitantly, she lifted one finger and touched his naked skin. The bare chin conspired with the unruly curls to present an illusion of youth, yet this was no boy. A few strands of silver were visible in his dark mane. Fine wrinkles crimped the corners of his eyes.

Those eyes gleamed rich and brown, the color of stones washed by a stream, but soft, like the summer coat of an otter. Some emotion stirred deep in her breast. She caught her bottom lip with her teeth. She'd seen this man before; she was sure of it. But how? She didn't know him. Her gaze drifted lower to the glint of metal at his chest.

Roman armor, dark with stains that looked like blood.

Terror crashed through the fog in her brain. With it came the memory of the battle. She'd followed the men, but had arrived too late to prevent Owein's mad attack on the Roman commander. She'd aided her brother with her bow, only to have the Roman's sword fall on her. She flung herself back, but there was no escape. One strong palm caught her shoulder, the other her stomach.

"*Quies,*" he said again.

She kicked and pain shot through her leg. "Filth!" she snarled in the Roman's own tongue, glad for the first time that Madog had taught her the foul language. "Take your hands from me." She tore at his face.

The Roman swore. Catching her wrists in his hands, he pinned them on either side of her head and shifted his torso over her. The sharp edges of his armor cut into her breast. She lay beneath him, chest heaving, caught like a mountain hare in a trap. The thought enraged her. Dear Briga, if only her arrow had pierced his neck instead of his arse! She writhed, cursing, but his hold was sure and his body as steady as an oak.

Her captor looked down at her, a smile tugging at one corner of his mouth. The dog dared to mock her? She gathered what moisture she could on her tongue and spat in his face.

His smile vanished into an oath to some Roman god. He hauled her wrists over her head and held them with one hand. He used the other to wipe the spittle from his cheek. His dark eyes never left her face.

"Hurry," he said.

Rhiannon understood, but couldn't guess his meaning. Hurry? How, when she lay trapped? Then a second man's voice emerged from behind the Roman and she realized her captor's command had not been meant for her.

Hands grasped her wounded leg, bringing a spike of pain so vivid that lights burst in her vision. She gasped, trying to catch enough air to breathe. The Roman barked another word and swung his head to the side.

The sudden movement sent the room spinning.

Lucius gazed at the barbarian woman's pale face, a stark contrast to the wild flame of her hair. He'd thought her a girl, but now, as he examined his prize more closely, he saw her figure was that of a woman. A sylvan nymph, born of fire and mist.

"She's fainted," he said, as if Demetrius didn't have eyes and ears of his own.

"So I see," the old Greek replied. With professional precision, he tore the woman's checkered tunic from waist to hem, completing the rip from the neckline Lucius had begun.

Her breasts were small and exquisite, her navel a gentle dip in the curve of her belly. Lucius's gaze touched the coppery thatch of hair at the apex of her thighs, but didn't linger. At the moment, the ugly gash on her leg was a much more compelling sight.

Demetrius dipped a length of linen into the basin of warm water and wine at his elbow. "Thank the gods she's quiet at last. Now, perhaps, I can attend to my labor in peace." He wiped the cloth over the wound, clearing the worst of the blood.

Lucius stood, his gaze probing the shadows at the corners of the chamber. Aulus hadn't reappeared after the battle. Where in Hades had he gone? The irony of Lucius's reaction didn't escape him. For half a year he'd sought to banish his brother's ghost. Now, perversely, Aulus's absence left him wary.

He rubbed the pounding pulse in his right temple. "Will she live?" he asked, trying not to care.

The physician shrugged without looking up from his task. "She seems strong enough and the cut is not deep." He drew apart the edges of the wound. A trickle of fresh blood stained his hands.

"Stitch it and be done, then."

"The wound must be cleared of debris, else it will corrupt. As well you know." Demetrius's grizzled eyebrows arched above his hawklike nose as he probed the gash with his fingers.

More blood oozed, streaking over the nymph's pale skin like veins through marble. Lucius was no stranger to battle injuries, but to see such a wound on a woman . . .

He looked away.

Demetrius caught the movement and snickered. "The mighty warrior grows faint?"

Lucius glared at him. "I've seen far worse."

"No doubt." Demetrius threaded a thin strand of sinew through the eye of a bronze needle. "Be of some use to me, boy. Bring that hand lamp closer."

Lucius obeyed without hesitation. He'd been taking orders from the ancient scholar since childhood. Old habits died hard.

Demetrius pulled the edges of the wound together and made one careful stitch, then another. "I'm glad you sharpened your sword before hacking at her," he said in a conversational tone. "A ragged edge would have been much harder to close."

Lucius gripped the lamp and refused to take the bait.

23

"She spoke in the Roman tongue," Demetrius continued.

"That's not surprising. Many *Brittunculi* do. Her clan must have dealings in the fort village."

"The barbarians provide grain one day, a spear in the back the next."

"It's the way of things on the frontier. Assyria was no different."

Demetrius finished stitching the wound. He put the needle aside and took up a strip of linen. "Raise her leg, Luc, so I may bind it."

Lucius set the hand lamp near the basin of water and slid his hands under the nymph's leg. Her ankle nestled in his left palm, his right hand caressed her thigh. Carefully, so as not to disturb the new stitches, he lifted the wounded limb.

The movement parted her legs, giving him a glimpse of the dark mystery hidden by the triangle of curls guarding her sex. His breath caught and he leaned closer.

"Enough time for drooling once the girl awakens," Demetrius said with a cackle.

Lucius jerked his head back. The old man's mirth far outweighed his wit, he thought darkly. Then the barbarian woman sighed and he leaned forward again, his gaze fixed on her face.

Her eyelids fluttered and opened. She stared for a moment, dazed. Then comprehension dawned in her golden eyes and she bucked. Her arm shot forward.

Lucius jumped back, the nymph's fist missing his jaw by a hairsbreadth. No gentle goddess here. He grabbed her wrist in time to prevent a second attack. "Quiet, little wild thing. I'm not going to hurt you."

Demetrius chuckled. "She'll make a lively bed-slave, if you can tame her."

"Canis!" she hissed. "Roman dog!" She wrenched her head to the side and sank her teeth into his forearm.

Lucius swore. He inserted the fingers of his free hand

24

into her mouth and pressed deep, forcing her to gag. Leaning forward, he pinned her shoulders to the bed and gave her a slight shake.

"Cease, or I will have you bound."

She stilled. Demetrius shook his gray head. "I suggest you brand her now. She will run when she is able."

The nymph's eyes blazed and her head gave a violent shake. The dark flame of her hair had fallen from its braid. It shimmered in waves about her shoulders, obscuring his hands. Her breasts, firm and pink-tipped, heaved with fury.

By the gods, she was magnificent.

He shot a quelling look in Demetrius's direction. "Your jest lacks humor, old man. You know I never mark my slaves."

"You've marked this one already, boy. That scar won't fade." The physician gathered his tools, wiping them carefully with a clean cloth.

Lucius removed his hands from the woman's shoulders. He straightened but kept his gaze locked with hers, daring her to move. "She brought that wound upon herself."

Demetrius snorted. "As you say."

A knock sounded at the door.

"Come," Lucius called.

Two women entered, carrying clean water and bed linens. The pair, along with more than a dozen others, had been Aulus's slaves. Now the entire household belonged to Lucius and with them the contents of a richly furnished residence. His brother might have embraced the wilds of Britannia, but he'd been loath to discard the luxuries of Rome.

Lucius watched the slaves set out the bathwater. The Celt nymph scowled at him, then reddened as the older slave woman peeled away the remnants of the checkered tunic. Lucius turned away so as to afford her some semblance of privacy.

The chamber's single window looked out onto a starless night. From his vantage point on the upper story of the fort commander's house, he could distinguish the shadowed roofs of the barracks, the northern gate, and the torch-studded rim of the fort's perimeter wall. A night sentry passed on the high battlement, his helmet catching the glare of torchlight. Beyond, silent hills rose on the horizon.

He rested a hand on the window frame. By rights, he should have installed his new slave on a mean cot in the slaves' quarters. Instead, he had carried the barbarian woman up the narrow stairs and into the room adjoining Aulus's former bedchamber, now Lucius's own. Demetrius had raised his eyebrows but had made no comment.

After a moment, Lucius turned back to the physician. The Greek had moved from the nymph's bedside to a table set before a mural of Cupid and Psyche. His saffron mantle was torn and streaked with blood and his striped tunic had fared little better. Fatigue showed in the line of his shoulders, but his gnarled fingers were steady as he fitted his surgical instruments into a small wooden chest.

The slave women finished their labors. Gathering the soiled linens and water, they looked to Lucius. At his nod, they left the room.

Demetrius caught his gaze. "There are too many others in need of my skills for me to tarry here. I will offer my assistance at the fort hospital."

Lucius shook his head, but knew any order he gave would be ignored. "Go if you must, but don't tire yourself unduly. Seek your bed before dawn."

The heavy oak door thudded shut, leaving him alone with the nymph. Her pallid face put him in mind of his brother's ghost, who, to Lucius's great puzzlement, still hadn't reappeared. He took a step toward the bed. The nymph went rigid, clutching the thin woolen sheet to her chest and staring at Lucius as if he were some foul beast escaped from Tartarus.

Her eyes spit fury, but Lucius did not miss the wash of

terror behind her anger. Did she expect he would abuse her? If so, her fear was unfounded. He preferred a willing woman. In the twelve years of his military career he'd sampled the charms of females from every corner of the empire. Not one had left his bed disappointed. This forest nymph might hate him now, but in the end she would welcome him gladly enough.

The embers in the brazier had gone white, leaving the room chilly. Lucius closed the shutters against the night air. The barbarian woman would be calmer after taking her rest. He would send a boy to replenish the coals.

He retrieved a second blanket from an ornate wood chest near the window. The nymph flinched when he wrapped the soft material about her shoulders, but otherwise offered no resistance. Her wounded leg must hurt like Hades, yet no tears filled her eyes. His admiration of her rose another notch.

"Rest," he said. "We will talk in the morning."

"You cannot hold me here. My people will come."

"Your people are counting their dead."

"As are yours."

He inclined his head. "But I count also the living." He leaned closer. She smelled of roses. The slave women must have perfumed her bathwater. Suddenly, Lucius became all too aware of his own aroma—the stink of sweat and battle grime.

He straightened. "I've no desire to harm you. Just the opposite." Then, since he couldn't bear to leave without touching her, he brushed the back of his hand across her cheek.

She drew a sharp breath, a flicker of something like recognition showing in her eyes. Curious. He'd expected her to strike him again, but instead she'd gone still. Encouraged, he traced a line along her jaw, stroking his thumb under her chin and down the column of her throat. Her eyelids fluttered closed and her lips parted on a quick intake of breath.

His rod stiffened.

His secretary's voice sounded at the door. "My lord!"

"Yes, Candidus?"

"My lord, you wished to be informed when the porter admitted Tribune Vetus. The tribune awaits you now in the reception chamber."

Vetus. The man who had penned the improbable account of Aulus's death. Lucius's hand dropped to his side. "Tell the tribune I will greet him at once."

"Yes, my lord."

Lucius took a step toward the door, then halted and returned to the bed. With a swift movement designed to preclude any protest, he dipped his head and placed a brief kiss on the nymph's lips. "Until tomorrow."

She stared up at him, eyes wide, her fingers clutching the edges of her blanket until her knuckles turned white. "I will kill you for that, Roman."

Her expression was so serious that Lucius couldn't suppress a smile. "You're welcome to try, little one. I'll look forward to it."

Aulus was waiting outside the chamber door.

Lucius shot him a dark look. "Have you been lurking out here the entire time?"

The specter shrugged.

"Come along, then," Lucius said in disgust. He headed toward the stairwell at the far end of the upper gallery, navigating the passage by the light of the torches burning in the courtyard garden below. Once on the ground floor, his footsteps slowed outside the reception chamber.

Tribune Vetus lounged in a low chair, his face half turned from the open door. Though dressed in full military uniform, the young patrician somehow managed to project an air of graceful indolence. A bronze goblet rested in his right hand; his left stroked the intricate carvings on the chair's armrest. A junior officer, two years into his obligatory decade of military service, if Lucius's memory served.

Aulus glided past Lucius to the threshold and halted, his transparent shoulders nearly filling the doorframe. Lucius eyed his brother uneasily, loath to step through bone-numbing cold to gain entry to the chamber.

Vetus's head turned. "Aquila. At last. Why do you hover on the threshold like an old woman? Come in, man."

Lucius took a cautious step forward and let out a sigh of relief when Aulus moved aside. *"Salve,* Vetus."

The tribune rose. He was not a tall man, but carried himself as though he were. "I'm relieved to see you unharmed." He took a closer look at Lucius and frowned. "There's a private bath in the house. I might suggest you pay it a visit."

Lucius spread his palms. "A fine suggestion. But as you see, I've yet to remove my armor. You've been at the hospital?"

"And to the morgue. Rome lost far too many men today."

"We were ill prepared," Lucius said bluntly. "The commander at Eburacum assured me the Celts raided in small bands."

Vetus peered into his goblet. "Yes. Well. Most Celt attacks are erratic affairs."

"There was nothing erratic about this one. The barbarians numbered fifty men at the least."

"So I was told." Vetus took a delicate sip from his cup. "More than one local clan was certainly involved. Very surprising. It's been my experience that the *Brittunculi* fight each other more fiercely than they've ever battled Rome."

"They were united today."

Vetus made a dismissive gesture. "An aberration, I'm sure. They are a wretched, undisciplined people. Hardly worth the trouble of conquering." He took another draught of wine. "I cannot conceive why the emperor does not abandon this frontier."

Lucius crossed the room and lifted a pitcher from a granite table carved in the image of an Egyptian temple. "The strength of Rome lies in her victories, not her retreats."

"Perhaps, but the riches of the East command Trajan's attention these days. There's nothing in Britannia outside of a few lead mines."

Aulus drifted to the far end of the Egyptian table. Lucius considered the hideous piece of furniture. His brother's previous post had been as tribune in Egypt.

"That monstrosity is heavy enough to put a strain on any wagon axle," Lucius muttered. "I cannot imagine how or why you transported it north."

Aulus sent him a repressive look. He stretched out his hand and stroked the red stone lovingly.

"Eh? What did you say, Aquila?"

By Pollux. He'd addressed the ghost in Vetus's presence, without even being aware of what he was doing. He covered his dismay by splashing wine into an empty goblet. "I said, the land seems fertile enough here in the north."

Vetus snorted. "If the barbarians would exploit their resources, perhaps a man could make a profit. As it is, the natives are content to wallow in the mud. Their largest village is a dismal cluster of sheep-dung huts." The tribune joined Lucius at the table. "And the winter is as cold as a spinster's tit. At least Assyria was warm."

"You were in the East?"

"Attached to the Fourth Legion." His gaze drifted to the granite table. "I would have preferred Egypt," he said softly.

"What brought you to Britannia?"

"I arrived late last summer to assess the fortifications from Segedunum to Maia. Seventy-five miles of misery. According to my scouts, a barbarian lurks behind every tree."

"You didn't travel the road yourself?"

"Are you mad? I much prefer my head attached to my body than dangling from some Celt war chief's saddle."

Lucius regarded the tribune in silence for a long moment. "Your report is complete, then?" he said at last.

"Yes. I'm to deliver it directly to General Hadrian. I'll leave as soon as an escort can be arranged."

"I'm afraid I can't allow that," Lucius said. At least not before he investigated the circumstances of Aulus's death.

Vetus's head shot up, the first swift movement Lucius had seen the man make. "What do you mean?"

"After today's attack, I must assume the local chieftains have banded together. They could strike again. I won't be able to spare sufficient men for your safe passage south."

Vetus swore. "I was to have left a month ago, but the road was flooded." He refilled his goblet and stared morosely into his wine. "Barely a day passes without rain here. It's a far cry from the Eastern deserts." He looked up. "You've come lately from Assyria as well, have you not?"

"Yes," Lucius said. "I commanded the Thirtieth Legion."

"You left a prestigious post to come north. A step in the wrong direction, most would say. All of Rome expected you to claim your father's seat in the Senate after his death last year."

Lucius could hardly reveal that a ghost's urgings had brought him to Vindolanda. "I came to retrieve my brother's belongings."

The tribune gave a sidelong glance to the Egyptian table. "A prodigious undertaking, I'm sure, but you need not have taken over his command as well."

"A temporary position. The governor's permanent replacement will arrive before winter." If Lucius couldn't avenge Aulus's death and send the ghost to its rest by then, he would surely go insane.

Vetus's expression turned hooded. "You resemble your brother quite keenly, you know."

"It was always so, though he was eight years my junior."

Vetus's gaze darted toward Aulus.

Lucius froze. Had the tribune sensed the specter's pres-

31

ence? If so, it would be the first indication that another person shared Lucius's vision. He searched for a glimmer of recognition in Vetus's eyes.

But the tribune's attention slid to the high window set in the outside wall. "Aulus's death was a grievous waste."

Lucius narrowed his gaze. Only close family members dared to call a man by his forename. Just what type of relationship had Aulus and Vetus shared during their brief association?

"Did you witness my brother's death?"

Vetus twisted his goblet in his hands. "No. The First Centurion and two junior officers issued him an invitation to hunt. Your brother felt he could not refuse."

Aulus moved more fully into Lucius's line of vision and gave a swift shake of his head. Why? Because he had declined the invitation? Or because Vetus knew the outing had been a sham?

With an effort, Lucius tore his gaze from the ghost. "What happened?"

"The hounds flushed a boar from a thicket. Aulus took up his spear and pursued the beast. He never rejoined the group. By the time his body was located, it had been badly gored." Vetus placed his goblet on the table, leaving it teetering dangerously close to the edge. "A waste."

Lucius moved the cup to the center of the table, near his own. "I would speak with the First Centurion."

"You'll need to travel to Hades then, for he is also dead. Thrown from his mount while on patrol. As for the others . . ." Vetus shrugged, but it seemed to Lucius the gesture was forced. "I cannot recall. Speak with the quartermaster, Gaius Brennus. He is—was—acting commander."

"Brennus? That's a Gaulish name, is it not?"

"Yes. He's of the Tungri tribe, from Belgica, as are most of the men stationed here. The unit has been in Britannia for several generations."

Lucius nodded. Conscripted soldiers were routinely

posted far from their homelands, lest they join with the local populace in revolt against their conquerors.

Vetus poured himself another cup of wine, then paced toward the door with the bowl of the goblet cradled in his palm. "The hour grows late. If we wish more than a brief rest before cockcrow, I suggest we seek our beds."

"Of course."

Vetus exited the receiving room and disappeared in the direction of the stairs. Lucius set out across the courtyard. At the moment, a bath appealed to him far more than sleep.

A slave boy started awake when the door to the bath's anteroom opened. He ran to load the furnace. The fire had been stoked earlier, however, for fragrant steam already wafted from the hot room. A fresh tunic and sandals, along with a linen towel, lay in the changing cubicle, causing Lucius to bless Candidus's unobtrusive efficiency.

He removed his sword, war belt, and armor and gave it to the boy for cleaning, along with additional instructions to replenish the coals in the nymph's brazier.

The boy scampered from the room. Lucius retrieved his dagger from the changing alcove and set it at the edge of the pool. He would take no chances, even in his own residence.

He stripped off the remainder of his soiled clothing and plunged into the hot pool. Settling himself onto the seat, he heaved a resigned sigh as Aulus shed his own toga and tunic. The ghost sank into the water, taking the bench opposite.

Lucius grabbed a bottle of oil from a niche at the water's edge and smoothed the fragrant balm over his battle-stained skin. Picking up the accompanying bronze strigil, he pointed the curved blade at his brother. "I'd offer to scrape your back, but I'm afraid I might run you through. Of course," he added, "since you're already dead, it hardly would matter."

Aulus opened one eye and shot Lucius a disgruntled

look. Lucius laughed, the sound echoing off the tiles of the bath chamber. By Pollux, if he had to go insane, at least he could take some small pleasure in it. He drew the blade over his skin, scraping away the odor of death along with the oil.

The blood and grime of the skirmish dissolved into the scented water. Lucius's tense muscles relaxed, leaving him free to pursue his thoughts. Vetus's mantle of innocence covered him like the whitest candidate's toga, and yet . . .

He looked at Aulus. "I'm certain he was lying. You would sooner scour a latrine with a toothpick than charge a wild boar with a spear."

The Horned God's favor was capricious.

The thought weighed heavily on Owein as he leaned on the sturdy branch he'd chosen as a walking stick. His breath was short and his chest ached, but he had no choice but to go on foot. His pony carried one of the wounded warriors rescued from the scavenging Romans.

A reluctant dawn cast gray light over the fens. The Romans had resumed their march toward Vindolanda just before sunset. The Celts had hunkered in the forest most of the night, tending their wounded. Some warriors had slept, but Owein hadn't been among them. His head had ached with the dull pain that preceded a vision. He'd had no desire to close his eyes and look upon yet more blood.

"How many?" Owein heard Madog ask.

"Eight of our clan is missing," Edmyg replied grimly, striding to the Druid's side. "Though only six that I am sure died in battle. The others will have fallen on their swords rather than be taken."

Madog spit on the ground. "Yet the Roman commander walks free." His pale blue eyes flashed with annoyance. "Could ye nay have taken him yourself, Edmyg, rather than let Owein be attempting the task? The lad is lucky to be among the living. Rhiannon will flay ye alive when she hears of it."

Edmyg's expression, already set in stone, grew even harder. "I killed more than any, old man."

Owein caught his breath. No one dared insult a Druid, not even a king. Did Edmyg wish a curse on his head?

An older warrior, scarred by more years of battle than Owein wished to count, chose that moment to approach the duo. Kynan stood as tall as Edmyg, but his frame was much leaner, as if time had burned away his bulk along with the impetuousness of his youth. Owein repressed a shudder. The man's nose had been severed in some long-ago battle, leaving him with a visage few could dwell on for long.

"Near half my warriors be lost, Edmyg," Kynan said. "Had ye sent a competent scout to verify the enemy's strength, no doubt my kin would walk still."

Owein gripped his walking stick and edged closer, his heart pounding. How would his arrogant brother-in-law react to Kynan's challenge? Owein half hoped the older warrior would strike Edmyg down.

"The Romans ne'er march with so many," Edmyg retorted, his face flushing dangerously. "The commander's escort was to number no more than twenty men."

"An' who was it telling ye this?"

"Cormac."

Kynan let out a bark of disgust. "The misbegotten gnome?"

Edmyg bristled. "My *brother* is inside the Roman fort."

"A poor spy he is, then. His blunder killed twelve of my kinsmen. The rest will be loath to join ye in warring again." With that, Kynan spun about, barking orders to his warriors. The band vanished into the clouded depths of the forest.

Edmyg uttered a curse, his fist clenched at his side. "If Kynan turns the other chieftains against us, 'tis little hope of taking the fort we'll be having, even with the alliance Cormac has gained us."

Madog stroked his beard. To Owein's surprise, the Druid

didn't seem perturbed at this revelation. "The clans will come," he said. "They willna turn away from Rhiannon."

Edmyg snorted. "Rhiannon is a woman, not a warrior."

"Aye," Madog replied. "A woman who represents all that the Brigantes have lost. All they can regain. Our people look to her and see their freedom. When the time is right, they willna look away, no matter what path Kynan urges."

"I hope ye have the right of it," Edmyg said. He retrieved a Roman sword from his saddle and ran a thumb along the edge of its blade. "At least we've increased our store of arms."

The bedraggled company started along a path skirting the ridge above the fens. Owein set his eyes to the north, where two peaks formed what looked like twin thrones. There, according to the Old Ones, Briga, the Great Mother, once sat with her consort, Kernunnos, the Horned God. The Druid circle lay in the shadow of the crags, sheltered by the sacred oaks and guarded by the skull of the Roman slaughtered at Samhain.

Owein trudged just to the fore of his uncle, Bryan. The sooner home, the better. Rhiannon would be sick with worry until he returned. He allowed himself a small smile. When his sister saw him, she would run her fingers through his hair as she'd done since before he could remember. He would protest, of course, but in truth her touch would chase away the horror of yesterday's battle, if only for a moment.

A slight figure dropped into step beside him. Reese, Bryan's youngest son. Born two winters after Owein, he was the youngest member of the raiding party. The lad's boots thudded on the sodden cushion of last year's leaves, the crook of his bow slung over his shoulder as he walked. Reese hadn't been allowed in the thick of the battle, but had used his weapon to cover the older warriors.

Owein slid a glance sideways and nodded. "I'm much obliged to ye, cousin. If not for your arrows, I'd be riding yon pony, or worse."

Reese squinted up at him. "I dinna understand ye, Owein."

"Ye shot when I dropped from the trees onto the Roman commander." Owein's heart pounded at the memory. A reckless move it had been, but the hot urge to show up Rhiannon's loutish mate had gripped him like a fever. "Your arrows distracted him. Had your hand not been quick on the bow, the foreign dog would have surely gutted me."

His cousin's gaze remained puzzled. "But I shot nowhere near ye. I was hidden on the opposite side of the road."

Owein frowned. None of the older warriors carried a bow—he'd been sure Reese's arrows had saved him. He set his stick in the mud and hoisted himself over the jumble of rocks blocking the trail. *Someone* had been concealed in the willows during his mad skirmish. The unknown archer had harassed the commander and saved Owein's life. But who—

A soft whinny came from the brush, followed by a crackle of twigs. Owein whipped his head around as Bryan gave a low whistle. Another nicker, and then a snow-white mare crashed through the branches. The pony didn't stop until she reached Owein's side.

"Derwa," he whispered. Rhiannon's pony. A horrible suspicion formed in Owein's mind. His sister had a steady hand on the bow—she'd often shot targets with him when he was a lad. His gut contracted on a stab of nausea more painful than the slice of a Roman sword.

Reese grabbed Derwa's reins. "This be Rhiannon's pony."

"Aye," replied Owein. "How did the beast come to be so far from the village?"

The mare nudged Owein's shoulder with her nose. Then she tossed her head and turned, as if expecting him to follow.

"No," Owein croaked. *Dear Briga, don't let it be true.* Did Rhiannon think so little of his battle skills that she would follow him to war?

He grabbed the pouch tied at Derwa's neck and tore it open. The bitter scent of coltsfoot and silverweed, herbs Rhiannon had brewed for him just two days before, assaulted his senses. She'd come after him, but where was she now? She would never have let her pony wander without a rider.

His sister was dead or taken prisoner.

Owein's nausea surged anew. He doubled over and emptied his stomach on the trail.

Chapter Three

The Roman bedchamber was at once wondrous and terrifying.

Sunlight streamed through the shuttered windows, casting bright stripes across a floor paved with bits of colored stone. Beyond, a smooth wall rose to a ceiling ribbed with square-hewn timbers. Exquisite paintings danced across the flat walls, images of tiny men and women so breathtakingly real that Rhiannon half expected them to move.

She marveled at the floor. The shining stone fragments wove a fearsome beast from the colors of the rainbow. The enormous catlike monster bared long, sharp teeth as it swatted at its prey, its mane of golden fur glittering with the reflected light of the sun. Did such a monster truly exist? Or had it been conjured from the artist's nightmares?

A shiver ran the length of Rhiannon's spine. She shifted on her raised pallet. Her wounded leg throbbed, but the pain was not unbearable. The soft wool of her blanket warmed her naked skin. The women who had bathed her had taken her ruined tunic and left no replacement. Had the oversight been deliberate? The thought brought a rush of dread.

She pushed herself upright, one hand gripping the curved end of the bed that rose a handsbreadth above the mattress. Intricate carvings etched the wood, twining vines painted so realistically she could almost smell the clusters of small, round fruits nestled among the leaves. A matching terminal rose at the foot of the mattress, giving the bed the aspect of a boat. And indeed Rhiannon had never felt quite so adrift as at that moment.

There was but one door—had it been barred? One window on the opposite wall. The square chamber was small and sparsely furnished, but the few items it held were, like the bed, luxurious. A long wooden table, bearing a tall ewer, stood against the wall. A smaller bench was within reach of the bed, as was a wide stool with crossed legs. A metal tray, filled with glowing coals and supported on squat legs, lay on the floor. Languid heat rose from it into the air, without the haze and odor of smoke that accompanied a hearth fire.

The hairs on Rhiannon's nape lifted despite the warmth. Never in her life had she been enclosed by flat walls. Her own dwelling was comprised of circular walls and capped by a high conical peak. She gazed at the shadowed corners of the chamber. Who knew what dread beings lurked in the unnatural angles of this place, untouched by the spirals of the Great Mother's spirit?

Rhiannon forced a swallow past her dry tongue and gathered what courage she could. It would do her no good to worry about unseen demons. The all-too-real Roman commander provided the greater threat. She had to flee before he returned. Pulling the blanket about her, she pushed herself to a sitting position. She would try the door. Perhaps it would open.

She swung her legs over the edge of the cushions. The movement sent a hot poker of pain through her wounded leg. Dark patches clouded her vision. She leaned heavily on the raised end of the bed and waited for the blotches to clear.

A creak of hinges sounded behind her, then, *"Ut vales?"*

She wrenched her body toward the voice, gasping as another burst of brilliant pain enflamed her right thigh. A lad some years younger than Owein had slipped into the chamber and closed the door behind him. He stood now with his back pressed against the smooth wood, as if needing the strength of the oak to remain on his feet. One hand clasped something hung on a leather thong about his neck, the other gripped the door's latch as if he were ready to flee should Rhiannon prove to be a threat.

She blinked at the thought. He stared back at her with the dark, bright eyes of a bird—frightened yet at the same time fascinated. Black curls tumbled about his face. He wore a plain white tunic, tied at the waist with a leather cord and edged at the hem and sleeves with stripes of crimson. Leather sandals clad his feet.

She drew the blanket more firmly across her breasts and sank back onto the cushions. She'd seen this lad. She frowned, trying to remember.

"Ut vales?" he asked again, hesitant. "Are you well?"

Rhiannon tried to answer, but her mouth felt dry and foul, like new-shorn wool, and she managed only a dull croak. She wet her lips with her tongue and tried again, forming the Roman words with care. *"Parum bene."* Not well enough.

The lad's face registered his surprise. "Do you speak Latin?" His hand dropped from the door latch. At Rhiannon's nod, he took a tentative step in her direction.

She swallowed again, thickly. *"Aqua?"*

He frowned, then crossed to the table, where he grasped the high curving handle of the ewer and filled an accompanying cup, all the while keeping one hand clasped on the object strung at his neck. He approached her bed, halting a few steps away and offering the drink with one outstretched arm.

"Wine," he said.

She anchored the blanket with one arm and leaned forward, ignoring the stab of pain in her leg. When her fin-

41

gers closed on the cup, the lad snatched his hand away and retreated a few paces.

He watched as she drank. Rhiannon took a cautious sip, letting the cool, sweet liquid bathe her tongue before she swallowed. So this was wine. She'd heard of the drink. She had imagined its flavor to be similar to *cervesia*, the barley beer she brewed for Owein and Edmyg. In reality, the two drinks couldn't have been more different.

She took another long draught. Roman wine tasted like the summer sun, bright and sparkling. Its scent teased her nose with enticing flavor and bubbling mirth. If *cervesia* were a drink of the earth, dark and vital, then wine was a drink of the sky, playful and capricious.

She drained the cup, catching every precious drop of moisture. Only when she had finished did she think to look more closely at the vessel that had held it.

Another wonder.

The cup was wrought of a clear material like ice, yet it was warm in her hand. Frozen ripples within it scattered the sunlight like faerie lights. Surely some goddess had crafted the cup in Annwyn, the magical land beyond the setting sun.

She raised her gaze to the lad. "What is this?" she asked, stroking the smooth rim of the cup with one finger.

"Glass. Have you never seen it?"

She shook her head and handed the treasure back to him. The lad returned it to the table; then, struck by sudden boldness, he edged closer to the bed. "I'm Marcus."

"*Salve*, Marcus."

He gave her a cautious smile. The hand at his throat loosened, revealing a gold ornament.

"Have you a name as well?" he asked in a rush. "Or are your people like beasts that have no need of them?"

She followed the rapid flow of his words with growing amusement. "I'm called Rhiannon."

"Rhiannon." Marcus rolled her name on his tongue as if

testing its flavor. "Rhiannon." He frowned. "That doesn't sound like a girl's name."

She bit back a smile. Marcus's expression was clear and guileless, much like Owein's had been at that age. "It is, I assure you." She let her gaze roam over the lad. His hands and feet were large, as if they had sprouted in advance of the rest of his frame. He would not grow to be so tall as Owein, she guessed, but one day his shoulders would be broader and his arms as strong.

The smooth skin of his forehead puckered over his eyebrows. "What do you eat?" he asked, his eyes bright with anticipation. "Do you tear the flesh from a man's bones and boil it in your cauldron?"

Rhiannon did smile at that. "That's a meal I've yet to try," she said with mock gravity. "Do you suppose it tastes better than venison?"

Marcus paled, his fingers tightening once again on the charm at his neck. "I've heard tell your women eat their children if they're not good, then birth fairer ones from their bones. Uncle Aulus sent such a story to me in Rome. Is it true?"

Rhiannon raised her brows. Marcus spoke of the crone Cerridwen, one of the many faces of the Great Mother. After eating one disobedient child, she birthed another of great beauty. Who was this lad's uncle to have known such a story? "That story holds truth, but not in the way you mean," she said. "My people love their children. We eat venison, boar, and grouse. Never babies."

"Oh." Marcus looked relieved and disappointed at the same time. "But your blue warriors are fierce," he said as if to console her. He shifted his gaze to the window, but not before Rhiannon saw a flash of terror in his eyes.

All at once, she knew him. The Roman commander had fought like a madman to protect this lad during the battle, much as she had fought to protect Owein.

He turned back to her. "Even so, Father says the blue

men lack discipline. They cannot stand against the Roman army."

Of course. She should have known at once who he was. He looked so like his sire. And like another man, whose identity flitted about the corner of her memory like a swarm of midges, refusing to take form. A tendril of unease unfurled in her chest. She wished she could remember.

Marcus was clenching and unclenching his fingers on the gold charm so fiercely that Rhiannon thought its thong might snap.

"What do you wear about your neck?" she asked.

The lad looked down at the ornament as if he'd never seen it before. "Oh." His hand dropped away, revealing a golden ball. "It's a *bulla*. It protects me from evil."

Rhiannon chuckled. "And you think you have need of it in my presence?"

The lad had the good grace to blush. "I've worn it always, since before I can remember." He forged on with painful honesty. "But you're right, I thought perhaps I might need it here." He grinned, showing a deep dimple in one cheek. "You're much nicer than I thought you would be."

The hinges on the door groaned again, saving Rhiannon from a reply. Marcus gave a guilty start. An old man strode into the chamber with a sure step, a small wooden bowl nestled in his hands. Rhiannon recognized him as the healer, much improved in appearance, who had tended her wound the night before. His short gray beard had been washed and combed and his bloodied mantle replaced with a clean one. An ornate pin held the saffron fabric fast at one shoulder, drawing up the folds to reveal a floor-length striped tunic decorated with wide bands of embroidery at the neck, sleeves and hem. The incongruous scent of spring flowers clung to his wizened form.

Rhiannon looked at Marcus and resisted the urge to laugh. The lad looked as if he would rather sink into the tiled floor and fight the cat-beast than face the old man.

The healer turned a fierce eye on him. "Why are you here?"

Marcus swallowed. "I'm . . . I'm talking to Father's new slave, Magister Demetrius."

Slave. Rhiannon closed her eyes. Yesterday she'd been a queen.

The healer spoke again, this time in a language Rhiannon didn't understand. After a slight hesitation, Marcus answered in the same tongue.

The old man snorted. "Your Greek is abysmal, young Marcus. Go to the library and take up your Aristotle. I will come to you when I am finished here."

"As you wish, Magister." Marcus scooted past the healer and collided with a woman who had suddenly appeared in the doorway. Water sloshed up over the edge of the large clay bowl she carried and hit him in the face. He sputtered, ducked around her, and disappeared.

The healer shook his head. "Zeus help me."

He moved to Rhiannon's bedside, gesturing for the slave woman to enter the chamber. She advanced, setting her bowl of water on the low table near Rhiannon's bed. A younger woman laden with linens followed in her wake, bare feet slapping on the wet floor.

The first woman crossed the room and flung open the shutters. Light flooded the room, sending blessed illumination into the shadowed corners. Rhiannon drew a deep breath, feeling her courage strengthen. The second woman gave Rhiannon a shy smile and placed her bundles on the bed.

Demetrius dismissed the slave women and they hurried from the room. Rhiannon watched the healer's approach with wary eyes.

"How fares your leg today?" Without waiting for an answer, the old man grasped the lower edge of Rhiannon's makeshift cloak and pushed it to one side.

She snatched the blanket's hem from his fingers. Her

fingers curled into a fist, ready to strike should he reach for her a second time.

The healer spread his arms, palms up. "I mean no disrespect," he said gently. "I must examine the injury. Surely you realize that."

Rhiannon's shoulders hunched. His words were true enough. She knew only too well what became of wounds left untended. And no doubt both the healer and the commander had seen her unclothed the night before, when she lay unconscious. Her face flamed at the thought.

"Very well." Anchoring the top of her blanket about her throat, she drew back the lower portion with her free hand.

"You must lie down, girl."

Rhiannon shook her head. She would not put herself in such a vulnerable position.

"As you wish." He slid his hands under her leg, straightened it at the knee, and unwound the bandage with practiced precision. To Rhiannon's surprise, the gash was neatly closed with precise stitches, as if her skin were a length of fabric mended with the finest of needles.

The healer took a clean cloth from the bundle on the bed and dipped it in the bowl of water the slave woman had left. He washed the last traces of blood from the wound, then smeared the contents of the smaller wooden bowl over his handiwork. The remedy soothed immediately.

"The gash is not deep," he said. "It should heal without causing a limp. Do not put undue weight on your leg for a full day at least." He replaced the discarded bandage with a clean length of cloth, nodding toward the remaining linens as he worked. "Clothing, I believe—one of the women must have located something suitable for you."

When she did not answer, he clucked softly. "What has happened to your tongue, girl? It wagged freely enough yesterday."

"I find I have little to say this day."

He let out a barking laugh, showing a tooth encased in gold. "The gods be praised."

She glared at him, lips pressed together.

His expression softened. "You are fearful now, of course, but you will adjust quickly enough to your new situation. You may even find it preferable to the life you left." He snorted. "And since Zeus knows this household is overrun with slaves, your duties are not likely to be taxing."

"Save for those I will perform on my back."

The healer's grizzled eyebrows shot up. "So. The fire has not quite died." He chuckled at some private amusement as he wiped his hands on a discarded cloth.

A third slave woman arrived, her sturdy arms bearing a tray laden with enough food to feed Rhiannon and several others besides—savory pork roasted with nuts, two soft round loaves, winter apples, and a large clay mug. The woman set the tray on the table by the bed. She threw a wide smile in Rhiannon's direction before collecting the soiled linens and exiting the chamber.

"Eat, then, and rest your leg," the healer said. "I will look in on you later."

When he had gone, Rhiannon slipped the blanket from her shoulders. She shook out the folded fabric on her bed and found a long tunic of the softest linen she'd ever held in her hands. It had been dyed an apple green and stitched so carefully that its seams were all but invisible. She slipped it quickly over her head, eager to cover herself. It slid over her skin like a caress. She belted it at her waist with a braided leather cord.

Though clothing had been quite welcome, her stomach protested the smell of food. She suspected any nourishment she tried would not remain long in her stomach. The mug, however, was filled with *cervesia*, not wine. She could probably keep that down. She lifted it to her lips and took a cautious sip.

Feeling somewhat fortified, she swung her legs over the side of the bed and stood, balancing on her good leg. No matter what the healer instructed, she would not stay abed. Escape was her paramount goal and she could not achieve it lying on her back. Edmyg's brother, Cormac, was some-where in the fort. Did he know of her capture? Had he passed news of it to the clan? She would need to locate him this very day, if possible, while the Roman commander went about fort business. She dared not dwell on his re-turn to her chamber or on what the night hours would bring.

Grasping the raised end of the bed for balance, she eased her weight onto her uninjured limb. Her wounded leg throbbed, but she resolutely ignored it and took a step toward the window. She needed an idea of the fort's layout before she could escape it.

The first step on her wounded leg sent a shooting pain into her thigh. She gritted her teeth and stepped forward on her uninjured limb. On the third step her balance fal-tered. She landed on the hard tiles with a thump, her hand striking the tail of the glittering cat-beast. Pain exploded behind her eyes. She clutched her leg and forced back a cry as she waited for the sting to recede.

The door opened at that precise moment. She peered under the bed frame, her heart pounding in her throat. A pair of masculine feet, encased in short leather boots, ad-vanced a few steps into the chamber. Bronzed skin, sprin-kled with dark hair, covered calves hard with muscle. The hem of a blood-red tunic fell above the knee, affording her a tantalizing glimpse of long thighs roped with sinew.

The owner of the magnificent limbs moved unerringly in Rhiannon's direction. She jerked herself upright, ignor-ing the fresh spurt of pain in her leg. She would not meet her captor while sprawled on her arse.

The Roman commander rounded the bed and looked down at her, his dark brows drawn together in a disbeliev-ing scowl. "Are you insane? You should be in bed." With-out waiting for a reply, he bent and scooped her into his arms.

He lifted her easily, his arms flexing around her like a

living cage, and for a moment Rhiannon forgot to breathe. Her fingers closed on his upper arms. His skin was smooth and golden, stretched taut over iron-hard muscles. Rhiannon willed her racing heart to slow and, as she filled her lungs with air, she thought she had succeeded.

Then she looked up into his eyes.

His steady gaze enveloped her like a fur cloak on a winter night. His frown softened, drawing her attention once again to his smooth chin. One corner of his mouth lifted with the promise of a smile. She shifted in his arms. His lips parted on a quick intake of breath, revealing a row of even white teeth.

He smelled of the wind in the pines and of leather freshly cured. His powerful, blunt-fingered hand closed on her arm. His skin was dark against her fairer coloring, but his grip was not harsh. His fingernails were clean and trimmed short.

Rhiannon's heart set to pounding harder than before. She thought perhaps she should be afraid, but, oddly, she was not. When his callused warrior's hands lowered her to the bed, she thought only that this Roman's touch was softer than Edmyg's had ever been.

He straightened, the frown returning to his eyes. He swiveled his head to the right and left—searching, it seemed, but for what, Rhiannon couldn't imagine. He hunted, prowling to the window, then back to the door. He bent to inspect the underside of the long table against the wall.

"Gone again," he said, his tone abrupt. He turned on her with a swift movement. "Could it be you?"

Rhiannon's confusion grew. "What do you mean? Who is gone? The healer?"

He didn't answer. His shoulders slumped and his hand passed over his eyes as if to wipe away some unwanted vision. She'd seen only his strength when he had first entered the chamber, but now, looking closer, she noted the weariness in his stance, the slight tremble of his hand as it curled into a fist. After a long moment, he raised his head and met her gaze. Again recognition sparked in Rhiannon's heart, along with an overwhelming desire to ease the raw pain that showed so clearly in his soft, dark eyes. Eyes she was certain she'd looked upon before.

Then, suddenly, she knew.

The Roman commander bore an uncanny resemblance to the young officer Madog had slaughtered at Samhain. The man whose soul had cried out to Rhiannon at the moment of his death. Was the new fort commander kin to the murdered man, come to avenge his death? A sound of distress escaped her lips.

Her captor's features smoothed, as if he'd exerted a sudden effort to wipe them clean. "I'm sorry if I frightened you," he said. Then, a heartbeat later, "You shouldn't walk. I'm sure Demetrius told you."

"He did."

"But you thought to try anyway."

"Yes."

The smile returned to his eyes. "My esteemed physician will not be pleased to find you think so little of his advice."

"Then he should refrain from giving it."

The corners of his mouth lifted, first one side, then the other. The result was a lopsided smile and a dimple that was identical to his son's. One dark curl fell over his forehead. He brushed it aside only to have it fall back again.

"Forgive me if I don't relay that sentiment to Demetrius. I know from hard experience he wouldn't take it kindly." He took a step toward her. His hand came to rest on the bed, very close to her arm.

She inched in the opposite direction. Did he think after a bit of light banter she would welcome him into her bed? If so, he was to be disappointed. At the same time, she wondered why he bothered with polite pretenses at all. He'd claimed her as a battle prize. He could take her whenever he wished and there was precious little she could do to stop him.

"Rhiannon," he said. "A beautiful name."

She looked up to find him watching her. "How did you—Oh. The lad told you."

He nodded. "My son."

"Marcus."

"Yes." He paused. "You may call me Lucius."

Lucius. It fit him. A bold name, but not a rough one. Rhiannon was drawn to the sound of it in spite of a fierce wish to snap the thread of fate that joined her soul to his. She shifted backward on the bed, away from him. No matter what he was called, no matter what connection his kinsman's blood had forged between them, he was her enemy.

The heat in his gaze told Rhiannon that he desired her and the knowledge of it filled her with dread. Her captor was above all a man, and like all men he would take what he wanted. But she would not yield easily.

She kept her expression neutral. "How is your arse, Lucius, where it was struck by my arrow?"

His eyes narrowed. "Improving."

"I'm sorry to hear it."

He snorted, but to her relief moved away to the window. Supporting his weight with one hand on the frame, he peered through the opening as if contemplating the scenery. Beyond his dark head, Rhiannon caught a glimpse of the green hills she called home. How simple her escape could be if she had the wings of a bird.

"Where did you learn to speak the language of Rome?" Lucius asked without turning.

She bit her lip, thinking belatedly that perhaps she should have feigned ignorance. She could hardly reveal the truth—that she had been taught by a Druid master so as to better understand her enemies. Druidry had been banned by Roman law well before her birth.

"Many of my people speak Latin," she hedged.

He turned and fixed her with a piercing gaze. "A few words, perhaps. Enough to trade in the fort village."

"My grandparents had dealings with the Romans." That, at least, was no lie. Cartimandua had been an ally of Rome. "I learned your language as a child."

To her relief, he didn't press further. But his next question proved even more disturbing. "Who was the young warrior you protected on the battlefield?"

Rhiannon didn't answer.

"Too old for a son, too young for a lover. A brother, perhaps?"

She shrugged.

"He owes you his life. If not for your arrows, I would have killed him."

"A pity none of my shots pierced your neck."

That brought a smile to his lips. He moved from the window, closing the distance between them with two quick strides. "You are a brave woman." He lifted his hand and grazed her cheek with one finger. Just a feather touch, but it conveyed a wealth of honest esteem.

An odd spark jumped in Rhiannon's belly. It took all her strength not to lean into his caress.

"Such a beautiful nymph," he said. "You're mine now."

Rhiannon stiffened. "Your bed-slave?"

His soft eyes glittered like a wash of stars in the winter sky. "If you wish it."

"A slave has little choice as to her duties."

"True enough, but I'm not in the habit of forcing women into my bed, slave or free."

She forced a laugh. "You're a Roman." She let her contempt show in her eyes. "A defiler."

His hand dropped from her cheek. He placed his palms on the bed, one on either side of her body and leaned close, so close that his hot breath grazed her neck, though he didn't touch her.

"I am a man, like any other."

A man. Niall's face, twisted with lust, flashed before her eyes. How many times had she lain beneath her husband as he took his pleasure with no thought to hers? "I know the ways of men, Roman."

He caught a strand of her hair and let it slide between his fingers. "Do you, my nymph?"

"Yes. They sate their needs with a few quick thrusts. Afterwards, they run to their mugs and boast."

He frowned.

Rhiannon closed her eyes, berating herself for her quick tongue. She'd wanted to buy herself time in the hope that she could contact Cormac before the Roman forced himself on her. Instead she'd provoked her captor past any man's patience. She braced herself for his assault. He would press her into the cushions and part her legs. She would fight, but in the end she would not escape his lust.

"A few quick thrusts?" His incredulous whisper stroked her ear. "Not all men expire so soon, little one. You and I will enjoy a far more leisurely lovemaking." He drew back slightly and captured her with his dark gaze. "First I'll explore you with my fingertips, learning your body until it becomes as familiar as my own. Then I'll lower my lips to your sweet flesh. Your scent will fill my nostrils. I'll savor your taste on my tongue until you writhe beneath me."

His words were as heady as the wine Rhiannon had tasted earlier. They poured like sparkling heat through her veins. Taste her? Dear Briga! Surely he did not mean . . .

She shifted, trying to assuage the restless ache that had sprung up between her thighs. What was happening to her? Neither Edmyg's words nor his touch had ever provoked such a reaction.

Lucius's voice dipped low and she found herself leaning forward, closer to his heat. Still, he did not touch her.

"Your moans will be sweet music in my ears, your fingertips like fire on my skin," he whispered. "My flesh will harden, longing to find its home within you."

The words painted a vivid image in Rhiannon's mind.

Instinctively she reached for him, if only to steady herself on the strength of his body.

He stepped back. Cool air rushed over her skin. The door closed with a soft thud, leaving her alone.

Rosebushes hardly belonged in Britannia.

Lucius leaned on the wooden rail opposite the nymph's chamber door and looked down into the courtyard below. Clusters of bare canes, studded with thorns, ringed a small fountain pool. In Rome, no doubt, gardens were already resplendent with roses. Here in Britannia, the first tentative leaves had scarcely begun to unfurl.

A flicker of white settled beside him.

"The roses are too large for you to have brought them with you three years ago," he commented without turning his head. Aulus had reappeared the instant he'd emerged from the nymph's chamber.

"One of our hapless predecessors must have transported the shrubs north for his wife." Lucius snorted. "I hope she polished his sword well for his trouble."

He turned in time to catch his brother's answering grin. His heart slammed in his chest at the familiar sight. Lucius would have given much to be able to throw his arm around Aulus's shoulders, but the chill that accompanied the specter kept him from closing the distance between them.

He pushed himself back from the railing. "Why do you stay away from the nymph?"

Aulus shrugged.

"Ah, so I am right, you are avoiding her. Why?"

Aulus looked away, into the courtyard, as if studying the roses.

"Perhaps," Lucius mused as he paced toward his chamber, "you wish to afford me a modicum of privacy at last. Jupiter knows I've been loath to bed a woman in your presence." He paused to shoot a glare at his brother. "Though I suspect you wouldn't have protested."

Aulus glanced back at the nymph's door and smirked.

Lucius's own gaze followed his brother's. His rod was still hard from his encounter with Rhiannon; he'd barely escaped the room without ravishing her. He'd approached her too soon, of course. Too soon for both of them. He'd been intending to allow her a few days to become accustomed to her new situation, but he'd found himself unable to stay away.

Rhiannon. She was as mysterious as the forest from which she'd sprung. She brought to mind fingers of mist sifting through the trees, beckoning him to explore wild places he had never known. He was as eager to taste her as a man dying of thirst was to drink from a mountain spring. She'd been gloriously savage in her resistance to him— how much more so would she be in surrender?

His mind raced with plans for her seduction, his rod springing upward once again. He would gentle her like a new colt, drawing her closer each day, until she rested in his arms. He had no doubt of his ultimate success. Women varied little from one end of the empire to the other. They were creatures of sensation, susceptible to flattery. Rhiannon would revel in his endearments and the luxuries a civilized household provided. And she would no doubt enjoy making love to a man who lasted beyond a few swift thrusts.

He crossed the threshold to his bedchamber. Aulus drifted in behind before Lucius could shut the door. The room was crowded with Egyptian-styled furniture even more hideous than the table in the receiving chamber. A wide bed, another table, a padded bench. A tall cabinet opened to reveal trinkets, jewelry and small works of art.

A golden chain hung with a perfect teardrop of amber caught his attention. The color reminded him of Rhiannon's eyes.

"Just how many wagonloads of useless items did you bring to Britannia?" he asked Aulus.

Aulus, of course, gave no response. He floated about, inspecting the corners of the chamber as if lately returned from a long holiday. Lucius sighed and reached for his armor. He fastened the hammered metal over his short war tunic and cinched his war belt about his waist. He slid his battle dagger into its sheath.

His hand closed next on his sword. The hilt was fashioned in the shape of a wolf's head, the emblem both of Lucius's family name—Ulpius—and of the Roman Empire itself. The artist who had crafted it had been clever—the blade seemed to spring from the beast's jaws.

"Do you remember when you gave me this?" he asked Aulus, rubbing his thumb along the gilded edge of the cross guard. "It was on my twenty-second . . . no," he amended, "my twenty-third birthday, when you had but fifteen years. Seven years ago. You told me I was the warrior, you the dreamer. I was to buy you a new translation of Homer for your birthday."

Had he done so? Lucius couldn't remember. He thought not.

He moved one jerky step to the low table on which the contents of his toilet kit lay scattered. He dragged a comb through his hair, then slid it into its leather case. With careful precision, he retrieved the other items one by one and fitted them into their proper slots in the polished wooden toiletry case. Razor and strop. Toothpick. Tweezers. A small mirror of polished silver.

He looked up from his task to find Aulus watching him with sad eyes. "I grew to manhood basking in your adoration," he said, his chest constricting painfully. "Was there ever a time when I didn't take your love for granted?"

His throat burned. He swallowed hard and closed the toiletry case, taking care to fit the corners in place despite the slight tremor in his hands. He lifted his crested Legionary helmet and left the room, too cowardly to dare another glance at the ghost drifting by his side.

He let out a long, frustrated breath as he passed Rhiannon's chamber. He'd been far too long without a woman. Five months and twenty-one days, to be exact, since the night prior to Aulus's first appearance on the Kalends of

November. It was now well past the Ides of Aprilis. Small wonder he was losing his mind.

He laughed, throwing his head back and emitting a brittle, hopeless sound. It echoed through the stairwell, fading only as he reached the lower level of the house. Aulus shot him a sharp look.

A fine state of affairs, when even a dead man thought him mad.

Demetrius's calm voice drifted from the library, exhorting the beauty of Aristotle's discourses. An elegant lecture, for all that it was wasted on Marcus. Lucius could well imagine the glazed expression in his son's eyes.

"He prefers folklores and fantasy to logic," Lucius told Aulus as he strode to the foyer. "As you did."

Candidus stood by the front door with Lucius's newly laundered military cloak over his arm. "Where is Tribune Vetus?" Lucius asked him.

"In the baths, my lord."

"So early?"

"I'm told he receives a massage and bath each morning, and again each afternoon."

Lucius snorted. "He must be the sweetest-smelling officer in the Roman army."

"Quite so," Candidus replied. He extended Lucius's cloak. "Your *sagum*, my lord? The skies promise rain." Aulus drifted into Lucius's line of vision and nodded vigorously.

"I'm well able to dress on my own," Lucius retorted.

Candidus started. "Of course, my lord."

Lucius ripped his gaze from the ghost. "No need for the *sagum*, Candidus," he said, exerting considerable effort to keep his voice calm. "Britannia's sky delivers rain almost daily. I may as well get used to it. How have you found my brother's household?"

"The kitchen is well stocked, my lord, as are the storerooms. As for the slaves . . ." He tapped his palm with his forefinger. "Six women, four men, and two boys are Celts from the south, near Londinium. Another man is a misshapen half-witted brute from a local tribe. A woman in the fort village takes the laundry every fourth day. And the cook—praise Jupiter! She is Roman."

"Have the Celts become shiftless since my brother's death?"

"No, my lord, they seem industrious enough. Tribune Vetus has kept them active, I would imagine. But they do like their beer." He shuddered. "A noxious liquid fermented from barley, if you can imagine such a thing."

Lucius's lips twitched. "I assure you, I cannot. I trust there's wine in the storerooms for the rest of us."

Candidus inclined his head. "Yes, my lord. Master Aulus had nothing but the best vintages and I thank Bacchus for it. Otherwise, we would be forced to drink water."

"A grim thought indeed," Lucius said dryly. He fell silent for a moment, considering. "What do the slaves say of my brother's death?"

"Nothing out of the ordinary, my lord, at least not yet. It may be they are reluctant to confide in me so soon."

"Keep me apprised, then." Lucius dismissed the man. As his footsteps faded, Aulus, who had been hovering at the edge of the courtyard, drifted toward an alcove near the door.

Lucius followed, halting at his brother's side before the house altar. There, on a polished stone slab, tiny gods and goddesses clustered about an offering bowl like soldiers drawn to a game of chance. Lucius gritted his teeth. The lares were charged with the guardianship of all who lived in the household. They had failed miserably in their duties toward Aulus.

Aulus lifted one hand and touched a goddess fashioned from a fragment of alabaster. Lucius sent a sharp glance toward his brother. He recognized the figurine and what she represented.

"Justice," he said. "I'll find it, brother. Without the aid of fickle spirits."

58

He backed away from the altar and strode to the door, nodding to the porter as he stepped into a day of miserable weather. Ponderous clouds spat moisture but couldn't seem to commit themselves to rain.

The passage onto which his residence fronted cut a wide, straight line from the east gate to the west. Six long barracks faced him, obscuring the towers of the northern gate. Even without prior exploration, Lucius knew the headquarters and hospital lay to the left, the stables and granaries to the south. Every fort in which he'd served had shared essentially the same arrangement.

Vindolanda was a frontier outpost. As such, it didn't approach the dignity of the great stone fortress at Londinium or even the smaller fortress at Eburacum. Its walls were thick turf topped by a sturdy wooden palisade and battlement that provided a clear view of the surrounding countryside.

Though modest in size, the post's strategic importance could not be underestimated—Vindolanda commanded the center of the road linking the eastern waters to the Hibernian Sea, at the narrowest point in Britannia's core—a mere seventy-five miles. With the surrounding lands secure, Rome controlled the intercourse of the docile southern tribes and their more warlike northern neighbors. In return for the taxes Rome exacted from the local Celts, the army provided secure trade routes and the chance for profit by all.

The sentry at the headquarters' gate saluted as Lucius passed into the unroofed center yard. In contrast to the fort commander's residence, no graceful plantings graced the wide space. Lucius gave the fort commander's office a cursory glance, wondering if Aulus had spent much time there. If he were to cast lots on the question, he would wager against it.

He approached a second, smaller cubicle, where a guard snapped to attention. Lucius looked past the footsoldier at Vindolanda's interim commander, the man who was now his second-in-command.

Gaius Brennus sat behind a battered desk far too small for his bulk, marking notes on one of the thin wooden tablets used for military records and correspondence. A number of identical tablets were scattered haphazardly before him. An open inkwell perched dangerously close to his right elbow. Smudges of ink and dirt showed on his fingers.

At Lucius's approach, Brennus set his stylus aside, got to his feet, and raised a hand in salute. The Gaulish officer was tall, even taller than Lucius, who was considered almost a giant among his Roman companions. His eyes were a watery gray, his face ruddy and pitted with scars.

A Celtic torc of twisted gold glinted behind his short, red-blond beard. The terminals had been fashioned in the shape of horned serpents with rubies for eyes. The neck ornament appeared old and in need of cleaning, Lucius noted. In that last detail, it matched the officer's tunic and mail overshirt.

"At ease," Lucius said.

"Commander Aquila. I await your orders."

Aulus brushed past Lucius and drifted to the far wall, where a large map of the fort and its surroundings had been affixed. Leaning forward, the ghost peered at the papyrus as if he were searching for some hidden path.

"What are you doing?" Lucius asked.

"Sir?"

Lucius clenched his jaw and sucked in an angry breath between his teeth. If he couldn't control his babbling, the fort would soon be as rife with rumors about his sanity as his Legion had been. With effort, he refocused on Brennus. "What is the report from the hospital?"

"Two of the men wounded in yesterday's attack died in the night. A third will most likely lose a leg. Fully half your escort from Eburacum is either dead or injured." Brennus's palm connected with the desk, causing the inkwell to lurch dangerously close to the edge. "Those men were the first reinforcements Vindolanda has seen in nearly a year. Every spare soldier in Britannia has been seconded to Gaul or Germania as replacements for the Legions bound for the East."

Lucius nodded. He was one of the few officers who had recently traveled the route in reverse. "I would examine the current duty roster."

After much shuffling, Brennus extracted a tablet from the clutter on his desk. "This is the status as of the Kalends of Aprilis," he said, frowning down at the sprawling list. "Since then, seven or eight men have been taken ill with fever. The medics have had little success treating it."

"Is there no physician?"

"He died last winter, sir."

Lucius suppressed a sigh of frustration as he scanned the roster. Of the 437 soldiers who had been attached to Vindolanda the past autumn, fifty-six were dead, as many killed in accidents as in skirmishes with the Celts. Were Aulus's men so poorly trained as that? The discipline of Rome's auxiliary troops was notably less strict than that of the citizen soldiers in the Legions, but even so Lucius expected at least a semblance of competence. Apparently, Aulus had spent his three years in Britannia scribbling stories and puttering in his garden, to the detriment of his duty as a commanding officer. He shot his brother a dark look, barely managing to bite back the reproof that sprang to his lips. Aulus blinked back at him, unperturbed.

The miserable report continued: ten men on leave, thirty-six seconded to Maia to assist in the construction of a seawall. Twenty-seven were in Londinium at the governor's command; fifteen were sick or wounded; eleven suffered from inflamed eyes. Twelve were listed simply as "unfit." Even with the addition of the surviving reinforcements, Vindolanda stood at barely more than half its optimal strength.

"Less than an ideal situation," Lucius told Brennus, not bothering to conceal his disgust.

"Yes, sir."

"Especially as the recent attack on my party certainly signifies an increase in hostilities with the local tribes."

"I'm not convinced that's the case, sir. A few spring raids are only to be expected."

Lucius kept one eye on Aulus, who had drifted toward Brennus and was regarding him with a distinctly disgruntled expression. "Nonetheless, caution is warranted. The gates will remain closed and the intercourse with the fort village must be closely monitored. Post a double guard on all shifts."

Brennus looked for a moment as if he would argue. Then he saluted. "As you say, sir."

Lucius paced a few steps to the wall map. A bold black square indicated the fort. The crooked line nearby traced the course of the small river that provided the garrison with water for drinking and bathing. Neat barley fields, tended by the relatively friendly locals who inhabited the fort village, ringed the fort walls. Beyond the fields lay the forest, thick and nearly impenetrable.

Aulus had been studying the northern portion of the map. There, rocky crags and deep ravines—most likely blanketed with Britannia's infernal fog—provided enough cover to hide several Legions' worth of barbarian warriors. Quite unlike the bleak Assyrian desert, in which the enemy had precious few places to hide.

By Pollux, he wished his brother had never come to this place. He turned back to Brennus. "What can you tell me of my brother's death?"

Brennus shifted his weight. "It was an unfortunate accident, sir."

"This garrison seems prone to accidents. Were you in the commander's hunting party that day?"

"No, sir. Commander Aquila rode out with the First Centurion and two junior officers. Sextus Gallus and Petronius Rufus."

"I understand the First Centurion was killed last autumn."

"Yes, sir. An accident."

"I would speak with the others, then," he said, his gaze drifting back to the map. Perhaps Aulus was trying to tell him something about that fateful day.

Brennus cleared his throat. "I'm sorry, sir, that won't be possible. Both men were injured in training during the winter. Their wounds proved fatal."

Lucius regarded Brennus in silence for a long moment. "More unfortunate accidents," he said at last.

"Yes, sir."

He strode toward the door. "It seems the First Cohort of Tungrians is in sore need of discipline. Call the men to the parade grounds. I wish to inspect those who have some-how managed to stay alive."

The raven cackled in Owein's dream, driving shards of pain into his skull.

It had been the same every night since Rhiannon had been lost, but tonight his vision had taken an ominous turn. The great black bird no longer spread its wings in flight. Instead, it swooped low to the ground and landed. Darting forward on its twig legs, it dipped its beak and speared the eye of a newborn lamb. Its gruesome meal complete, the hulking creature rose into the air. It soared across the treetops, only to dive again almost immediately. It alighted on the rack of a magnificent stag.

"Kernunnos," Madog said when Owein told him. "The Horned God may take the shape of any creature, but the hart is his favorite." He stroked his beard with one long, crooked finger. "A good omen it is. What form the power will be taking is yet to be revealed."

Owein let out a long breath and stared moodily into the fire in the center of Madog's forest hut. The cloying scent of the bundled herbs drying over the flames mingled with the moldy smell of the mud and dauble walls, which leaned inward so precariously that Owein wondered if a

Druid spell kept them upright. The skull of a stag guarded the only opening, a low portal hung with the skin of a wildcat. The Druid master's iron sword and silver dagger lay on a low table. A wooden-handled scythe with a blade of gold hung from the twisted rafters. Madog's staff—fashioned, Owein knew, from the heart of an oak struck by lightning—was not far from his hand.

The severed head of the Roman commander perched atop it.

Owein wondered at the skull's presence in Madog's hut. Until their return from the disastrous raid, the gruesome talisman had been displayed atop a stake inside the Druid circle. Now the Roman's hollow eyes surveyed Madog's sacred sanctuary. Dark patches on its surface—scraps of oiled skin and matted hair—seemed to dissolve in the shadows, leaving glimpses of smooth white bone.

Owein shuddered. So long as the Roman's head remained unburied, his soul was trapped in the formless land between death and life. His spirit was forced to lend its power to the cause of his destroyers. The dark slavery stretched into eternity with little hope for freedom.

He closed his eyes, remembering the man's hideous death dance. Rhiannon had cried for three full nights after Madog had thrust his sword into the prisoner's back. Owein's own visions had begun soon after. By chance, or were his nightmares a consequence of the Rite?

Madog's hand stretched toward his prize. Gnarled fingers stroked the dead Roman's rotted skin with the exuberant pride of a man touching his firstborn son. "Soon," he told it. "Soon."

Owein's scalp prickled.

"If Kernunnos comes to ye this night," Madog said, "attend him well."

"What good be visions that speak in riddles?" Owein asked, a plaintive note creeping into his tone. "If Kernunnos had spoken more clearly before the raid, I could have prevented Rhiannon's capture."

"Ye must not blame yourself that she was taken, lad."

Owein slammed his fist into the dirt floor. The shock of the blow traveled up his arm, but the spike of pain brought him no respite from his guilt. "I should have recognized my own arrows, at the least," he said, his voice rising. "If I had, I could have brought my sister safely home."

A grunt was Madog's only reply.

Owein shifted on his stool. The walls of the hut seemed to draw closer. His breath rattled in his lungs, proving, much as he hated to admit it, that Rhiannon's concern for his health had not been unfounded. He should never have joined the raid, no matter Edmyg's taunts. He should have cowered in the dun with the women. If he had, Rhiannon would be safe within the village palisade, brewing her potions or weaving at her loom.

He leaned forward, his forearms resting on his thighs, hands dangling uselessly between his knees. His foolhardy attack on the Roman commander had cost Rhiannon her freedom, her dignity, perhaps even her life.

"Edmyg holds me at fault," he muttered. "For once he has the right of it."

Madog stabbed a sharp stick into the fire, sending up a shower of sparks. "Edmyg hurls blame like other men throw spittle, with no regard for the direction of the wind. Your dreams foretold Rhiannon's capture, Owein. I am thinking it could nay have been avoided."

"What do ye mean?"

"Kernunnos has taken Rhiannon and placed her inside the Roman fort. Cormac reports her injury is not grave"— he stabbed the fire a second time—"and that she has caught the eye of the Roman commander."

Owein sprang to his feet. "If the bastard dares touch her—" He ended with a foul oath, his bravado fading. Most likely, the foreign dog had already forced himself on Rhiannon.

The blood rushed in his ears so fiercely that he almost

didn't hear Madog's murmured reply. "Ye and your sister share one blood, Owein." His fingers caressed the oiled skull. "Kernunnos leads you with visions. Rhiannon is close to the enemy's throat."

The old Druid's eyes shone red in the dancing light of the fire. "Such favors are nay to be wasted."

Chapter Four

"What are you doing?"

Rhiannon looked up to see Lucius's son perched on the low roof covering the courtyard garden's perimeter walkway. She'd been kneeling in the cool, moist dirt, so absorbed with loosening a choking vine from a clump of betony that she hadn't heard his approach.

"How did you get up there?" she asked.

He pointed to the upper gallery fronting Rhiannon's bedchamber. A stout vine climbed from the garden to entwine the railing.

"It wasn't hard," he said. "I can get up on the high roof, too."

"You're a resourceful lad."

"I suppose." He clambered across the slates and down the vine. His dark head bobbed between the plantings as he approached. The sun's muted rays were not yet strong in the square patch of gray sky framed by the walls of the Roman house, but morning light sparkled in the lad's eyes.

Rhiannon sat back on her heels and brushed a damp

strand of hair out of her face. She'd awakened at dawn on this, the second day of her captivity. She'd spent the first confined to her chamber, attended by a young slave woman. In response to Rhiannon's careful questioning, the girl—Bronwyn—revealed a fact that caused Rhiannon's heart to leap. A man of Cormac's description—and surely only one man fit that image—was a slave in the fort commander's dwelling.

She'd made her way to the garden to await him. He would come to her when he was able, she was sure of it. Rhiannon only hoped Lucius didn't find her first.

A pool of water shone in the center of the courtyard. Around it, rigid garden plots overflowed with clumps of a thorny shrub Rhiannon had never seen before. A few red-green leaves had unfurled, but many more were wanted before the unsightly canes would be covered. Nestled among the roots of the odd plants were clusters of more familiar greenery—betony, coltsfoot and meadowsweet, among others.

"What are you doing?" Marcus asked again.

She smiled up at him. "See this bit of betony? It can't take a breath for want of space. I'm clearing a path around it."

"Do plants breathe like people, then?"

She nodded. "They speak as well, at least to those who know how to listen."

"What do they say?"

"They tell why Briga, the Great Mother, has granted them life. Like people, each has its purpose—healing, coloring cloth, or flavoring food."

The lad hunkered down beside her and cocked his head to one side. "I don't hear anything."

Rhiannon's smile deepened. "Plants don't speak in words. It takes much patience to learn their language."

"Oh." Marcus pondered this revelation. "Will you teach me? I think I would prefer the language of the garden to that of the Greeks."

Rhiannon laughed at that. "Perhaps," she hedged. If all

went well, her time in the fort would be far too short to allow it.

"I wonder if Uncle Aulus could hear them. He never wrote to me of it, but he knew a lot about plants. I'm sure he tended these himself."

"Your uncle lived here?" Rhiannon asked.

Marcus's eyes clouded. "He was the fort commander. He was killed last autumn."

So the man who had fallen to Madog's sword was not only Lucius's kinsman but also his brother. The revelation hit Rhiannon like a blast of winter wind. For a moment, she stood again in the shadow of the great stones, the dying man's bloody fingers clutching her hem, his despair echoing in her heart.

He'd spoken to her before he died. *Tell him.* Had he been speaking of Lucius? Had the dying man's torment called his brother north to seek vengeance? An icy chill settled about her.

At that moment, as if she'd summoned it, Lucius's rich voice drifted from the far corner of the courtyard. Rhiannon sought him with her gaze, heart pounding. A door giving out onto the covered walkway opened. Demetrius emerged with Lucius a step behind.

Marcus shrank down behind a cluster of bare canes. "Quiet," he whispered fervently. "I'm supposed to be in the library translating Aristotle. If Magister Demetrius sees me, he'll skin my hide. And take pleasure in tanning it."

Rhiannon ducked her head—she certainly had no desire to attract attention. She peered through the thorn branches and watched the two men traverse the edge of the courtyard.

Her heart tripped a beat at the sight of Lucius in full uniform. Silver armor gleamed over a tunic the color of Roman wine. A sword and dagger hung at his hip and a short crimson cloak, fastened with a gold pin, fell over his shoulders. His crested helmet was nestled under one arm. His shining dark hair curled at his nape and at the edges of his strong, clean-shaven jaw. His bearing was powerful, but not overbearing as Edmyg's was. He moved with the grace of a sleek, exotic cat akin to the one portrayed in stone on Rhiannon's chamber floor.

Without her conscious assent, Rhiannon's gaze drifted lower, taking in Lucius's bare thighs and calves and the dark sprinkling of hair on his bronzed skin. Long muscles flexed as he walked, leaving her throat dry. Roman men didn't encase their legs in *braccas* as her kinsmen did. They preferred, it seemed, to leave their lower limbs bare at all times.

No doubt Roman women were glad of it.

Beside her, Marcus was barely breathing. "What will you do when the healer enters the library and discovers your absence?" she whispered.

"He won't, if Fortuna smiles on me. Magister Demetrius is bound for the fort hospital."

Lucius and Demetrius halted in the foyer, before a wide portal that most likely was the domicile's main entrance. At Lucius's command, a slave stepped from an alcove and lifted the latch.

The door swung open. Demetrius passed under the lintel into the patch of daylight beyond. Lucius made as if to follow, then stopped. He looked to the right, then the left, then pivoted in a full circle as if looking for someone. Rhiannon's brow furrowed. He'd performed the same odd movements in her room the day before.

A scowl appeared on Lucius's brow. "Go on ahead, Demetrius. I will follow shortly."

The door closed. Lucius wheeled about and walked to the edge of the courtyard, his attention fixed unerringly on the shrub behind which Rhiannon and Marcus crouched.

"By Pollux," Marcus muttered.

The lad's attempt at manly disgruntlement had Rhiannon stifling a laugh. Her amusement rapidly diminished as Lucius closed the distance between them and circled the shrub. His gaze flicked briefly over her and settled on his son. Marcus jumped to his feet, a blush spreading across his cheeks.

Rhiannon tried to rise. Dull pain shot through her thigh, accompanied by a rush of lightheadedness. She'd eaten little since her capture, not trusting her churning stomach to retain the rich Roman food. Her body was beginning to feel the effects of her fast.

She swayed on her feet, putting out one hand to catch Marcus's shoulder. She missed and would have fallen if Lucius hadn't stepped forward and caught her. She felt his touch far more keenly than she should have. His grasp was firm yet gentle, gifting her with the unconscious strength that seemed so much a part of him.

He steered her to a bench at the edge of the fountain. Rhiannon sank onto the smooth stone. She felt his steady scrutiny, but dared not lift her eyes to meet his gaze. If she did, she would see the eyes of his brother as she so often had in her nightmares. So she kept her face averted, staring at the ripples on the surface of the water.

"How in Hades did you get down the stairs?" he asked her.

"Slowly." She dared a quick peek at his face. His frown could have blistered the hide from a pig. No doubt it sent enemies and allies alike into spasms of terror but, curiously, Rhiannon felt no fear.

"You might have reopened your wound," he said. "Are you mad?"

"No. But another hour in that chamber might have made me so."

"Ah. You sought the garden."

"Yes." Rhiannon glanced toward Marcus, who was watching the exchange with undisguised interest.

"You are welcome to it, then. Stay as long as you like," Lucius said.

She nodded, keeping perfectly still while his gaze raked over her. Her unruly heart calmed only when he turned his attention to Marcus.

"Why are you not in the library?"

Marcus seemed to shrink under his father's disapproval. "I needed to visit the latrine," he mumbled. "I was just on my way back."

Lucius's gaze narrowed. "By a roundabout path, I see."

Marcus's blush deepened. "Yes, sir."

"Then continue on your way, by all means. Aristotle awaits you. Impatiently, I'm sure."

The lad wasted no time in fleeing the courtyard. Lucius watched him disappear through a doorway near the foyer, then sighed. He turned back to Rhiannon. "I must depart. If you've need of anything, hail one of the slave women. They've been instructed to serve you."

Alone once more, Rhiannon tugged another weed from the betony. She'd expected rough treatment from her captor. Instead, he gave her careful politeness. His respect was perhaps more unsettling than violence. It diluted the terror that had sustained her in the first hours of her capture and left room for her to feel the other, more disturbing emotions he invoked.

She pulled another root free from the dirt. He'd ordered the household staff to serve her. Another surprise. She'd expected to be given a slave's work. Instead, she had been handed more leisure than she'd had in her entire life. Of course, her true duties, those to be performed in Lucius's bed, hadn't yet begun.

She imagined his strong, gentle hands on her bare skin, and a pleasant ache settled in her loins. What would Lucius's loving be like? She sensed it would not resemble Niall's fierce coupling. The Roman's whispered words of two days before flooded through her senses. He'd said he wanted to taste her. Dear Briga . . .

Her musings fizzled in a rush of horror. Did she want this man in her bed? How could she view her clan's enemy with anything less than loathing?

Leaning forward, she splashed her fingers in the cool waters of the garden pool to steady herself. Water was the sacred gift of the Great Mother to her children. Even here, surrounded by Roman walls, Briga's peace flowed.

A door at the rear of the courtyard opened. Bronwyn appeared, arms laden with linens. A squat figure of a man followed, a misshapen brute with limbs half the length of Rhiannon's. His hands and feet, however, were huge. His head perched on his shoulders like a precarious boulder ornamented with dirty blond hair. His eyes, sharp and blue, glittered in his face like gems on the bottom of a still pond. Despite his small stature, he hefted an impressive load of firewood in his arms. Rhiannon snatched her fingers from the water, her heartbeat accelerating.

Cormac.

She started to rise. Edmyg's brother swiveled his head in her direction. His gaze caught hers briefly as he gave an almost imperceptible shake of his head. She nodded and sank down again on the bench.

"Come along, ye lout!" Bronwyn's tone was teasing.

Cormac leered at her, showing a wide gap in his front teeth. He murmured a lewd suggestion.

To Rhiannon's surprise, Bronwyn giggled and blushed. "Lucky it is that yer cock is as strong as yer wits are weak," she said.

Rhiannon's brows shot up. Cormac, witless? Hardly. He was the eldest of the three brothers and the cleverest by far. He had far more cunning than Niall or Edmyg, though he barely cleared his brothers' navels. If he'd been born without deformities, he would have been chieftain. As it was, she'd heard tell that he'd barely escaped being killed at birth.

The pair disappeared through yet another doorway. Rhiannon eased off the bench and onto the ground, renewing her efforts to free the betony from the grip of the weeds while watching the portal for Cormac's return. Now that she'd found him, it was possible she would escape the fort before the day was out.

She'd finished weeding the first garden bed and had

moved to a second before he reappeared. Rhiannon nearly jumped out of her skin when Cormac crept around one of the columns lining the edge of the courtyard and whispered her name. Though she'd been watching, she hadn't seen his approach. He carried a large wooden bucket in his hands.

"Ye must get me away," she said.

"How is your leg?"

"Better."

He eyed her speculatively. "And the Roman? Has he bedded ye yet?"

Rhiannon nearly choked. "No! Nor will he, if ye get me free of these walls before nightfall."

"I've sent word of yer capture to Edmyg." His tone turned mocking. "I await my noble chieftain's instruction."

"Instruction? Are ye daft? He'll be telling ye to bring me home."

Cormac flicked one sausage finger in a dismissive gesture. " 'Tis not possible for ye to leave this day."

"Then when?"

He shot a glance across the courtyard. "Lower yer voice, woman. The entire household will be hearing ye."

Rhiannon grasped a particularly stubborn weed and gave it a sharp tug. "I must get out of here," she said through clenched teeth. "Now."

He lifted his bucket and approached the fountain, brushing Rhiannon's arm as he passed. "The guard at the gates has been doubled. Every Celt who approaches is questioned at length. I'm able to pass only because I assist the Roman cook in her endless quest for fresh vegetables."

"Smuggle me in a cart, then."

"A fine plan, sister, if my sacks were nay empty on the way out."

Rhiannon smothered a sound of frustration. "There must be another way."

"I might persuade the village laundress to claim ye as her assistant. But nay until the guard is lightened."

"How long before 'tis safe to try?"

"No telling." He hopped up on the low wall surrounding the fountain and slid his bucket under the stream of clear water that spouted from the mouth of a fish. "Perhaps in a sennight if my idiot brother lies low and doesna provoke the Romans further. Ye'll have to make the best of it 'til then."

Rhiannon's heart gave a strange shudder. She was sure Lucius's careful politeness would not last seven more nights. He'd said he wouldn't force her to his bed, but he was a man, after all, and she had seen the heat in his eyes. And, to her shame, had felt her own body warm in response.

She watched water bubble over the rim of Cormac's bucket. "A spring within walls," she said, trying to turn her thoughts from Lucius. "A splendid convenience."

"No spring," said Cormac, scuttling back to the ground. He lifted the full bucket as if it weighed nothing. "This water's diverted from the burn."

"The burn that runs through the valley below the fort?" Rhiannon could not hide her amazement. "Are the Romans so powerful that they command water to run uphill?"

Cormac shrugged. "I ken not how the dogs manage it." He nodded toward the chamber into which he had carried the firewood. "But beyond that door the stream runs through their bathing rooms and latrine."

"They bathe within the house?" Rhiannon couldn't fathom it. She washed in a clear lake under the sky. Did Romans enclose their entire existence with flat walls?

"Aye, in a great pool of steaming water. Even the slaves are permitted—nay, required—to make use of it one day out of thirty."

Rhiannon imagined floating in such a cushion of warmth. Like a babe not yet born, surrounded by the waters of its mother's body. Surely even the goddesses of Annwyn did not know such luxury.

The door to the baths squeaked open a bit. Cormac caught Rhiannon's wrist and drew her down behind one of the thorn bushes. "Tribune Vetus emerges from his bath at last. Have ye seen him?"

Rhiannon shook her head.

"He passed the entire winter with his arse submerged." Cormac snorted. "No Roman lady could be finer."

He fell silent as Vetus emerged from the bathing room. A billow of perfumed steam followed him. A dark man, shorter than Lucius, with features far less handsome. He wore the crimson tunic of a Roman soldier, but moved with a graceful gait more suited to a woman. His short black hair, slicked with moisture, clung to his scalp. His chin was as smooth as a babe's. As she watched, the tribune glided to the corner of the courtyard and disappeared up the stairs.

"Hardly a man at all," Cormac said, spitting into a flowerbed. " 'Tis to be wondered why his cock doesna shrivel and fall off."

"The First Cohort of Tungrians is a disgrace to its standard." Lucius placed his palms on the scarred desk in his office and leaned forward, fixing Aulus with a scowl designed to bring him to his ghostly knees.

Aulus responded by glancing down and rearranging the folds of his toga.

Lucius's ire rose. He'd spent the better part of the day inspecting his brother's miserable troops, an activity that had left him disinclined to cater to the moods of a dead man. "If you were standing here in the flesh, I would throttle you."

Aulus made a rude gesture.

Lucius swore. "I'm sorry I ever wrote the recommendation that got you this command. I was a fool. I'd thought your years in Egypt had made a man of you." He rounded the desk, advancing on Aulus. "I was mistaken. You failed in your duty to Vindolanda."

Aulus sent him a look of reproach along with an icy chill

that stopped Lucius in his tracks. "Oh, I'm well aware you're dead," he said, disgusted. "But the fact remains that a disciplined garrison would not have fallen apart in six months." He gave his brother a wide berth and strode out of the chamber.

He halted in the headquarters' courtyard and looked back. "You should have made training your first priority."

Aulus rolled his eyes toward the gray sky, which at the moment was fading into a mottled dusk. His pale lips compressed in an unrepentant line. Lucius could almost hear his brother berating him for his obsession with discipline. Jupiter knew he'd heard the lecture often enough when Aulus was alive.

He exited the headquarters building, drawing an inquisitive look from the sentry. The first torches were sparking to life on the high battlement above the west gate. "At least my love of order has kept me breathing," he muttered. "Which is more than I can say for you. If you'd had a care for something other than fantasy and roses, you might be alive rather than rotting in a fort cemetery on the edge of the Empire."

The words had no sooner left his lips than Lucius wished them unsaid. Aulus's expression had gone hollow, his eyes bleak. His fingers worried the purple stripe on the edge of his toga.

Lucius halted at the door to his residence and braced his arm on the cold wood, a fierce wave of loss breaking over him. The pale figure tormenting him wasn't Aulus. Aulus was dead. Gone. But until his shade was banished, Lucius would not be able to mourn. His arm began to shake.

"Commander?"

Lucius whirled about. Gaius Brennus stood a few paces away, eyeing him curiously.

"Is there a problem, Quartermaster?"

"I thought to ask the same of you, sir."

Lucius waited a beat, until Brennus looked away. "The difficulty lies entirely with your troops," he said succinctly. "They are a disgrace. I expect to see every able-bodied man—save those on sentry duty—mustered on the parade grounds at cockcrow. In full battle dress."

"Yes, sir." Brennus pivoted and took a step toward the barracks.

Lucius's brows shot up. No soldier in the Legions would turn his back on a senior officer. He cleared his throat. "Quartermaster. You have not been dismissed."

Brennus halted. "Your pardon, sir."

"I'll see you tomorrow at dawn, soldier. Clean your armor before then."

The quartermaster's expression hardened. "As you say, sir."

"Dismissed."

The sentry at the northern gatehouse called a faint, "All's well." After a pause that was a fraction too long, the cry was repeated by the guard at the east gate. Lucius's hand clenched into a fist, but when he rapped on the door of his residence, the force of his blow was controlled, the sound precise.

The porter, a lean Celt with an unruly mane of blond hair, admitted him immediately. Lucius gave instructions for a late supper to be laid in the dining room. The man bowed and hastened in the direction of the kitchens.

Habit prompted Lucius to approach the house altar, where he lifted one of the lares at random and murmured a rote prayer he didn't believe would be heard. It was only when he replaced the figurine on the stone table that he took a good look at the brass god. An unclothed man in his prime, sporting a grotesquely huge erection.

"Potency." Lucius glanced toward Aulus, anticipating his brother's smirk. A warm wash of air, rather than the chill to which he'd grown accustomed, caressed his skin. The foyer was empty.

His gaze immediately sought Rhiannon. Did the Celt

nymph wield some dark power over the dead? Could she be a witch? The thought unsettled him. She hardly fit the description of such a creature that Horace had given in his *Epodes*.

He found her in the courtyard garden. She was sitting on a bench near the fountain, so still she might have been chiseled from marble, save for a wary flicker in her golden eyes. He drew closer, removing his helmet and abandoning it at the base of a rosebush. Perhaps she would be more at ease if his head was bare.

She'd tamed her fiery mane into a thick braid that fell over her shoulder to curl at her waist. Lucius much preferred it unbound. He imagined sifting his fingers through the strands and spreading them over her naked body like a curtain of flame. He'd gladly plunge through such a barrier to claim her.

Never before had a woman stirred Lucius's lust so completely. Julia had not, and Lucius had wanted his first wife with a rare fervor, even though their marriage had been a political pact arranged by their fathers. Once married, however, he'd found Julia to be spoiled and petulant, more of a girl than a woman. After Marcus was born he'd hardly cared when his wife barred him from her bed. The brief sorrow he'd felt at her death had been purely for his son's sake.

The women of the East, in contrast, had been lush and inviting, and knew bedchamber secrets unheard of in Rome, but Lucius had found their docility tiring. Now, faced with this slip of a woman who hadn't hesitated to put an arrow in his ass, his rod hardened so painfully he feared it would snap. If he slaked his need on her body, would his obsession fade?

He seated himself beside her on the stone bench. She made no response to his presence.

"The night falls far later here in the north than it does in Rome," he said at length.

She did not answer.

"Have you eaten this evening?" When she didn't respond, Lucius sighed and stretched out his legs. The dusk settled silently around them. He was prepared to wait all night for her response, but he doubted it would be necessary. No woman could remain silent that long. In the meantime, a few moments free of his brother's unrelenting presence would be pleasure enough.

A slave exited the kitchens and made the rounds of the courtyard, touching a lit taper to the pitch-soaked torches set about the perimeter of the garden. Lucius waited until the man had disappeared before placing his hand on Rhiannon's arm.

Her head turned and her gaze met his. "Do not touch me."

Lucius smiled. "The hour grows late. You should be seeking your bed. I'll carry you above stairs."

"I prefer to sleep with the kitchen women." She shook off his touch and rose.

"Ah, so the little bird can hop from its perch. I'd begun to wonder if you'd spent the entire day motionless on this bench."

Rhiannon's chin went up, accentuating its sharpness. "Hardly that. I cleared your garden."

She'd been pulling at weeds when he'd found her with Marcus this morning, Lucius recalled. He couldn't fathom it. He'd given no order for her to do so.

"Why?"

"The herbs have been neglected."

Lucius peered through the torchlight. One of the planting beds looked less crowded, perhaps, but beyond that he could discern little difference from its appearance the day before. The unruly clumps of greenery in no way resembled a garden, especially since the roses had yet to bloom. "No doubt my brother tended the garden himself."

His comment seemed to cause Rhiannon such distress that Lucius found himself replaying the words in his mind. He could find nothing untoward, though his nymph seemed close to tears. "By all means," he said hastily, "do whatever you like. I recognize little beyond the roses."

"Roses?"

He nodded toward the arching canes. "The shrubs covered with thorns."

"They are hideous."

"Flowers will soon improve their appearance." He extended one hand. "Come. I'll carry you above stairs."

Rhiannon took a swift step backward and ducked her head. The shy gesture charmed him. Was that a blush spreading across her cheeks? She took a second, more hesitant step, then drew a sharp breath. Swaying on her feet, she grabbed for the bench and missed.

Lucius sprang forward. As his arms tightened around her he willed her not to struggle, and perhaps she read his thoughts, for she went as still in his embrace as a mouse stunned by the cat's claws.

"Your leg pains you?" he asked, frowning.

She blinked up at him. "No." A flicker of alarm showed in her eyes. She twisted and Lucius reluctantly freed her, only to grasp her upper arm when he feared she would not keep her balance alone.

"I'm . . . I'm just lightheaded. 'Twill soon pass."

His gaze narrowed. "What have you eaten today?"

"A mug of *cervesia* at midday."

Lucius swore.

"I wasn't hungry."

"Hungry or not, you must eat."

" 'Tis no concern of yours."

"It is." Before she could open her mouth to protest further, he lifted her in his arms.

"Put me down!"

"No." He carried her across the courtyard toward the dining chamber, approaching the door at the same time as a man and a woman exited the kitchens bearing the late meal he'd ordered.

"You'll share my supper," Lucius announced in a tone that broached no argument.

The dining chamber gleamed in the soft light of the hanging lamps. Three wide couches, draped in fine linens, were clustered about a central table. On the walls Bacchus reigned, feasting merrily in a forest grove with his scantily clad supplicants. Some of the figures weren't clothed at all and taking full advantage of that happy fact. Rhiannon's eyes widened when she saw the painting, but she said nothing. Lucius eased her onto the nearest couch and tucked the bolster under her left arm as the slaves laid out the meal on the table.

She rolled onto her stomach and peered up at him. "I'm to eat while reclining?"

Lucius smiled. "It will enhance the pleasure of your meal." A heady mix of aromas rose from the table: broiled fish swimming in dark sauce, roasted eggs, and flat loaves arranged with artistic perfection. Lucius nodded his approval. His brother's Roman cook had a fine hand indeed.

He removed his armor, handing the torso shield along with his sword belt to the male slave with instructions for their care. The man bowed and left the chamber.

Clad only in his tunic, Lucius settled himself to Rhiannon's left, not touching, but close enough to wrap his arm around her waist if he so chose. "Your presence will enhance my own pleasure," he whispered in her ear.

As if in response, Rhiannon's stomach growled loudly. Lucius chuckled. "Your appetite seems to have recovered," he said, drawing close.

"It seems so," she said faintly, moving away.

The female slave stepped forward to fill their goblets. "Leave us for now," Lucius commanded. "We'll serve ourselves."

He reached over the bolster and used a flat knife to transfer various selections from the platters to a shared plate. When he'd finished, he lifted a plump morsel of fish with his thumb and forefinger and raised it to Rhiannon's lips. He held it just slightly out of reach.

She caught the offering on her tongue, laving the pad of Lucius's thumb as she drew the succulent fish into her mouth. Fire shot through his loins. He shifted on the cushions until he felt the whisper of her body along the length of his own.

He chose another small piece from the plate, but before he could present it, Rhiannon made a sound of distress. She snatched a goblet from the table and downed a hefty draught of wine.

"Dear Briga!" She swiped the back of her hand across her tearing eyes.

Lucius rubbed her back. "Have you never tasted fish?"

"None that swim in fire," she replied. Lucius chuckled and ate from his own dish while Rhiannon nibbled at the bread and ate a small portion of egg. At length, the slave woman returned bearing a platter of roasted boar's meat.

"Perhaps you will find the second course more to your liking," Lucius said. His finger brushed a tendril of hair from her cheek.

She went very still. "I've never been fond of boar's meat."

Lucius ordered the woman to take away the platter and bring the final course. Rhiannon's eyes widened when a bowl of poached pears soaked in honey and wine appeared before her. She dipped her spoon into the confection and did not stop until it was gone. She closed her eyes as she brought the final taste to her mouth. Lucius watched the pink tip of her tongue move over her lips to catch the last drop of syrup.

His arm brushed Rhiannon's shoulder as he nudged his own untouched plate in front of her. Her eyes flew open. He placed the palm of his hand on her nape. "I'm glad you found a dish to your liking at last," he said, his lips close to her ear.

She shivered. He slid his palm to her shoulder for the briefest of caresses before breaking contact. When the second dish of pears was empty he rose from the couch and, leaning, once again lifted her into his arms.

"I need no help," she said, twisting in his grasp.

"Perhaps not, but I wish to give it."

He stepped onto the path bordering the courtyard and strode toward the stairs. Once in the upper gallery, he paused and captured her gaze.

"Shall I carry you to my chamber, nymph?"

Rhiannon's heart pounded so violently, she feared it would leap out of her chest. She went very still, hoping that a dearth of movement would calm it. It did not.

Lucius's arms tightened about her. His steady pulse beat against her breast, not so rapidly as her own but swift nonetheless. One hand cupped her buttocks. Its heat burned through her, feeding the torturous fire that had been kindled by their intimate supper.

Lying on the Roman dining couch with Lucius had been far too much like lying abed. Every sip of wine had been flavored by his scent; every taste of honeyed fruit had been spiced by his touch. Rhiannon had eaten too little and drunk too much, and she had clung too tightly to Lucius's shoulders as he'd ascended the stairs.

His arousal had nudged her hip with every step and even now lay heavy between them. She struggled to remember that he was her clan's enemy and that this blatant evidence of his lust should repulse, not tempt her. But floating as she was in the pleasant haze of the Roman wine, the thought held little meaning.

Sweet fire raced through her veins, a desire so unfamiliar and fierce that it stole her breath. Lucius looked down at her, a splash of light from the courtyard playing about his face. His dark, exotic eyes gleamed.

"Shall I carry you to my chamber?" he repeated. His

voice, low and vibrant, cloaked her like a mantle of darkest midnight.

Rhiannon wondered that he had asked at all. Certainly Niall would not have. The thought sliced through the wine-induced fog like an icy wind. Dear Briga. What manner of woman was she to lust after her clan's foe?

She went rigid in his arms. "No. I would pass the night alone."

Lucius swore under his breath. In two swift paces he was at her chamber door, shoving it open. Midnight shadows shrouded the small space, relieved only by the red glow of the coals in the brazier. He strode to the bed, footsteps harsh on the tile, movements rough. He deposited her on the narrow mattress so abruptly that she fell back into the cushions. He braced his arms on either side of her head and leaned over her. His breath bathed her face with heat. He inhaled deeply as if to imprint her scent on his memory.

His lips parted, showing a glint of teeth. "I would stay with you." His head dipped slowly, and in the taut, endless moment before his lips touched hers, Rhiannon could think only that she could not turn away even if her very life had hung in the balance.

His kiss teased like the tantalizing flight of a butterfly. His possession eased, then advanced, a sensual assault both urgent and enticing. Desire flowed into Rhiannon's loins. Lucius's teeth nipped her lower lip, creating tiny darts of pleasure. His tongue soothed, then probed the slick lining, demanding more.

Rhiannon trembled beneath him. Her mouth opened as if in welcome, her arms entwined his neck as if in need. His body came down on hers, the ridge of his arousal pressing against her thigh. The small part of her brain that had been protesting her surrender fell silent. She was a woman, he a man, and the night was dark.

Yet even as the sweet ache in her breasts rose and the liquid heat pooled low in the hidden place between her thighs, the scornful whisper returned, taunting. How fitting that the granddaughter of Cartimandua should open her legs for her enemy.

Shame seared her. She gave a sharp cry of protest. When Lucius gave no response, she slapped his chest with her palm. She tore her lips from his, twisting as she fought to free herself from his weight.

He swore softly and shoved himself off the bed. His gait was angry as he strode to the window. He stood, unmoving, hands fisted at his sides and stared out into the black night. Rhiannon swallowed hard, her fingers knotting the edge of the coverlet. Had she gained another day's reprieve? Or had she succeeded only in tapping his rage?

At length he turned and approached her. She tensed as he drew near, but he merely took up a brass handlamp from the table near the bed. Crouching at the brazier, he touched the wick to the coals and blew gently until the flame leapt to life.

He repositioned the lamp on the table with careful precision. His eyes were hard, his expression grim. When he reached for her with an abrupt motion, she flinched.

He frowned and drew back. Rhiannon struggled to remain calm. Would he force her now? Would it have been better to yield to his advances when his mood had been light?

"What manner of man do you belong to, Rhiannon?"

She drew a shaky breath. "None."

"Every woman belongs to a man. Have you a husband?" When she didn't answer, he added softly, "I won't hurt you as he did."

"What?"

"I won't beat you. You needn't fear my hands."

Dear Briga. How could Lucius know that Niall had indeed taken to striking out at her? Not often, and never in the company of others, but Rhiannon suspected that Owein had known. The fault was her own. If her womb had provided Niall with a living babe, he'd never have felt the urge to hit her. And Edmyg never would have gone to Glynis's pallet to seek a son.

"He should be castrated." The compassion in Lucius's eyes was harder to bear than his anger. "Put your thoughts of him aside. I promise you will enjoy every moment in my bed."

"Your vanity is astounding," Rhiannon whispered.

He grinned suddenly, the dimple in his cheek deepening and his eyes taking on the impish glint of a lad. "Why not put my arrogance to the test? You may well find yourself begging for my conceit."

An unexpected laugh bubbled into her throat. "You are far too sure of yourself."

He touched her face, the roughened callus on the pad of his thumb curiously gentle on her cheekbone while his fingers caressed the sensitive skin behind her ear. Against her will, her eyelids fluttered shut.

Abruptly, he stepped back, leaving her bereft before she recalled she should be glad of his withdrawal.

"Please leave," she said, but the words held little force.

In answer, he lowered himself onto the bed and took her hand in his. He began a thorough kneading of her palm, first stroking with firm pressure, then tracing the skew of lines with a feathering touch. An aching response pulled low in Rhiannon's belly. The small smile tugging at one corner of Lucius's mouth told her that he was well aware of the effect of his touch.

Her face flamed and she snatched her hand away. "Why do you woo me? You are a Roman defiler. You have only to spread my legs."

"I wish your pleasure."

"You seek your own."

His teeth bared in a smile that looked almost painful. "True enough. Yet I find I anticipate your satisfaction even more." His voice dropped to an intimate whisper. "Would you care to know what I dreamed last night?"

She drew her knees up and wrapped her arms around them. "No."

Lucius rose and paced around the bed until he stood behind her, not touching, but close enough that the heat of his body seeped through the thin barrier of her tunic. "You came to me while I lay abed. You flowed over me like wine and I drank you in." The heat of his breath was on her neck, the musk of his sweat in her nostrils. "First, I savored your lips. . . ."

He paused on an inhale. Rhiannon licked her lips. They had gone suddenly dry.

"Then I moved to your breasts. . . ."

Her nipples tautened as if they'd been touched. She clutched her knees tighter, pressing them into her chest.

"Then your navel . . ." Lucius's breathing was rougher now and his tone had taken on a sharp edge. "I circled it with the tip of my tongue." His voice dipped to a bare whisper. "The taste was sweet, but I knew there were hidden places that would taste sweeter still." Rhiannon eased back slightly, her grip on her legs loosening as she strained to catch his words. Her hands moved to the cushion to balance her weight.

"I followed the scent of your need." His low, vibrant voice stroked like a caress. "I drank honey from the cup of your womanhood." His breath fanned over her nape, but still he did not touch her. "No wine could compare."

Her breath grew ragged and the fire between her thighs flared hot and slick. She imagined Lucius's tongue there, lapping and probing in that forbidden place. She bit hard on her lower lip, stifling a moan.

"I lay back and you rose over me. You sank onto my shaft and rode me into a storm."

Rhiannon's knees fell apart. She leaned back, into his arms, her body pleading for that which her lips could not beg.

He tasted her at last, his mouth searing the hollow between her neck and collarbone. His tongue stroked over her in delicious waves. His scent, spiced and dangerous, filled her senses with the promise of dark ecstasy. She twisted, threading her fingers through his hair and drawing him close.

He made a sound of feral satisfaction. He surged onto the mattress, his weight pressing her to the cushions as his tongue plunged and retreated. He delved into her mouth—a hot, wet promise of pleasures yet to come.

He eased back, kissing a line from the corner of her mouth to her earlobe. "Your past is gone. You belong to me now, Rhiannon."

His whispered words shattered the erotic fog hazing her brain, even as his shameless tongue sent another tremor of need coursing through her. She blinked and looked up at him. His eyes glittered down at her, alight with pure arrogance.

How many times had she seen the same expression on Niall's face?

She gave a sharp cry and struck him, throwing her full weight into the blow. Her fist connected with his jaw. His head whipped to the side and he lost his balance. He rolled over the edge of the mattress and struck the floor with a sickening smack. Rhiannon scrambled off the opposite side of the bed, putting its bulk between them as he leaped to his feet.

He rubbed the back of his head and glared at her. "By Pollux! Why did you do that?"

"I don't belong to you, Roman."

"You do." Anger radiated from his body with the force of a wildfire. Deliberately, he leaned across the narrow bed and caught her chin between his fingers. "Do not forget it. My patience is not infinite. You are mine and I mean to have you."

"Shall I lift my hem for you then, master?" She spat out the word as if it were dung. "A quick plunge should soften your temper. My wishes hardly signify. A Roman never shrinks from lands where he is not welcome."

"So you say. Yet I wonder—were I to slip my finger between your thighs, would I find myself unwanted?"

"Yes," she said, but she twisted her chin from his fingers and dropped her gaze.

He gave a short, harsh laugh. "Soon, Rhiannon, you'll beg me to conquer you. When I slip my sword into your sheath, you will writhe with the glory of it."

Dear Briga, what arrogance. Yet even as she condemned him, she feared his words might very well be true.

He half turned and when he spoke again, it was as if to himself. "Another man would have taken you so often he would have tired of you by now." He laughed again, and the brittle sound echoed off the walls. "Perhaps it is the final proof of my insanity that I intend to leave you untouched."

She dared not risk a response to that.

He strode to the door. "No doubt I'll see you in a dream again tonight." Another chilling burst of laughter. "By Pollux, it is sure to be a nightmare."

Chapter Five

The following morning, Rhiannon entered the kitchen shortly after dawn, intent on tracking down her brother-in-law.

"Is Cormac about, Alara?" she asked the stout Celt woman who had tried to coax her appetite the day before.

Alara looked up from the bread she was kneading and blinked in surprise. "Have ye discovered the man's talents already then?"

Rhiannon gave her a sharp glance. Did the woman suspect Cormac was more than he seemed? "Talents?"

Alara chuckled. "Yer a coy one, aren't ye? There's only one reason a lass as fair as ye would be seeking that misshapen lout. His cock's near as long as his legs."

Rhiannon's faced flamed scarlet, but she bit back the protest that sprang to her lips. Pretending a tryst with Cormac was perhaps the safest way to speak privately with him. "Aye," she said. "Bronwyn twittered so when she spoke of him. I mean to see for myself if her tales are true."

"Take a care, lass, lest the new master find ye out. He doesna look to be a man to share his woman."

Rhiannon's face reddened even more. Was the entire

91

household aware of Lucius's pursuit? No doubt they were casting lots as to the hour of his success. "The Roman's nay here," she informed the woman. "Do ye know where Cormac is?"

Alara upended a wooden bowl over her dough. "Gone with Claudia to the fort village," she said, nodding to the cook's empty place by the main oven. " 'Tis his job to haul her selections from the market."

The market. Cormac would be meeting his contact there, who surely would have word from Edmyg by now. Rhiannon lifted a winter apple from a basket on the floor and examined it thoughtfully. "When will he return?"

"Nay afore midday."

Rhiannon took a bite of the tart fruit and watched as Alara assaulted a second mound of dough with the energy of a dog attacking a bone. It was hardly past dawn, but already the kitchen women were abuzz with preparations for the evening meal. She shook her head in amazement. The Roman kitchen contained easily as much space as an entire Celt roundhouse. Long worktables marched down the center of the room, bundles of herbs hung from the rafters, and a row of stone ovens lined the outside wall.

She dropped her apple core in the garbage trough. "Will ye tell Cormac to seek me out?"

Alara gave her a disapproving look. "Aye, I'll tell him, but 'tis a dangerous game ye be playing, lass."

It was indeed, Rhiannon reflected, but not for the reason Alara suspected. She wandered through the door to the courtyard and stared into a shroud of rain. No garden work would distract her this day. With her hands idle, her thoughts should have been consumed with the prospect of her imminent escape, but to her great shame they were not. Instead images of Lucius filled her mind.

Lucius, who had aroused her with dark whispers. Lucius, who had kindled forbidden fire in her loins. Lucius, who had left her untouched despite his obvious desire to share her bed.

A small part of Rhiannon wished he had ignored her protests. Dear Briga! She shook her head as if to shake the notion from her brain. She should be nothing but relieved that she had escaped his lust for another night. If all went well, Cormac would smuggle her out of the fort today and by dark she would be lying on her own pallet.

Soon after, Edmyg would take Niall's place and lie there with her. A knot of dread tightened in her stomach. Edmyg wouldn't be pleased that she'd followed the raiders and put herself in danger. Her duty had been to remain in the dun, awaiting the injured. How many of her wounded kinsmen had died because she hadn't been there to heal them? And what of Owein? Edmyg would surely blame him for Rhiannon's capture. She stared into the rain. If she found he'd laid a hand on the lad . . .

"What are you looking at?"

With an effort, Rhiannon pulled herself from her dark broodings. Marcus stood a few paces away, fingering his gold talisman.

"Am I to be feared this day?" she asked him.

He dropped the charm and flushed. "No. It's just—the expression on your face a moment ago. I might have thought you were staring into the jaws of a lion."

"A lion?"

"A great beast from the lands across the southern sea. Like a cat, only much larger. There's one done in mosaic on your bedchamber floor."

Rhiannon shivered, imagining such a creature sprung to life. She glanced behind her, as if half expecting the animal to be lying in wait. Marcus chuckled.

She narrowed her gaze at him, biting off a laugh at the mischief flashing in his eyes. "Where is your tutor, miscreant?"

"Magister Demetrius went again to the hospital. Did you

know there is no fort physician here? The last one choked on a boar's knuckle." He snickered.

"That hardly seems like a cause for mirth," Rhiannon pointed out.

The lad sobered. "I know. But I can't help laughing when I think of it. One of the slaves told me the physician was a great, fat man, with a red face and jowls that waved when he walked." He looked to the courtyard. "It's too wet for you to work in the garden today."

"Yes."

He sighed. "Aristotle, however, can be read in any weather."

"Are you shirking your studies again?"

Marcus shrugged. "Rain makes my mind wander."

"As does the sun, I imagine."

The lad grimaced. "Aristotle was an uncommonly dull man, and there's a whole shelf of him in the library. In the original Greek. Magister Demetrius will probably make me translate every scroll."

"You can read Greek runes?"

"Yes. Though I wish I didn't have to." He stared gloomily into the rain. "Will you come to the library? I'm sure my studies will go easier with you there."

"I very much doubt that," Rhiannon said, but she allowed Marcus to lead her to a small chamber near the entrance foyer.

She blinked at the fantastic scene that greeted her there. Shelves piled with slender brass tubes spanned the walls from floor to ceiling. A tall cupboard stood near the door. A large hanging lamp, sporting more flames than Rhiannon could count, threw its dancing light onto a long stone table. Ink pots and pens were scattered across its surface, along with a number of hinged wooden tablets.

Marcus sank down on a cushioned stool and scowled at an open scroll. Rhiannon had seen papyrus only once before, when a peddler had passed through her village. That had been just a tiny scrap compared to the wide roll that lay on the table, weighted with polished stones and scrawled with precise dark markings. So many more waited on the shelves. It was a treasure beyond imagining.

"Father will be terribly angry if I don't finish my lessons," Marcus said. He picked up a hinged wooden tablet and opened it. The inside surfaces were coated with wax.

"He wants the best for you, no doubt."

"So Magister Demetrius says. But Father's always angry with me for something, no matter what I do. What use is there in trying to please him?"

Rhiannon couldn't think of a reply to that, so she nodded toward the tablet in Marcus's hand. "May I see?"

Marcus handed it to her. Three scrawling lines of runes had been scratched into the wax.

"Are these Greek runes?"

"No," Marcus said. "This is the Latin. The Greek is there." He pointed to the scroll laid out on the table.

Rhiannon took the stool opposite Marcus and peered at the delicate papyrus. Black letters crawled across the creamy surface in neat rows like ants, offering their knowledge to any with the skill to decipher them. The concept amazed her—Celts carried their stories in their hearts. Madog had once told her that Romans and Greeks were possessed with brains softer than sand. Rather than exert the discipline needed to commit their sacred stories to memory, they scratched them in ink. Still, to Rhiannon's mind, writing seemed a wondrous thing.

She touched the runes. "What does it say?"

Marcus made a face. "It's Aristotle's discourse on prior analytics." His brow creased as he read. " 'If no beta is alpha, neither can any alpha be beta. For if some alpha were beta, it would not be true that no beta is alpha.' And more of the same. I'm to copy each line of the Greek and translate it into Latin. As you can see, it's an exceedingly dull work."

Rhiannon was inclined to agree. "Are there no stories on the shelves?" she asked.

Marcus shot her a glum look. "Yes, but I'm forbidden to read them. Uncle Aulus collected tales from all over the Empire." He slumped down on his stool, his eyes suddenly bleak. "I can't believe he's gone."

Rhiannon stilled. "Your uncle?"

Marcus nodded. "His death didn't seem real until we arrived at the fort. Before he came here, he served as a tribune in Egypt, but he visited Rome as often as he could and always brought me a new story. I used to wish he were my father."

"You don't mean that."

"I do. I hardly know Father. He's been on campaign for as long as I can remember."

"Did you not travel with him?"

"No," Marcus replied, pressing his fingernail into the wax at the edge of his tablet. "Mother would never have allowed it. But she's dead now," he added matter-of-factly. "That's why I'm here in the North."

Rhiannon touched his arm, not one bit fooled by the lad's careless tone. "I'm sorry your mother is gone."

"She died last summer, giving birth to my sister. Demetrius said the babe was turned the wrong way and Mama didn't have the strength to endure the pain." His voice trembled. "The baby came out dead anyway, so perhaps it was best that Mama never knew."

Without pausing to think, Rhiannon left her stool and knelt at Marcus's side, pulling him into her arms and ruffling his hair as she had done with Owein so many times. "And your father?" she heard herself ask. "Was he distraught?"

"Father wasn't there. He was in Assyria with the emperor. Magister Demetrius wrote to him when Mama got sick, but he didn't get home until a month after her burial."

"How awful!"

Marcus sniffed. "Father was so angry when he arrived home that I wished he had stayed in Assyria. He'd been there a year and a half already—why bother to come at all?"

Rhiannon drew back. "Your father had been in the East for a year?"

"Longer. He'd been gone for two turns of the New Year."

"And your mother went to visit him during that time?"

Marcus gave her an odd look. "Mama? No. She would never have gone to the frontier. She didn't even like the countryside. She preferred Rome."

Rhiannon rose from her stool and paced a few steps away, not wanting Marcus to see the surprise she knew must show on her face. Dear Briga. Lucius's wife had died birthing another man's child. No wonder he'd been angry.

Marcus picked up a smooth stick with a metal nib and made some random marks on his tablet. "But then Father said he'd had word that Uncle Aulus was dead. He was to leave for Britannia and I didn't want him to go. At least not without me. He didn't want to bring me, but I begged until he gave in." He sighed. "I thought I could make him proud of me."

Rhiannon came up behind Marcus and laid a hand on his shoulder. "I'm sure that he is."

"No." Marcus studied the tip of his stylus with exaggerated care. "He's not. I'm a disappointment."

"Surely he didn't tell you such a thing."

"He doesn't have to. I can tell."

Rhiannon took hold of his shoulders and turned him toward her. "You're mistaken."

"No, I'm not. I can ride a horse, but I hate history and logic and I'm terrible with a sword. I'll make a poor soldier."

"It matters not. You'll be a fine man."

Marcus dragged the back of his hand across his eyes and blinked up at her. "Do you think so?"

"I know it," Rhiannon said firmly, rising. "You have a great curiosity. That's the mark of the wise."

He gave her a small smile, though the expression in his

eyes told her he was unconvinced. Turning back to the table, he picked up his stylus and tablet. Rhiannon scrutinized Aristotle's indecipherable writings. When she raised her head, she found Marcus watching her, the mischievous light restored to his eyes.

He broke into a wide grin, complete with Lucius's dimple. Rhiannon's breath caught.

"Here," he said, turning his tablet around. "Look."

He'd smoothed out the Roman runes and replaced them with the image of a woman's face. Though the rendition was only a few quick strokes, his hand had been so skillful that the drawing seemed almost to breathe. Rhiannon stared at it in amazement. Such skill was powerful magick indeed.

"Do you like it?"

"Very much." Then, hesitantly, "Is it your mother?"

Marcus's face fell. "No. It's you. Can you not tell?"

Rhiannon's eyes widened. She had never seen an image of her own face, save in a wavering pool of water. Was this truly her likeness?

Marcus turned the tablet around and regarded it with a critical air. Then he made a sound of exasperation and passed the flat edge of his stylus over the wax, obliterating his work. "You're right. I did the eyes all wrong."

"I didn't mean—" Rhiannon began.

"But it's hardly my fault." Marcus tilted his head to one side and gave her a shy smile. "You're far too beautiful to draw."

The innocent compliment made Rhiannon blush. "Thank you, Marcus."

"My father thinks so too, you know." He affected a nonchalant tone, but his gaze wandered the room as if afraid to rest. "I saw the way he looked at you in the courtyard yesterday. As if you were Venus herself."

"Venus?"

"A goddess," Marcus clarified. "Of love."

Rhiannon's face flamed even hotter. She turned back to the scroll. "Aristotle grows weary with waiting."

Marcus rolled his eyes. "Aristotle is dead." He dropped his tablet and stylus onto the table. "Though I suspect he's not buried deeply enough."

Rhiannon chuckled. "Then what will you do, if not study?"

"Would you like to play a game?"

"What game?"

Marcus slid off his stool and moved to the cupboard. "I'm not allowed to go through the scrolls, but Magister Demetrius didn't say anything about Uncle Aulus's games." He opened the cupboard's tall doors and rummaged through the contents.

He extracted a wooden board and two leather pouches. "I knew there would be a Robbers board in there," he said, returning to Rhiannon's side. "Uncle Aulus taught me to play. It was his favorite."

He frowned at the crowded table, then simply pushed his stool to one side and sat on the floor, setting the checkered square of wood in front of him. Rhiannon seated herself opposite him and leaned forward. "How do you play?"

Marcus upended the larger pouch, releasing a shower of black and white tiles. He took the black squares for himself and pushed the white ones toward Rhiannon. Then he fished around in the second pouch and drew out two round stone disks, one of each color.

"This is your leader, the *Dux,*" he said. "He's in charge of your band of robbers. If you lose him, the game's over." He began placing his tiles on the board, one by one. Rhiannon did the same. As she set down her last token, Marcus broke into a wide grin.

Her men were surely doomed.

She was right—Marcus's robbers made short work of hers in the first battle. Rhiannon lost a second round, but managed to take the third match.

"You learn far too quickly," Marcus grumbled.

She laughed and leaned forward to ruffle his curls. "I have a good teacher."

"Let's see if you're any good at Knucklebones." He rummaged once more in the cupboard and returned with a pouch of small bones. "Sheep's knuckles," Marcus explained. He chose five and held them in one palm.

With a sharp motion, he tossed the bones in the air and tried to catch them on the back of the same hand. Three clattered to the floor, but the remaining two stuck.

"I can do better," he said. He scooped up the bones and tried again.

Rhiannon fished more bones from the pouch and imitated Marcus's toss. All five bounced off her knuckles and skittered under the table. Marcus giggled. Rhiannon retrieved the bones and tried again, sending the lad into a fit of laughter when her second attempt failed as miserably as the first.

He made a noise of superiority and tossed his own set. Rhiannon swatted at the bones in midtoss, knocking three across the room.

"Hey! You can't do that!" Marcus said.

"I just did," Rhiannon replied, tossing her own bones well out of Marcus's reach.

The lad lunged for them, but Rhiannon still managed to catch one on the back of her hand. She threw him a triumphant look.

Marcus dove for the bone, slamming into Rhiannon with his full weight. They fell together in a heap on the Robbers board, scattering the tiles across the floor. Marcus scrambled to one side. Rhiannon hoisted herself onto her elbows, met his startled gaze, and burst into laughter.

Marcus hooted and dropped onto his back on the floor, arms flung wide. Rhiannon leaned back against a leg of the table, giggling like a lass.

"Clearly," Marcus said, chortling, "I'm the winner."

"No, let me try again." She gathered five of the bones

and tried again to catch them on the back of her hand. When they bounced off her knuckles, she dissolved once more into laughter. "Truly, Marcus. No one could succeed at this game!"

Marcus sat up and collected another handful. "Uncle Aulus could catch all five," he said. "So can Father. I saw them playing once late at night."

Rhiannon could scarcely imagine it. She readied her pieces for a third try. "You jest. I'm not so foolish as to believe your father excels in such a frivolous pastime."

"Well, you should, because—"

"It is true," a man's voice said.

Rhiannon's head snapped up. Lucius stood in the doorway—how long had he been there? Mud stained his bare legs and marred the shine of his armor. He'd yet to remove his helmet—the plumes of its crest brushed the door's stone lintel. The side guards shaded his expression, but she felt his scrutiny with every fiber of her being.

"Father!" Marcus's voice hit a high note.

Rhiannon scrambled to her feet, her fist closed tightly on her set of bones.

Marcus leaped up as well. His foot slipped on a heap of Robbers tiles, sending him skidding across the floor. He grabbed for the edge of the table, missed, and went sprawling atop it. A writing tablet skittered across the stone and crashed to the floor.

"Jupiter help me," Lucius muttered.

Marcus shot him a fearful glance and dove under the table to retrieve the tablet.

"Marcus," Lucius said.

Marcus jerked his head around and it hit the underside of the table with a crack. He sucked in a breath and emerged slowly, clutching the tablet like a lifeline. Rising to his feet, he placed it on the table with exaggerated care.

"Marcus, come to me," Lucius commanded. Marcus stiffened as though he feared his father would run him through with his sword.

Rhiannon stepped between them. Lucius's startled gaze focused on her. "Stand aside," he said.

"No." Behind her, Marcus gasped. She held out her palm and offered Lucius the knucklebones. "I would see you perform the feat of which you boast."

His expression turned as dark as a thundercloud. "Very well."

She dropped the bones into his palm and retreated to Marcus's side. Lucius weighed the set in his hand. When he looked up, his expression was inscrutable. "What is learned as a child is seldom forgotten."

With a swift flick of his wrist, he sent the bones aloft. His palm flipped downward. All five knucklebones landed, neatly balanced, on the back of his hand.

Marcus gave a gasp of delight. Lucius's opposite palm closed over the bones. Retrieving a pouch from the floor, he slid the pieces inside and handed the bag to Marcus. "Put this room in order and return to your studies."

The lad took the bag, his shoulders visibly relaxing. "At once, Father."

Lucius turned to Rhiannon. "Come."

She shot a sidelong glance at Marcus. "No. I'll stay and help Marcus tidy the room."

Marcus made a strangled sound. Rhiannon snorted. Did no one ever contradict Lucius? If not, it was time someone did.

Lucius fixed Rhiannon with a glare that would have caused even the most battle-hardened soldier to drop to his knees. And indeed, Rhiannon did drop to her knees, but not to cower. She began gathering the scattered Robbers pieces.

Lucius grasped her by the elbow and hauled her back to her feet. The game tiles she held clattered to the floor. "Come," he repeated in a tone that brooked no defiance.

He propelled her out the door. When it had shut behind them, Rhiannon wrenched her arm from Lucius's grip. "What are you about? You scared Marcus half to death."

Lucius shot her a dark glance. "I only wish you were as easy to frighten. Why were you disturbing my son's studies?"

"He sought me out." She strode past him into the courtyard. The rain had lightened. Only a few stray drops stirred the puddles.

She stopped at the edge of the fountain. Lucius came to a halt behind her, not touching, but so close she could smell the musk of the day's exertion on his skin. Warmth pooled low in her belly. He set one hand on her shoulder and an odd restlessness shot through her. Feigning nonchalance, she moved away, breaking the contact.

"The boy needs to attend his studies," Lucius said.

"He needs a father more. Especially since he has lost his mother." She sank down onto the stone bench and dabbled her fingertips in the water. A measure of the Great Mother's calm flowed into her, enough that she dared a look into Lucius's eyes.

She saw sorrow there, and regret, before his gaze shuttered. "Demetrius thought the journey north might turn Marcus's mind from his mother's death." He bent and picked up a pebble that had strayed from the path to nestle in the dirt. "He was very attached to her." He tossed the pebble from hand to hand, not meeting her gaze.

"Yet she lay with another man while you were at war. She died bearing his child."

He started. The pebble glanced off his arm and plunked into the pool, splattering water over the edge. "Marcus told you that?"

"No. He's far too innocent. He told me only that you'd been gone more than a year before the babe's birth."

"Another reason why I consented to bring Marcus to Britannia," Lucius said. "Rome is a city built as much of gossip and rumor as it is of stone. Sooner or later Marcus would have realized the truth. I would rather his memory of Julia be unsullied, at least while he is young."

"Even after she shamed you?"

Lucius shrugged. "I hadn't visited my wife's bed since before Marcus's birth and Jupiter knows I was not celibate all that time. I could hardly expect Julia to comport herself like a Vestal in a city where bed partners change more frequently than the weather." He met Rhiannon's gaze. "But I did expect her to use whatever means necessary to avoid bearing a bastard."

"Oh." She kept her eyes fixed on the surface of the pool. "Did you not love her?"

He was silent for a time. Rhiannon's breath grew shallow, though she tried to tell herself that his answer was of no matter to her.

"I loved her once," he replied finally. "Or thought I did. Long ago, when I was young and blind with lust. Before I discovered she was a gilded box that didn't contain the treasure I'd hoped for." He shook his head, as if clearing the memory from his mind. "Julia was a good mother; I cannot fault her on that score. I know Marcus feels her loss."

"That's all the more reason for you to be gentle with him."

"And encourage his weakness?" Lucius replied. "No. I think not. He's better served by putting sentiment aside and applying his mind to Aristotle's logic. I fear for his future if he does not. Every day he grows more like . . ."

"His mother?" Rhiannon ventured when Lucius fell silent.

"No," he replied sharply. "Not like Julia. Like Aulus. My brother. Marcus cares more for tales of fancy than for the world before his eyes. Like the story of a Celt woman who ate a bad child and birthed a beautiful one from his bones."

Rhiannon's eyes widened. "Marcus told you that story?"

Lucius snorted. "He babbled incessantly of it on the road."

"The story of the crone mother teaches that good is

104

birthed from the bones of evil, even as day rises from night."

"Evil brings only more of the same," Lucius replied. "Marcus must learn that."

"He's yet a lad, and seeking his purpose. His sensitivity is a strength, not a failing. It will lead him to wisdom."

"Or to disaster. My brother's death proves it."

A vivid image of Aulus's death flashed through Rhiannon's mind. "How so?" she asked, struggling to keep her voice steady.

Lucius drew his dagger and tested its edge with his thumb, an unconscious gesture that raised the hairs on Rhiannon's nape. "There's a man residing in this house. Tribune Vetus. Perhaps you have seen him?"

"The officer who frequents the baths?"

Lucius gave a short, mirthless laugh. "None other. I came north believing Vetus had murdered my brother." His fingers flexed on the dagger's hilt.

"Why would you think such a thing?"

Lucius swiped his blade into the air and then to the side in one sleek motion, fighting an unseen enemy. "Vetus penned the report of my brother's death. Aulus supposedly died while hunting for boar. A sport he abhorred. I suspected Tribune Vetus invented the story. I came north to discover why." He pressed the tip of his dagger to his thumb, piercing his flesh. A single drop of crimson blood welled from the cut and dropped to the earth.

Rhiannon sucked in a breath. Could it be that Lucius was unaware of the true circumstances surrounding his brother's death? But why would the tribune invent such a fiction? "What have you found out?" she asked. Her voice sounded strange to her ears.

"So far, little." Lucius resheathed his blade with a brutal motion and began to pace the gravel path. Stones crunched under his boots. "Aulus's bones lie in the fort cemetery, yet all witnesses to his death have conveniently disappeared. Vetus is an indolent fool. If he betrayed my brother, I have yet to discover his motive. But the fact remains that someone is lying." His dark eyes glittered. "If there is a man in this fort who knows the truth, I will find him."

And if the truth is known only by a woman? Rhiannon withdrew her finger from the pool and crossed her arms over her middle, feeling suddenly ill.

He stopped pacing, pausing in front of Rhiannon's bench and meeting her gaze. "Justice will be served. When it is, I will leave this wretched island and return to Rome as a civilian. A seat in the Senate awaits me. I can no longer avoid the duty of occupying it." His expression softened. "I'll take you with me when I go, of course. I think I would enjoy showing you my homeland."

Rome. If the luxury of this house was any measure, the capital must hold wonders far beyond her dreams. Part of her longed to see such glory, but she knew such a thing would never come to pass. She refrained from saying as much to Lucius. It mattered little.

She would soon be gone.

At midday, Rhiannon renewed her search for Cormac. Surely he'd returned from the fort-village by now. She would corner him in the storeroom and hear a plan of escape from his thick lips, even if it meant the entire household believed they coupled between the shelves.

She found him outside the rear entrance to the kitchens, maneuvering a heavily laden cart. It was the first time Rhiannon had seen the door unbarred. She looked past her brother-in-law's stubby frame to the unfettered daylight beyond. Even the narrow alley between the house and the stables glowed with freedom.

"Have ye heard from Edmyg?" she asked, rescuing a delicate bundle of spring greens from his rough hands.

"Aye. He came to the village himself. I had words with him while Claudia fussed over a fisherman's morning catch." Cormac set his shoulders under a cask of *cervesia* and heaved it from the cart and into the kitchen. Bronwyn looked up from tending the oven fires and giggled. Claudia, an enormous Roman woman with strong beefy arms and swarthy skin, frowned at the girl.

"And?" Rhiannon said, following her brother-in-law into the storeroom.

Cormac set the cask on the plank floor. "How fares yer leg?"

" 'Tis well enough. I'll be having no problem escaping, if that's what is worrying ye."

He didn't meet her gaze. "Ye'll nay be leaving just yet."

"Not leaving? I must!"

"Nay. Edmyg bids ye stay."

Rhiannon's mouth dropped open. "Stay?" Bronwyn entered the storeroom and made a great show of scooping a measure of beans from a bin. Rhiannon waited until the girl had returned to the kitchen, then said, "What madness are ye talking?"

Cormac straightened to his full height and peered up at her. "Edmyg is thinking to use yer capture to the clan's advantage."

"How so?"

He returned to the cart and laid his hands on a haunch of fresh venison. "He seeks to rally the chieftains for an attack on the fort, but Kynan—" He spit into the dirt. "Kynan cowers like a dog with his tail between his legs. He's afeared of the fort's new commander."

Rhiannon pitched her voice low. "As well he should be. But what has this to do with my escape?"

Cormac hefted the venison and waddled to the rear of the storeroom, well away from the heat of the ovens and the ears of the kitchen women. "The soldiers of Vindolanda are Gauls. Celts. They share one blood with the Brigantes, worship Kernunnos as we do. If they can be persuaded to mutiny when the clans attack, the fort will fall faster than a house of twigs in a gale."

"Mutiny! They are soldiers of Rome, no matter their ancestry." She shook her head. "They would pay a grave price for such treachery."

Cormac grinned, showing a rotten gap in his yellowed teeth. "Every beast has its price. If the bait is set carefully, a meal will be had."

"What bait could ye have set to turn the garrison against Rome?"

He climbed onto a tottering stool and hung the meat on an iron hook. "Ye need not know. Ye've only to play yer part."

A knot of apprehension settled in Rhiannon's stomach. "Which is?"

Cormac hoisted himself onto a crate that afforded him the height of a warrior. He leaned back against the wall, folded his arms across his chest and regarded Rhiannon with a hard expression. For an instant, he looked so much like Niall and Edmyg that she almost forgot his deformed body.

"What am I to do?" she whispered.

"Has the Roman taken ye yet?"

"No! Nor will he!"

Cormac regarded her steadily. "He was in yer chamber last night."

Rhiannon's hands fisted in her skirt. "And what do ye know of that?"

"I'm a spy, dear sister. 'Tis my business to ken all that passes in my domain." He leaned toward her, his thick lips curling upward. "Does the Roman's cock thrust as deep as my dear brother's did?"

"Ye are a brute," Rhiannon said, furious. "I have nay lain with Lucius."

"Lucius, eh? So the Roman allows ye to call him by a name other than 'master' while ye spread yer legs, does he?"

Rhiannon clenched her fingers into a ball and swung. Cormac's stubby arm moved like a blur and caught her wrist.

"What lies have ye told Edmyg?" she said through gritted teeth.

"Only the truth," Cormac replied. "But dinna fret. Edmyg craves the title of king. He'll nay be setting his queen aside, no matter who she lies with."

" 'Tis I who should be setting him aside! He sowed his seed in Glynis."

"Five years ye were wed to Niall and ye have no babe to show fer it. When Edmyg weds ye, he will plow a barren field. No one condemns him for seeking a son on a willing woman. Ye'll nay dare be refusing to join hands with him, I am thinking—he is Niall's heir and the only warrior fit to lead the Brigantes."

"There are other warriors," Rhiannon said tersely.

Cormac shook his head. "None who willna split the tribe in two. Would ye be repeating your grandmother's folly, lass?"

" 'Tis not the same at all," Rhiannon countered. "Cartimandua spurned her king to satisfy her lust. If I reject Edmyg, 'twill be his perfidy, not mine, that causes the rift."

Cormac spat. "The result will be the same. War among the clans rather than war against the Romans. The foreign dogs will emerge the victors without even having to unsheathe their swords."

Rhiannon bit her lip. Cormac was right. If she refused Edmyg, the Brigantes would never drive the Romans south.

"Listen well, lass. There is little time to lose. The new commander has been in residence only a few days, but he's already begun to unravel my entire winter's work with his dawn drills and barracks inspections. If I'm to turn the garrison against Rome, we need to be rid of him. He'll nay be expecting a woman to best him."

The blood drained from Rhiannon's face. "What would ye have me do?"

"Distract him with yer body. Then, when I give ye the signal, lure him outside the fort gates for a tryst in the forest—alone. Once he is"—a leer twisted Cormac's lips—"bare-assed and pumping, Edmyg will take him."

Rhiannon stared at him, aghast. "I'm to lure Luc—the Roman to his death?"

"Aye, that's the short of it."

A wave of nausea buffeted her. "No. I will not."

Cormac's fleshy fingers closed on Rhiannon's wrist. "Ye will."

"I won't." She glared at him, her fury building. "I'm a healer, not a murderess."

His grip tightened until she thought her bones would snap. "Ye'll do as yer told, lass."

She twisted her arm from his grasp. "Nay. Ye have no need of me to kill him. Ye may sneak into the Roman's room any night the fancy strikes ye." The thought made her ill.

"Aye, I could slip a knife betwixt his ribs—perhaps even escape with my life after. But Madog wants the man alive."

Alive. "For the circle," Rhiannon whispered.

"Aye. At the summer fires. With the Roman's blood offered in tribute to Kernunnos, we willna fail."

An image of Lucius's bloodied body sprawled in the Druid circle flashed before Rhiannon's eyes. Her gorge rose.

Cormac jumped down from his perch on the crate. "Even barring the Horned One's blessing, any fool can see that the fort will fall much quicker with the Roman gone—he's far more able than his predecessor. Ye must do yer part, Rhiannon. Think on the clansmen who will die if ye do not."

Rhiannon swallowed past the painful lump in her throat, not daring to answer.

Cormac's gaze narrowed. "So much concern ye have for an enemy. Yet ye've nay asked after yer own brother."

"Owein? What of him?"

Cormac waddled past her toward the door to the kitchen. Rhiannon overtook him with two quick strides and barred his path. "Is he ill?"

The dwarf halted and peered up at her. "Not ailing, exactly, as I heard tell."

Icy fingers squeezed Rhiannon's heart. "What then?"

"Edmyg has turned him out of the dun."

"Turned him out? For what cause?"

"The lad woke the entire village two nights past, raving like a mad wolf in the mud. The clan gathered 'round him as he screamed his Druid curses."

Rhiannon's stomach rolled. "What do ye mean?"

"A death wish it was. For Glynis and her babe."

"Nay," Rhiannon whispered. "No curse. A vision. He canna help it. They come unbidden."

"Owein has the Sight?" Cormac asked sharply. "Does Madog know?"

"Aye. Where is Owein now?"

"I dinna ken, but Edmyg vows he will kill the lad if he comes near the village. He's forbidden any to speak to him."

"He'll have sought Madog," Rhiannon said, her mind racing. "I must go to him."

"Aye," Cormac said. "Ye must. Deliver the Roman into Edmyg's hands and I'll see ye safe to the Druid's door."

Chapter Six

Twilight deepened into night as Lucius stood outside Rhiannon's bedchamber, wanting more than anything to enter.

Walking through her door would mean leaving Aulus outside. Once within, the aura of futility Lucius breathed like murky air would vanish. The lilting cadence of Rhiannon's voice would drive the self-reproach from his head. Her warmth would banish the chill failures from his heart. He would catch her scent, a shimmer of forest greenery and summer mist. Her body would tremble with need when he touched her, even as she pushed him away. The very thought of it caused Lucius's rod to harden with pleasure akin to pain. To feel his nymph's surrender, to bury himself inside her . . .

Lucius had no doubt that making love to Rhiannon would fill the aching chasm that had become his soul.

Yet still he hesitated and, after another long moment, left her door untouched. He shoved open his own. The heavy wood thudded shut behind him, but not before Aulus had slipped into the room. Lucius lit the handlamp and watched the shadows retreat to the corners.

He told himself Rhiannon needed more time to accept

the idea of becoming his concubine. He rationalized that patience would bring her to his bed far more quickly than heavy-handed persuasion.

Fine tales, but lies. In truth, he'd grown wary of the nymph and the power she seemed to wield over Aulus.

In the world he inhabited, logic ruled. As a senator's son, he'd been born to a life of tradition and duty. Schooling in rhetoric and philosophy, a decade of military service, a political career that commenced by the thirtieth year—the age Lucius had currently attained. Lucius had never questioned the path mapped out for him until Aulus's ghost had sprung from the sands of the Eastern desert.

His brother's unrest had cracked the very foundation of Lucius's ordered world view. If the dead did not stay safely within their graves, what prevented any part of life from violation? And if one beautiful nymph could command his brother's soul . . .

He sent Aulus a piercing look. "What power does she wield over you?"

Aulus developed a sudden interest in the ceiling beams.

Lucius fought the urge to grasp his brother by his ghostly shoulders and shake some life into him. "Is she a witch?" He stepped closer. "Do you fear her?"

Aulus drifted toward the bed. The creation was another Egyptian monstrosity, gilded and garish, double the size of any bed Lucius had ever seen.

"Look at me when I speak to you, by Pollux!"

With an air of infinite weariness, Aulus sank to the cushions, still avoiding Lucius's gaze.

"She's hardly one of the hideous daughters of Diana described by Horace," Lucius muttered. He strode to the side table and poured himself a cup of wine. "Still, who's to say a beautiful woman cannot command witch's powers as easily as a hag?"

He drained the cup and refilled it. "If she has the power to keep you from her presence, perhaps she can banish you from mine as well."

Aulus's head snapped up. Fear illuminated his pale eyes. His shoulders had gone rigid, giving him an eerie semblance of solidity. Lucius looked closer. His brother looked weary, haggard. Haunted, even, if such an irony were possible. Lucius set his cup on the table and moved as close as he dared.

Ice and despair enveloped him.

The smoldering veil of peat smoke skulked into Owein's lungs, dragging at his breath like a wolf bitch hauling her kill to her young. He shifted on his lumpy pallet and drew his blanket over his head. The thick woolen fabric might have blocked the worst of the haze, but it did little to muffle the wet rasp of Madog's snores.

Searing pain spread through Owein's temple, a sensation by now so familiar that he could barely remember a time when agony had not been his companion. A vision of Glynis's still body rose in the sight of Owein's inner eye. The image of a newborn babe strangled by its birth cord joined it. The child was a lad, a son Edmyg should have planted in Rhiannon's womb.

Owein's face went hot with rage. He'd seen Edmyg and Glynis coupling in the forest on more than one occasion. He'd told Rhiannon, hoping she would renounce him. But she'd refused, despite Edmyg's betrayal. Why?

Guilt that her own babe had died before its first breath had been drawn? Shame that a second child had refused to take root in her body? Or did Rhiannon believe that as the Brigantes' strongest warrior and Niall's brother, Edmyg deserved the title of king? Owein knew most of the clansmen thought as much, but he didn't agree. To his mind, Edmyg's arrogance, quick temper, and slow wit were poor traits for a ruler.

His fingers tested the taut muscles encased in his upper arm. For a man of fifteen winters, he was strong, but he was no match for a seasoned warrior who had seen nearly twice as many years.

If only he were older, stronger, he would challenge Edmyg for the right to lead the clan and hold the dun for Rhiannon. Then his sister could choose another mate. A man worthy to be called king.

The magnificent battle played out in Owein's imagination. In the scene he was a giant of a warrior, broader and fiercer than any the Brigantes had ever known. He swaggered toward Edmyg, buoyed by the cheers of his kin. He unsheathed his sword like lightning. His thrust was swift and merciless. Edmyg crumpled, clutching his chest, blood streaming from the wound. Owein lowered his weapon and turned to Rhiannon. Her eyes were shining with tears.

Her eyes were shining with tears.

Owein jerked upright, his breath coming in gasps, his right temple pounding so violently that he thought it would burst. A dream image of Rhiannon's face hovered before him, but Owein knew beyond a doubt that he was seeing his sister as she was, at that very moment.

The tears she cried were real. He squeezed his eyes shut, willing them to remain dry as he watched his sister sob. What abuse had her Roman captor visited upon her? When the vision faded, he threw off his blanket and crawled toward the door.

Once free of the hut Owein sucked in a clear breath of midnight air and let it out in a long stream. The cries of the night creatures throbbed about him. Above, a hazy gibbous moon tried to break free of the clouds.

Rhiannon's absence ached like the ghost of a severed limb. No balm could hope to soothe it. He stifled a sob, longing to feel her arms come about him in a swift hug or her fingers, light as a breeze, ruffling his hair. To his shame, he'd begun protesting such attentions. He'd told Rhiannon that as a man he would no longer tolerate such an overt show of affection. Her response had been naught but lilting laughter.

Tears threatened again. If Rhiannon were here now, Owein would let her pet him to her heart's content.

His throat burned with unvoiced grief. He found his feet moving toward Madog's drinking spring, a bubbling pool of clear water sprung from the heart of the Great Mother.

Had the Druid master truly forgotten Briga in his eagerness to cultivate Kernunnos's favor? Rhiannon had thought it. Owein knelt by the water and lifted a handful in his cupped fingers. Murmuring the prayer of thanks Rhiannon had taught him, he raised the earth's most precious gift to his lips.

"Drink deep, my son."

Owein lifted his head. Madog loomed over him, dark and forbidding, one hand anchored on the staff that bore the dead Roman's skull. Owein wondered at the Druid's stealth. He'd not heard even a whisper of his approach.

"Drink," he said again.

Owein dipped his head and gulped the sweet, cool water, drinking until he'd had his fill.

"I've Seen a true vision," he said. "Of Rhiannon. Not of the future, but as she is at this moment."

Madog did not seem surprised at this revelation. He nodded at the water's surface. "Look into the pool, lad. The past, the present, the future. All are there. What else do you see?"

A dim shaft of moonlight broke the clouds, casting a misty sheen on the black water. Owein drew a deep breath and cast his gaze on the pool, looking deep.

"Nothing," he said after a moment.

"Clear yer mind and look again," Madog instructed. He lifted his staff and set it in the mud at the water's edge.

Owein obeyed. At first the water seemed as black as before. Then the fleeting glimpse of a spark flashed. Owein couldn't tell if he'd seen the light with his eyes or his mind.

The pounding in his temple intensified. Rhiannon's face swam into focus. Tears no longer stained her cheeks, but her eyes held sadness beyond bearing as she sat huddled on a high pallet. Behind her crouched a fearsome beast—a giant wildcat with tufts of savage hair bristling about its face. The monster stood with one enormous paw raised, poised to attack. . . .

He cried out a warning as the vision vanished.

Madog's hand clawed Owein's arm. "What did ye see, lad?"

Owein drew a shaking breath and told him.

"Rhiannon draws the beast to her," the Druid said thoughtfully. "Though she understands little of its danger."

The tears Owein had vowed not to shed tracked down his cheeks. "Is the monster real, then? Has it been conjured by Roman magick? How can she fight it?"

Madog made no reply. Owein covered the fist of one hand with the palm of the other, well aware that he was trembling. After a long moment, the Druid stepped away from the pool. Owein followed. When the old man set foot on a steep descending trail, it was clear where the journey would end.

The stones ringing the Druid circle gleamed in somber majesty. Madog's head dipped as he passed between them. The base of his staff sank into the mud and sucked free with each step. The skull riding it rattled against the twisted wood.

Owein halted at the edge of the stones, reluctant to enter. A faint, foul odor, the smell of death, rose from within. He remembered only too well the agony the Roman's death had brought Rhiannon. Dark powers had been loosed that night.

From the moment Madog had lifted the doomed man's severed head to the night sky, the Druid's eyes had gleamed with an eager light Owein had come to fear.

"Come, lad. Do not tarry." Madog's voice held more than a note of impatience. Owein drew a deep breath and stepped into the circle.

A ray of moonlight pierced the clouds, splashing

through the oak canopy to pool in a bright puddle at Owein's feet. A chant began, rising from Madog's throat and fading, thin and distant, into the sky.

The Words were of a language long unspoken save within the circle of protection afforded by the stones. Words, Owein knew, that could bless or kill with a single, ancient sound. Their fearful power burned in his ears, thudded in his chest.

Madog paced to the center of the sacred ring, chanting, halting before each stone and dipping his staff. The Roman's skull cracked against each rock as if in obeisance. He approached the eastern stone last. The sentinel that faced the rising sun did not match the height of its brethren. Deep, round gouges scored its squat girth, remnants of the Old Ones who had set their mark forever in this valley. Owein could only guess at what purpose the markings had once served.

His scalp tingled as the skull slapped against the weathered rock. Madog's chant grew deeper and more vibrant, his tone expanding as if another's voice had joined him. Moving to the center of the circle, he lifted his staff to the night sky. His call climbed to a shrieking crescendo.

The wind rose with it, circling the stones, whipping the old man's pale cloak about his skeletal frame. "I summon the soul enslaved to the clan," Madog shouted. "I bid ye return to the circle and hear the command of yer master."

The wind gusted, whistling through the oaks with a ghastly wail.

"Come to me, lad." The staff and its ghastly ornament dipped in Owein's direction.

Owein tensed as if a lash had licked his skin. He didn't dare disobey, though his every sense screamed to resist. On trembling legs, he crept forward.

Madog sank his staff into the mud in the very center of the circle and stepped away. The skull swung on the point of the wood, then stilled.

118

"Place your hands upon the shaft," the Druid commanded.

Owein wrapped his palms around Madog's staff. The twisted oak was warm to his touch, but when he raised his head and looked into the Roman's hollow eyes, his breath froze in his lungs. A spark lit the shadow of the sunken orbs. The soul of the man enslaved by Madog's killing sword had returned to the shattered vessel it had once claimed as its own.

A bolt of intense pain darted through Owein's temple, forcing a cry from his lips and nearly dislodging his grip on the staff. Madog placed a steady hand on Owein's shoulder.

"Look deep," he said. "See."

Owein's world tilted. Violent tremors wracked his body and the roar of blood swept through his head. Before this night, he'd never sought a vision. The images had come unwanted, surging on agony. Yet if it were possible to See a path to Rhiannon's safety, Owein would gladly suffer any pain.

Staring into the Roman's dead eyes, he reached with his mind into the world of the spirits. Light exploded behind his eyes. Glittering sparks fell in a spiral pattern. Sweet music floated past, drowning the wind. His arms grew heavy, as if they'd suddenly been turned to stone, but somehow he kept his grip on Madog's staff.

Color swirled about him, brighter than a rainbow, then coalesced into a shining road set with gems. Golden trees crowded the path; silver branches overhung it. A sweet aroma filled the air. In the distance, at the peak of a high bluff, a shining gate gleamed in the light of a thousand suns.

Annwyn.

The land of faeries and gods, the wondrous world where pain and suffering did not exist. Annwyn was a place for which men searched but seldom found. Owein shuddered at the beauty of it, and he'd caught but a glimpse.

A bolt of lightning flashed. The gate opened; a flicker of light passed through the portal and took an animal's shape. Owein might have named the creature a buck, for it had the look of the proud lord of the forest, but to do so would have fallen woefully short of describing the beast's grandeur. The stag was enormous, much bigger and more glorious than any Owein had ever glimpsed.

The beast pawed the ground and dipped its head with regal grace, inviting Owein to come closer. He swallowed his fear and inched forward.

"What do ye See?" Madog's forgotten voice rumbled in Owein's ear.

"A gate. To a shining land."

"The Otherworld," the Druid murmured. "What else?"

"A buck."

"The Horned One," Madog breathed. "'Tis a rare honor. Request a sign. Ask Kernunnos what we must do to gain his favor in the battle against Rome. Speak in the tongue of the Old Ones."

Owen said the Words, surprised his voice did not falter.

The buck dipped its head as if in acknowledgment. The next instant, swirls of blackness seeped into the scene, obscuring the path, blotting the shining oaks. The music faltered and turned discordant. The foul scent of excrement filled Owein's nostrils.

The dark form of a Roman soldier coalesced in front of the buck. The mighty beast lowered its antlers. The warrior drew his sword.

The buck charged. A fierce, deadly battle ensued. Kernunnos drove forward. The edge of the Roman's weapon bit through the stag's flank, drawing blood. Kernunnos shook free and reared, striking the soldier to the ground. The Horned God's antlers tore into the Roman's gut, pulling bloody entrails from the soldier's body.

The man gave a hideous cry and vanished into mist.

The buck lifted its head and looked at Owein. With slow, halting steps the injured animal approached, blood oozing from its flank. When the animal stood but an arm's length away, Owein stretched out his hand and touched the thick stream of its blood.

He felt a pulling sensation in the vicinity of his chest, then a tingle that ran down his arm to the tips of his fingers. His life essence flowed along the path. The Horned God's blood slowed, then stopped.

The gash closed, taking the last of Owein's strength with it. His knees buckled. His grip on Madog's staff loosened. He struck the ground with a painful jolt and the vision shattered.

A long moment passed before Owein found the strength to open his eyes. Madog's face swam above him.

"What have ye Seen, lad?"

Somehow Owein told him.

The Druid's eyes sparked with the fire Owein had come to dread. "Few See the Undying Spirits," the old man murmured. "Blessed ye be." He grasped Owein's hand and pulled him upright.

The ground lurched, then settled into place. Owein steadied himself with one hand on Madog's staff, then snatched his arm back when he realized what he'd done. "What does it mean?" he asked.

"Kernunnos has chosen ye as his messenger. A hard path it is, but 'tis a road that leads to victory." His face drew closer, his eyes searching Owein with piercing intensity. "What would ye give to travel such a road, if it led ye to yer sister's side?"

An image of Rhiannon's face, twisted with sorrow, sprang into Owein's mind. Hate for all things Roman surged through his veins, more potent than a river of fire, more deadly than a sharpened sword.

"What would ye give, lad?"

"My life," Owein whispered. "My soul."

Violence danced on the edge of Lucius's dream. A man clashed with a stag, sword striking flank in a flash of cold steel. The beast reacted with wild fury, pitching its magnificent rack low and gouging the soldier's metal armor as if it were linen.

Aulus's entrails spilled with his blood onto the dark earth. His shrieks rang out into the night, unanswered.

Chapter Seven

"Are you a witch?"

Lucius lifted the lamp with a shaking hand and cast a thin stream of light across Rhiannon's bed. She was asleep, a fur coverlet draped over her hips. Her face was pale against its flowing halo. Soft ripples of lamplight lapped at her breasts like the moon on the sea. Venus herself had never looked so beautiful.

He brought the lamp closer. She awoke with a start, jerking upright and scooting back in one motion. Her golden eyes widened as she looked at his nakedness. She opened her mouth as if to scream, then shut it again. She swallowed.

"I'm not here to ravish you." Lucius rubbed the fingers of his free hand across his eyes and stifled a laugh bordering on hysteria. Rhiannon had only to look at his shriveled rod to realize he told no lie. "But I will have the truth. Are you in service to dark powers?"

Rhiannon's fingers found the edge of the blanket and inched it higher. "Why would you think such a thing?"

Why, indeed? He'd once been a man of logic. Now, it

seemed, he saw only impossibly twisted patterns where once clarity had ruled. "It's said a witch may speak with the dead."

Some emotion—guilt? fear?—flicked briefly over her face. "I've no reason to do such a thing."

"But you are able."

"No! I didn't say that."

He took a step closer. "Did you drive Aulus into my dreams this night?"

"You've seen your brother in a dream?"

Lucius did laugh then, filling the room with his black mirth. "I see my brother everywhere," he said. "But tonight, in my dream, he fought a great stag. When the beast killed him, his cries ripped into my soul."

He lunged for her, but Rhiannon moved faster, evading his grasp. The fingers of his free hand closed on air, then curled into a fist and dropped to his side. The lamplight shuddered and he realized that the hand that held the flame was shaking so badly, the blankets were in danger of being set afire.

He lowered the handlamp to the table. Brass met polished wood with a harsh clatter.

When he looked back at Rhiannon, he saw her pale face had gone even whiter. "You say you see your brother everywhere. What do you mean?"

"A witch may call spirits. Can she banish them as well?"

"I . . ."

He braced his hands on the edge of the bed frame and leaned over her, close enough to smell the aroma of her fear. "What spell sends a spirit to its rest?"

Rhiannon drew in a breath and met his gaze. "You've been visited by your brother's ghost?"

He hesitated, then nodded. "Since the Kalends of November." If she thought him mad, so be it. Perhaps it was true.

But she didn't seem to doubt his words. Her gaze flicked into the shadows. "Do you see him now?"

"No," he said. "He flees your presence."

"Dear Briga," she breathed and shut her eyes.

"I ask again. Are you a witch?"

"I know only healing spells. None that would banish a ghost. My gift touches only the living."

His laughter echoed off the ceiling. "Your foul power touches my brother and he is dead enough." He reached for her again and this time managed to snare her wrist. "Send him to his rest."

"I tell you, I cannot."

His grip tightened. "You must. I order you to make it so. For six months Aulus has shadowed my existence, turning it into a waking nightmare. Now he's invaded my dreams. I can stand it no longer. I wake and stroke the edge of my sword. I imagine its kiss on my flesh."

"You must not speak so."

His fingers pressed still deeper into her white flesh, but if his touch pained her, she gave no sign of it. "The dream stag gored Aulus. I watched—watched!—unable to help him. Then the beast vanished and the scene changed. I stood in a cavern split by a dark river. Roman soldiers roamed the banks calling for the boatman, but Charon gave them no notice. Aulus was among them."

"Lucius, let go. You're hurting me."

He looked down at his hand, surprised to see Rhiannon's wrist nearly crushed in his grasp. His fingers uncurled slowly. "My apologies," he said stiffly. He moved away to the table set before the mural of Cupid and Psyche. The image of the lovers blurred as he fumbled for the handle of the wine pitcher. Red liquid sloshed over the rim of the glass goblet and spilled like blood on the silver tray.

"Your brother's ghost comes to you often?"

He drained the wine. "He's with me always," he said without turning. "Save when I'm with you. What power do you wield over him?"

She inhaled sharply. "None."

He spun about and hurled the goblet across the room.

The delicate glass exploded with brittle fury against the far wall. Rhiannon gave a cry and dove under the blanket.

He strode toward the bed. "Do not lie to me," he snarled. He snatched up the coverlet and flung it to the ground.

She straightened and glared at him. "I speak the truth."

"I do not believe you." But when his gaze swept over her, he found he hardly cared. With her chest heaving and her red hair tumbling about her shoulders, she glowed like fire and life, a beacon of hope in the dark night that had become his existence.

He ached for her then, wanting nothing so much as to bury himself in her heat and forget the haunting specter that waited outside her door. His rod responded to the wish. Her gaze flicked downward, then back to his face, and her eyes widened.

He caught a handful of her hair in his fist. Breathing harshly, he wound the tresses slowly around his wrist, forcing her closer. "Truth or not," he said, "I can only wonder—if I take you here, make you a part of me, will Aulus vanish for good?"

Rhiannon's eyes closed and her lips parted. She made a mewling sound in her throat. A moan born of desire, or fear, or equal measures of both? The murmur shattered Lucius's thin control. He pressed her against his naked body and took her mouth, devouring its sweetness. He drew her down into the bed cushions.

She braced her hands on his chest, not protesting yet not welcoming either. Lucius gentled his assault, stroking her lips, kissing the line of her jaw.

His tongue found her ear and swirled into it. His arousal settled between her thighs. Rhiannon's hips shifted against him in a hint of welcome. He fisted her tunic in his hand and drew the hem upward, baring her legs to his touch. Her arms snaked around his neck. His fingers stroked a path up her thigh.

She stilled beneath him even as she clung to him. "No, Lucius, please, I . . ."

"Hush, little one," he whispered, his fury sputtering like a dying flame. "There's nothing to fear. I would never hurt you." He hoped it was true.

His mouth covered hers, seeking silence and surrender. His tongue plunged and receded. She tasted like wind and honey. It would be no hardship to drink from her cup for a lifetime. He dipped his head to taste her again.

She bit his lip.

He jerked away and uttered an oath. Rhiannon scrambled to the far end of the bed. He stared at her as he touched his mouth. When he drew his finger away, it was streaked with blood.

"By Pollux," he said, but the wild urge to subdue her had shattered. A glimmer of respect rose in its place.

Rhiannon met his gaze. "You told me you had no need to force your attentions on a woman."

"Your response led me to believe no force would be necessary."

She blushed. "I'm sorry."

"For what?"

She looked down at her clasped hands. "I . . . I don't know."

"You feel it as I do, do you not? When I draw near. When I touch you."

"Yes," she whispered, still avoiding his gaze. "When you touch me. I feel . . . more. Everything. Like I'm dying inside." She lifted her head and he saw anguish in her eyes. "You must believe me, Lucius. I know no spell that will ease your brother's soul."

A weight like a heavy stone settled on Lucius's shoulders. He regarded her in silence, sickened that he'd come so close to snapping the thin threads of his control. After a moment, he forced his legs to carry him to the door. Shards of glass cut into his bare soles. He welcomed the

127

pain. It was infinitely preferable to the numbness that had taken over his heart.

He set his hand on the latch, but couldn't bring himself to lift it. Aulus waited outside.

He pressed his forehead against the polished wood. Long heartbeats passed, pulsing against silence. When he spoke, his voice trembled.

"May I stay?"

"Stay?" Rhiannon's voice held a note of panic.

He turned, supporting his back against the door, not sure his legs would take his full weight. His fingers gripped the door latch. "Not in your bed, Rhiannon, unless you want me there. On the floor." He jerked his chin toward the door. "Aulus awaits me in the passageway. I cannot . . ." He choked, unable to finish.

Rhiannon's hand crept to her throat.

"I'm sorry," he said when she did not answer. "I forget myself." He turned, steeling himself to open the door.

"Wait."

He looked back at her.

"I'd bid you sleep on my floor, Lucius, but it seems to be covered with bits of glass." She offered him a shaky smile. "Perhaps if I go to your chamber . . ."

Relief nearly drove him to his knees. "You don't fear me? Think me mad?"

"No more mad than I am."

"You cannot know that—you've not seen me speaking to the air. Sometimes Aulus seems more real than the living men before me." He loosened his grip on the door latch and laid his palm flat against the wood. "More solid than this barrier. I relinquished command of my Legion to come north, but if truth be told, I was on the verge of being dismissed. My men no longer trusted me. And though I knew it, I didn't care. I thought only of Aulus."

"You loved him."

Lucius closed his eyes against the familiar wave of guilt. "Not enough. He loved me far better."

Rhiannon held out her arms. "Come. Carry me to your chamber. I dare not step off the bed for fear of cutting my feet."

Lucius straightened away from the door and lifted her, pausing to blow out the lamp flame. He moved through the darkness swiftly, shouldering open her door and striding down the blessedly deserted passage to his own chamber.

His door stood ajar. He pushed through it and kicked it shut behind him. Aulus's hideous Egyptian furnishings hulked in the darkness. He lowered Rhiannon onto the wide bed and covered her with one of the furs. He lingered at her side, wishing he could make out her expression in the dim light slanting through the shutters.

She caught his hand and brought it to her cheek. "This bed is large. Will you not share it with me?"

Shock flashed through him, leaving flames of violent hope in its wake. A long moment passed before he reined in his lust and gave Rhiannon a swift shake of his head. His control was far too close to the breaking point. Making love to her now would surely shatter it. If that happened, Lucius feared he would never regain his equilibrium.

"Lucius?"

"I would be a poor lover this night, my nymph. I'll take my rest on the bench." He bent low and brushed a chaste kiss across Rhiannon's lips. "But I'll promise you tomorrow."

Chapter Eight

"Consorting with ghosts in the night, Luc?"

Lucius's gaze jerked to the library door. Demetrius stood there, the weariness of his features a match to the limp drape of his mantle. His tone, however, had not lost its customary caustic wit. Lucius's senses went on alert, but it seemed the old man's comment regarding spirits had been an innocent one. Demetrius took no particular notice of Aulus's pale form slumped at the far end of the reading table.

The specter lifted its head and stared dispassionately at the physician for a heartbeat, then looked away.

"So you've taken leave of the hospital at last," Lucius said, his attention fixed on his brother. Aulus had been lurking in the upper passageway when Lucius had let himself out of his room a few hours earlier, all but fleeing from the woman asleep in his bed. He'd not trusted himself to pass the rest of the night in Rhiannon's presence without making love to her.

One look at Aulus had been more than sufficient to drive any amount of lust from Lucius's mind. His brother looked as if he'd met the wrong end of a centurion's cane. Welts and bruises covered his face and forearms. A gash below his right eye dripped gray blood. His ethereal toga was torn in several places and his tunic sagged on one shoulder.

Demetrius stepped into the room and moved toward Aulus's motionless form. Lucius half rose, ready to intervene, but at the last moment the physician frowned and chose another stool. Lucius let out a long, slow breath.

"You look fit to be washed down a sewer," Demetrius commented. "Why are you not abed?"

"I might ask the same of you. Surely there are medics to care for the wounded."

The Greek's grizzled brows drew together. "Certainly, if you wish Vindolanda to lose even more men. As it is, two soldiers died today, despite my efforts."

"Of wounds sustained in the skirmish?" Lucius asked.

"No. These men were not part of our escort. They had been ill with fever since before our arrival. Had they been properly cared for, I suspect they would be playing at dice rather than awaiting their eulogies."

Lucius put aside the scroll he'd been reading. "Are conditions in the hospital so deplorable?"

Demetrius made a sound of distaste. "The pharmacy is depleted. The herb plot is crowded with weeds and it seems the dead physician is the only man in the fort who knew their uses. Zeus knows the soldiers who call themselves medics are idiots." He gazed meditatively at his hands. "Perhaps there's a healer in the fort village who can instruct me in local herblore."

"Rhiannon is a healer," Lucius heard himself say.

"Indeed? She may be of some use to me, then." He shook his head. "But that is but a part of the problem. The sickroom is filthy—the pallets crawl with vermin. I have ordered a thorough cleaning of the entire facility. It will be a start, at least."

"Good," Lucius said. "And now I'll give you an order. Seek your bed. It will do Vindolanda no good if its sole physician takes ill."

Demetrius flicked a hand to the side. "Sleep! As my years advance, its allure diminishes. All too soon I will close my eyes for good. I'm loath to waste my remaining hours."

Aulus stirred. Struggling to his feet, he began a slow circuit of the room. Lucius frowned. Was his brother favoring his left leg?

"You're far too ornery for the grave," he told Demetrius, forcing a light tone. "Hades himself will take leave of the underworld once you arrive."

Demetrius snorted. "We shall see." He waved at the neat row of scrolls lined up like soldiers. "So, my fellow insomniac—what are you about?"

Lucius shot a glance toward Aulus. The ghost had come to a halt behind Demetrius and was gazing wistfully at the pitcher of wine set out near the old man's elbow. "Aulus wrote constantly, about everything."

"Ah, yes," Demetrius said. "To the detriment of serious study, as I well recall."

"He was in the habit of recording every fanciful story he discovered, but wrote of his daily life as well. I hoped he might have recorded an account of the days before his death."

"Ah." Demetrius lifted the pitcher and poured a draught into the accompanying goblet. "Did he?"

Lucius rose with an abrupt motion and paced to the nearest shelf, giving Aulus a wide berth. "Not that I can tell." He slid yet another scroll from its tube and checked its subject against its label. "You might trouble yourself to point a finger," he muttered in his brother's direction.

"What's that, Lucius?"

"Nothing."

Demetrius set down his drink and got to his feet. Halting at Lucius's side, he squinted at the volumes Lucius had slid partway off the shelves. "Phaedrus and Plautus. Fable and comedy." He shook his head. "How like Aulus. Have you found nothing useful?"

"No," he replied. "Aulus seldom wrote anything useful."

Lucius reshelved the two scrolls and chose a third. When he unrolled it, his brother's bold scrawl leapt off the papyrus, so alive that his breath caught. He sat down, weighted the corners, and began to read. "This one appears to be a local fable," he said.

"Indeed?"

Lucius scanned the page. "A horseman pursued a woman for three days, yet couldn't catch his quarry." He made a sound of derision. "A sorry rider he must have been."

Demetrius cocked his head to one side. "The women of Britannia are not like those of Rome."

Lucius was inclined to agree.

"Have you bedded her yet?"

"That, old man, is no business of yours."

The physician chuckled. "I thought you had not. You fare about as well as that hapless horseman." He pulled the scroll across the table and rolled the papyrus to reveal the next passage. "You would do well not to underestimate any woman of Britannia," he said, peering at the script. "Do you remember Boudicca?"

"Who could not?" Lucius asked irritably. "Thousands fell when the Iceni queen led her tribe into battle against Rome after the death of her husband. But that was in the south, where the Celts thrust their swords with one arm before Rome subdued them. Here in the north, the *Brittunculi* are scattered and lawless. At least they have always acted so before the attack on our party."

"Do you think their show of unity will continue?"

"I'm planning for that possibility," Lucius replied.

"As well you should," Demetrius said after a moment. "If this story has any truth behind it."

133

"What have you found?"

"A bit of local history." The physician's bent finger traced a path across the papyrus. " 'The queen of the Brigantes tribe, Cartimandua, a client of Rome, ruled by right of her mother's bloodlines. Her carnal appetite was vast but tolerated by her people until she renounced Venutius, her king and consort, in favor of the beardless youth who cleaned his armor. A civil war among the Brigantes ensued. Cartimandua, belly swollen with the child of her young lover, was taken prisoner by Venutius's clansmen. The Roman governor sent a Legion to her aid and put down the revolt. The territory of the Brigantes was placed under Roman rule, but not before a female infant, the daughter of Cartimandua, vanished into the northlands.' "

Aulus stopped pacing and came to peer over Demetrius's shoulder. Not for the first time, Lucius wondered why the physician didn't feel the same icy chill that gripped Lucius whenever the ghost neared. "I read as much in a volume published by Tacitus last year," he replied. "Save for the claim of a child. All this took place over fifty years ago. It has no bearing on the present situation."

"There is more," Demetrius said. Aulus drew closer, his fingers tearing at the purple stripe on his ragged toga. " 'Local lore holds that the line of Cartimandua is not extinct. The Brigantes await the day a hidden queen will unite the clans and drive Rome south.' "

"You expect me to believe that a queen is hiding in a sheep-dung hut, waiting to claim her throne?"

Demetrius's finger trailed farther down the papyrus. "Your brother also writes of the Druids." At this pronouncement, Aulus jerked as if he'd been struck.

Lucius only just managed to stop from reaching out to him. "Druids? That foul cult was outlawed after Gaius Suetonius burned their sanctuary on the Isle of Mona."

"Some say they are scholars and priests, equal in learning to Rome's."

"That's preposterous. They may speak Greek and Latin,

but their religious practices include offering the blood of men to their gods. Dark altars were found on Mona, hidden deep in the forest and strewn with human bones. No civilized people would countenance such rites."

"Aulus claims the Brigantes hold the Druids in high esteem." Demetrius came to the end of the scroll, rerolled it, and slid it back into its brass tube.

Lucius rubbed the stubble on his chin as he looked from Aulus to the physician. "Despite the fascinating nature of local superstition, I would prefer to find an account of my brother's dealings with the fort officers, or anyone else who might have meant him harm. But it seems no such volume exists. I've already searched my bedchamber and my office at the fort headquarters." He walked the length of the shelf and back again, inspecting tags. His brother drifted beside him, shaking his head. "You never wrote about anything practical, did you?" he asked Aulus.

"I? Lucius, I think you need some sleep. You make no sense."

Lucius started. "You are right, Demetrius. I am fatigued." He took a step back toward the table, then changed course abruptly when Aulus barred his path.

Demetrius gestured to the stool. "Luc. For the love of Aphrodite, stop pacing. You are upsetting my stomach."

Lucius dropped onto the stool sideways, straddling it with one leg on either side. "My apologies, old man. We must safeguard your digestion at all costs. I wouldn't wish the aroma of the latrine to worsen."

"Insolent wretch," Demetrius said affectionately. He fell silent for a moment, then asked, "What information has Candidus gleaned from the slaves?"

Lucius frowned. "Aulus kept largely to himself, in the garden or library, until Vetus's arrival late last summer. After that, the tribune was often in my brother's company. The pair dined alone on the night before Aulus's death."

"Their conversation?"

"Light banter." He spread his palms on his knees and

rose. "It seems Aulus and the tribune were"—he grimaced—"the closest of friends."

"Ah," Demetrius said, understanding. "Aulus never was one to turn from pleasure."

"Indeed." Lucius had nothing against pleasure-seeking, but Aulus's predilection for male companionship in his bed was a subject upon which he'd never cared to dwell.

"Do you suspect a crime of passion?"

Lucius sighed. "It's difficult to say. I have a hard time believing Vetus capable of any passion save that for cleanliness. I doubt he killed Aulus over the temperature of the baths." He squinted at the narrow window set high in the outside wall. The sky was lightening. Dawn could not be far off.

Demetrius stood wearily. "Perhaps the dilemma will seem clearer after a few hours' rest."

Lucius glanced at Aulus. He'd sunk to his knees. His upper body rested on the cushion of a stool, face buried in his crossed arms.

"You go," he said. "I'm to address the garrison at cockcrow."

"Very well."

"What has gotten into you?" he asked Aulus once Demetrius had gone. "Did my nightmare affect you?"

Aulus didn't look up. Lucius inched closer. He had the sense that his brother had changed in more than demeanor. His shoulders shook with emotion, causing his toga to slip off his shoulder and onto the floor. There were wounds on Aulus's upper arms Lucius hadn't seen before and as he stared at the vicious welts in horror, his mind dimly registered that the blood oozing from Aulus's wounds was no longer gray, but pink. His brother's body seemed almost solid. Almost alive.

Lucius's blood turned to ice in his veins.

Aulus sobbed and though no sound stirred the chamber, Lucius heard the echoes of his brother's grief in his mind. Without thinking, he reached out and laid a comforting hand on Aulus's shoulder. His palm cooled, but the chill was not unbearable. Lucius could almost imagine that something other than air brushed his fingers.

"I'm trying to help you, brother, though I've begun to wonder what good it will do."

Aulus looked up, his pale eyes wet with tears.

Chapter Nine

The pilfered brass knife sliced easily, piercing a fine network of roots. Rhiannon lifted the fragile clump of greenery from the garden bed, murmuring soothing words to the plant as if it were a babe. Meadowsweet should catch the sun, not hide in the shade. She settled the herb into the shallow hole she'd prepared earlier and swaddled its roots with a blanket of soil. It would thrive here, away from the spreading branches of the apple tree.

Unless, of course, Edmyg was successful in taking the fort. If that happened, one of his warriors would surely trample it.

She sat back on her heels. In the short time she'd been in the fort, the Roman thorn shrubs—roses, Lucius had called them—had begun to fill out. Tiny leaves covered the arching canes. They were edged in red, as if an unseen hand had dipped them in blood.

Blood. She'd dreamed of blood as she'd slept in Lucius's bed. Once again she'd seen the Druid circle. Madog's sword had thrust deep, plunging through the fragile flesh of Lucius's brother. A red river had flowed from his stomach, even as his hand reached for her. . . .

Dear Briga. Aulus's soul clung to his brother's side and

Lucius suspected she was to blame. He wasn't so far from the truth. She'd awoken at dawn, chilled to her soul, choking for breath.

She'd found Lucius gone. She knew she should be glad of it, but she was not.

Tell him. Aulus's dying plea echoed in her skull. Had he been speaking of Lucius? Did he haunt his brother now, hoping to draw him to the Druid circle, where his skull rode the point of a wooden spike? Unless that skull was buried, neither brother would have peace.

What she'd told Lucius was only part of the truth. She knew no spell to banish his brother's ghost, but she knew how to release Aulus from his gruesome prison. Lucius had only to bury the skull in some secret place, far from Madog's influence. Such a simple task, yet he would never perform it. She would not lead a Roman sword into the soft belly of her kin. By rights she should lead him to his death.

Her knuckles went white on the handle of her knife. She was born of a long line of queens, many of whom would not have hesitated to deliver their enemies to the sword. Yet she knew she could not bear to watch Lucius suffer in the Druid circle as his brother had. She would sooner slit his throat with her own hand.

"Have you a knowledge of herbs?"

She dropped the blade and whipped her head around.

Magister Demetrius's black eyes frowned down on her. "Are you feeling quite well, child? Your wound has not putrefied, has it?"

"No," she said faintly, shoving a damp lock of hair from her eyes. "It's healing quite well. You startled me, that is all."

To her surprise, the old man adjusted his elegant mantle and hunkered down at her side. His age-spotted fingers touched the thin leaves she'd just settled in their new nest. "I am unfamiliar with this herb. What is it called?"

"Meadowsweet. It eases pain. I've moved it from the shade. It prefers a sunny location."

Demetrius uttered a gruff sound that might have been a laugh. "If that is true, you should waste no time in carrying it to Greece. I vow Apollo has not shown his face in Britannia for more than a few hours since I set foot on the island."

" 'Tis the season for rain," Rhiannon said. "The sun will show itself once summer is here."

"One can only hope." He straightened, pressing one hand against his back. Rhiannon rose quickly and offered him her arm. He took it, his lips curving in a genuine smile at odds with his weathered features. "Lucius tells me you are a healer."

"I am," she said, wondering what else Lucius had told him.

"Are you skilled in herb lore?"

"Yes." She moved her hand from his arm. "There are many healing plants here. I wonder who planted them."

"Lucius's brother, most likely."

"Truly?"

He nodded. "Aulus loved to tend his garden."

"Did he have a healer's hand?" Perhaps that was why his soul had touched hers so readily.

"No." Demetrius's smile was sad. "But not for lack of instruction on my part. He had no interest in crushing roots and steeping teas. He preferred to capture the rose with his pen."

She gave the thorny canes a doubtful glance.

"Ah, you have never seen a rose in bloom, I imagine." He pointed to the thorn bushes. "They do not grow wild in Britannia. These were brought from Rome."

"Why would anyone bother to transport shrubs as ugly as those such a long way?"

Demetrius chuckled. "They are not much to look at now, I'll grant you that, but come summer, the thorns will be hidden by flowers too numerous to count. The scent of them will fill the air."

"That is hard to imagine."

"Wait and see," Demetrius replied and Rhiannon felt her gut clench. If Edmyg's siege was successful, there would be no summer garden.

"There is a plot in the fort hospital," Demetrius was saying. "Planted with herbs I've never seen. Perhaps you would accompany me there and tell me of their uses."

Rhiannon's eyes widened. She'd tried this morning to leave Lucius's house, but had been denied by the porters at both the front and rear doors. Now the perfect opportunity had presented itself. If she could gain an idea of Vindolanda's layout, she could figure an escape plan without Cormac's help.

"I'm most happy to help you, if it means I may leave this house." As soon as the words left her lips she wished she could call them back. Would the healer suspect she meant to escape?

Demetrius only chuckled. "Lucius should know better than to expect a wild bird to be happy in a cage," he said. "Though I fear the trip to the hospital will not be a pleasant affair. Shall we go now? Marcus is translating a passage from Aristotle's discourse on metaphysics. That should give us plenty of time," he added dryly.

As if on cue, Marcus's head appeared from behind the low wall encircling the fountain. "If you please, Magister, might I accompany you and Rhiannon to the hospital? I should be glad to learn of medicine rather than metaphysics today."

Rhiannon hid a smile as the healer glowered at his young charge. "How long have you been crouching in the dirt?"

"Not long. I had to use the latrine."

"Again?"

"I heard you ask Rhiannon to visit the hospital," the lad persisted. "May I go with you? I promise not to get in your way."

Demetrius let out a long-suffering sigh. "Go back to

your studies, young Marcus. The hospital is rife with fever. Your father would have my head if you were to fall ill."

Rhiannon exited the house with the healer. The wide, graveled path beyond the door was no wilderness trail, but the rush of freedom Rhiannon felt upon stepping into the open air was keen. A slice of sky arched over the road. Swallows were diving dizzy circles through it, their plaintive cries carrying on the breeze.

A pair of soldiers strolled by, eyeing Rhiannon curiously before nodding to Demetrius and moving on. The healer guided her past a massive building he described as the fort's headquarters. Two guards stood at attention before its gated entrance.

"What lies beyond the headquarters?"

"Barracks to the north," Demetrius replied. "To the south, granaries, stables, and workshops." Rhiannon fixed the location of each building in her memory. Such information might prove useful.

"The fort village lies beyond the south gate," Demetrius said.

She knew as much from Cormac's description. "Do the soldiers guard the village as well as the fort?" she asked casually.

Demetrius nodded. "Many have families living there. Not legally, mind you, since only officers may marry. Ah, here we are."

The hospital was a wide, squat structure in the shadow of Vindolanda's western gate. Inside, the odor of illness hung in the air. The groans issuing from the sickrooms roused Rhiannon's sympathy. She'd never been able to shield her heart from others' suffering. It mattered not that the afflicted were her enemies.

A soldier hurried forward to meet Demetrius, sparing Rhiannon the briefest of glances. "*Medicus,* the man you examined yesterday is worse."

Demetrius's brows furrowed. "In what way?"

"He shakes, then goes rigid. His skin is covered with welts as fine as sand and he burns with fever."

"Did you place him away from the others as I ordered?"

"Yes, *Medicus*. This way."

Demetrius waved Rhiannon back when she started to follow. "You need not accompany me—see to the garden." He indicated an open gate, beyond which lay an unkempt plot. "I will come to you when I finish with my patient."

Rhiannon hesitated. The medic had described an illness similar to one that had swept through her village last summer after a traveling peddler had taken ill. Perhaps she could be of help.

But Demetrius had already turned away. Rhiannon stifled the urge to go after him. The health of a Roman soldier was no concern of hers—indeed, she should wish for his demise rather than his recovery. But though the faceless man was her enemy, Rhiannon found she could not despise him.

She passed through the gate into the walled court that enclosed the hospital garden. The layout was smaller and more utilitarian than the courtyard in Lucius's residence and boasted no fountain. Rhiannon was relieved to see no soldiers about.

Judging from the condition of the plots, the garden received few visitors. Weeds overran the herbs and choked the narrow paths. Rhiannon waded through the chaos, picking out familiar remedies—coltsfoot and horehound for cough, foxglove for chest pain, mugwort to purify the sickroom. Silverweed for fever, but when the peddler's illness had afflicted the dun, silverweed alone had not been sufficient to quell both the fever and convulsions. Only mistletoe cut from the sacred grove had eased the malady. Even so, several of the elders and two of the children had died.

Footsteps crunched on the gravel behind her. She turned, expecting to see Demetrius, but the newcomer was not the healer returning from his ministrations. A soldier stood watching her, his eyes shaded by the jutting visor on his helmet. He was tall and broad-shouldered—of a size with Edmyg, Rhiannon guessed. His mail shirt molded his torso as if it were a part of him. His beard was clipped short, but its relative neatness did little to quell the subtle threat Rhiannon perceived in his stance. He projected the menace of a predator waiting to pounce.

A shudder raced through her. She straightened, holding her ground as he approached, his step quiet despite his bulk. When at last he stood before her, the glint of a gold torc at his neck caught her attention. It was old and finely wrought with terminals in the shape of horned serpents' heads. A symbol, along with the stag, of the Horned God, Kernunnos.

She blinked in astonishment. "What manner of Roman soldier wears the torc of a Celtic king?"

"Ye are the woman the commander captured in battle," the man replied. It was not a question.

She made no reply.

With a swift motion, he caught her chin in his hand. When Rhiannon tried to twist her head, his grip tightened.

"Let go!" She kicked, striking his knee.

"I enjoy a woman with some fire about her," he said, unmoved by her struggle.

He caught her wrists and shoved her against the garden wall, pinning her arms above her head and trapping her lower body with his hips. His arousal, hot and hard beneath the leather strips of his war belt, pressed into her belly.

She gave a cry of dismay and tried to free herself, but his fingers only tightened. He gave her no quarter, transferring both her wrists to one of his powerful hands. The other found her breast and palmed it through the thin fabric of her tunic. His fingers tightened on her nipple and his hips jerked against hers with short, brutal thrusts.

His breath, sour with *cervesia*, came hot on Rhiannon's

neck. Her stomach lurched. She struggled again, then stilled when she realized her movements only increased his excitement. "Take your foul hands from me," she said from between clenched teeth. "Or I will scream."

In reply, he covered her mouth with his, thrusting his tongue deep. Rhiannon gagged and fought anew. When he withdrew for a breath, she clamped her teeth on his lower lip and bit as hard as her jaw allowed.

He jerked his head back and swore. His fingers squeezed her wrists with a punishing grip as he wiped the back of his free hand across his mouth, catching a trickle of blood. His lips curved in the parody of a smile. The expression chilled Rhiannon more than his anger had done.

"A firebrand," he said, his cock hardening even more against her stomach. "Cormac told me as much. Yet I had to see for myself."

"Cormac? What has he—"

The sound of voices cut off her words. Abruptly, the soldier released her and stepped away.

Demetrius and the fort medic appeared in the doorway. Upon sighting Rhiannon's attacker, the medic came to attention and saluted. "Quartermaster. I did not know you were here. How may I help you?"

Rhiannon's attacker nodded to the footsoldier. "At ease." He turned to Demetrius. "*Medicus.* How fares your patient?"

Demetrius's voice was grave. "Worse, and three more have fallen to the same illness. I will do my best to heal them, but the fever comes on like a Fury. I promise nothing."

"I understand. Nevertheless, we are fortunate to have the benefit of your wisdom." He turned to the medic. "Commander Aquila requests a full account of the garrison's health status. Have your report in my office before the seventh hour."

"Yes, sir."

His gaze raked over Rhiannon with an air of carnal propriety, leaving her with an urge to scrub her skin until the memory of his touch faded. The brute nodded once more to Demetrius, then turned on his heel and strode from the garden. The medic trailed after him.

"Who is that man?" she asked Demetrius once he'd gone.

"Gaius Brennus, the fort's quartermaster."

"An officer?"

The healer nodded. "Lucius's second-in-command." His gaze narrowed. "Did he interfere with you?"

"No," Rhiannon replied quickly. Cormac had spoken about her to the brute. That fact rankled, but she could not afford to accuse the foul-breathed officer of misconduct without knowing what sort of association he had with her brother-in-law.

"He is not Roman," she said.

"Not a citizen, but he serves the Empire as his father did before him. He is a Gaul from Belgica, as are most of the soldiers stationed here." He pointed to the first garden bed. "Shall we begin?"

Rhiannon spent the next few hours identifying the herbs in the hospital garden, hardly aware of the information she imparted. Her mind spun with the implications of Brennus's acquaintance with Cormac. She'd thought the prospect of mutiny unlikely, but now doubt crept into her mind. Gaulish Celts manned Vindolanda. Perhaps, despite their allegiance to Rome, they had not forgotten their blood.

Chapter Ten

Night fell grudgingly in the northlands, coming late and creeping through the sky like a thief. Lucius rubbed one hand over his eyes as Candidus lit a lamp against the gathering gloom in the headquarters office. Aulus paced behind the secretary, the hem of his shredded toga trailing across the floor. The bruises on his face had turned a mottled purple over the white sheen of his skin. Lucius wished Rhiannon were here to banish him.

I'll promise you tomorrow. His own words haunted him as thoroughly as Aulus did. Was Rhiannon waiting for him as night fell and the house grew still? If she was, why was Lucius dictating correspondence in the fort headquarters office in an effort to avoid her?

Lucius had an uneasy suspicion that the reason was fear. He tidied the stack of wood tablets on his desk, checked the cap on the inkwell, then lined up his writing instruments in a neat row.

"—ready to continue, my lord?"

Lucius refocused on Candidus. The secretary had reinked his stylus and was holding the pen's sharpened nib poised above the shaved wood tablet, waiting for Lucius's reply.

"Where was I?" he asked.

"Your last words were, 'In summary, I find the garrison at Vindolanda to be in a deplorable state.'"

"Yes. Continue with, 'In light of the increased barbarian threat, I request immediate deployment of reinforcements from Eburacum, numbering no less than eighty men.'" Little good the request would do, for Lucius knew the commander at Eburacum did not have a full century's worth of men to spare. Still, perhaps forty might be sent. Provided the messengers bearing the letter managed to reach the fortress.

A young foot soldier approached the doorway, requesting entrance.

"Come," Lucius said. The man moved forward and placed a clay mug at Lucius's elbow. "The refreshment you requested, sir."

Lucius lifted the mug and without looking took a long draught. The next instant he choked, spewing a putrid yellow froth across the desktop.

"What swill is this?" he thundered.

The young foot soldier took several steps backward. "*Cervesia*, sir."

"Tastes like piss," Lucius muttered. "Looks like it, too. Have you no wine about?"

"No, sir."

Lucius thrust the mug in the man's direction. "Get this out of here." He turned to Candidus, who was already mopping the desk with a rag. "Fetch meat and drink from the residence."

The secretary straightened. "I'll go at once, my lord, if you wish, but the correspondence is complete. Why not quit your office for the night?"

Why not indeed? He watched Aulus limp to the doorway, pivot, then start back across the room.

I'll promise you tomorrow.

Lucius might as well have promised Rhiannon his soul, for he suspected that was what he would lose if he touched her again. She knew of Aulus. She'd seen Lucius frightened, nearly sobbing. That fact alone should have made him despise her, but just the opposite had happened. His uncharacteristic vulnerability had loosed something inside him that had long lain buried. He ached for Rhiannon even more than before.

He felt his control slip with every notch his desire rose. Once he gave in to his yearning and lost himself in her arms, he would be completely ensnared in her witch's spell.

The thought terrified him.

"My lord? Shall I put away my pen?"

"No. I wish to dictate another letter, to the governor at Londinium. I'll proceed once you return with our supper."

The vision coalesced slowly, gaining form and depth by slow degrees until it claimed more solidity than the ground beneath Owein's knees. It burned with fervor, like the heat that rolled in merciless waves from Madog's fire. The scent of blood hung in the air as the flames leapt into the night sky. Hideous wails filled the Druid circle—wind in the trees, or the spirits of those long dead? Owein didn't know, didn't question.

Madog's voice creaked like winter branches. "Look into the past this night, lad. See what horrors the Romans visited upon the sacred Isle of Mona fifty long years ago. See what must be avenged."

Owein struggled against the harsh spear of pain in his head. He peered through the veils of time and he Saw.

The Romans came in the night.

Their Legions massed at the foot of the sacred mountains and rippled on the shore like a sinuous beast. The glare of a thousand torches stained the black waves. Shouts echoed against the stones.

The moon, a shivering crescent, cowered above the thin line of water that separated the isle from the mainland. A foul wind blew, sweeping the call of the night creatures into the arms of the sea.

The children of the Horned God gathered beneath the spreading branches of the oaks, erect and unafraid. The hand of Kernunnos shielded them; the invaders could not prevail. The Druid men took their places on the beach, aligned according to power. The women shook loose their braids and smeared mud on their flesh. Sacred fire, lit in the bowels of the forest, licked to the top of the Druidesses' pitch-soaked branches and flashed against the sky. Their children hid in the shadows, silent.

The conquerors set flat-bottomed boats upon the restless waters. Horses swam alongside. Slowly, one by one, the Romans slid across the strait.

Unnoticed by his elders, a small lad crawled from the shelter of the forest and clawed his way to the rocky coastline. Trembling with fear and exhilaration, he huddled in the cleft between two stones and watched as the Romans emerged from the sea like some fearsome fiend of legend, armor glinting like scales, talon swords unsheathed.

As the last warrior gained the shore, the Druid women came alive. They hurled themselves through the ranks of their men, shrieking, torches sparking fiery trails behind them. The lad thought their surge a fierce and beautiful fury, not unlike the violence of the storms that rolled from the sea each winter. He'd always loved watching the sea. He flattened his palms on the smooth, damp stone and leaned forward, hoping to catch sight of his mother and sisters.

The Romans halted as if frozen by a wintry blast. The soldiers looked at their leaders, sword points dipping to the rocks. Sparks fell from their torches to sputter and die on the ground.

The sons of the Horned God lifted their arms and faces

to the sky. The lad's great-grandfather, an Elder far beyond the memory of his birth, shouted a Word of unimaginable power. The lad had never before heard the sound. He whispered it in his hiding place and felt the stones tremble.

The ground shook. Kernunnos, the Horned God of the forest, stirred. The Druid men called to him, hurling prayers into the night sky like spears. The women ran through the ranks of their men, shrieks echoing across the water. The wind howled. The ancient curse rose.

The Roman beast on the shore shuddered.

For one pure, shining moment, the conquerors staggered under the weight of their fear, their weapons as heavy as grinding stones in their hands. The lad eased from his lair, shifting to get a better view of the spectacle. The Horned God was the greatest of all and his victory was at hand.

At that moment, a dark figure separated itself from the cowering Legions. The lad gasped as the man gave his back to the Druids. How did he dare to insult Kernunnos in this way? The dog would surely be struck dead. The lad held his breath, waiting for a bolt of lightning to drop from the sky.

It didn't come.

The Roman, pacing, waved his sword before his troops. His voice pierced the air, a thin reed above the wild prayers and savage wails of the Druids. Yet like a reed, it did not break before the brunt of the storm. The man waded through puddles of torchlight, red cloak whipping about his shoulders. He barked harsh words, slicing the night with his blade in emphasis. Then he spun about, pointed his weapon at the Druids, and gave a shout.

The Roman horde roared in response as they surged across the beach with all the fury of a winter tide. The defiant shrieks of the lad's mother and sisters turned to cries of terror. The prayers of his father and uncles shattered as the Roman swords struck.

Blood flowed in rivers on the ground, seeping into the sea. The lad smelled death. Bile rose in his throat as flames engulfed the forest, racing to the tops of the ancient oaks to snap at the sky, shouting to any that would listen that the glory of Rome was stronger than any barbarian god.

The lad shrank into his meager cleft in the rocks, choking on terror. The odor of burning flesh met his nostrils. His gut heaved.

He huddled in a pool of his own vomit, awaiting the end.

Owein clawed through the suffocating remnants of the vision, gulping great shuddering breaths of air. His arms shook when he tried to lift himself from the rain-soaked earth. The first gray cobwebs of dawn stretched across the sky, binding the limbs of the oaks. Clumps of mistletoe perched on the branches like giant spiders, hairy limbs trailing.

"Steady, lad."

Madog grasped Owein's arm and heaved him into a sitting position. Owein concentrated on his next breath, then the one after that. Finally he looked into the old Druid's eyes.

"Tell me," Madog said. One of the old man's hands remained on Owein's arm, imparting strength; the other was wrapped like a vine about the twisted staff bearing the Roman skull.

Though the nightmare had seared itself in Owein's memory, its description didn't come easily. He bit out the words between gasps. "Romans. Set ashore on a Druid isle. The Holy Ones called Kernunnos, but he did not answer."

" 'Tis the Druid stronghold at Mona ye saw, lad. The Romans burned its sacred groves. Killed its Elders. Raped its women. In the end, only charred stumps and ashes remained."

"A true vision?" Owein asked.

"Aye."

Owein shut his eyes. "Death," he whispered. "Always death. Why can I See naught else?"

Madog sank to his knees by Owein's side. "With power comes pain. 'Tis the way of Kernunnos."

Owein bowed his head and prayed he would be worthy of the Horned God's favor. He would gladly give all that he had, bear any hurt to bring Rhiannon home. He prayed in the language of the Old Ones, speaking the Words of power as Madog had taught him. When he had finished, he looked up.

"The lad I saw—did he survive?"

The Druid's gray eyes turned flat. His hand trembled as he brushed a tear from his craggy cheek. He held silent so long that Owein wondered if he would answer at all.

"Aye," he said at last, his voice distant, as if speaking to those who had died on that dread day.

"That he did, lad. That he did."

Chapter Eleven

"Hurry!"

A fragile thread of dawn hung over the fort as Marcus slipped into the alley between the barracks. Rhiannon hurried after him, wondering at the lad's destination. He'd crept into her bedchamber as the night sky lightened, begging her to rise and follow quickly in silence. His dark eyes had flashed with the same mischievious light Rhiannon had seen so many times in Owein's blue gaze.

She could not help acquiescing to his appeal. To her amazement, he'd commanded the slave at the front entrance in a tone so like his father's that the porter had unlocked the door and allowed them to pass without question. Once in the street, Marcus had broken into a run.

She lifted her skirt and sprinted after him. "Marcus! Where are we going?"

He paused at the corner of a long, low building, his hand gripping the end of the brass tube he sheltered with one arm. "Over there," he said, pointing. "The gate tower."

The gate tower. Dear Briga! Could Marcus get them both through it? Her heart pounded in her throat. "Are we leaving the fort?"

154

GET UP TO
4 FREE BOOKS!

You can have the best romance delivered to your door for less than what you'd pay in a bookstore or online. Sign up for one of our book clubs today, and we'll send you **FREE* BOOKS** just for trying it out...**with no obligation to buy, ever!**

HISTORICAL ROMANCE BOOK CLUB

Travel from the Scottish Highlands to the American West, the decadent ballrooms of Regency England to Viking ships. Your shipments will include authors such as CONNIE MASON, CASSIE EDWARDS, LYNSAY SANDS, LEIGH GREENWOOD, and many, many more.

LOVE SPELL BOOK CLUB

Bring a little magic into your life with the romances of Love Spell—fun contemporaries, paranormals, time-travels, futuristics, and more. Your shipments will include authors such as KATIE MACALISTER, SUSAN GRANT, NINA BANGS, SANDRA HILL, and more.

As a book club member you also receive the following special benefits:

- **30% OFF all orders through our website & telecenter!**
  (Plus, you still get 1 book FREE for every 5 books you buy!)

- **Exclusive access to special discounts!**

- **Convenient home delivery and 10 days to return any books you don't want to keep.**

There is no minimum number of books to buy, and you may cancel membership at any time. See back to sign up!

*Please include $2.00 for shipping and handling.

YES! ☐

Sign me up for the **Historical Romance Book Club** and send my TWO FREE BOOKS! If I choose to stay in the club, I will pay only $8.50* each month, a savings of $5.48!

YES! ☐

Sign me up for the **Love Spell Book Club** and send my TWO FREE BOOKS! If I choose to stay in the club, I will pay only $8.50* each month, a savings of $5.48!

NAME: _____

ADDRESS: _____

_____

TELEPHONE: _____

E-MAIL: _____

☐ **I WANT TO PAY BY CREDIT CARD.**

☐ VISA   ☐ MasterCard   ☐ DISCOVER

ACCOUNT #: _____

EXPIRATION DATE: _____

SIGNATURE: _____

Send this card along with $2.00 shipping & handling for each club you wish to join, to:

**Romance Book Clubs
1 Mechanic Street
Norwalk, CT 06850-3431**

Or fax (must include credit card information!) to: 610.995.9274.
You can also sign up online at www.dorchesterpub.com.

*Plus $2.00 for shipping. Offer open to residents of the U.S. and Canada only.
Canadian residents please call 1.800.481.9191 for pricing information.
If under 18, a parent or guardian must sign. Terms, prices and conditions subject to change. Subscription subject
to acceptance. Dorchester Publishing reserves the right to reject any order or cancel any subscription.

JOIN NOW!

He shook his head. "The guards would never let me pass! We're going up onto the battlements."

"Why?" Rhiannon asked, but Marcus had already grabbed her hand and was towing her across the wide gap between the edge of the barracks and the perimeter wall.

"You'll see. Come on."

They inched along the earthen foundation past the row of ovens built into the turf where a shaggy black dog snuffled for scraps. Rhiannon threw a longing glance toward the stout timber gate. Just beyond, so close she could almost taste it, lay freedom.

Marcus halted in the long shadow of the gate tower and squared his shoulders. "Follow me," he whispered. "Act as though we have the right to be here."

He approached the guards—one a burly man with a bored expression and one a tall, slender youth whose beard had not yet fully grown. After some minutes of finagling, the burly man nodded and opened a door behind him. Marcus entered. Rhiannon followed, slapping away the guard's hand when it strayed too close to her breast.

The room within the tower was little more than a shaft with a wooden ladder propped up against the wall. Marcus placed his foot on the lower rung and began to climb. Rhiannon waited for the door's thud before she hiked up her skirt and followed him.

They emerged on an intermediary platform and, after negotiating a second ladder, gained the upper level. The high walkway ringed the fort in an unbroken path, with bridges spanning the towers flanking the gates. Rhiannon looked to the north and drank in the sight of her home for the first time since her capture.

Her breath caught. Towering crags stood like blue mist on the horizon. The rains would not come this day, for the clouds had fled in the night. The sky was a rare deep blue, tinged with rose where the sun had yet to rise. Birds dipped and soared, calling madly. One long-tailed swallow landed on the rail and blinked at her. Rhiannon sighed. If she had wings, she would lift herself from the battlements and fly home to Owein.

Below her, a man's voice shouted. Marcus nudged her excitedly. "Look."

Rhiannon blinked past the hills and the wide sweep of barley fields and focused on the trampled area just outside Vindolanda's wall. Neat rows of soldiers lined the clearing like sticks set in the mud. Off to one side stood the unmistakable form of Brennus. Rhiannon curled her fingers, fighting the urge to scratch the foul itch that crawled across her skin at the memory of his touch.

"Father and Quartermaster Brennus are to cross swords."

Rhiannon's gaze snapped to Marcus. "Indeed? For what cause?"

"Father wishes to show the troops how a Legionary soldier fights. The quartermaster is his second-in-command. The men will be in awe of Father when Brennus falls."

"For that your father will risk his life?"

Marcus shot her a disbelieving look. "Father had the command of the Thirtieth Legion. He's hardly at risk fighting an auxiliary quartermaster. Besides," he added, "I imagine they'll be using practice swords, not real ones."

Rhiannon's gaze narrowed. "And how is it that you know all about this?"

Marcus had the grace to look guilty. "I went out yesterday while you and Magister Demetrius were at the hospital. I heard some soldiers laying wagers on the fight."

"Demetrius wouldn't be pleased to know you've been sneaking about the fort."

"You won't tell him, will you?"

Rhiannon laughed. "No."

"Good." He turned his attention back to the assembly. "Look. There's Father."

Rhiannon leaned over the railing. Lucius paced the rows of men, sword drawn. "Why is your father's uniform different from that of Brennus and the others?" she asked Marcus.

"Father wears the armor of a Legionary. The auxiliary soldiers wear only mail shirts and leather."

Lucius stopped before one unfortunate wretch and flicked the tip of his blade at some imperfection on the soldier's chest. The man's spine stiffened. Lucius regarded him in silence for a long moment before moving down the line and repeating the scene.

A warm sensation flooded Rhiannon's belly as she watched him. *I'll promise you tomorrow.* Two nights had passed. Why had he not come to fulfill his pledge?

Lucius reached the end of the row directly below Rhiannon's perch on the battlement, glanced to the rear, and went very still. Then his gaze lifted, meeting hers as if she'd called out to him.

The ghost. When it fled, he knew she was near. Rhiannon raised a tentative hand in greeting. Beside her, Marcus blanched and sank to the plank floor.

"Do you think he saw me?"

"I'm sure of it," Rhiannon replied, still watching Lucius. She thought she saw a hint of amusement in his expression, but because of the distance and the shadow of his face guard, she couldn't be sure. Pivoting, he started in on the next row of soldiers.

"He'll flay me alive," Marcus said miserably.

Rhiannon chuckled. "Then may I know why you are taking such a grave risk to be here?"

The lad slid the brass tube from his belt, where he'd secured it before scaling the ladders. Carefully, he removed the cap and slid out the contents: several scraps of papyrus, a pen, and a small pot of ink.

"You've climbed to the battlements to write?"

"Not write. Draw." He gathered his equipment. "I overheard Father telling Demetrius that Vindolanda houses the sorriest collection of auxiliary bastards he's ever had the misfortune to command." At Rhiannon's raised brows, he grinned. "He said he'll drill them like dogs until he's satisfied they can distinguish their heads from their asses."

"Is that so?"

Marcus nodded vigorously. "Yes. I've always wanted to draw a real swordfight, not one copied from some Greek vase."

"Ah," said Rhiannon, understanding at last. "But why did you need my company? It would have been much simpler to come on your own."

The lad busied himself opening the inkwell and setting it with care on the ground. He rolled open a piece of papyrus and weighted it with several small stones. Then he straightened and peered over the battlements onto the parade grounds.

"I don't know exactly. I did think to come alone, but when I woke this morning I thought you might enjoy sharing the adventure."

She smiled. "I do. I also like to watch you draw."

He grinned up at her shyly. "Knowing that will make me draw all the better."

She ruffled his hair, aware of a sweet tug in the vicinity of her heart. *It would be so easy to love this lad. As easy as it would be to love his father.*

The thought, so unexpected and yet so natural, set her heart pounding. She snatched her hand from Marcus's dark curls. Fortunately, he'd already returned his attention to the soldiers and didn't seem to notice Rhiannon's sudden discomfort.

She steeled herself to look down at the assembly. As she watched, the men exchanged their battle swords for wooden blades and separated into sparring pairs. Grunts and shouts peppered the combat, which to Rhiannon looked as fierce as the battle in the fens, if not as bloody. If these men fell far short of Lucius's ideal, she shuddered to imagine the carnage his Legion in the East had wreaked.

After a time, Lucius barked an order, causing the men to

cease their battle-play and fall into a wide arc. He retrieved a wooden practice sword from the ground and lifted its tip waist-high.

"Gaius Brennus, advance."

A murmur rippled through the assembled garrison as Brennus swaggered into the circle. The slanting rays of the sun glinted off the twisted gold of his torc. "Commander."

"Take up a wooden blade," Lucius said.

"I'll not spar with a child's toy." Brennus spat into the dirt, then slid his battle sword from its hilt and set it at the ready. The men at his back shifted forward, a current of anticipation rippling through them.

"Very well." Lucius flung the practice sword away and drew his own blade.

Beside her, Marcus's breath caught. "Father will carve that Gaul's heart out!"

Rhiannon clung to the lad's confidence as the two men circled. Brennus stood taller than Lucius and outweighed him as well. Lucius's plated armor provided a far better defense than Brennus's mail, yet it would provide scant protection if the garrison mutinied. Her gaze moved to the foot soldiers. How many of them had rejected Rome and pledged their secret allegiance to the quartermaster? Would they come to his aid if he fell today?

The two men circled slowly, like winter wolves. Behind, men jostled for the best view, discipline forgotten. In the rear of the pack, wagers were being cast and recast furiously.

Brennus's arm whipped toward Lucius.

Lucius parried easily. He dodged the next slice as well, then darted forward more quickly than Rhiannon would have thought possible for a man weighted in full battle armor. Brennus spun away, but even so the edge of Lucius's blade caught the larger man's leather breast shield, carving a path through it to the mail beneath.

Enraged, Brennus lifted his sword with both hands and brought it down and to one side, the edge angled toward Lucius's neck.

Rhiannon's cry mingled with Marcus's gasp. Lucius lunged to one side, unscathed. In the same motion, he spun about. Taking advantage of Brennus's forward motion, he slammed the flat of his sword into the quartermaster's back.

Brennus hit the ground with a dull thump, drawing a mixture of shouts and groans from the audience. The large man lay motionless, the point of Lucius's sword pricking his neck. Rhiannon let out a long breath.

Marcus took one last look, then dropped to the ground and snatched up his pen. "Magnificent!" he breathed.

Rhiannon was inclined to agree. Lucius's hard body had been a breathless combination of strength and grace, his sword but a flash of light. Had he wished Brennus dead, she had no doubt that the larger man's blood would now be soaking the earth.

Lucius looked to the battlements and speared her with his dark gaze. Heat washed through her veins in a flood. She gripped the edge of the railing, sending a splinter of wood into her palm. On the first night of her captivity and every night after, Lucius could have forced her to his bed far more easily than he'd thrown Brennus to the mud. Yet he hadn't. He had stepped back and waited.

She watched him now, heart pounding with a violence that left her gasping. She wanted him—she could deny it no longer. Yet perhaps it was better that Lucius hadn't come to her last night, whatever his reason. He would soon be locked in battle with her kin. How could she give her heart to her tribe's enemy?

He lifted his sword. Silence fell as Brennus heaved himself from the ground and retrieved his own weapon. Lucius turned his back on the man and barked an order for the soldiers to resume their sparring. The command afforded his opponent some measure of dignity, Rhiannon thought.

Brennus didn't seem to appreciate the gesture. The glare he shot at Lucius's back spit venom.

She now had no doubt Brennus meant to betray Lucius.

A wash of nausea stole over her as she realized that when Brennus joined forces with Edmyg, the quartermaster would be in a position to exact revenge on Lucius for to-day's humiliation. Dear Briga. Peril circled Lucius like a hawk for the kill, yet he walked through his enemies unconcerned, as though a Legion guarded his back.

What fate awaited Marcus should his father be killed? Only death, of that she was certain. There would be no mercy for a Roman commander's son.

Nausea surged. She could not bear to allow either father or son to come to harm. But how could she warn Lucius of the danger without betraying her clan? By some miracle she had to convince Lucius to take Marcus and travel south before the moon of Beltane, four nights hence.

Rhiannon swallowed a sudden rise of bile. Shakily, she tore her gaze from Lucius and hunkered down beside Marcus. He was sprawled on the planks, dipping pen to ink and drawing furiously.

"There," he said, carefully wiping the ink from his pen with a bit of cloth. "What do you think?"

She examined his drawing. His lines were simple. If taken separately, each was hardly more than a swirl of ink. Seen together, the strokes took on a life beyond the boundaries of the papyrus. They danced and leapt, clashed and collided. Gazing at the trapped fury of the swordsmen, Rhiannon almost expected the figures to soar from the page.

"Truly, Marcus, you do magick with your pen."

He gave her an uncertain look, as if unsure of her sincerity but wanting more than anything to believe. "Do you really think so?"

"Your father will be proud," she said, her voice catching.

The lad's hopeful expression crumpled. "No, he won't. He hates my drawings."

"Truly?" *How could anyone frown on such a talent?*

Marcus waved one hand over the papyrus to dry the ink. "He says they're nonsense. But I won't stop," he added

161

fiercely. "Uncle Aulus said I should draw every day, as he did."

"Your uncle was an artist, too?"

"Yes. And a storyteller. Father called him frivolous." Marcus recapped the inkwell and stowed it with his pen in the bottom of the brass tube. Carefully, he picked up the papyrus and passed it back and forth through the air until he was satisfied it was dry. Then, placing a blank sheet atop it, he rolled it tightly and slid it into the tube with the rest of his supplies.

"We should be going back." He grimaced. "No doubt Magister Demetrius is already searching for me."

They retraced their steps along the battlement and down the ladder. As they stepped clear of the gate tower, the black dog they'd seen earlier raised its head. Rhiannon smiled at the creature. It looked underfed, but its golden eyes held a soulful light. The animal tracked their progress, ears erect. Then, as if coming to some canine decision, it loped toward them.

Marcus laughed in delight. "Come, boy." He held out his hand and stood as still as a whisper. The dog nuzzled Marcus's hand, then turned its attention on Rhiannon. She allowed the beast its exploration, then scratched its ears. When they turned down the alley between the barracks, the dog followed. A few minutes later Marcus stood at the front door to the fort commander's residence, frowning down at the animal.

"I don't think he wants to leave you," Rhiannon observed.

"Father will be furious if I let him in the house." A spark of longing showed in his eyes. "We had hounds at our country home outside Rome, for hunting, but they stayed in the stables. I used to sneak out to play with them. Mother never allowed me one in the city."

The dog leaned against Marcus, tail wagging, nose in the air while the lad's fingers tangled in its dirty mane. The scruffy fur about its head gave it a comical air. Despite her anxiety, Rhiannon smiled. The beast's head came nearly to Marcus's chest.

"We'll bring him to the storeroom and bathe him," she said on impulse. "I'm sure your father won't mind having a dog about if it stays out of sight."

Marcus shot her a look that said he feared for her wits; then he giggled. "All right," he said and pounded on the door.

The porter gave them a startled glance but made no comment as Marcus scurried through the foyer, the dog at his heels. He had no trouble coaxing the beast into the kitchen, where it promptly rose on its hind legs and snatched a hunk of raw meat from a platter on the worktable.

Claudia grabbed a knife in her beefy hands and shrieked. Bronwyn, slack-jawed, dropped the container she'd been wrestling to the stove, splashing water over the loaves ready for the oven. Seizing the scruff of the dog's neck, Rhiannon helped Marcus wrestle his new pet to an open area in the rear of the storeroom.

She found a pair of hide buckets and returned a few moments later with water from the courtyard fountain. "What will you call him, Marcus?"

"Hercules," he said with a decided air. The dog looked at him and thumped his tail once on the ground.

"He seems to approve."

Hercules did not approve of his bath, however, deciding if he were to be drenched, it was only fair Rhiannon and Marcus be soaked as well. After much wrestling and laughter, the brute shook off the last drops of water and settled in a dry corner of the storeroom, chewing on a bone Marcus had pilfered from the kitchen.

Rhiannon surveyed the soggy ruins and shook her head. "Where shall we have him sleep?" she mused. "I doubt if Lucius's dour-faced man will allow him a place with the servants."

Marcus giggled. "No, Candidus will likely give birth to a cow when he sees Hercules. I'll let him sleep in my room."

The unbounded joy on Marcus's face was contagious and Rhiannon grinned in response, despite her fears for the future. At the same time, her heart clenched and she sent a prayer to Briga for wisdom. How could she get the lad and his father away from the fort?

"Great Zeus!" Demetrius appeared in the doorway, a look of pure astonishment on his face. If his grizzled brows rose any farther, Rhiannon thought, they would disappear into his scalp.

"Do you like him?" Marcus asked ingenuously.

The healer let out a word that Rhiannon suspected wasn't part of Marcus's Greek vocabulary. "Your father—"

"—won't even notice he's here," Marcus supplied quickly. "I'll keep him out of the way."

"A fiend of that size can hardly be kept hidden," Demetrius said, "but I suppose it may stay until Lucius removes it. The brute could hardly distract you from your lessons any more than usual."

"Oh, thank you, Magister! Hercules won't be any trouble, I promise!" Marcus jumped up and threw an impulsive hug about the old man's waist. Hercules, sensing his young master's excitement, bounded to his feet.

Demetrius made a strangled sound. "Have a care, boy! You are soaked through."

"Oh!" Marcus sprang away. Rhiannon launched herself at Hercules and barely managed to hold him at bay while Demetrius beat a prudent retreat to the protection of the doorway.

"Marcus, change your tunic and go to the library at once," he ordered. "I will await you there."

After Marcus left, towing his new companion, Rhiannon wrung out the wet washrags. She was hanging them to dry when Cormac found her.

"The Roman slept alone last night," he said. "Surely ye can do better than that."

Rhiannon pushed past him. "Leave me be."

He caught her arm. "I care not how distasteful ye be finding the task, Rhiannon. Ye are to go to his bed this eve."

"I'll nay lure a man to his death."

"He's a dead man already. Would ye let him be taking your kin to the grave with him?"

Rhiannon turned and looked down at her brother-in-law, wondering not for the first time how a man so grotesquely undersized could loom so large. "What dealings have ye with the fort quartermaster?" she asked.

His gaze narrowed. "Brennus? What ken ye of him?"

"He wears the torc."

"Aye. Fashioned with the serpents of Kernunnos."

"Is he your ally? The one who will turn the garrison against Rome?"

Cormac swore softly. "Keep yer voice down, lass. The less ye be speaking of it, the safer ye will be." He peered into the kitchen before continuing. "Brennus is descended from the old chieftains of Gaul. He's a fine warrior, trained by Rome."

"All the same, Lucius bested him with ease this morn. How can ye be so sure the garrison will side with Brennus? If they are loyal to Lucius, the siege will be a bloodbath."

"The Gauls call Brennus king. They willna be shifting their allegiance. Do yer part, Rhiannon, and this fort will fall quickly enough." He waddled toward the door, then turned back. "Ye had me almost forgetting. I had a message yesterday."

"From Edmyg?"

"Nay. From Madog."

Rhiannon's heart skipped a beat. "Owein."

Cormac grunted. "Glynis died birthing Edmyg's babe, as yer brother predicted. Owein collapsed when he learned of it. He calls for ye. He needs yer magick."

"Madog knows far more of magick than I could ever hope to," Rhiannon whispered.

"That may be, but he hasna yer touch, Rhiannon, especially with Owein." A touch of impatience strengthened his voice. "Madog bids ye deliver the Roman to Edmyg and come as soon as ye can."

When she didn't answer right away, he shook his head. "Do what ye must and then put it from yer mind."

" 'Tis not possible."

"Ye are far too softhearted," Cormac replied, not unkindly. "Do ye remember when ye were a lass and ye mended a bird's wing, only to have the wee creature die a moon later?"

Rhiannon nodded.

"Had ye been truly merciful, ye would have wrung its neck."

Chapter Twelve

Aulus looked like Hades. Prometheus chained to the rock could hardly have looked worse.

The ghost had become so solid, Lucius could hardly credit the fact that no one but he perceived his brother's presence. Aulus no longer glided through the air; he staggered through the mud as if weighted by the burden of Atlas. His toga was gone and his tunic hung in limp shreds, revealing a torso covered with angry bruises. A week's worth of stubble clung to his chin. Blood oozed from a gash on his temple.

The ghost's color approached that of a living man. The chill that had prevented Lucius's approach had evaporated like mist burned away by the morning sun. But most disturbing of all was the specter's scent, a sickening fusion of vomit, blood, and despair.

Aulus had reappeared the moment Rhiannon and Marcus had quit the battlement after Lucius's bout with Brennus. The ghost's lifelike demeanor had been so startling that Lucius had hardly heard the cheers of the men as they'd saluted his victory. He hadn't, however, missed the savage glint in Brennus's eyes as he'd pushed himself out of the mud. Lucius regretted the necessity of humiliating the man in front of the entire garrison, but he'd had little choice in the matter. The quartermaster had ignored his direct order to use practice swords. That was a challenge Lucius couldn't afford to let pass. And in truth, if the defeat caused Brennus to train that much harder in anticipation of a rematch, so much the better. Vindolanda needed every one of its warriors in top form.

Aulus staggered into Lucius's path. Lucius gritted his teeth and drew up short. Stepping neatly to one side, he kept his eyes fixed firmly to the fore as he strode toward his residence. He feared if he caught sight of his brother's tortured countenance one more time, he wouldn't have to worry about going mad. He would draw his sword and plunge it into his own belly if only for the slim hope that once he was safely dead, Charon might row him across the River Styx and into oblivion.

The porter admitted him to the foyer and Lucius nearly knocked the man to the tiles in his haste to slam the door. Yet for all his solidity, Aulus simply plodded through the wood and resumed his post at Lucius's side.

The porter cleared his throat. "Is everything all right, my lord?"

Lucius muttered an oath in place of an answer. The man withdrew hastily.

A women's scream pierced the air.

Lucius darted toward the sound. An enormously fat woman—Aulus's Roman cook, he thought—tottered on the bench by the courtyard fountain. Her face was contorted with terror. Her hands, knotted into her skirt, shook so badly, Lucius wondered that the fabric of her tunic hadn't ripped.

Nosing about at her feet was the apparent source of the woman's terror. A hulking black dog sniffed at her toes, its ragged tail whipping back and forth. Just beyond, one of the flower beds Rhiannon had so painstakingly weeded lay in ruins, its dirt and greenery strewn across the gravel path. Lucius let out an aggravated sigh. How had the misbegotten canine gotten into the house?

Rolling mounds of flesh quivered at the cook's heaving breast as she drew in a great gulp of air. Lucius watched, half fascinated, half repulsed, as she prepared to shatter his ears a second time.

"Cease!" Lucius spoke a moment too late. His command was lost in the unholy shriek that emerged from the woman's throat.

The porter had entered the courtyard on Lucius's heels and now stood cowering behind him. The rest of the household had also appeared—Candidus from the receiving room, the rest of the slaves from the kitchen. Vetus, clad only in a linen towel, scowled from the entrance to the baths. Even Demetrius had dashed out of the library, scroll in hand, moving faster than Lucius would have thought possible.

The dog placed one enormous paw on the bench near the cook's fleshy foot and barked. The woman snatched up the skirt of her long tunic, revealing calves of which Lucius would have preferred to remain ignorant. She screamed a third time, but not one spectator moved to her aid. Apparently none had the courage to interfere with a hulking creature the size of a small bear.

"For the love of Jupiter," Lucius muttered, striding forward. He drew up sharply when Aulus staggered into his path, his ghostly mouth open in a silent scream. The scent of fresh blood poured off him. Lucius's gut heaved.

Then Rhiannon came into sight at the corner of his vision, her footsteps light on the stairway. She leapt over the bottom step and ran into the garden. Aulus vanished.

Lucius's relief at his brother's disappearance was so intense that he staggered back, nearly falling. By the time he'd recovered his balance, Rhiannon had caught the scruff of the dog's neck and was tugging furiously. To Lucius's surprise, the beast allowed her to haul it away from the bench.

He reached her side just as she'd persuaded the dog to lie down.

"He won't hurt you," Rhiannon was telling the cook. "He's quite docile."

"Did you bring that creature into my house?" Lucius demanded. Rhiannon blinked up at him, but before she could answer, Marcus came running from the direction of the latrine.

"I'm sorry," he said, panting. "I just left him for a moment. I won't do it again." He threw his arms around the animal's neck and raised his wide dark eyes to Lucius. "Please don't send Hercules away."

"Hercules?" Lucius asked, dumbfounded. It was about the unlikeliest name for the sorry beast he could imagine. The dog lifted its head and added its appeal to Marcus's, its tail beating an even rhythm in the dirt.

"Please, Father?"

Demetrius camouflaged a chuckle with a cough. Lucius shot the old man a quelling look. The last thing Lucius needed was a flea-bitten monster disrupting his household. He opened his mouth to deny his son's request.

The words never came. They died on his tongue when he looked into Rhiannon's golden eyes.

"Please, Lucius?" she whispered.

Her voice, soft and pleading, sent an erotic image spinning through his brain. He imagined her naked on his bed, opening her thighs to him, saying those exact words. He held her gaze and let his desire flow into his eyes. A slow blush crept up her neck, as if his fantasy had leapt from his mind into hers.

"Yes," he said and she colored even more.

Marcus let out a whoop. "Oh, thank you, Father. I promise Hercules won't be any trouble."

The cook's eyes bulged. Something akin to a growl issued from her throat, along with a string of profanity as foul as any Lucius had heard during his entire military service. She halted abruptly when he raised his eyebrows at her. With a huff of annoyance, the woman climbed from the bench and maneuvered her bulk toward the kitchens. Her assistants trailed behind, all but cowering in the wake of her fury.

"No doubt tonight's dinner will not be worth the effort of eating it," Demetrius commented.

The dog's wet nose touched Lucius's palm. He bent and scratched its head. The beast collapsed on the ground and offered him its belly. He snorted. "Hercules? Whatever possessed you to call him that, Marcus? This overgrown rag has little hope of honoring his namesake."

"I don't know about that," his son replied with a cheeky grin. He glanced toward the kitchen. "He's already vanquished the Erymanthian Boar."

Lucius threw back his head and laughed out loud. The cook did indeed bear more than a passing resemblance to one of the legendary hero's larger foes. He chuckled again and then, without thinking, placed his hand on his son's shoulder and gave an affectionate squeeze.

Marcus stiffened, but didn't pull away. Color crept into his cheeks. Lucius removed his hand abruptly, feeling suddenly foolish. Marcus looked up at him and grinned, his dark eyes glowing with adoration. His expression was a mirror of the one Lucius had so often seen shining forth from Aulus's face.

Suddenly it was very difficult to breathe.

"Just make sure our hero stays out of the kitchen," he muttered. "Else we may find ourselves on barley rations."

"Oh, I will, Father," Marcus said fervently.

"Now then. Magister Demetrius has already returned to the library. No doubt you and Hercules should join him."

"Yes, sir." Marcus led his dubious companion out of the courtyard. Lucius looked about. Candidus had dispersed the remainder of the household. Even Vetus had disappeared—Lucius had caught a glimpse of the tribune retreating to his bath some moments before.

He stood alone in the garden with Rhiannon. She met

171

his gaze, her golden eyes glowing with approval. "Thank you," she said. "Your kindness meant so much to Marcus."

"It's but a dog," Lucius replied. He rubbed the back of his neck.

"I wasn't speaking of Hercules," she said softly.

Lucius frowned. "What then?"

"The embrace you gave your son."

His face heated. "I didn't stop to consider it."

"That's only how it should be! Did you not see how Marcus reacted to your touch?"

"Yes. He was embarrassed."

"Less so than his father," Rhiannon said in a teasing tone. Her lilting laughter wrapped around his heart, causing a heady lightness he hadn't felt in what seemed like an eternity.

It was happiness, he realized.

Rhiannon turned toward the kitchen. Without thinking, Lucius put out his hand and stopped her with a touch on her arm. Once she disappeared through the doorway, Aulus would return, and he didn't think he had the strength to bear it.

"Don't go."

She gestured to the ruined flower bed. "I thought to find a trowel."

"There's no need. One of the other women will attend to it." His voice sounded strangely hoarse.

He stepped close enough to catch her scent. Forest mist, mysterious and eternal. Her coppery lashes swept upward. Her eyes locked with his and he searched the clear depths of her gaze, seeking refuge.

His hand still rested on her arm. He slid it to her shoulder and kneaded the muscles there, turning her and drawing her in until her breasts flattened against his breastplate. Despite the mud that spattered his armor, she leaned into him, her lips parting in a soft gasp.

He bent his head and kissed her. She tasted of fruit forbidden by the gods, so tantalizing that a man would gladly offer his life for just one morsel of it. He suckled her lower lip, drinking her sweetness. She returned his ardor, opening her mouth to his questing tongue. He plunged deep, taking what she offered and more.

A shudder passed through her body. In the next instant she turned to flame in his arms, searing him with her kisses, tangling her fingers into the hair at his nape and tugging so hard he wondered that the strands did not pull from his scalp. His rod, already hard, grew stiffer. He cupped her buttocks in his palms and pulled her hips flush against him, cursing the barrier of his war belt.

Need gripped him like a fever. In the dim recesses of his mind he heard a voice warning caution, but he gave it no heed. At that moment he no longer cared if his sanity shattered or if his soul was lost forever. He only wondered why he'd fought so hard to keep it.

Lust surged through his veins, demanding that he claim Rhiannon on the very ground upon which they stood. He choked back the urge. Half the household could be watching from the shadowed doorways ringing the courtyard.

He gripped her waist with both hands and thrust her away. She looked up at him, a dazed expression on her face.

"Not here," he gasped. "Above stairs."

Her eyes widened as if she'd suddenly realized what they'd been doing and now thought better of it. "No, I . . ."

He forced his fingers to loosen his grip on her waist. "I'll not hurt you," he said in a fierce whisper. "I would protect you with my life. Say you believe me."

Her expression changed to one he might have sworn was guilt. "I do."

He swallowed hard. "Then will you have me, Rhiannon?"

Tears were on her lashes. He thought for one dreadful moment that she would refuse him yet again, but after a brief hesitation she nodded and the relief he felt was sweet. She lifted her hand and traced a trembling path along the line of his jaw. When she ventured too near his mouth, he caught her fingertip between his lips. He watched her eyes widen as he suckled, then darken when he captured her hand in his and flicked his tongue into the center of her palm.

Her breath quickened. "Will you have me?" he asked again, needing to hear her acceptance.

Her gaze fell to his mouth, and her tongue flicked out to lick lips already swollen with his kisses. "Yes," she said. "I'll have you, Lucius."

He needed no more encouragement. Bending low, he swept her into his arms. She clutched at his shoulders and buried her face in the curve of his neck, her long curls brushing a tantalizing caress over his bare arms. He took the steps to his bedchamber three at a time, but even so it seemed like an eternity before he emerged on the upper level. Her heat seeped around the edges of his armor, causing his heart to race and his thoughts to cloud. His rod hardened beyond endurance. He reached for the door and fumbled with the latch, cursing when the simple mechanism refused to yield.

Rhiannon laughed softly and nudged his fingers aside. "Let me do it."

The door swung open. He shoved his way into the chamber, wanting nothing so much as to fall on the woman in his arms like a stag in rut, marking her as his own and obliterating the memories—both good and ill—of any who might have come before him. He denied his craving. Rhiannon needed a tender lover, not a savage brute who would take his own pleasure with no thought of hers.

He tumbled her onto Aulus's wide bed. She lay on her back on the coverlet, gazing up at him with eyes as heated as a summer night. Her hair was a wild blaze of fire, her tunic hiked up past her knees. His control faltered.

Then Rhiannon smiled. She lifted her arms, beckoning him closer, and all restraint fled.

* * *

Rhiannon lay trapped by Lucius's hungry gaze. Her heart pounded as she watched his shaking fingers loosen the fastenings of his war belt. She could not have looked away for her life, even if she had desired such a thing. She didn't. She wanted nothing more than to be lost in the dark glitter of his eyes, surrounded by a thousand stars, seeking the mysterious pleasures she knew were hidden there.

His sword and belt fell to the floor with a thud. The sound carried a finality Rhiannon no longer wished to deny. For good or ill, she would give herself to her clan's enemy, not because she'd been ordered to seduce him, but for the simple reason that she could no longer hold herself away.

Soon enough she would return to her people and the duty she owed to them. Soon enough she would welcome Edmyg to her bed as her king and consort. That was her future and she could not gainsay it. But here, this night, in this place, the future would not intrude.

Here, tonight, she belonged only to Lucius.

When he'd laughed and touched his son with love, her heart had melted. She'd seen his soul in that instant as she had two nights before when he'd pleaded with her to banish Aulus's ghost. His façade of cool discipline was a sham, no more a real part of him than the armor he donned to shield his body. Once stripped of its protection, he was revealed as a man whose emotions ran so deep he feared he would drown in them.

His strength mingled with his aching vulnerability drew her to him more surely than any command he might have thought to issue. A flame of yearning came to life in her womb as he stripped off his armor and tunic. When both had fallen to the floor, she sucked in a breath between her teeth.

He stood before her naked and aroused, like some virile god of midnight. His golden-dark skin stretched over the hard muscles of a warrior. Black, springy curls danced across his chest and dipped in a tight V over his flat stomach to the dark nest below. His cock, smooth and erect, rose in unrepentant glory.

Lassitude stole across her limbs, weighting them, while at the same time a curious restlessness stirred in her belly. Her hips shifted forward, seeking relief from the fierce ache that had settled there. The slight movement did not go unnoticed by Lucius. He caught her gaze and his lips parted, baring his teeth.

He moved toward her, slow and silent as a wolf. Sudden apprehension stole Rhiannon's breath as he advanced. He'd vowed not to hurt her, but he was a man, with a man's lusts. Would he take her fast and hard, completing the act before she found more than a whisper of pleasure? Or, worse, would he demand more of her, more than she knew how to give?

She'd never given her heart to Niall, had never allowed him to touch her deepest secrets. Instinctively, she knew Lucius would not be satisfied with such a pale surrender. He would strip her soul to its essence.

The thought terrified her.

It also aroused her beyond bearing. Desire shot through her veins like fire-tipped arrows. She felt hot, and empty, and aching. She writhed as she caught the scent of him, the peaks of her breasts hardening. The fabric of her tunic chafed the sensitive tips. She longed for Lucius to slip the garment over her heated skin.

She knew by the fierce expression in his eyes he desired it, too, but he did not close the last bit of distance between them. Instead he moved away to the foot of the bed and gripped the raised end of the frame with both hands. His cock rested on the top edge of the intricate woodcarvings, pointing at her loins. The thought of its wide head penetrating her slick folds made her throat go dry.

"Remove your tunic," Lucius said hoarsely. "If I attempt the task, the garment will surely be shredded past repair."

Rhiannon blushed, but she could no more deny his request than she could refuse her lungs air. She pushed herself to a sitting position and unknotted the length of cord at her waist. Her fingers found the hem of her tunic and drew it slowly upward. Cool air brushed her thighs, then caressed the curls between her legs.

Lucius went still, watching, his breath growing rougher with each pass. A giddy sense of power filled Rhiannon. Bunching the linen in her fists, she eased it higher by infinite degrees over her hips, her stomach, her breasts. A gasp escaped her lips as the fabric grazed her swollen nipples. Then the garment whispered over her head, slid a slow path down her arm, and disappeared onto the floor.

"So beautiful," Lucius said, but he made no move toward her. His dark gaze caressed her from head to foot. Rhiannon's body responded to his scrutiny with a longing so violent she began to tremble.

"Please," she said.

"Please?"

"I want—"

"What?" He leaned forward. "What is it you want from me, Rhiannon?"

Everything, Rhiannon thought, but she couldn't bring herself to say the word. She suspected there was no need—surely Lucius could see the answer in her eyes.

"Lie back and place your hands above your head."

The soft command coiled around her like the first murmur of a storm. Dizzily, she complied, lowering herself to the cushions and stretching like a cat. Her fingers reached up behind her and sought purchase in the carved terminal of the bed frame.

"Part your legs." Lucius's voice thrummed with urgency. Moisture seeped onto Rhiannon's thighs and her blood rushed in her ears. She groaned but lay still, staring up at him, too embarrassed to comply.

Lucius's heated gaze burned a path down her body, halting, she knew, at the bright triangle of curls that guarded her sex.

"Open for me, Rhiannon."

As if of their own accord, her knees fell apart.

"Wider."

She flushed hot and her breath came in shallow gasps, but she did as he asked, opening herself to his hunger.

His gaze consumed her. And though it hardly seemed possible, his cock swelled even larger. Rhiannon went slick and wet with the wanting of him, even as she wondered if he would fit within.

He leaned close, but didn't reach for her. His white-knuckled fists gripped the bed frame so tightly she feared the wood was in danger of splintering.

"Touch yourself for me, Rhiannon."

She looked up at him in dazed confusion. "What?"

"Cup your breasts with your palms."

Lightning need, mingled with fear, shot through her. Emotions she'd never bared to the day fought to rise, called by a man she'd known but a sennight. Yet her soul leapt to his, finding some reflection of its own essence. She knew not why this should be so. She only knew that when Lucius spoke his dark, shameful commands, she was helpless to resist him.

Slowly, she unclenched her fingers from the bed frame and smoothed her palms over her flushed skin. Sliding her hands under her breasts, she lifted the mounds like an offering.

"Brush your fingertips across the peaks."

The fiery jolt she felt when she complied took her breath away. "Come to me now, Lucius." She touched her breasts again, aching for his hands upon her.

His dark eyes flared with satisfaction. "Soon." He drew a long breath. "First, part your folds for me." He loosened his grip on the bed frame long enough to brush an agonizing stroke over the curls between her thighs. "Here."

She clenched deep inside, wanting to beg him to fill her there, where she felt nothing but emptiness. But the hard, almost painful expression on his face told her he wouldn't comply until she'd done as he'd asked. She moved her trembling hand downward by slow degrees. Her fingers touched her own soft, bare flesh and slid along the hot dew of her desire.

His breath left in a rush. His body, already strung tight as a bow, tautened further. Beads of perspiration appeared on his brow, but still he didn't reach for her. His eyes consumed her, urged her on.

She stroked herself again, finding the hidden nub that seemed to be the center of her torment. She touched it once and cried out. Her hips arched, her legs parted even wider.

Then Lucius was upon her, his hands skimming the surface of her skin, his body covering hers with its heat. He kissed a hot trail down her neck to her breast and suckled, and if Rhiannon had thought her want unbearable before, she found her anguish now to be beyond anything she could have imagined. She writhed under Lucius's touch, wrapping her legs about his body and trying to capture his shaft between her thighs.

Coherent thought scattered in a gale of need. It was a storm she'd never before ridden, indeed, had never even known existed.

"Lucius—" Her plea ended in a moan when his teeth grazed her nipple.

"Steady, my nymph." He rose over her, supporting himself on forearms braced on either side of her head. "It's but evening and we have all night. There's no need to hurry."

She bit back a sob of frustration. Her palms skittered with urgency over his shoulders and across his chest. "I want you now." Nay, she *needed* him—more than pride, more than sanity, more than breath. Her questing hand found the tip of his shaft, her finger catching a bead of moisture. A sound like a low growl tore from Lucius's throat.

"Now," she said. The word was a plea, a prayer. She inhaled. The scent of his desire inflamed her. He was rough leather and restless energy, sweet balsam and hot sun. He knelt between her open thighs, but still he held himself apart from her. Too far. She needed him closer.

She wrapped her fingers around his shaft and hissed with satisfaction when it leapt hotly in her palm. He shuddered and buried his face in the crook of her neck, catching her flesh between his teeth and nipping hard enough to send a dart of pleasure to her loins.

"You are fire and mist at once," he said in a tone filled with wonder. He raised his head just far enough to look into her eyes. "Are you truly mortal? Or are you Diana, come to torture me?"

"Diana?"

"A wild goddess. The dark forest is her realm."

"No goddess," Rhiannon whispered. "I'm but a woman."

"Then I am content to be a man."

The hot tip of his shaft touched her at last, teasing, probing. Exquisite ripples of sensation overtook her as her hips tilted upward. He entered her slowly in one endless thrust, opening and stretching her flesh until he lay hot and full inside her.

The feel of him was like the summer dawn, sweet and wild. She clenched his cock with her body, sending a spasm of pleasure through her, and she knew he felt it, too, because his arms began to tremble with the exertion of holding himself motionless within her.

She opened herself further, lifting her hips and spreading her knees as she stretched to take in all of him. She gripped his buttocks and pulled him closer, wanting more.

"For the love of Jupiter, be still but a moment," Lucius said. His expression was fierce, but his lips curved in a rueful half smile. "Or you'll end your pleasure before it's begun."

Low laughter bubbled in her throat. She circled her

180

hips and smiled when his growl sounded in her ear. He uttered an oath and surrendered to her. His mouth claimed hers in a punishing kiss as he began to move.

Her body responded with a flood of sensation, a turbulent combination of bliss and agony. Lucius's tongue plunged and retreated with excruciating leisure. His cock matched the rhythm, thrusting and withdrawing in long, slow strokes. Rhiannon gripped his shoulders and bucked against him. If he didn't increase the tempo of their joining, she would surely die before she reached . . . what? She could not fathom the answer, but suspected Lucius knew all too well what her body craved.

She moved again, desperate to put an end to her fevered quest. Lucius answered her plea by sliding his hands to her hips and holding her motionless beneath him. She cried out in protest, but his grip only tightened and she could do little but accept the pace he'd set.

He broke their kiss and drew back. His eyes glittered with triumph. A wash of vulnerability assailed Rhiannon, but then he moved inside her again, faster this time, and the wave of intense pleasure eclipsed her fears. He repeated the movement, thrusting forward, then back quickly several times before returning once again to a slow, ruthless slide.

Rhiannon nearly screamed in frustration. She fisted her hands in the blanket. "Faster," she begged.

A half smile lifted one corner of his mouth, but his eyes had gone dark and held no hint of humor. He granted her wish, increasing his tempo, at the same time easing his grip on her body. Rhiannon sent a prayer of thanks to Briga.

She closed her eyes. Raising her hips, she met him thrust for thrust and gasped with the glory of it. His hand stole to her breast and plucked her taut nipple. Another wave of agonizing pleasure broke, driving her up the spiral, lifting her to darkest ecstasy. She knew not where the storm would end. Yet she yearned for Lucius to carry her through it, though she suspected she would emerge battered and broken.

She reached for her destruction with her whole being.

Lucius's cock stiffened between her legs. He was thrusting now with feverish speed, shaking the bed. The taut spiral of need inside her stretched to its limits, caught and stretched even more. He thrust one more time, driving himself deep, and the coil snapped.

She clung to him as the final shattering crash of pleasure broke over her. He cried her name and braced himself on rigid arms as his hot seed spilled into her womb. She gripped his torso and arched against him, crushing her breasts against his chest, no longer certain where he ended and she began and no longer caring.

They existed for a glorious moment as one being, entwined and complete for all eternity. Then reality whispered, pulling Rhiannon back to awareness. She collapsed onto the cushions, Lucius atop her, their legs still entwined, their bodies still joined.

"My nymph," Lucius murmured. "You are everything I imagined, and more." His breathing deepened and slowed and Rhiannon realized he'd fallen asleep.

With the loss of Lucius's attentions, the walls of the bedchamber seemed to draw inward, cold and threatening. Rhiannon pressed her body against her lover's warmth, but her own rest eluded her. Tears came instead and she could do nothing to stop them.

Chapter Thirteen

The slanting rays of the setting sun bathed the stones of the Old Ones in red. The sky above, framed by a fringe of oak leaves, darkened. Owein lay on his back at the center of the circle and squinted up at the night as the first star winked to life, an ember in a sea of ash. The cool earth, fed by the blood of his enemies, cradled his bare skin like a mother's arms.

Five iron swords encircled him. The first skewered the soil at his head, the flat of its blade grazing his scalp. Two more touched the soles of his feet; two others rested at the farthest reach of his outstretched arms. The power of the stones gathered, leaping across the circle to the swords. Owein could feel the might of the Old Ones, crackling, ready to make a second leap into his flesh.

Pain beat a tattoo in his skull, causing his vision to pulse red. The agony had begun the moment his head touched the soil within the Druid circle. His crown lay closest to the eastern stone. His splayed legs pointed west toward the setting sun and the gates of Annwyn.

A cool breeze stole into the glen, raising the hairs on Owein's naked body. His cock stiffened slightly, then relaxed. An itch crept into his right foot—a niggling annoyance, but he gave it scant notice. Madog had ordered him to remain motionless.

As the last glow of twilight faded, Owein's mentor stepped from the shadows of the oaks and passed into the circle. He halted at Owein's feet, just beyond the blades. His right hand encircled his staff, holding aloft the skull of the Roman commander.

The Druid's breath came hard. Owein's own breathing was shallow, spiked with the pain that threatened to cleave his skull in two. Madog made a circuit of the stones, bowing and chanting in the old tongue. He tapped each ancient sentinel with his staff, then moved toward the center of the circle. With a sudden motion, he sank the twisted shaft into the soft earth between Owein's legs, barely a finger's breadth from his cock.

Owein flinched but managed to keep his hands pinned to the ground. Madog's staff had united earth and sky, opening a path through which the power of creation flowed. The Druid nodded once, then paced to the east, beyond Owein's vision. His voice lifted in prayer. Words, ancient and powerful, moved through the forest like the winds before a storm. When the shrill entreaty fell silent, Owein drew a breath and took up the chant.

The syllables flowed from his tongue like a language remembered. The learning of it had been like a homecoming—each sound Madog had taught resonated in Owein's soul.

Crackling energy leapt from the swords to his limbs. It coursed to his heart, igniting wild desire and fierce hope. A comet trail arched across the sky. Owein tracked it with his gaze, his lips never faltering in the chant. His summons must be perfect if it was to be worthy of Kernunnos's answer.

The last syllable faded into darkness. Far above, stars illuminated the skies, but little of their light reached into the embrace of the oaks. The Horned God's forest realm, thick with the scents of life and death, filled Owein's senses.

The wind gusted, sending a swirl of mist into his vision. The branches and the sky faded, leaving nothing but darkness, cold and eternal. The throbbing agony in his skull spread like a fire through his body, blending with the power of the stones. Light burst in his vision. He reached for it with his mind.

He felt a wrenching sensation, like his soul being torn from his body. He floated free of his corporeal burden, rising over the treetops in a dizzying spiral. Pain vanished, swept away by the wind. The same gust bore him over the forest, past the crags, following the path of the burn as it snaked through the valley.

He halted above the barren patch of land where the conquerors had ripped the forest from Briga's embrace. The high, square walls of Vindolanda stood in the midst of the desolation. Tracking like a hawk, he circled above the fort, searching the shadows with his mind. A woman's sorrow floated skyward.

Rhiannon.

He swooped down into darkness and found himself hovering above a pool of water surrounded by greenery. His sister was not there, but his sense of her had grown stronger. She was close. Very close.

Higher. He floated to an upper passage lined with doors and surged toward the one that enclosed Rhiannon's essence. He glided through it, barely noticing the breadth of the wood as his spirit-body passed through it.

The room beyond lay in shadow, but Owein's spirit-eyes needed no light. An unclothed man sprawled on a raised pallet, sleeping. Rhiannon huddled at his side, sobbing, her naked body wrapped with naught but a thin blanket. The scent of the Roman's seed was upon her.

Rage raced like lightning in Owein's veins. He flung

himself at his enemy's throat, but the hands of his spirit passed harmlessly through the Roman's body. Rhiannon sobbed harder.

Owein watched, horrified, as Rhiannon's defiler stirred. The brute lifted himself on one elbow and peered at her, then dared to raise his hand and smooth a lock of hair from her forehead.

Owein's fury exploded, flinging him upward through the timber and slate roof and into the night sky. Rage flashed through his soul with the light of a thousand suns.

He screamed his curse in the tongue of the ancients. The Words darkened the sky and sent a tremor coursing through the sacred oaks.

The Roman dog would die. Owein would give his last breath to make it so.

Rhiannon was crying.

The sound twisted in Lucius's heart like the blade of a battle dagger. She'd given him pleasure beyond anything he'd ever experienced. Had he caused her pain? He smoothed a strand of hair from her face, but rather than comforting, his touch only seemed to make her tears fall faster.

He climbed from the bed and found the hand lamp. Touching the wick to the coals in the brazier, he blew gently until the flame sprang to life. Shadows leaped to the corners of the chamber. He set the lamp on the table and eased back onto the bed.

Rhiannon blinked up at him through wet lashes. He lifted her chin up with his knuckles. "Is my lovemaking so terrible then, little one?"

Her tears welled anew.

He leaned forward and kissed her eyelids, tasting salt. "Tell me why you cry. Did I hurt you?"

She cupped the side of his face with her hand. He turned his face into her palm and kissed it.

"No," she said. "Your touch caused me only happiness. 'Tis only . . ." She bit her lip and fell silent.

"What?"

"I never knew," she said softly.

"You've never taken pleasure in lovemaking before?"

She picked at the edge of the coverlet, tearing loose a tuft of wool. The blanket lay in her lap, leaving her breasts and belly exposed. Lucius forced himself to focus on Rhiannon's face as she spoke.

"I was wed for five winters," she said, "and the first months after my handclasping were not unpleasant. But I never—" She blushed, swallowed hard, then continued. "I welcomed Niall whenever he sought me. I longed for his seed to grow within me."

Lucius's gaze fell to Rhiannon's belly and for the first time he noticed the faint silvery lines on her skin. His finger traced the length of one from hip to navel.

"You have a child," he said, hating himself. He'd thought only of his own desire for Rhiannon and his need to keep Aulus away. He'd never considered she might have left a babe behind. Did the little one cry for her now?

But she shook her head. "Four years ago a difficult birth came upon me. Two nights, the midwife told me later, though I hardly knew if the sun rose or set. At the end of it, the babe was born broken. Dead. Niall blamed me."

"He should have been glad he didn't lose you as well."

"No. He was right to despise me. The lad was large and I too small to bear him. By rights, I should have died and given my son the chance to live." Her fingers ripped another tuft of wool from the blanket. "I prayed that Briga— the Great Mother—would send me another child. I sought Niall again and for a time he obliged me. His seed took root twice more. But each time, the babe passed from my body before two moons had passed."

"I'm sorry."

"The last time Niall came to me—" She closed her eyes and shuddered.

"He hurt you."

"No. Not truly." But she didn't meet his gaze.

"Lead me to him and I will kill him."

"He is already dead." Rhiannon lifted her head. "Killed by a soldier of Rome. As so many of my people have been."

Lucius could find no reply to that.

"Leave the northlands, Lucius. Take Marcus and the healer and go back to Rome. It's not safe for you here."

"I am not so easy to kill. The fort is secure."

She searched his gaze. "Can you be sure of that? Truly certain?"

He took her hand and the chill of her touch caused the hairs on his nape to rise. "What do you mean?"

"My people will never stop fighting."

He made a sound of dismissal. "Once the Celts of the north taste the riches of Rome, they will join their brethren to the south in welcoming a civilized life."

"Many believe death would be preferable."

"They are fools."

"Not fools. Men who fight for their lives and homes."

Lucius shook his head. "If Caesar hadn't landed on this island, the tribes would be busy enough fighting among themselves like children in need of a nursemaid. Rome has brought an end to strife in the south of Britannia."

"So long as the people pay taxes and answer to a Roman governor." Her voice betrayed her bitterness.

"Yes." He gave her a long, level look. "Is that so terrible a price to pay for peace?"

"Must you Romans take all you see, Lucius? Will you never stop?"

"Rome's strength lies in expansion. The emperor seeks glory in all lands."

" 'Tis glory purchased with the blood of his countrymen.

And for what? A moment's rest before the killing begins anew?" She extracted her hand from his and rose from the bed. She paced to the window, wrapping the blanket around her shoulders as she went.

After a long moment, Lucius came up behind her and laid his palms on her shoulders. Dipping his head, he dropped hot kisses on the curve of her neck. "Let's not argue, sweet. Come back to bed and I'll make you forget any thought of discord."

"Go back to Rome, Lucius," Rhiannon said without turning. "Let me return to my people. There's nothing for you here."

"You would have me leave you? After what we shared last night?" He wouldn't be able to do it, of that he was certain. What he'd felt in Rhiannon's arms had been beyond compare.

She said nothing.

He turned her toward him with one swift motion, far more roughly than he'd intended. "Rhiannon. You are like no woman I've ever known. I . . . I died in your embrace last night."

"Oh, Lucius."

"The slowest and sweetest of deaths, not the quick agony I've longed to inflict upon myself with my sword."

Rhiannon gave a cry of dismay. "You cannot truly wish to put an end to your life."

"I have seriously considered it." He looked at the door. Aulus, he had no doubt, crouched behind it. "Never more than yesterday."

He released her and stepped away. "Six months ago, when my brother's ghost first appeared, it was a wisp of mist. With every northward step I took, Aulus grew clearer. Now—" Lucius's hand clenched in a fist. "He appears to me as solid as a living man. He's been beaten—tortured—but I cannot see his tormentors. His clothing is in shreds. He stumbles about and I wonder that his blood does not stain the tile. If I don't find my brother's killer, I'll be forced to watch while he dies a second time."

Rhiannon looked ill. "Go back to Rome, Lucius. Perhaps then the vision will fade."

"I made a vow to avenge Aulus's death."

"And if you cannot?"

"I must, and soon. I've but a few short months before my successor arrives."

Her breath caught. "Truly?"

He gazed into her eyes and felt comforted despite the turmoil he saw there. Though she spoke words to the contrary, he couldn't believe she wished him to go. "This post will be my last. Come winter, I'll return to Rome and take my father's seat in the Senate." For the first time, the thought held some appeal. He smiled. "You'll come with me. I'll show you a city beyond anything you can imagine."

Her eyes clouded before they dropped to his chest. "Surely there are women enough in Rome."

He lifted her chin with one fingertip. "None like you."

She regarded him steadily with her golden eyes, but try as he might he couldn't read her thoughts. She traced his lips with the pad of her thumb.

"You are so proud," she said, almost to herself.

His tongue darted forward and gave her thumb a playful lap. "I am. Let me prove it to you. Come to bed."

Amusement chased away the shadows on her face. "Lucius . . ."

"On your lips, my name sounds like music." Caught by a sudden urge, he laced her fingers in his and tugged her toward Aulus's massive Egyptian wardrobe. "Come, I wish to show you something."

"What—"

"You'll see." He opened the brightly colored doors and searched through Aulus's collection of jewelry until he found the one piece he sought. A teardrop pendant of amber.

He dropped the chain around her neck. She cradled the

amber in her fingers and looked up at him in awe. " 'Tis beautiful."

"When I first saw it among my brother's things, the color of the stone reminded me of your eyes. I want you to have it."

She shook her head. "I cannot wear this." But her fingers gripped the pendant tightly, as if she dared not let it go.

"You can. I wish you to." He tugged the blanket aside and placed a kiss just below the stone in the valley between her breasts. "Please."

A tremor passed through her. "As you wish." When he raised his head she placed a kiss of her own upon his chest.

"Be careful," he muttered, "or you will find yourself impaled on my sword a second time."

"Such a threat will do little to deter me," she said, her voice thick. She flicked her tongue over his nipple.

He groaned. "You were forewarned." His slipped his hand between her legs and she gasped as he teased her there. Her knees gave way. He steadied her with his hands on her waist and guided her to the bed.

He stretched out on his back and lifted her atop him. She sprawled on his stomach, legs spread wide, hair cascading over her shoulders. Her skin was the finest alabaster, touched with rose, the dark flame of curls between her thighs held fire enough to sear any man. No goddess could be lovelier.

His gaze drifted to the angry red scar on her thigh, bordered by bruises just beginning to fade. He traced it with his fingertip. "I'm sorry for this."

She gave a wry smile. "Don't trouble yourself overmuch. I'm not sorry for the arrow I put in your arse."

His gaze narrowed, but her eyes held only laughter. He smiled, tension draining from his body. Rhiannon's fingers found his shaft and stroked upward. He needed no more encouragement. He slid into her body and lost himself in her welcoming heat.

Chapter Fourteen

"Vindolanda has no need for reinforcements. My scouts found no evidence of barbarian activity in the area. Sir."

"I'd be surprised if your men could find their way out of a latrine," Lucius told Brennus. He pressed his seal into the soft wax covering his letter to the fortress commander at Eburacum. "And even if nothing was found, it hardly signifies. By your own admission, there was no advance warning of the attack on my party."

Brennus rocked back on his heels, his expression unreadable. Lucius's attention drifted to Aulus, sprawled on the floor boards in the corner of the office. A loose knot was all that prevented the remnants of his shredded tunic from slipping over his hips.

"You dealt your attackers a severe blow, sir. Twenty barbarians dead by our count. More certainly died of their injuries. The Celts will not soon attack again."

"Your opinion is noted," Lucius replied. He closed the sealbox and set it with a second parcel addressed to the governor in Londinium. "Select three of your fastest riders for the journey."

"But sir . . ."

"That will be all, quartermaster. You are dismissed."

Brennus hesitated, then apparently thought better of further argument. He saluted, gathered the sealboxes from Lucius's desk, and left the room.

Aulus stirred, his chest heaving with labored breath. Lucius could almost imagine he heard the rasp of air as it dragged into his brother's lungs.

He stared at Aulus's battered form. "By Pollux. Who did this to you?"

Aulus tried to rise, stumbled, and fell to the ground. Lucius jumped from his stool and grabbed for his brother's arm. It was like trying to seize a swarm of bees—a violent shimmer of energy with no sensation of weight or form. He shook his tingling fingers and gaped at Aulus. The ghost was writhing on the floor, hands raised as if shielding himself from unseen fists. Lucius's throat closed on a feeling of utter helplessness.

He fled the chamber. Aulus struggled to his feet and staggered after him into the courtyard. The rain that had begun in the night fell in gray sheets from a mottled sky, but Lucius scarcely cared if he got soaked. He turned his steps toward the south gate, dreading his intended destination but unable to turn from his path. Some primitive instinct compelled him.

He ordered the gate sentry to unbar the stout timber doors, revealing a cluster of huts huddled along a muddy road. At the far end of the village, a path veered off a short distance to the edge of the forest, where a low stone wall encircled the remains of Vindolanda's dead. To Lucius's surprise, a figure stood within the enclosure, head bowed.

Vetus. What lunacy could have caused the tribune to stir from his bath on such a miserable day? Lucius approached slowly, suddenly hesitant to complete the last few steps to the cemetery.

But he found he could not turn away. He halted at Vetus's side and gazed on the stone column bearing Aulus's name. Distant thunder rolled.

193

Vetus raised his head. "How I miss him. It's odd, really. I knew Aulus only a few short weeks and yet . . ." He raised his head and Lucius saw that tears mingled with rain on the tribune's face.

"You loved him."

"Yes."

Lucius touched Vetus's shoulder. "Then we are brothers in grief."

They stood in silence for a time before Lucius spoke again. "Aulus's death must not go unavenged."

Vetus gave a furtive glance in Lucius's direction. "What do you mean? It was an accident."

"I don't believe that," Lucius said. "Do you know anyone in the fort who might have wished him harm?"

Vetus hesitated, then shook his head. "No one. Only . . ."

Lucius caught his arm. "What?"

"The men with whom Aulus went that day . . ."

"Sextus Gallus and Petronius Rufus."

"Yes."

"They are dead."

"Yes. I know." Vetus glanced toward the fort's high battlement, where a sentry was just visible through the rain. "The two of them hunted often."

Lucius's fingers loosened their grip. "There's nothing unusual in that."

Vetus's shoulders shook. "Aulus abhorred the hunt. I should have tried harder to dissuade him from accompanying them." He touched Aulus's monument. "I had it erected at my own expense."

"Thank you," Lucius said softly.

A bolt of lightning flashed and Vetus started as if suddenly coming awake. "It's as if the gods are always angry in this place. I'll not rest easy until I reach Rome. Until then . . ." He turned toward the gate. "I'll warm myself in the bath." He paused. "Will you join me?"

Lucius shook his head. "I think not."

"Then I'll take my leave." Lucius watched Vetus move

off. His gut told him the tribune had had nothing to do with Aulus's death. But if not Vetus, who? The two men who had seen Aulus die, only to meet with fatal accidents soon after? That was far too convenient a circumstance.

He watched the rivulets of muddy water course over his brother's grave. It made little sense that life should turn to ashes so easily, but Lucius had seen far too much death on the battlefield to doubt the power of the Fates. Life: a fragile thread, easily snapped.

Lucius stood motionless a moment longer before realizing Aulus had not entered the cemetery. The ghost huddled at the perimeter of the burial ground, fingers gripping the top of the stone wall. His shredded tunic hung in limp scraps about his hips.

Lucius shuddered, but could not tear his gaze from his brother's tortured eyes. "What ghost is frightened of a cemetery? Most especially of its own grave?"

Aulus swayed from side to side, his ethereal body trembling, whispers of perspiration glistening on his brow. His eyes, almost black now, locked with Lucius's as he shook his head. One trembling hand raised and pointed north.

Lucius looked toward the hills, then back at the grave, a dread suspicion forming in his gut.

"What are you telling me, brother?"

Dear Briga, what am I to do?

Rhiannon stood at the kitchen worktable, kneading dough. Or, more accurately, pounding it. She would have much preferred working in the courtyard garden, but heavy rains forbade that activity. Marcus, accompanied by Hercules, had plodded into the library after Demetrius had ignored the lad's complaints of a headache. Not wanting to remain alone and idle above stairs, Rhiannon had offered her services in the kitchen.

Claudia, the cook, was by now recovered from the trauma of Hercules's attentions. She hovered at the stove, fleshy arms bared, preparing pastries for the ovens. Alara sat on a stool by the door, cleaning peas. Bronwyn, like Rhiannon, stood at the worktable, kneading.

Rhiannon squeezed the soft wheat dough, so unlike the coarse barley mixture she was accustomed to preparing for Owein and Edmyg. As she worked, her mind wandered, seeking out dark memories of Lucius's mouth and tongue on her body. The man had been shameless, licking her skin, tasting her everywhere. When he'd dipped his head between her thighs, she'd cried out so loudly it was a wonder the entire household hadn't come running.

Heat rose at the thought, spreading up Rhiannon's neck and into her cheeks. She bent her head and worked the dough harder, praying Bronwyn wouldn't notice.

He'd taken her thrice last night and already she wanted more. What had come over her? She'd never before felt such a yearning to be with a man. Her muscles ached with the exertion of loving in ways she'd never dreamed were possible. Niall had always sank atop her, rutting swiftly, then rolling to the side. Lucius's teasing voice and clever hands had stretched the night into eternity.

Now, when she walked, the soft skin on her inner thigh stung from the scrape of his morning beard. Each time she thrust the dough against the table, the sensitized peaks of her nipples brushed the fabric of her tunic, reminding her of her lover's touch. The mere thought of Lucius's heated gaze kindled an answering fire low in her belly. Her thighs grew damp, her breathing shallow, and she cursed herself as the worst of fools.

She lusted after a Roman. How could the daughter of queens have sunk so low?

But dear Briga, how he'd watched her! His eyes had glittered in the light of the hand lamps he'd placed around the bed. She'd been embarrassed, then aroused by his scrutiny. Then he'd touched her and she'd seen her own pleasure reflected on his face.

That a lover could take such satisfaction in a partner's

bliss was a new concept for Rhiannon. She'd come to understand it quickly enough, though, when she'd moved to stroke Lucius's warrior's body in ways she never before dreamed of touching a man. She'd felt his response in her heart. It was as if they inhabited one skin, shared one soul. A fanciful notion, but one Rhiannon couldn't seem to shake.

Was this love?

Rhiannon punched the dough with the heel of her hand and folded the flattened mound in half with a vengeful twist. How had her situation become such a tangled mess? She could not love Lucius. She couldn't love his harsh self-discipline and the glory she'd found when he'd lost it. She couldn't love his crooked smile and the way laughter leaped to his eyes an instant before his lips curved. She couldn't revel in the feel of his clean-shaven jaw, his unruly dark curls, the sinew and muscle that roped his shoulders and chest, his hands. . . .

Dear Briga. She had to escape.

The door to the alley opened. Cormac waddled into the room, a sack of wheat from the fort granaries slung over his shoulder. He upended his burden into the bin near the oven, then surreptitiously swiped his finger through a bowl of cream at Claudia's elbow. The cook pivoted as fast as her girth allowed, wooden spoon raised. The dwarf raised a brow and sucked suggestively on his finger. Claudia blushed crimson and giggled.

Rhiannon eyed her brother-in-law with amazement. Was there no woman in the house, save herself, that Cormac hadn't taken?

He dipped his finger in the bowl a second time and lapped the froth with the tip of his tongue. This time the spoon did fall, on his head, but the blow was a mere tap.

"Take yourself away," Claudia said, "or dinner won't arrive at table this eve."

Cormac flashed her a grin and sauntered to the worktable. "I've plover eggs from the village to bring in," he said to Rhiannon. "I'm worrying they'll be crushed if I lift them from the cart. Come help me, lass."

Rhiannon wiped her hands on a rag and followed him into the alley. The high walls on either side gave shelter from the worst of the rain, but the runoff from the slanting roof was nearly a deluge in itself.

Cormac climbed onto the wheel of the cart. "I've seen Edmyg," he said, his voice tight. "Pray that he doesna find yer brother."

Dread blossomed in Rhiannon's stomach. "What has happened?"

"Edmyg's son followed its mother yestereve."

Rhiannon sucked in a breath. "Dead?"

"Aye. The second part of Owein's curse has come to pass." He thrust a basket of eggs into her hands. Rhiannon took it automatically, clutching it to her chest with fingers gone suddenly numb.

" 'Tis not his fault!"

"Edmyg's not of that mind."

"He canna think Owein would harm a mother and babe."

Cormac leaned over the cart's rail, close enough that Rhiannon could smell the stale scent of last night's *cervesia* on his breath. "If ye were at yer man's side, perhaps he'd be seeing the truth of that. As it is, the chieftains gather for war and find their queen missing. There are some what are wondering if ye've rejected Edmyg."

Rhiannon lowered her gaze. It would not do for Cormac to know that in her heart she had done just that. " 'Twas Edmyg who bade me stay here."

"True enough, but 'tis also true ye could have been safely home by now, had ye done as he ordered." He set one large bony hand on her shoulder and squeezed hard. "Does Roman cock please ye so much that ye forget the clan?"

Rhiannon nearly dropped the egg basket in her struggle to evade his grip. "Let me go. I'll not listen to your foul mouth."

Cormac's fingers tightened. "Think ye I care where ye take yer pleasure? I dinna fault ye for enjoying a cock larger than Niall's sorry stump."

When Rhiannon did not reply, Cormac gave a harsh laugh. "I saw the Roman this morn. Besotted, he looked to be. He'll follow ye into the hills like a dog."

Rhiannon twisted again and this time Cormac's hand fell away. "In case ye had not noticed," she said, " 'tis raining. I'll nay be convincing any man to lie with me in the mud."

"Rain or no, the chieftains are gathering their warriors and there is much quarreling among them. Kynan is of a mind to abandon the attack if the Roman is not taken from the fort beforehand, and many side with him. It wants but three nights to the summer moon."

He squinted into the sky. "Edmyg says if ye deliver the Roman within that time, he'll nay seek Owein's life in payment for his son's."

"Great Zeus, Lucius. Can we not wait until the storm passes?" Demetrius sent a look of disgruntlement at the cascade of mud flowing across the path.

Lucius shifted his shovel on his shoulder and strode through the dirty stream. "That happy event might not occur for a solid week. I must have my answer now." He shoved open the gate of the cemetery.

Demetrius gathered his tunic in one fist and lifted the embroidered hem clear of the ground before following. "Tell me again why we have embarked on this folly."

Lucius stole a glance at Aulus. The ghost stood on his own grave, leaning heavily on the monument. The last shreds of his tunic had fallen away, leaving him naked. Lucius's stomach twisted. His brother's skin was mottled with purple bruises and a harsh pattern of welts had risen on his back as if he'd been beaten long and cruelly.

"Luc?" Demetrius's sharp tone pulled Lucius back. "Did you hear me? Why do you suspect Aulus lies elsewhere?"

The ghost plodded to the north corner of the cemetery and looked to the hills, then turned and stretched one hand, palm upward, toward Lucius. "I cannot say," Lucius told Demetrius. "A hunch."

The physician snorted. "I've never known you to go to so much trouble on a whim. There is something you are not telling me."

Lucius replied with a thrust of his shovel into the dirt. "At least this cursed weather keeps the ground soft."

He dug, heaving sodden shovelfuls to one side. Rainwater rushed into the hole. He bent lower, boots sinking into the muck, and liberated another clod of earth. He stabbed at the dirt with fevered urgency, not stopping for breath until he'd sunk waist-deep in the hole.

"Your labor does not go unnoticed," Demetrius murmured. Lucius lifted his head. A cluster of Celts stood on the fringe of the village, peering at him through the rain. "They're welcome to their curiosity," he said. He shoved his spade into the earth yet again. This time the blade hit something other than mud.

He threw the tool aside and plunged his hands into the muck. Aulus's body had been cremated and his bones wrapped in linen. He hoped the bones would be enough to identify his brother.

"You need not lift it all." Demetrius crouched on the edge of the pit. "The lower half of the right legbone should be sufficient."

Lucius nodded. Aulus had broken his leg as a youth and Demetrius had splinted the injury. Lucius wrenched the remains of the skeleton's right limb upward. Drawing his dagger, he sliced through the knee joint as if he were butchering a stag. Bile rose in his throat, but he forced it back. His need to be certain far outweighed his disgust.

He handed the leg bones to Demetrius, then set to the task of climbing the slippery walls of the grave. By the time he'd heaved himself out of the pit, Demetrius had finished his examination.

"Well?"

The physician lifted his eyebrows. "Your hunch is correct. These are not Aulus's remains." He rubbed the corner of his sodden mantle over the shinbone, then thrust it into Lucius's hands. "See?" he said, pointing. "Unmarred. If this were Aulus's leg, there would be a bump, right here, at the site of the break."

"You are sure."

"Yes."

Lucius closed his eyes and let out a sigh. When he looked up again, it was toward Aulus, who had moved from the gravesite and fallen in a crumpled heap against the cemetery wall. He twisted, trying to avoid an unseen boot or stick.

His lips parted. Lucius heard his brother's cry in his mind as clearly as if it had sounded in his ear.

Chapter Fifteen

"Please, Gwenda, ye must help me."

"Nay. The Roman will be having my head if I do."

Rhiannon grasped the laundress's arm. "He'll not be knowing 'twas you, nor will any of the others. The kitchen is nearly deserted." It was the day of the month allotted for the slaves' use of the bathing rooms and everyone save the porters had gathered at the pool.

Gwenda shifted the bundle of soiled clothing in her arms. "I dinna know. . . . There's Cormac to be considering as well." She glanced about the storeroom as if expecting the dwarf to leap from behind a flank of boar's meat.

"Do ye know? About Cormac?"

Gwenda lowered her voice. "Aye. 'Tis my brother that carries his messages to Edmyg."

"He'll not know ye helped me." After a moment's hesitation, she touched the amber pendant at her throat. "I'll give ye this for your trouble."

"By Briga! Such a piece would feed my family for a year." Gwenda's eyes narrowed. "Where did ye come by it? If 'tis stolen, I want no part of it."

"Nay. 'Twas a gift." Rhiannon's hands shook as she drew

the chain over her head. She couldn't shake the memory of Lucius's face as he'd placed it there. How hurt he would be to see her give it away! But if parting with a bit of gold and amber might save his life, she had little choice.

She had to leave, had to get to Owein's side. But she wouldn't forfeit Lucius's life to do it—couldn't let him face the clans and the betrayal of his own men if there were another path. If Lucius wouldn't leave Vindolanda, it was up to Rhiannon to stop the attack on the fort. She had a plan to do just that.

The warriors Edmyg gathered came to fight in her name. If she ordered their swords sheathed, she was not sure whether they would obey her or follow the man who was to be their king. But if she renounced Edmyg and chose another, less militant chieftain to be her consort, some would shift their allegiance. If she chose a man with a steadier hand on his sword, the attack on the fort might be abandoned. But who? Her consort must be a chieftain who was a strong warrior and respected by many, but one who would not bow to Edmyg.

Kynan was the only man who fit that description. Rhiannon shuddered as she thought of the older warrior's mutilated face, but there was little choice. He was the only chieftain who dared to spit in Edmyg's face.

Yes. It would have to be Kynan, and even then Rhiannon was not so sure the attack on Vindolanda could be entirely avoided. Her people had borne the weight of Rome for far too long to give up their thirst for vengeance. But even if the clans didn't abandon the siege, her actions would cause a delay at the least. During that time, she would steal Aulus's head from the Druid circle and bury it, ending Lucius's torment. By the time the chieftains finished quarreling and staged their attack, Lucius and Marcus would be long gone.

The strategy was a good one. Rhiannon's kinsmen could fight amongst themselves for years without ceasing. They had done as much when Cartimandua renounced one king and took another. Her heart plummeted. Despite Madog's careful tutelage, she would repeat her grandmother's folly. Would her people end by hating her for it?

"Aye," Gwenda was saying. "I'll help ye leave the fort." She quickly divided her laundry and held one of the bundles out to Rhiannon.

Rhiannon dropped the chain over Gwenda's head and took the laundry in exchange. The woman shoved the amber pendant into the neckline of her tunic.

"We'd best be going," the laundress said in a whisper, "afore the women return from the baths."

Rhiannon nodded, not without a pang of regret. She'd not seen the inside of the bathing rooms, as Vetus was nearly always within, but the kitchen women spoke of the pool's heated waters in the most reverent of whispers.

She wished she could delay long enough to experience the bath's pleasures for herself, but there would be no better time to make her escape. Lucius had left the house several hours earlier. Even Cormac was gone. Claudia had sent him to one of the outlying farms in search of an herb he'd been unable to procure in the village. He'd been none too happy to receive the order, as the task took him far from the fort.

She had to act now or not at all.

"How will ye distract Dermot?" she asked Gwenda.

The woman chuckled. "'Tis no problem I'll be having on that score. Just slip out and don' be stopping until ye turn the corner past the stables. I'll follow as soon as I'm able. Here," she said, unpinning her checkered cloak. "Take this."

Rhiannon drew the garment's hood over her head. "Will the gate sentries remark upon two laundresses leaving the fort when only one entered?"

"Nay. The guard changed at midday. The new ones will not be knowing I came alone." She stepped to the door. "Wait here a spell until ye see it's safe to pass."

Gwenda went into the kitchen, hips swaying, as Rhiannon peeked around the doorframe. Dermot sat near the alley door, back propped against the wall, his weight balanced on two legs of a stool. His eyes were closed.

"Good day to ye, Dermot." Gwenda's voice was a husky whisper.

Dermot's stool crashed to the floor as he leapt to his feet. "Gwenda." Heat flared in his blue eyes.

Gwenda smiled up at him. Dermot took the bundle of laundry from her arms and set it aside, then bent low for a kiss. Gwenda responded, wrapping her arms about the man's broad shoulders. He backed her up against the worktable and tugged the neck of her tunic down over one shoulder. His head dipped and Rhiannon heard the sound of suckling mingled with Gwenda's sigh of satisfaction. The laundress's fingers tangled in the stout man's blond hair, holding him close.

Rhiannon stood rooted to the spot. Gwenda opened her eyes. She sent Rhiannon a grin and a pointed glance at the alley door over the top of Dermot's head. Rhiannon drew a sharp breath, then went still. Dear Briga! Had Dermot heard her? No. He was oblivious to anything but Gwenda, at least for the moment.

Rhiannon crept toward the door, scarcely daring to breathe. How in the name of the Great Mother would she be able to open it unnoticed? Surely Dermot would hear the creaking hinges and feel the rush of moist air, no matter how intent he was on Gwenda's ample breasts.

She sent the laundress a questioning look. Gwenda's eyes unglazed long enough for her to respond with a brief nod. She wriggled in Dermot's arms, coaxing him toward the storeroom where Rhiannon had stood but a moment before. Rhiannon eased open the latch as silently as she could and stepped into the alley.

The morning's downpour had eased to a sullen drizzle. Thank Briga, the narrow path was deserted. With luck, the garrison soldiers would be within their barracks until the rain stopped completely. She glanced to her left and caught sight of the wide road fronting the residence, then turned to the right and made her way along the wall of the stables.

Soft whinnies and snorts drifted from a bank of high windows. She crept to the corner and peeked around it. No one. She slipped into the intersecting alley, flattened her spine against the wall, and waited.

Gwenda arrived a few moments later, breathless and glowing, one breast all but spilling from her tunic. Rhiannon cast about for words to cover her embarrassment, but the laundress just gave her a cheeky grin. "The others rave about Cormac, but I've no complaint with Dermot," she said. "My last babe was his."

Rhiannon followed Gwenda past the rear of Lucius's house and into another alley between the granaries. Only one barrier remained—the south gate. Once through, it would be an easy task to slip through the fort village and into the forest.

Gwenda traded bawdy jests with the sentries, introducing Rhiannon as her cousin visiting from a village to the south. Rhiannon forced a smile and a few suggestive comments to her lips. One soldier patted her behind as she passed, but Rhiannon barely noticed the liberty in her haste to clear the gate. She drew a deep breath and murmured a prayer of thanks as the stout timber doors closed behind her.

"Ye'll stay in my home until nightfall," Gwenda said, drawing Rhiannon into the shelter of the nearest dwelling. "Ye don' want to be attracting notice."

Rhiannon shook her head. "Ye've done enough, Gwenda. I'll not be putting your family in danger. I'll be gone at once."

"The lookouts atop the wall might be seeing ye."

"They'll be thinking nothing of a village woman entering the forest." She thrust her bundle of laundry at Gwenda.

The laundress hesitated, then took the bundle and nodded. "Keep my cloak, then, and go swiftly. May Briga go with ye."

Rhiannon whispered a final word of thanks and slipped through the alley into the barley field beyond. The young plants, ankle-high and drooping with rain, soaked her skirt as she passed. Though every instinct screamed for haste, she forced herself to go slowly. She could not afford to attract attention.

The path between the planting rows ended at the tree line, quite near a patch of ground strewn with high markers and encircled by a stone wall. A cemetery?

A dark shadow moved just beyond, in the trees. A shiver of dread went up Rhiannon's spine. Changing course, she picked her way across the rows and entered the forest by a separate path, head bent against the rain. She'd taken but two steps into the blessed shadows when a man stepped from behind an elm and clamped his fingers around her wrist.

Lucius wanted Rhiannon's terror.

Instead, he received her disdain. Her chin lifted and her spine stiffened. The hood of her checkered cloak fell to her shoulders. She looked past him, into the forest, as if his hand restraining her arm was but a momentary inconvenience.

He caught her chin with his free hand and forced her to meet his gaze. Her golden eyes, usually so expressive, showed not a trace of emotion. Neither fear, nor anger, nor even regret. Had she played him for a fool? Was it so easy for her to walk away after she'd opened her thighs to him?

His own emotions, in contrast, churned in a cauldron of conflict. He snatched the one closest to the surface—anger—and clung to it.

"Lucius. Why are you here?"

His grip tightened on her wrist and the flare of pain he saw in her eyes brought satisfaction as well as guilt. "I

207

might ask the same of you," he said, keeping his voice carefully neutral.

She wrenched her chin from his grasp. "I am going home."

"Your home is with me."

"No. I am a free Celt, not a Roman slave. You have no right to keep me here."

"By Pollux, I have every right. I claimed you from the field of battle." He bent his head low and let his breath brush her temple. "You are mine." He released her wrist and trailed his fingers up the inside of her arm, under her cloak. He brushed the outside curve of her breast.

He felt rather than heard her sharp intake of breath. With it rose the scent of her need.

His rod hardened.

She must have known, for her eyes went dark and when she spoke, her voice trembled. "How did you find me? Did you follow from the fort?"

"No. I was in the cemetery. Digging."

Her eyes widened as she took in his mud-slicked armor. "Why?"

"Aulus is not in his grave."

The tip of her tongue darted forward to wet her lips. "He is not?"

"No. An interesting turn of events, don't you agree?"

"Indeed."

"My brother watched my labors, of course. Then, as I finished refilling the pit, he vanished."

Understanding dawned in her eyes. "You knew I was near."

His fingers drifted across the swell of her breast and stroked through the fabric of her tunic. "Yes." He teased her nipple into a tight nub, then flicked his thumb roughly across the hardened peak. "But I hardly need my brother to lead me to you. I scented you like the buck scents the doe."

She gasped and arched into his touch, though he suspected she would have much preferred to remain unmoved. "Lucius . . ."

"I knew you were near," he repeated, "but I didn't know why, or how." He plucked one nipple, then brought his left hand up to pinch the other, taking no care to be gentle. "You had help."

"How did you—"

"Your cloak. Who was she? No, don't answer. It will be easy enough to discover."

Rhiannon tried to move away. "Nay! She did only as I asked."

"No doubt." His hands stole upward, encircling the delicate column of her neck. His thumbs covered the pulse at her throat. "Where is the amber necklace, Rhiannon?" His voice was deadly calm, but his fury crouched like a wildcat behind it. "Will I find it in your bedchamber? Or around the neck of the deceiving wench who gave you this cloak?" He made a disapproving sound. "What punishment should I mete out to such a woman?"

"Nay," Rhiannon whispered. "You must not harm her. She knew nothing of where I came by the treasure, only that I bartered it for my freedom."

The sense of betrayal bit deep. Anger surged so hot he wondered that the rain did not sizzle as it struck his skin. He crowded her against the trunk of a broad elm, his heart black with fury.

He raised one hand to touch her face and she flung up her arms as if to ward off a blow. He stared for a moment, stunned, then threw back his head and laughed. She feared him. No matter that he'd never lifted a hand against her. No matter that he hadn't forced her into his bed when another man would have used her until she broke. No matter that he had whispered soft endearments and heard them spoken in return. He'd told her of Aulus's haunting and of his own guilt and despair. He'd trusted her with the darkest secrets of his soul.

Yet despite what they'd shared, she still believed him to be the basest of criminals, a Roman dog, a defiler.

Fire raged through his veins, along with a dark purpose born of anger and need. He would give her what she expected of him, no more, no less. It was only what she deserved.

With a swift motion, he grasped her cloak in both hands and tore the fabric free of the pin at her throat. The garment landed on the ground, a bright heap on the mud.

"Lucius, nay—" Rhiannon's eyes were wide, startled. Afraid.

He couldn't bear to look into them any more than he could stop himself from reaching for her. He caged her with his arms. She resisted, twisting, but her frantic struggle only caused him to tighten his hold. He spun her around and pressed her spine against his muddy armor. Her buttocks nestled at his groin, his hands splayed over her breasts and stomach, holding her immobile.

"Release me," she gasped.

"No." He lifted her instead, carrying her deeper into the forest with two quick strides. His hand sought the hidden place between her thighs and stroked the heat he found there. She squirmed and twisted, striking him as she was able. Her efforts succeeded only in causing his rod to go even harder.

He increased the tempo of his fingers, concentrating on the hard nub at her center. He scraped the fabric of her tunic across her sex until the linen dampened in his hand. A moan tore from deep in her throat.

Her entreaty, when it came, was breathless. "Lucius. Please. Put me"—she moaned again as he touched her—"down."

"As you wish." He set her, face down, over the wide trunk of a fallen oak and lifted her hem.

Rain fell in glistening drops on the smooth white skin of Rhiannon's buttocks. She struggled furiously, but his hand on the small of her back conspired with her awkward position to prevent her escape. She braced her hands on the ground but gained little leverage. "Let me go."

He palmed over one smooth globe. "How could you leave me, Rhiannon?" He slipped his hand into her cleft and stroked downward. Slick heat gripped him when he slid his finger into her sheath.

She went still. He added a second finger to the first and flexed his knuckles. She let out a cry, not of anger or pain, but of need.

His eyes burned. "How could you leave me," he said again, "when you want me as much as I want you?" He flexed a second time. "Tell me, Rhiannon. Tell me that you want me inside you."

"No."

He bent low, his hand still pulsing inside her. Raindrops fell on his arm and coursed along his wrist and into her heat. "Tell me to whom you belong."

"No." The word was a bare breath.

His low chuckle contained no mirth. "Then I will show you." His hand left her tight passage. She made a small sound, a whimper she tried but failed to contain. He cupped her buttocks with his palms, kneading, watching as the rain pelted her skin. He followed the path of one droplet with his finger into the crease at the top of her thigh.

Her hips lifted into his touch. "Lucius . . . please."

"What do you want, Rhiannon?"

Another moan as he reached between her legs to stroke where her need was greatest. "You, Lucius. Within me. Now. I cannot bear it any longer."

He shifted his war belt and lifted his tunic. Grasping her hips with both hands, he plunged into her with one sure, swift stroke, burying himself to the hilt. She let out a soft cry and clamped tight around him, hot, wet, and demanding. He withdrew until he was nearly unsheathed, then paused, waiting, gripping her hips and holding her still.

She was sobbing now. "Please, Lucius. I want—"

His fingers tightened. "What?"

"You."

A heady flare of satisfaction pulsed through him. He entered her again, driving deep, losing himself in her heat. He withdrew and thrust again, savoring her cry of relief as he filled her. He bucked hard and fast, urging her surrender, until she sobbed his name a final time and came apart in his hands. His own climax followed, pulsing, unending, until his legs gave way and he collapsed atop her, gasping for breath.

Rhiannon made little protest when at last he pushed himself off her and hoisted her to her feet. Her tunic was smeared with mud, soaked through and plastered to her skin. He snatched the sodden cloak from the ground and wrapped it around her shoulders. She looked up at him, a bemused expression on her face.

"Did I hurt you?" he asked, suddenly ashamed. He'd intended only to prevent her escape, not to rut with her in the dirt like a beast. Had he lost his dignity along with his mind?

"Nay," she whispered, but she turned away from him. The gesture tore at his heart.

He took her by the elbow and propelled her out of the forest and through the village. She offered no complaint, indeed, she gripped his arm as if it were a lifeline. He guided her between the south gate towers, ignoring the stares of the sentries. He pounded on the door of his residence as rain sluiced out of the sky, harder than before.

Rhiannon shivered and drew her arms tight across her chest. A scant moment later they stood in the foyer, dripping onto the mosaic floor. Lucius waved the porter away.

Only then did Rhiannon finally raise her head and look at him. Her dazed expression was gone, replaced with anger.

"You are a brute."

"Then you crave a brute's touch."

"You cannot keep me here."

Lucius snorted. "I disagree. Henceforth a military guard will be posted at each door. I suggest you do not try to pass."

"And if I do, what will happen? Will you beat me with your son and the rest of the household looking on?"

"Don't speak to me of Marcus. The boy adores you. You surely didn't take his feelings into consideration when you decided to run from me."

"I considered more than his feelings," she said quietly. "I considered his life."

He narrowed his gaze. "What do you mean?"

She drew a deep breath. "What if I told you that you were right in naming me a witch? If I promised that if you release me, I will see your brother's spirit sent to rest?"

"If you were to say such a thing . . ." His hands fisted at his sides. "If you did, then I would tell you to cast your spell now, while I stand before you."

Panic flashed in her eyes. "The words must be spoken in the forest." She bit her lip and looked past him to the door. "I cannot cast such a spell within walls."

"Cannot? Or will not?" He stepped close and gripped her shoulders. "Tell me the truth, Rhiannon. Did you imprison Aulus? Is his suffering at your hand?"

When she didn't respond, he gave her a rough shake. "Answer me, by Pollux!"

"No!" she said. " 'Tis not I, I vow! But I can free your brother, Lucius, if you let me go."

"Why should I believe you?"

"You must! I didn't imprison your brother's spirit, but . . ." She shut her eyes briefly. "I know how he died."

Lucius stilled. "What?"

"I've always known. I . . . I saw it."

"Tell me."

She went deathly pale. His grip on her shoulders tightened. "I will have the truth. Now."

"I saw Aulus die. It was no hunting accident."

"How, then?"

Her lips opened, then closed. "I can tell you no more than that."

In the vicinity of Lucius's heart, something broke. All this time Rhiannon had known how Aulus had met his death. She knew his murderers but had said nothing, even as he had bared his soul to her. The betrayal cut deep, though he supposed he should have expected it. He'd admired her pride and her loyalty, but she'd gifted neither to him. She would protect her people with her dying breath. And despite her deception, he loved her for it.

He was worse than a fool. He was an idiot.

"So Aulus was killed by barbarians," he said quietly. "Your people?"

Her silence was acknowledgment enough.

"I will find my brother's murderers. You will lead me to them."

"Nay. I will not." She gathered her sodden skirt in one hand and took a step toward the stair.

"Rhiannon."

She stopped, but didn't look back.

"I would have your loyalty."

Her spine stiffened. "I cannot give it to you."

"Then seek your bed with the rest of the slaves."

Chapter Sixteen

"What did you do to Rhiannon?"

Lucius's exit from his bedchamber was halted by the agitated presence of his son. The hour was early; dawn was only a dull sheen in the cloudy sky. Had the boy been lying in wait all night? His hair was damp, the dark curls plastered to his forehead. The insect-infested pile of fur he'd claimed for a pet stood nearby. When Aulus staggered into the passageway, the animal issued a low growl.

"I've done nothing to her. Why? Is she ill?"

"She's crying." Marcus seemed almost ready to break into tears himself. Red patches adorned his cheeks and his eyes were unnaturally bright. "She's huddled in the back of the storeroom, weeping, and nothing I say will make her stop."

A pang of guilt stabbed Lucius, but it was a small prick compared to the horror he'd felt when Rhiannon had admitted being a witness to Aulus's death. His mind was still reeling from the shock of it. Once his sense of betrayal had settled to a dull ache, a new thought had arisen. His brother had been murdered by Celts, not mangled by a boar. Who in the fort had concocted the false report? And why?

"Go to her, Father. Tell her you're sorry."

"Marcus—"

"She's my friend."

Lucius started for the stair with Aulus limping after him. "Go begin your studies, Marcus."

Marcus drew a deep breath. "No."

Lucius halted, staring at his son in disbelief. The boy had never dared to defy him so openly. "I'll repeat my order only once," he said slowly. "Go to the library and take up your Aristotle."

"No. I'll make you go to her." Marcus launched himself forward, fists raised. Hercules, apparently sensing a romp, bounded forward at the same time. Lucius watched, stunned, as boy collided with dog and landed in a heap at his feet.

He caught Marcus by the arm and hauled him upright. His tunic was damp, his body shaking. When the boy looked up, his eyes were not quite focused.

"I . . . I thought you liked Rhiannon."

Lucius ignored the tightness in his chest. "She's but a slave, Marcus."

"So was Magister Demetrius, long ago. He told me."

"True, but—" He broke off to take a closer look at the boy. The crimson flush on his face was not entirely due to emotion. His anger at Marcus's outburst quickly turned to fear. "Marcus, are you feeling quite well?"

"Well enough, but . . ." He frowned. "One moment it's so hot I can't bear it, the next so cold that I'm shaking."

Lucius pressed his palm to his son's cheek. By Pollux, he was burning up. Looking up, he met Aulus's gaze and was chilled to the bone by the expression he saw there.

Marcus swayed and would have fallen if Lucius hadn't caught him. "Where is Magister Demetrius?" he asked the boy.

"Hospital," Marcus mumbled.

Lucius swept his son into his arms. He carried him to his own bedchamber and lowered him onto Aulus's bed. Marcus gave a shuddering sigh and went limp.

Terror blacker than a storm-ridden sea churned in Lucius's gut. He covered his son with a blanket and made for the fort hospital.

"More water. Hotter than before."

Rhiannon heaved the bucket of water to the stove and filled the boiling pot. "Marcus is worse?"

Demetrius emptied the contents of a glass vial into the water, releasing the odor of spoiled eggs. "He grows delirious."

"And the fever?"

"Increasing. There is a blockage of fluids in Marcus's body. This purge should allow the humours to flow." His hand shook so violently that the stopper missed the hole.

Rhiannon took the vial and plugged it herself. "You fear for his life."

"This malady has claimed ten men since I arrived at Vindolanda. I could save none of them, neither with the medicines I brought from Rome nor the remedies you showed me in the hospital garden." He rubbed his eyes. "Marcus is asking for you."

"Truly?"

"Yes. Come with me above stairs. Perhaps your presence will sooth him."

"But Lucius forbade . . ."

"Lucius left for headquarters an hour past."

"Oh." He'd left his son's side while the lad was so ill?

She followed Demetrius to the upper level. Marcus lay in Lucius's bedchamber, the shutters drawn tight against the day. The five braziers that had been set in a circle about his bed threw off waves of heat but little light. A thick, fetid odor hung in the air—a combination of herbs and vomit. A bucket of noxious fluids stood by the door.

Bronwyn sat on a stool, closer to the door than the bed, and the expression on her face clearly said she wished to be elsewhere. At Demetrius's nod she took hold of the bucket's handle and disappeared through the doorway.

"The chamber wants cooling," Rhiannon said.

"Marcus's constitution suffers from an excess of water," Demetrius replied. "Heat aids its release."

Rhiannon couldn't fathom how anyone could hope to survive when already shut in a tomb. In her opinion, fresh air would be far more helpful. That and a potion brewed from mistletoe harvested from the branches of the sacred oaks near the Druid circle. She crossed the room swiftly and knelt at Marcus's side. His face was dry and hot to the touch, his pulse far too rapid.

"Marcus," she whispered. Then, when he didn't seem to hear her, "Marcus. 'Tis Rhiannon."

His swollen lids lifted, but it was a long moment before his eyes seemed to focus. "Rhiannon?"

She entwined her fingers with his. "Yes, love. I'm here."

"Stay." His eyes closed again.

She murmured a healing spell and sought the lad's soul with her own. When she found it, she held it tightly, appalled by how weak the spark of his essence was.

"Raise his head," Demetrius said, lifting the cup he had carried from the kitchens. "He needs to drink the purge."

"He is so weak. 'Twould be better to let him rest. Some cool air would help."

"Such a thing would surely kill him," Demetrius replied. He advanced toward the bed, bearing the purge. Rhiannon slipped onto the cushions and cradled Marcus in her arms, lifting his head so he could take the healer's remedy. Dear Briga, but he was hot! His head lolled to one side and he seemed hardly to know what was happening.

Demetrius coaxed the liquid down his patient's throat. Marcus sputtered but managed to swallow most of the vile brew. He slumped against Rhiannon, his breathing so shallow she had to bend her head to hear it.

She stroked the curls from his forehead. Demetrius located an empty bucket. A moment later, Marcus groaned, then went rigid. Vomit spewed from his mouth, soaking the coverlet. A second stream, tinged with blood, landed in the bucket.

The lad retched until Rhiannon feared for his life; then he lay back, exhausted, muscles twitching, face a vivid scarlet. Demetrius sank heavily onto the stool as Rhiannon began clearing the soiled linens.

"Now we wait," he said. "Zeus knows there is little more I can do."

Lucius's hand lay motionless on his bedchamber door for a long while before he found the courage to shove it open. When at last he did, the rank odor of vomit washed over him like a vengeful tide. Outside, the night sentry called the last hour before cockcrow.

Marcus's whimpering sounded from the bed. The piteous sound filled Lucius with relief. By some small favor of the gods, the boy had stayed alive during the long hours that his father had feigned industry in the fort headquarters, unable to face the sight of his only son lying on his deathbed. Lucius's steps dragged into the chamber. Aulus, naked and battered, limped to the threshold and disappeared.

Rhiannon half rose from the stool by the bed, then dropped down again as if Lucius's sudden appearance had weakened her legs. Her fair skin was deathly pale save for the dark smudges under her eyes. Her hair was disheveled, her tunic soiled. The sight of her sent a fierce pain crashing through his chest.

Her fingers were entwined with his son's. The boy's dog lay at her feet. As Lucius stepped forward, the ragged beast raised its head and thumped its tail once against the floor.

"Why are you here?" he asked her. Before she could open her mouth to reply, Marcus cried out and wrenched his hand from Rhiannon's grasp. He thrashed against his blankets, tangling them about his legs and arms as if wrestling a Fury.

219

Lucius strode to the bed and quickly loosened Marcus's limbs from their restraints. "Marcus. Lie still."

He began to shake. "Cold." He opened his eyes and looked wildly about the chamber, his teeth clashing so violently Lucius thought they would shatter. "So cold."

Rhiannon retrieved the blanket from the floor and tucked it over the bed, though with the boy's skin so hot it seemed a ludicrous thing to do. "Why are you here?" he asked again.

"Marcus asked for me."

"Where is Demetrius?"

"I told him to seek his bed, lest he collapse on the floor."

"But you stayed."

"Yes."

Lucius rubbed his hand over his eyes. "Leave now. Send another woman to tend my son."

She hesitated, then said, "None will come. They are too afraid."

Another moan drifted from the bed. Hercules's head came up. Lucius bent over Marcus. By the gods. The boy's face was as red as if he'd been stranded in the Eastern desert. His cracked lips parted, revealing a bloated tongue covered with a white sheen. His breath came shallow and rasping. A thick lump rose in Lucius's throat. His son was dying.

Rhiannon took a clean linen and dipped it in a bowl of water. She wrung it out and gently wiped Marcus's face, murmuring in her native tongue as she worked. Then she drew back the blankets and repeated the procedure on his chest. The boy seemed to relax under her ministrations.

She left the cloth draped on his forehead. Lucius sank onto the stool and without thinking caught Marcus's hand in his own. He stared at the boy's long fingers, so unlike his own blunt digits. He'd longed for a son who would be a warrior and a scholar. He'd gotten one who was an artist and a dreamer.

Lucius wondered why he hadn't been wise enough to cherish Marcus as he was.

If he could, he would take back all the sharp reprimands and replace them with words of love. But now, even if such a thing were possible, Marcus was not lucid enough to understand.

He spoke anyway. "Marcus, get well and I promise you may draw all day if you like. You can burn Aristotle for all I care."

Rhiannon's soft voice sounded behind him. "Lucius, I . . ."

Creaking hinges interrupted her speech, which was just as well. Lucius's emotions were stretched to the breaking point. Any words Rhiannon spoke to him would surely cause him to snap.

Demetrius's weary footsteps advanced. The physician came to a halt at Lucius's side and laid one gnarled hand on his shoulder.

"Can you do nothing more?" Lucius asked him.

"I am at the end of my wits, Luc. I've tried all the usual remedies, and some unusual ones as well, yet still the fever climbs."

Lucius's brain felt numb. "He will die."

"Perhaps not. He is young and strong."

He eased Marcus's hand onto the bed and rose, scraping the legs of his chair across the tiles. "Don't lie to me, old man. Is there nothing else?"

Rhiannon stepped into Lucius's line of vision and placed one hand on his arm. "Lucius."

He looked at her and his gut twisted. Even haggard from lack of sleep and covered with the stains of a sickroom, she was the most beautiful creature he'd ever laid eyes upon. He forced himself to remember that her loveliness hid deceit.

"Lucius, I know of an herb not found in the hospital plot. It is the remedy I used when the same illness struck my village last summer. All but the weakest lived."

He looked away from her, not wanting to trust, not daring to nurture the spark of hope she kindled.

"Why should I believe you?"

"You must!"

"She has no reason to lie," Demetrius put in. "Go on, girl. What manner of herb is it?"

"My people call it mistletoe. I know of a place—an oak grove fed by sacred waters—where plants of great power thrive. I can bring the remedy to you."

"Lucius, it is worth a try at the least," Demetrius said.

He hesitated, but in the end his shoulders slumped. "Very well. I'll order an escort to take you there."

"Nay. I must go alone."

His fragile ember of hope faded. "Do you think me a fool? There is no herb. You would use Marcus's illness as an excuse to escape."

Demetrius made a sound of protest. "I cannot believe Rhiannon would do such a thing. She cares for the boy."

Lucius snorted. "Unfortunately I know all too well how deceptive she can be. No. She's not to be trusted."

"Please, Lucius," Rhiannon said. "I beg you. Let me go before—"

Marcus let out a sharp cry, his spine arching from the bed. His limbs flailed, once again entangling with the blankets. Lucius sank onto the bed and gathered his son in his arms. The boy clung to his neck, whimpering, but his struggles eased with every soothing word Lucius whispered, until at last he lay still.

An eerie peace swept over Lucius. He'd never before cradled his son in his arms, not even when Marcus had been a babe. How was it, then, that the sensation of the young body pressed against his seemed as natural as breathing?

Demetrius retrieved the blanket from the floor and covered them both. "Rhiannon's remedy is Marcus's last hope," he said. "Perhaps she will allow me, if not a guard, to accompany her."

Rhiannon hesitated, then nodded once.

Lucius dragged a hand across his eyes. It came away wet. "Go," he said.

Rhiannon tipped her head back and took in the rain-washed scent of the forest in huge, lusty gulps. How she had missed it! She could hardly believe little more than a sennight had passed since Lucius had taken her from the battlefield. It seemed she had spent the better part of her lifetime enclosed by Vindolanda's walls.

The rain had passed, leaving the promise of summer warm and heavy in the air. Mist clung to the narrow forest trail. The large mare she rode was spirited, but well trained and responsive to her hand on the reins.

Beside her, Demetrius grumbled atop his own mount. "I can't abide horses. Never could. How far must we journey?"

"Not far," Rhiannon replied vaguely. "We'll return before nightfall." She cast him a sidelong glance. She should leave him now, while they were still close to the fort. If she waited until they neared the Druid circle, the healer might never find his way out of the forest.

She eased toward a dense growth of underbrush, then said, "I'm in need of a few moments' rest."

"Rest? You're but a girl and we've ridden only an hour."

She lowered her gaze, feigning embarrassment. "I didn't mean that I was tired. The wine I drank before we left the fort . . ."

"Ah," he said, understanding. His birdlike eyes took on a wicked gleam. "Luc told me not to let you out of my sight."

She forced a small smile. "He cannot stand to look at me himself. Why burden you with the task?"

His features softened. "It's not a hardship, my dear."

Rhiannon turned away, blinking back her tears.

"I've known Lucius more than twenty-two years," Demetrius said. "I came to his household as a slave, bought on the occasion of Lucius's eighth birthday to be his tutor."

"A slave? But Lucius respects you so."

"It's not the label that defines the man, but his attitude and actions. In my mind I was always a free man. Within nine years of coming to Lucius's father's household, I had earned enough by my skill as a physician to purchase my freedom." He smiled. "I beat out Lucius by a year. He had vowed to purchase me from his father and free me himself when he reached manhood."

"Why did you stay with him once you were free?"

"Why indeed? You would think I might have returned to Greece. But I had no family there. By then Lucius and Aulus had become like sons to me." He sighed. "Aulus was still young and in sore need of guidance. He was much like Marcus is now: generous, scheming, and forever falling into trouble."

"And Lucius? What was he like?"

The healer sent her a knowing glance. "The dutiful son, always. Athletic, good with a sword, and a scholar as well. Intensely private. He guarded his emotions closely even then. Aulus was the only one who could truly reach him, but only in rare moments."

"I see."

"Now I sense you are the one who holds that power. Lucius knows not how to deal with that, I think."

"You're wrong. He despises me." *With good reason.*

He snorted. "I've seen how he looks at you, girl. You've well and truly seduced him. In bed and out."

"I . . . didn't seek to bed him! He pursued me."

"And was caught in his own snare." Demetrius held her gaze. "I don't believe you regret it."

Rhiannon searched for words of denial but found none.

"Why did you try to leave him?" Demetrius asked. "Did you not know he would grant anything you asked?"

"Barring my freedom."

"Freedom? No woman is truly free. Few men are, either. You can live a fine life with him."

A wistful smile touched her lips. "In Rome?"

"Yes. Would you not like to see the heart of the empire? It's a grand and amazing city."

Rhiannon closed her eyes. Part of her did long to travel to the ends of the earth and look upon all the wonders she could find. Another part, just as strong, knew that to leave the northlands would cause an ache that would never fade. "I . . . I cannot say."

"Think on it, my dear." He blinked rapidly and Rhiannon realized he was crying. "If Marcus should . . . die . . . Lucius will need you."

Her chest tightened unbearably. She could think of no adequate response, so she swung her leg over her mare's flank and dismounted. "If you will give me but a moment, Magister . . ." She sent a meaningful glance toward the bushes.

"Do not be long."

"I won't." She ducked into the thicket, making sure to rustle the branches as she went. When she had gained a sufficient distance from the trail, she went still for several long heartbeats. When she moved again, it was with the silence of a ghost.

She did not look back.

Chapter Seventeen

For most, mist meant blindness. For Owein, the white shroud that crept over the landscape brought vision. The pictures behind his eyes no longer needed night shadows for a backdrop. He Saw as clearly during the days now.

He sat rigid in the small clearing outside Madog's hut, holding the Druid sword his mentor had given him. It was the sword that had killed the Roman at Samhain. The same blade that would kill Rhiannon's defiler at the rise of the summer moon.

The hand of Kernunnos lay heavy upon him. The pain in his temple was as familiar to him as breath and he'd begun to believe it would never retreat. He cared little, if his torment brought him the power to free his sister from the vile dog who had enslaved her.

"What do ye See, lad?" Madog's voice was Owein's only connection to the outside world when the visions took over. He felt the old Druid lean closer.

"A man. Dead."

"Roman or Celt?"

Owein waited for the scene's fragments to coalesce. "I canna . . . Nay, wait, I See him more clearly now. Roman, I am thinking." Rhiannon's captor? Owein couldn't be sure. The picture faded.

"Good." Madog rose and paced a circle about him. He chanted the ancient prayers, his form a shadow on the landscape of Owein's vision. "Look beyond, lad. Ye have Seen what will be. Now See what *can* be, and the path to it."

Cautiously Owein extended his mind and touched the mist. In the past he had never sought to birth the images that rose in his mind. But Madog had told Owein that his Sight revealed only a small portion of things to come. The larger part of the future could be shaped by those who had the favor of Kernunnos.

As Owein did.

Madog's steps tightened, forming a spiral of which Owein was the center. "*See,* Owein." He halted before him and lifted a frantic mountain hare overhead. "See the defeat of our enemy." The Druid's shadow arm slashed. The hare shrieked.

Hot blood spilled over Owein's bare shoulders and ran down his back. He inhaled deeply, drinking in the sweet scent of the hare's life, drawing strength from his animal brother's sacrifice. It was the way of things. Blood was spilled, power gained. It could not be otherwise.

The mist swirled. Images rose and vanished like puffs of winter breath. A man, wounded. A woman's face—Rhiannon? Her mouth opened in a soundless scream.

And blood. Always blood.

Owein's breathing slowed as he plunged deeper. The flash of Madog's Druid sword. His own hand on the hilt. The tip poised at the throat of a dark-skinned man. This time the man's features were unmistakable. It was the Roman commander. The foreign dog who had defiled the queen of the Brigantes.

He would die by Owein's hand.

"Rhiannon is gone, Luc. Left me in the forest with both our mounts. Took me half the day to find my way out."

Despite the fact that Lucius had anticipated Rhiannon's flight, Demetrius's words sliced like a finely honed battle sword. "I told you she would run," he replied wearily.

Demetrius lowered himself onto a stool on the opposite side of Marcus's bed, but Lucius didn't dare meet his friend's gaze. He stared instead at his son's limp hand clasped in his own rough palm. The boy was quiet now, having finally thrashed himself into a fitful slumber. Aulus hunched at the foot of his nephew's bed, silent and watchful. In the shrouded stillness of the sickroom, Lucius almost imagined he could hear the soft susurration of his brother's breath.

"You were right," Demetrius said finally. "As always. Yet I still find it hard to believe." He shook his head. "I was sure she cared for the boy."

"She cares only for her freedom. No doubt if she had given you an herb, it would have been a poisonous one."

"You cannot believe that."

"I don't know what to believe."

Demetrius's eyes showed his worry. "You look terrible, Luc. Like a man bound in Tartarus."

Lucius felt far worse. "A sojourn in Hades would be an improvement."

"Go to your chamber and get some rest while I look after Marcus. I'll call you if . . . if there's any change."

"No." The word came out more sharply than Lucius intended. "No. I've been absent for most of my son's life. I cannot turn from his death. It won't be long now."

Demetrius fell silent. He rose and adjusted the shutters, allowing a bit more light into the chamber, then resumed his seat. Lucius lifted Marcus's hand and laid it gently across the boy's chest. Then, since that position looked too corpselike, he repositioned it on the cushions.

He sat there, unmoving, watching his son—the future of his family's line—fade before his eyes. "What was I thinking, bringing Marcus to this wretched scrap of wilderness?"

"The boy begged to come north," Demetrius replied. "Don't torture yourself with what might have been. He could just as easily have fallen ill in Rome."

"No." Lucius's fist slammed onto the low table beside him, overturning a goblet of wine. "I am his father. It was my duty to ensure his safety."

"No one can foresee what the Fates have woven," Demetrius said. "We can guarantee nothing, not even our next breath."

They lapsed into silence. After a time, footsteps sounded beyond the door, but Lucius didn't bother to rise. No doubt it was Candidus, bearing yet another tray of food that Lucius wouldn't even glance at, let alone eat.

Aulus looked up, surprise evident on his bruised features. He flickered like a lamp flame in a breeze. Lucius sprang to his feet as his brother vanished in a puff of mist.

Demetrius looked up, startled. "Lucius, what—"

Lucius strode to the chamber door and flung it wide. Rhiannon stood before him, one hand lifted and poised to knock. Her face was streaked with grime, her tunic torn and muddy. Her hair blazed about her shoulders like a fire gone wild. She clutched a tangled clump of leaves and roots to her heaving chest.

Her eyes widened at the sight of him. No doubt he looked worse than she did. He'd neither slept nor shaved in two days. But now that she had returned, he felt his desperation fade.

"Lucius," Rhiannon breathed and swayed on her feet.

He caught her by the arm, holding her steady until she regained her balance. Then he drew his hand back, unsure if his touch was welcome. "You came back."

"Yes." She looked past him. "Marcus. Is he—"

"He lives still." Lucius stepped aside and allowed her to pass.

She bent low over Marcus's bed and smoothed one hand over his forehead. "I am sorry, Magister. It was necessary I gather the herb alone. The sacred grove lies close to my village."

"You might have trusted me to understand," Demetrius said.

"I couldn't take that chance."

Lucius understood only too well. Rhiannon dared not reveal the location of her village and risk the lives of Aulus's murderers.

Demetrius set his hands on the bed and pushed himself to his feet. "Do not speak of it further." He touched the knot of roots she'd laid on the blankets. "What will you need? Mortar and pestle?"

"Yes. And hot water," she said, not looking up from her examination of the boy.

Demetrius left them alone. Lucius told himself to keep his distance, but the siren call of Rhiannon's presence proved impossible to resist. Yes, she'd protected her murdering kinsmen, but she'd sacrificed her sudden freedom to return to the fort, for Marcus's sake if not for his own.

He moved to stand behind her, close but not touching. When she straightened and looked up at him, her face was flushed. She spoke, her voice so low he had to dip his head to make out the words. "Lucius, I must warn you. Marcus is weak and this cure is dangerous in itself. It may only hasten his death."

"Yet it has cured some?"

"Many."

Lucius paced around the bed, halting at the table upon which Demetrius's instruments had been set out. His hand closed on the goblet he'd overturned earlier. He righted the cup and busied himself mopping the spilt wine with a cloth. Twilight gloom was gathering swiftly. He relit the hand lamp, gathered the soiled rags, and placed them in a heap by the door.

When at last he turned back to Rhiannon, his surge of helplessness was, if not vanquished, then tightly under control. "Do what you must. Marcus has little time left as it is."

She moved toward him and cupped his cheek with her palm. "Thank you for your trust. I know I've done little to deserve it."

His jaw worked to force a swallow past the burning lump in his throat. He looked toward the newly lit lamp. The flame stung his eyes.

Rhiannon's hand dropped away and the loss of her touch brought an ache to Lucius's chest. As she peeled away the swath of blankets shrouding Marcus's upper body, he found himself wishing for Aulus's presence, however gruesome, at his side.

If he needed final proof of his insanity, the fact that he missed his brother's ghost was surely it.

Rhiannon wet a clean length of linen and began to sponge Marcus's face and torso. Lucius wondered at her actions—Demetrius had insisted the boy remain warm. Yet he didn't question her method. He had placed his son's life—and his own heart—in Rhiannon's hands. He could do no less than to trust her.

Marcus stirred and his eyelids fluttered open. "Rhiannon." The word was little more than a hoarse croak.

"I'm here, Marcus." She brushed a kiss on his forehead.

Lucius's heart clenched. She loved his son. He could see it in her eyes, in her touch. How Lucius wished he could earn even a half measure of that emotion.

Demetrius returned, followed by a slave woman carrying a steaming bowl of water.

"Both leaves and roots," Rhiannon said. Demetrius took up a pestle and crushed the first bit of root. Rhiannon leaned low, her lips grazing Marcus's ear. "I need you to take a draught. A potion."

Marcus's eyes were two wide pools. "A witch's brew?"

Rhiannon's lips curved, even as her tears welled. "Yes. It will be horrid, but it will make you better."

Demetrius finished his preparations and filled a cup with liquid. Rhiannon murmured her most potent healing spell as she slipped her arm under Marcus's shoulders. A

231

spasm gripped the lad's body. His arm flailed, striking her in the face.

Lucius was at her side in an instant. His arms closed about Marcus in gentle restraint. "Are you hurt?"

"No."

Marcus's fit passed. Lucius held him upright while Rhiannon dripped her brew down his throat. When she finished, he eased his son's head onto the cushions.

"How long?" he asked grimly.

Rhiannon met his gaze. "We will know by morning."

"It wants but two nights to the summer moon." Edmyg eyed the skull atop Madog's staff. "My warriors are eager."

Owein stood silent, watching the firelight paint the chieftain's arrogant features in wavering shadows. Even at a distance of twenty paces, Owein could see hatred burning in his kinsman's eyes. Pain spiked into his temple. The visions called. He leaned heavily on the rough doorframe of Madog's hut and fought against them. When they came upon him, he lay as helpless as a babe. He knew Edmyg wished to kill him. He dared not show his vulnerability.

"We will be ready," Madog said. His hand shifted on his staff, causing the dead man's visage to swivel in Owein's direction.

"How, when Rhiannon has failed to deliver the Roman?" Edmyg asked.

At that, Owein moved from the shadows into the firelight, fighting the pain with each step. "Deliver? How so?"

Madog's gaze shifted toward Owein before returning to Edmyg. "A stag will take the Roman's place," he said.

Edmyg spat in Owein's direction. "A poor substitute for an enemy's blood. The chieftains will nay be pleased."

Madog shrugged. "When warriors are discontented, the fault lies with their leader."

Edmyg bristled. "Watch your tongue, old man."

Another brilliant shaft of agony exploded in Owein's

head. He took a deep breath and waited for the worst of it to pass. "How was Rhiannon to deliver the Roman? She's his prisoner."

Edmyg paid him scant attention. "Dinna bring the lad to the circle," he told Madog. "He is no longer of the clan."

"Think ye that blood can be denied?" said Madog. "Ye will find otherwise."

"He killed Glynis and her babe. My son."

"True enough. Yet he did nay more than Kernunnos commanded."

Owein's blood ran cold. Madog believed his Sight had caused the death of Glynis and her bastard? Could it be true? He'd not sought to form the vision. It had come unbidden.

Edmyg snatched his dagger from its sheath and pressed the tip to Madog's throat. "Ye set him to it, old man. Dinna be denying it."

Owein seized the Druid sword from the scabbard at his belt. But Madog raised a palm to Owein and merely met Edmyg's gaze with a cold stare. Edmyg slammed his weapon back into its sheath.

He turned on Owein. "Yer precious sister plays the whore with the Roman."

"The dog forced himself on her."

"Nay. Cormac reports she takes her pleasure gladly. Cartimandua's blood runs strong in her veins."

" 'Tis a lie!"

Edmyg gave an unpleasant laugh. "Is it? Rhiannon kens she has but to lure her lover outside the fort to gain her freedom. Yet she doesna climb from his bed."

Owein stared at him. "What do ye mean?"

"I sent her word through Cormac instructing her to bed the Roman and contrive a way to lie with him in the forest, away from his guards." He made a slashing motion with one hand. "I was to be waiting, to take him alive."

"She will yet bring him to the circle," Madog said.

Owein spun toward him. "Ye knew of this?"

"Aye," answered Edmyg. "He knew."

Owein felt sick. "How could ye ask Rhiannon to debase herself so?"

Madog's eyes took on a hard glint. "How many Druid women suffered worse degradations at Mona only to have their throats slit by Roman swords after? 'Tis no shameful role Rhiannon takes in this. 'Tis vengeance. She wields a weapon only a woman can hold."

He caressed the skull atop his staff. "Revenge is precious. It canna be gained without sacrifice. Who better to offer it than a queen?"

Chapter Eighteen

Rhiannon awoke by small degrees, fighting a dream in which she searched the ground within the sacred stones, but could not find the Roman skull. *Nay.* It had to be there. But the spike that had once held Aulus's severed head was empty.

She jerked upright, heart pounding. It was no dream she saw, but a memory. She'd searched the Druid circle after gathering mistletoe from the oak grove. She'd intended to bury Lucius's brother's remains before returning to the fort, but had found the skull missing. Had Madog moved it? If so, why? She would have searched further, perhaps even ventured near the Druid's hut, but her fear for Marcus's life had driven her back to the fort.

Marcus. Did he live?

She could just make out his motionless form nestled on the bed at his father's side, but from her vantage point on the floor she couldn't tell if he breathed or not. Lucius lay stretched on his back, his arms flung over his head. Sleep softened the hard angles of his face, giving Rhiannon a glimpse of how he might have looked as a youth.

She flung aside her hasty pallet of blankets and forced

herself to her feet. Dreading what she might find, she inched toward the bed, steeling herself for the worst. Halting by Marcus's side, she looked down at the lad.

Her heart slammed into her chest. The lad slept. Not the fitful rest of the last days, but a deep, natural slumber. The heat and flush of his skin had receded and his breathing had eased. Rhiannon gripped the bed frame in a dizzying flood of relief.

Marcus would live.

At least until Edmyg laid siege to the fort.

The summer moon was but one night away. Rhiannon harbored no illusions that any Roman, no matter how young, would be spared her kinsmen's vengeance. And whether she watched the Celt warriors approach or stood behind their battle surge, she could only be a part of the losing side. There would be no winners in this war unless she could stop the fight entirely.

Could she escape Vindolanda a third time? She turned to the window as if she would find the answer somewhere in the lane below or the hills beyond the perimeter walls. She'd thrown open the shutters during the night, hoping to relieve the stench of the sickroom despite Demetrius's disapproval. Now she saw that the glow of dawn lay low on the horizon. The day would be clear. If only her heart were as well.

"My son lives. Thanks to you."

She spun around. Lucius had eased himself to a sitting position in the bed, his son nestled close to him. The sight of them together filled her heart to bursting.

The dark stubble on Lucius's chin gave him the look of some wild Roman god. His face was haggard, but his eyes spoke gentle whispers, dark and warm like a summer night. Truly, he was a king among men—strong and proud, with a heart that loved deeply and true.

She turned away.

A soft, bitter laugh reached her ears. "I deserve your disgust after my conduct in the forest, I am quite sure of that."

"No," she said, her voice breaking. "I could never hate you, Lucius."

She heard him rise, heard the sound of Marcus being shifted from his arms. She turned to see Lucius drawing a blanket over his son. Bending low, he placed a kiss on the lad's forehead.

He approached her slowly as if he thought she would bolt if he dared to get too close. "You have every right to despise me, yet you repay my harsh treatment by trading your freedom for my son's life."

"I love the lad," she said simply.

Lucius's eyes glittered like dark, brittle stars. "I envy him that. I would give much to hear you say the same of me."

An ache rose in Rhiannon's breast. She would give anything to say those words, but she dared not. Once said, there would be no going back to her people. No going back to Owein.

Lucius touched his finger to her chin and lifted it. There was heat in his gaze now, fused with another, deeper emotion. One that frightened her even more than his anger had done on the day he'd prevented her escape. She blinked, trying to quell the rise of her emotions before they caused her heart to break.

She caught his wrist. "I'm not what you think, Lucius."

"Do you know what I'm thinking?" He took her hand in his and turned it over, tracing circles on her palm with the tip of his forefinger. "Surely you do not. If you could look into my mind at this moment, you would not be standing so calmly before me."

She trembled as sweet sparks shot from his touch directly to her loins. Her tears began in earnest, streaming down her cheeks. Lucius bent his head and caught one on his tongue. "Why do you weep, my nymph?" He pulled back and looked into her eyes, his hands steady and warm on her shoulders.

She knew she should turn away. Knew she should step back and shatter the intimacy of his touch. But when she searched his gaze and read a note of uncertainty there, her limbs went weak. She could no more turn away from him than water could refuse to rush over the falls.

Slowly, she moved her palms up his torso, over the taut muscles of his stomach and the sleek strength of his chest. She explored the breadth of his shoulders. He stood motionless, neither inviting nor rejecting her advances. She stroked the column of his throat, finding the steady pulse there. Then she entwined her arms about his neck and pressed her body into his comforting heat.

Only then did he dip his head. His mouth took hers in a sweet, almost chaste kiss. His second kiss delved only a fraction deeper. He lingered on her lips, coaxing, teasing, for endless aching moments.

A fierce hunger came over her, an untamed craving so great she was powerless to resist it. She probed Lucius's lips with the tip of her tongue, hesitantly at first, then with growing passion, demanding entrance.

He opened to her at last, allowing her plunder and taking his own. His hands cupped her buttocks, lifting her slightly, then sliding her cleft along the hard ridge beneath his tunic. He repeated the motion, raising and lowering her in a sensuous rhythm until she thought she would go mad.

Her fingers caught the tangled curls at his nape and held tightly. She wrapped one leg around his, rubbing like a cat, desperate to get closer. Her arousal grew unbearable. She moved in sinuous rhythm against him, wanting him inside her, needing him to assuage her need.

A cautious rap sounded at the door. Rhiannon went rigid, passion draining as quickly as it had come. Dear Briga! What was she doing? Marcus lay sleeping but a few steps away. She fought Lucius's arms. "Release me."

He permitted her to turn but didn't let her step out of his embrace. He slipped one arm across her torso and pulled her against his body. Her spine pressed into his chest and stomach. His arousal prodded the small of her back.

"Come in," he said.

The door opened, admitting Demetrius. The healer had visited the bath sometime during the night. His soiled tunic and mantle had been exchanged for clean garments and his hair and beard had been washed and combed. His eyes, however, were red-rimmed, and Rhiannon guessed he'd had little rest. Rhiannon, rigid in Lucius's arms, felt her face go hot, but the healer's attention barely touched her before swinging to Marcus. He hastened to the bed and placed his hand on the lad's brow.

"The gods be praised," he said.

"The fever broke before dawn," Rhiannon said.

"Should we wake him now so he may take some nourishment?" Lucius asked.

Demetrius shook his head. "Better that he rest." His gaze strayed, at last, to Rhiannon, still held firm against Lucius's body.

She resisted the urge to squirm under his knowing gaze. "Sleep is healing," she told Lucius, trying desperately for calm. "He may eat when he wakes."

"Then we'll retire as well," Lucius said.

"Yes," said Demetrius dryly. "Please do. I will stay with the boy while you two, ah . . ."

Rhiannon blushed even more.

". . . rest," he finished.

Lucius tightened his hold on Rhiannon, hand splayed on her stomach, pressing her even more firmly against his arousal. "We'll return soon."

"No need. Take your time."

Lucius shifted Rhiannon to his side, positioning her between him and Demetrius. "I've no wish to display my rod before the old goat," he said against her ear.

Demetrius snorted. "Don't flatter yourself. I've seen it before."

Rhiannon nearly choked.

"Your hearing is far too sharp for an old man," Lucius muttered darkly. He propelled Rhiannon toward the door and lifted the latch.

"I suggest a shave and bath before you fall into her bed, Luc," Demetrius said, chuckling.

Lucius half turned as he shepherded Rhiannon out of the chamber. "As always, Magister, I bow to your wisdom."

The healer let out a bark of laughter. "Begone, boy. I'll tend your son while you tend your woman." He waggled his bristly brows. "Make your ancestors proud."

Lucius moved his hands over Rhiannon's body, dipping into her gentle curves and exploring her sleek, muscled limbs through the soft fabric of her tunic. The feel of her spun through his soul like an intoxicating fire. It would consume him, leaving little more than ash, but he no longer cared.

With Rhiannon in his arms he felt alive in a way he'd never before experienced: more vital than dawn, his mind sharper than the instant before a battle horn sounded. When he looked at the world through her eyes, the narrow path of his life split open. A myriad of possibilities spread out at his feet, each choice glittering like a gem. The expectations heaped upon him at birth faded. With Rhiannon by his side he would have the courage to become the man he longed to be, not the figurehead tradition and family demanded.

He nuzzled her breast.

She tried to push him away. "Lucius! Someone will see."

No doubt. They stood on the upper passageway in full view of anyone who might venture into the courtyard. Dawn's light painted the sky in shades of rose and violet. After the long, dark hours shut in Marcus's chamber, its effect on Lucius was like that of a drug.

"If some curious eye cares to watch, let it," he said, "as

long as Marcus and Demetrius are safely occupied." He buried his face in her hair, inhaling her scent—mist and flowers underlaid with the fiery musk of her arousal. He could hardly wait to lose himself inside her. But where? The chamber adjoining his own? No. He would not let Demetrius amuse himself by listening. On the stair?

Lucius was envisioning the possibilities when Rhiannon swatted his arm. "I assure you, Lucius, I will care if someone watches."

He toyed with her braid, plucking off the binding cord and separating the strands. "I want you, Rhiannon." He drew back and met her gaze. "I need you. Now."

He heard the soft hitch in her breathing, saw the light in her expression that quickly overlaid a flash of pain. Her hand drifted from his neck to his face, where her fingers scraped the stubble on his jaw. Her gaze darted to the courtyard, the tiles, the sky—anywhere but toward his eyes.

His urgency dimmed, but his determination increased. She had a right to fear him—he'd taken her in the forest like a green soldier pumping a whore. Perhaps she was afraid he'd do so again.

He swept her into his arms and strode toward the stairs. She clung to his neck. "My chamber lies in the opposite direction."

"I know," he said, taking the steps to the lower level two at a time.

When he halted before the door to the bathing rooms, Rhiannon looked up at him, confused. "Tribune Vetus—"

"Fled the house when Marcus fell ill," Lucius informed her. "He's ordered Brennus out of his private room in the barracks."

A shadow flitted across Rhiannon's face. "I doubt the quartermaster will take kindly to such an imposition."

"He has little choice unless he wishes to share his bed with the man." He snorted. "Vetus might enjoy that arrangement."

241

"What do you mean?"

"The tribune prefers men to women."

Rhiannon's eyes went wide. "For coupling? I've never heard of such a thing."

"It's common enough in Rome."

"Oh." She frowned. "Have you ever—"

"By Pollux! No."

He shouldered open the door to the baths. No slave boy slept in the antechamber, and Lucius was glad of it. He set Rhiannon on her feet. "Stay here. I'll return in but a moment."

Tepid water filled the bathing pool. In the furnace room, the fire that had heated Demetrius's bath water burned low. Lucius stirred the coals and stoked the reborn fire with logs from the wood pile.

He returned to the antechamber, half afraid Rhiannon might have fled. She hadn't. She'd taken a seat on a low stone bench in the changing alcove. He paced slowly toward her. She watched as he advanced, shifting her thighs on the bench in a way that made him wonder if she were already slick with wanting.

The thought pleased him immensely. By returning to the fort—even if concern for Marcus had been her first motive—she'd shown that she knew to whom she belonged. He resolved now to erase her last remnants of fear and bind her to him completely. From this moment forward, her loyalty to him would outweigh her sense of duty to her countrymen. She would lead him to Aulus's murderers and his brother's ghost would rest at last.

He dropped to his knees before her and loosened the leather ties on her shoes. He slid them from her feet and set them aside. He caressed one small foot, then the other, before his hand drifted to the hem of her tunic.

He slid his hands beneath the linen and stroked her calves with his palms. He kneaded the smooth skin, softening the taut muscles beneath. Her golden gaze heated as his hand moved higher. Her tunic bunched as he went, hiding his arms and hands. He teased the tender flesh at the back of her knees and the inside of her thighs. She let out a soft sigh and parted her legs.

When his fingers grazed the tight curls guarding her sex, she braced her hands on his shoulders and went very still. As he'd suspected, she was soft and wet. Her dew slicked his finger and he stroked deep, gathering it as if it were honey.

"You give me a king's welcome," he said. He stroked again, earning a gasp as he delved deeper. Her fingernails bit into his flesh.

He chuckled. "Do you like that, my love?"

"You mock me," she whispered. "You know that I do."

He lifted her tunic higher, baring her stomach, and swirled his tongue into the sweet indentation of her navel. Her hips arched. He seized the opportunity to glide the rear portion of her hem beneath her buttocks. "Raise your arms."

She obeyed, and he slipped the garment over her head. It fell to the floor in a languid flutter. But when she reached for him, he stopped her with another order. "Keep your hands above your head, clasped."

Once again, she obeyed without question. He sat back on his heels and drank in the sight of her. She sat before him, arms raised and legs parted, gloriously naked and more beautiful than Venus. Her unbound tresses were curls of flame that licked at one breast and covered the other. The taut peaks of those perfect mounds thrust forward invitingly. He imagined her budded nipples as ripe cherries, ready for the harvester's hand. Or mouth. He dipped his head and tasted one, then the other.

She abandoned her seductive pose to thread her fingers through his hair, urging him closer. He drew harder on her nipple. Her thighs opened. He felt one slim leg, then the other, rise to encircle his hips. Her boldness pleased him. She'd been so hesitant that first night, as if she'd never taken the initiative in lovemaking before. Perhaps she hadn't.

He left her breasts, inhaled a ragged breath, and moved lower, painting a trail with his tongue across her creamy skin. He buried his face in her belly and kissed her navel, then drew back and blew a cool stream of air across her wet skin.

She made a sound in her throat like the coo of a dove. He licked lower, lapping, then blowing across the path he'd traced with hot bursts of breath. Rhiannon squirmed, trying to lift her hips. He eased her legs from his waist and opened her completely, holding her thighs and keeping her bottom firmly anchored to the cool stone. He nuzzled her curls and inhaled a scent more intoxicating than wine. She'd guessed where his path was leading, for she clutched his hair in her fingers and tried to guide him lower.

He resisted, drawing another moan from her lips. "Lucius . . ." She all but tore the hair from his head.

He chuckled. "Have a care, sweet. Unless you prefer a bald lover." He licked a wet path along the upper edge of her Venus mound. He kissed the hooded place where her pleasure lay—once, twice, then again. "I'll give a thousand kisses, then another hundred," he whispered.

Her hips strained against his hands, inviting him in. A magnificent invitation, but one he wasn't yet ready to accept. He wanted her begging. Delirious. So stricken with need that she would never leave him. She would surrender to him at last, and if he could not quite subdue the niggling voice that told him she would never be completely his own, he could at least pretend he didn't hear it.

She tossed her head from side to side as he parted her sweet folds and kissed her again. "And yet a thousand kisses more." Withdrawing, he blew short puffs of air across her sensitized flesh, then turned his attention to the tender ivory skin of her inner thighs.

She groaned in protest, a low throaty growl that hardened his rod almost past bearing.

"Lucius—" Her tone was no longer breathless but demanding.

He laid his cheek against her thigh and circled one finger about her entrance. "Do you like this, I wonder?"

Her answer was a sharp intake of breath.

"No? Perhaps this, then?" He flicked his tongue gently over the exquisitely soft skin covering the swell at the opening of her sheath, then caught the tight bud between his lips and suckled.

Her cry rang off the tiles. Her fingernails dug into his nape. Triumph raced through him. No other before him had made her scream with pleasure; he was certain of it. No other after him would get the opportunity to try.

"Dear Briga. Lucius . . ."

He drew back until his touch on her was no more than the tantalizing movement of his breath across her swollen folds. "This?"

"No." She surprised him by slipping out from beneath his hands as easily as a water nymph. Before he could react she was behind him, pressing her breasts to his back and encircling his torso with her arms. She reached beneath his tunic and took hold of his rod. Her fingers stroked his length.

"Do you like this?" she said, giving his words back to him.

"By the gods!"

"No? Then perhaps . . ." She gripped his flesh in her hand and stroked upward.

"You are a vixen."

Her laughter fell on his ear like music. She danced away, her golden eyes flashing with mirth. He caught her by the arm, pulled her back to him, and lifted her in his arms. In two long strides he carried her through the door that led to the bathing room.

He descended the tiled steps. Rhiannon let out a sigh as the water lapped at her legs. Lucius lowered her onto the top step and reached for the flask set in a nearby niche.

"So warm," she murmured. "Like a dream."

He tipped a generous amount of fragrant oil into his

hand and rubbed his palms together, generating heat. He anointed her breasts, tracing circles around her areolas. She melted into his touch with a sigh.

He massaged the balm on her shoulders, stomach, legs. When he would have delved into more intimate places, Rhiannon shook her head and eased the bottle from his hands.

"Let me return your attentions."

Her fingers fluttered over his biceps, spreading the oil onto his skin. She massaged a trail over his shoulders and chest, a gentle siege before which he lay helpless. The tension of the last few days seeped away. In its place another, more pleasurable tension grew.

Her eyes glinted as she scrutinized his arousal. It crested the water's surface between her legs, dangerously close to her russet curls. She looked up at him and smiled. "Lie back."

He did as she commanded, spreading his arms on the edge of the pool, enjoying his passivity. She continued her ministrations, massaging oil onto his chest and stomach as he had done with her, sliding down his body with hands and lips. How far did she dare go? Anticipation coiled tightly as he watched her progress through half-closed eyelids.

Hot breath bathed his rod. She looked up at him, eyes glittering, the tips of her breasts just cresting the water. "Would you like this?" she murmured.

"Very much."

Her mouth closed on him and all sense of time stopped. The bathing room faded. There was only Rhiannon, until he could bear it no more.

He grasped her shoulders and hauled her into his arms. Shining rivulets cascaded over her skin to fall like raindrops on the water's surface. He pressed a kiss on her neck and eased her into the center of the pool where the water deepened. Her hair fanned out over the surface; her legs caged his hips. They were both slick with oil—one small movement and their bodies were joined. They moved slowly, in unison, seeking their deepest pleasure in the buoyant warmth. Flesh and bone, skin and water melded into one.

Then all thought fled. Somehow Lucius found the edge of the pool and anchored Rhiannon against it. He plunged faster, deeper, his chest sliding over her oiled breasts, his tongue ravaging her mouth. She made a soft mewling sound and he lifted his head to watch her passion. With her head flung back and her face a reflection of bliss, she seemed more than a mere woman. She was the nymph he'd once thought her to be. A goddess of the wild forest.

He worshiped her with his body, in the end offering his essence with each shudder of his heart until she broke in his arms like the fall of a thousand stars.

"I love you."

Lucius's whispered words fell on Rhiannon's ears like a curse. She squeezed her eyes closed and endured the stroke of his hand on her bare shoulder and back. She lay sprawled on the narrow bed in her chamber, her cheek pillowed on her lover's chest. Sunlight filtered through the closed shutters. It fell on the bed, warming her skin, but the brittle ice in her heart was beyond its touch. *I love you.* She'd never dared to hope to hear those words on his lips. If only she could give them back to him.

Lucius's wandering hand had moved from her back to the long fall of her hair. He lifted the tresses, weighing them in his palm. Rhiannon imagined raising her head and looking into his dark eyes. The corners of his mouth would lift—first one side, then the other, in the crooked smile that she loved. The dimple that made him look like a lad would show in his cheek. He would kiss her gently at first, and then . . .

She burrowed her face further into his chest. If those things happened, her heart would overflow and she would return his words of love. She couldn't allow that to happen. If it did, she would never find the courage to leave him.

"I love you," he said again.

His voice wrapped around her and for a moment she felt dazed, as if caught in a dream. Then, with the care one would use to ease away from a mad dog, she raised herself from his chest.

She wouldn't, couldn't, look at him. "You cannot love me."

"I can and I do. I want you as my wife."

Dear Briga. Her gaze darted to his despite her resolve. He looked as surprised as she to hear his words. "You would take me to wife?"

His tone gentled. "Yes. If you'll have me."

"Oh, Lucius."

He must have felt her withdrawal, for his arms tightened about her waist. "You returned to me when you might have fled. I thought . . ."

She disentangled herself from his arms and hugged her knees to her chest. "You would wed a slave?"

"You are no slave."

"You named me so."

"I was a fool to believe I could own you. I could more easily grasp the forest mist." His expression grew serious. "It matters not how we first came together. No one in Rome need know you were once my captive."

Rome.

"I'll return there before winter."

"To fill your father's seat in the Senate."

"Yes." The prospect didn't seem to please him.

"Do you wish to?"

He rose from the bed and paced to the window. "In truth? No. I spent a year as a magistrate after my first tour of military duty and found I preferred to face my enemies with a sword in my hand rather than words of flattery on my lips. When my term was finished, I left Rome to take command of my Legion."

"Then why do this thing now?"

"Family honor demands I serve the people of Rome. I've prepared for that duty all my life."

She tugged the blanket over herself. "Do many senators take barbarian wives?"

He laid one palm on the window frame. "It is not forbidden. I would ensure your welcome."

She hesitated, then asked, "Is it me that you want, Lucius, or a respite from your brother's ghost?"

He glanced at her, then away. "You claimed the words that would put Aulus's soul to rest had to be spoken in the forest. You were there, yet you didn't speak them."

Her gaze faltered. "There wasn't time."

He contemplated the scene in the street below and weighed his words carefully. "If you can truly send him to the underworld, then do it."

She rose, wrapping the blanket about her body. His hand dropped from the window as she took a step toward him. "I will send Aulus's soul to its rest if you and Marcus travel south. You must leave on the morrow." *Before Madog lights the summer fires.*

His voice hardened. "Without you?"

"Yes. You are in danger here."

His gaze narrowed. "What do you know?"

"Trust me, Lucius. Please. For your son's sake. More than that I cannot say."

"You expect me to abandon my post at a woman's word? No. I will stay until my replacement arrives. As will you."

Anger sparked. "Then it matters little whether you call me slave or free."

"Every woman must have a man for her master."

She drew a sharp breath. "I do not. I have a home. A clan. A brother."

He closed the distance between them with one swift stride. "A lover?"

If it would persuade Lucius to set her free . . . "Yes," she said. "A lover. We will soon join hands as equals."

"Equals." He shook his head. "How can a man and a woman be equals?" Lucius lifted his hand and cupped her breast through the blanket. "Does a woman wield a sword?" He squeezed gently and smiled at the gasp she could not suppress. "Does a woman strike down her enemies, watch their blood spill over the earth?"

He crowded her with the fierce strength of his body, dipping his head to bring his lips within a breath of hers. She smelled her scent on him, as if she'd marked him as her own.

"Equal," Lucius said, and laughed. "Does a woman face a brutal void when she looks into her heart? Does she yearn to fill it with her lover's touch, knowing her strength will fail when she does?" He anchored her head between his hands and took her mouth with the kiss of a conqueror, plunging deep, allowing only the breath he deigned to give. Rhiannon's traitorous body responded with a tremor of lust.

No. If he claimed her body again she would follow him to the corners of the earth. She clawed at his shoulders, desperate to break his hold.

"By Pollux! Perhaps you enjoyed our savage rut in the forest more than I thought. Was I too gentle last night? I can remedy that, I assure you." He caught the soft slope between her neck and shoulder between his teeth. She gasped as he bit the tender skin.

"Lucius, no, I—"

He tore the blanket from her body and shoved her against the wall. His body covered her, skin against slick skin, his arousal questing. He claimed her mouth, invading it with his tongue.

Dear Briga, how to stop him before she surrendered? Rhiannon drove her knee up into his groin.

He jerked back and snarled a curse.

"Take your hands from me, Roman dog." She saw her hateful words strike him as surely as if she'd dealt him a blow with a sword.

A flash of pain lit his eyes. It vanished almost immediately, leaving his expression devoid of emotion. He stepped away and gave a slight, ironic bow.

"Forgive me. My actions were inexcusable. Barbaric, one might say." He strode across the room and retrieved her tunic from the floor.

Her hand trembled as she took it. He turned away as she slipped the garment over her head. He located his own clothes and shrugged into them.

"Why did you return?" he asked.

"Marcus . . ."

"You should have let my son die. A Roman pup will become a dog in time."

She said nothing.

When he spoke again it was but a single word. "Go."

Her head snapped up. "What?"

"Take whatever provisions you need and leave the fort. I'll not stop you."

"Thank you," she whispered.

"No need," he said, already turning away.

Chapter Nineteen

The forest had shifted.

Rhiannon felt the subtle transformation with every step that took her away from Vindolanda, though she couldn't guess why or how the changes had come to pass. Surely the sunlight that peeked through the leafy canopy was no different. Oaks and elms still stretched their arms to the sky. Birds called; hares hopped. Yet in her heart she knew nothing would ever look the same.

A shiver tingled a path up her spine. She stopped. Some presence seemed to lurk nearby, just out of reach. She peered into the trees, circling slowly as she fought to keep her breathing steady. A wildcat or boar? Or was she being followed?

She slowed her steps, merging with the forest until her soul blended completely with Briga's spirit. Making a wide arc through the brush, she circled until she came up behind her pursuer. A scout from the fort.

Her anger flared. Lucius had set the man on her trail, no doubt intending to wreak his vengeance on her village in payment for the death of his brother. If he thought the heavy-footed Gaul was a match for her forest skills, he was sorely mistaken. Slipping silently into the brush, she blazed a false trail, then backtracked to a shallow burn. Stepping into the water, she waded north a short distance before resuming her trek.

She forded the burn at a shallow crossing in the shadow of the crags. When she bent to drink, she murmured a prayer to Briga. Not thanks for her freedom. An entreaty for Lucius.

Great Mother, keep him safe.

He loved her. She knew it was true, for he had said it and no matter his faults, deceit was not one of them. The only lies that lay between them were her own. What price had the proud Roman paid to put his heart in her hands? Did he curse her now? She'd fled the fort quickly. She hadn't even stopped to bid Marcus farewell.

She might have told Lucius outright that his men were poised to mutiny. If she had, he might not have brushed off her warnings as womanly hysterics. Yet if she'd told him the whole truth, he would have demanded to know whence her information had come. She wouldn't have been able to give him an answer without bringing his wrath down upon Cormac and the rest of her clan.

Would the decision to protect her kin cause Lucius's death? She hoped fervently she could yet prevent it. There was time to avert the siege. The uproar caused by her rejection of Edmyg would send the chieftains into debates that would last a full season at the least.

She would choose Kynan as consort immediately, or the clan might fall to warring among themselves. Kynan would be a strong leader but not a violent one. He was older and more cautious than Edmyg, and commanded great respect among the Brigantes. He had sons already, of an age with Owein, so he would not care too much about Rhiannon's barren womb. Most importantly, he valued the life of his people more than glory on the battlefield.

Aye, Kynan would make a fine king. There was only one fault with the plan.

Rhiannon would have to couple with him.

Bile rose in her throat at the thought of lying under the old warrior's unwashed body and watching his scarred face strain with lust. It would be no different from what she'd endured with Niall, but now that she knew the delight true lovemaking brought, the thought of opening her thighs to Kynan's cock sickened her. Yet the choice would protect Lucius and Marcus, and Owein would benefit as well. Even if Kynan had heard lies about her brother's visions, she would make Owein's welcome a condition of Kynan's kingship.

She resumed the trail at a quickened pace. The summer moon would rise on the morrow's eve. Kynan must become king before Madog kindled the fires of Beltane.

"I want Rhiannon. Where is she?"

Lucius squeezed his son's hand. "Gone, Marcus."

Marcus frowned and sat straight up in his bed. Rhiannon's mistletoe potion, which Demetrius continued to administer, had not only broken the boy's fever but had also improved his strength considerably. "When will she be back?"

"She'll not return. She's gone back to her people."

"The barbarians?"

Lucius nodded.

Marcus tugged his hand free of Lucius's grip. "You scared her away," he accused.

Lucius was silent for a moment, then heaved a sigh. "Most likely I did."

Tears welled in Marcus's eyes.

Without a word, Lucius opened his arms and pulled his son into his embrace.

By chance or fate, Rhiannon found Edmyg and Kynan together and nearly at blows.

They stood face-to-face in the grazing meadow, each

backed by a phalanx of hard-faced warriors. Rhiannon watched the two chieftains from a vantage point on the high ridge south of the clearing. An assembly of clansmen, spears in hand, formed shifting half circles behind their leaders. Swords and spears were drawn but not yet raised.

Rhiannon searched the gathering in vain for Madog and Owein. Most likely the pair were in the Druid circle gathering the power of Kernunnos to the stones in anticipation of the summer fire. She'd considered seeking them out before she faced Edmyg, but had decided against it. Her resolve was set, and if they did not agree to her plan, she would waste precious time.

She inched closer to Edmyg and the other men, keeping to the cover of the trees and avoiding the tents and brush shelters erected by the warriors who had come to attack Vindolanda. They counted in the hundreds—about equal, she thought, to the number of men in the fort. Even if the garrison were to prove loyal, Lucius faced a hard fight if the clansmen attacked as one.

That didn't seem likely. At present the formidable force faced off not against a common enemy but against each other. How did Edmyg imagine he could defeat Rome if he couldn't keep order within his own ranks?

She crept closer, scanning the stony expressions of her kinsmen as she descended the rocky slope. So many lads, so many old men! They might take Vindolanda if the garrison soldiers mutinied, but how did they hope to remove the conquerors permanently? For every Roman that fell, another would march from the south to take his place. Legionary soldiers, not auxiliary troops. If they fought with even half Lucius's skill, her people would be slaughtered.

"Ye are a coward." Edmyg hoisted his sword into the air as punctuation to his declaration. Rhiannon reached the bottom of the hill. She paused in the shelter of a broad oak and pulled herself onto the rise of a fallen limb.

"Ye'd best be watching yer words, lad," Kynan said.

Rhiannon reached for a higher branch, hoisting herself upward to get a better view of the old warrior. He was hard with muscle, but lean where Edmyg was bulky. His graying hair and beard were braided in dirty strands. In his youth he might have been handsome, but now, with his nose cut away, most would call him no less than hideous. Despite his appearance—or perhaps because of it—Kynan had the respect of the clans. His reputation was that of a cool-headed warrior and shrewd chieftain. She could choose no one more suited to serve the Brigantes as king.

"We'll ne'er be having a better chance to take the fort," Edmyg said. He lifted his sword and angled the tip toward Kynan's heart.

Kynan crossed his arms over his chest rather than drawing his own weapon. Edmyg's gaze narrowed at the insult. Muttering snaked through the onlookers.

"I'll nay act again on the advice of the misshapen brute ye call brother," Kynan said.

"Cormac willna fail us."

"As he didna fail us on the day of that ill-fated raid?" Kynan said. "I tell ye, Edmyg, I'll not be risking what kin I have yet living on the word of such a creature. By rights, he should have been exposed at birth."

Edmyg rose on the balls of his feet, shifting his weight subtly forward. The point of his sword darted upward and nicked the flesh at the base of Kynan's throat. The warrior standing at Kynan's right elbow unsheathed his sword. The older man waved him back.

"Will ye kill me, Edmyg, before our kin, for the sake of a plan destined to fail?"

"It willna fail. And even were the odds against us, we are honor-bound to see the attack to its end. Have ye forgotten that Rhiannon is held within the fort? Would ye be leaving her in Roman hands? She'll be lost to us if ye turn coward now."

Rhiannon stifled a gasp. Edmyg refused to aid her escape from Vindolanda—while he used her plight to rally the reluctant factions among the clans! An effective bit of strategy—no matter if Rhiannon delivered Lucius or not, Edmyg stood to gain from her capture. The subtlety of his thinking surprised her. Rhiannon never would have guessed Edmyg capable of it—his mind was as blunt and brutal as his manner. The scenario had the hallmarks of one of Cormac's plots. . . .

Dear Briga! Was Cormac the author of the scheme to use her as a whore? Did Edmyg even know of it?

"Tell me, Kynan," Edmyg said. "Will we suffer our queen to be taken as a bed-slave?"

For the first time, the old warrior hesitated.

Edmyg stepped back and lowered his sword. "Rhiannon seeks the courage of her warriors! Who among ye will aid her?"

His warriors sent up an answering shout. Kynan's men soon joined them. The old chieftain dropped his gaze, the slump of his shoulders signaling his defeat.

"We attack at the moon's rise," Edmyg shouted.

"Nay!" Rhiannon's cry couldn't pierce the ensuing uproar. She scrambled from the tree and into the throng, darting between the warriors until she stood panting at Edmyg's side. He stared at her as if she were an apparition. Kynan's expression was no less astonished.

Edmyg grabbed Rhiannon by the arm and hauled her aside. "What of Cormac?" he said in a low voice. "Has he brought the Roman to the circle?"

Rhiannon let out a gasp. "Ye knew. Ye bade me lie with another man."

"Of course I did, woman. 'Twas our best hope of capturing the dog alive. Madog said—"

"Madog consented?"

" 'Twas Madog's plan. Where is the Roman?"

"I dinna ken. I escaped the fort on my own." She wrenched her arm from his grasp. She caught one glimpse of his stunned expression before she turned to the assembled warriors and lifted her arms. "Brothers! Hear me!"

Silence fell over the crowd like a rippling shroud, as one by one the warriors realized who it was that stood in their midst. When the last man's voice was still, she spoke.

"Kynan speaks the truth! If Vindolanda is taken, do you imagine Rome will not send her Legions to recapture it? For every man you succeed in killing, two more will march from the south."

"Nay." Edmyg practically snarled the word. "In my father's day even the highlands far to the north crawled with Roman vermin. Now they've abandoned their forts there. Rome's tide retreats. We have but to hasten it."

" 'Twill not last. Like the tide, the Romans will return," Rhiannon said. "The clans must unite, 'tis true, but not for war. We can survive best as an ally of Rome."

Edmyg snorted. "The Romans have no allies. Only slaves."

Kynan stepped forward. "Nay. Rhiannon has the right of it. I can no longer count how many kinsmen I've lost to Roman swords. Shall our children go fatherless? They deserve a chance for peace."

Rhiannon laid her hand on the old warrior's arm. "Kynan, ye've the wisdom of a true king," she said, but it was Edmyg's face that she watched. "Before the witness of my kin, I choose you as my consort and king. Will ye have me to wife?"

The color drained from Edmyg's face, then returned as a dark rush of crimson. His knuckles went white on the hilt of his sword. Beside her, Rhiannon felt Kynan shift, drawing his own weapon. The older warrior moved swiftly, inserting his body between Rhiannon and Edmyg.

" 'Tis my place to be king in Niall's stead." Edmyg's voice shook. "Ye canna deny me."

Rhiannon squared her shoulders. "The Old Law gives me the right to choose the man worthy to be king. Ye are not that man, Edmyg. Ye fathered a bastard on Glynis."

"Aye, I did. A son murdered by yer foul brother."

"Nay! Owein has not that power."

"If ye truly believe that, yer a fool." His attention sliced to Kynan. "Step away from my woman, old man. I willna give her up."

Kynan stood his ground. "I accept Rhiannon's offer. I am her consort now by right of law."

Edmyg swore. "In one thing, at least, the Romans are wise. They keep their women locked away awaiting their pleasure." He looked at Rhiannon. "Is that not true?"

"You swine," Rhiannon whispered.

Edmyg's voice rose, mocking her. "A woman is nay a fit ruler. If Cartimandua had submitted to her consort and king, the Brigantes would rule their land to this day. Instead she opened her thighs to any who would enter. As her granddaughter has done."

Kynan's sword lifted. "Shut yer foul mouth, Edmyg."

Edmyg raised his own weapon. "Will ye fight for yer whore's honor, old man?"

Kynan shifted into a battle stance. "I will fight for my queen."

"Nay!" Rhiannon cried, but the two men paid her no heed. She lunged forward, but her kinsman Bryan restrained her. She twisted about. "Stop them."

"I willna," Bryan replied. "And nay will any of the others. They must resolve this feud with blood."

Edmyg's sword flashed. Kynan's answered. The older warrior's skill was keen, but Edmyg's prowess in battle had earned him the right to be called king. It took but a few strokes before Kynan lay sprawled in the dirt, the tip of Edmyg's sword pressing into the hollow of his throat.

A thin smile played about Edmyg's lips. "Ye might have picked a more worthy champion, my queen."

"Spare him, Edmyg. I beg ye."

"And let him be claiming a place by yer side? Nay." Kynan's eyes bulged as Edmyg pressed his sword deeper.

"Yer favor has doomed him," Edmyg declared. He

plunged his sword into Kynan's neck with a quick, deep thrust, nearly severing the old warrior's head with his ferocity. Blood spurted from the gash and sprayed onto Rhiannon's skirt.

She sank to her knees, struggling to draw breath into her stunned lungs. Kynan's spirit tore from his body with a violence that caused stars to burst in her vision. Pain pounded in her head. Tremors wracked her body, made worse by the knowledge that she alone was to blame for the honest warrior's death.

Edmyg lifted his bloodied blade to the sky. "Does anyone else dare challenge a king?"

When no answer came, he sheathed his sword and hauled Rhiannon to her feet. She grasped his shoulder for balance and fought the urge to vomit.

"Our queen has been defiled by the Roman dog who commands Vindolanda," Edmyg shouted.

"Nay," Rhiannon said, but a roar of outrage shattered her weak protest. Nausea surged and darkness swirled into her vision. She heard Edmyg's faraway voice as her consciousness faded.

"Who will join me in vengeance?"

Chapter Twenty

"Drink this."

Rhiannon grasped the wooden cup and brought it to her lips. A hand held the back of her head, supporting her as she drank a bitter potion. The light of a low fire cast flickering shadows over wattle-and-mud walls. Madog's forest hut.

"Owein," she said weakly.

"Hush. Dinna try to speak. Ye've suffered much today."

She nodded, closing her eyes against the memory of Kynan's slaughter. She drank again, swallowing deeply. Owein shifted on the pallet, drawing her against him in the reverse of an embrace she'd given him so often as a small lad. When had he grown so tall as to offer her the same comfort?

She laid her empty cup on the dirt floor. "Where is Madog?"

"Preparing the summer fires. This eve, your hand will spark the flames."

"Nay." Rhiannon sought Owein's gaze, but his eyes were shadowed and she could not make out his expression.

" 'Tis folly to attack the Romans. I'll not be part of it, Owein. Would ye join Edmyg in dooming the clan?"

He laughed, an unpleasant sound more suited to a man than a lad. "For once, Edmyg and I are of one mind. The Roman commander soiled ye. He must pay."

"He did naught but what I allowed him," Rhiannon whispered.

Owein swore. "Edmyg said as much, but I nay believed him. How could I, when I saw plain enough what he did? I heard your grief."

Rhiannon looked at him in confusion. "Ye saw, Owein? But how?"

"Ye know I have the Sight."

"Ye see shadows of the future."

"Aye, and those of the past and the present. I saw ye with him, Rhiannon. In his bed. Sobbing as if yer heart would break." His arms tensed around her. "I'll kill him for it."

"Nay," Rhiannon whispered, her mind reeling with the thought of Owein's unseen presence in the chamber she'd shared with Lucius. "He never harmed me. I went to him willingly."

"Willingly." He jerked to his feet. "I am ashamed of ye."

Rhiannon's temper flared. " 'Tis nay your place to approve of my union with Lucius."

"He will die for it. I promise ye that."

"Nay, Owein. Ye willna harm him."

He regarded her steadily. "The Roman fort will fall. Its commander will die. I have Seen it."

Cold dread seeped into Rhiannon's gut. "If Vindolanda falls, 'twill seal the Brigantes' doom. The Romans will not rest until we are all dead or enslaved. Can ye not See the truth?"

"The beasts killed our father. They slaughtered the Druids on Mona, raped their women. How can we forget?"

"Drawing blood from a wound will nay heal it! As queen I can negotiate peace. The Brigantes will once again be a free people within Rome, as we were under Cartimandua."

"A free people? Ye are mad to think it. Our grandmother believed Rome thought her an equal. Her trust cost her the throne."

Rhiannon closed her eyes as a swell of lightheadedness assaulted her. Owein spoke the truth. She'd little reason to believe the Roman governor would grant autonomy to the Brigantes. Still, she longed for the opportunity to intervene on her people's behalf. Perhaps with Lucius's help . . .

Nay. It was a dream that would never come true. Another wave of vertigo struck. She leaned forward and braced her palm on the floor.

Owein's hand pressed her shoulder. "Lie down, sister," he said. "The spinning will soon pass, leaving ye stronger than before. Ye'll be linked to Madog's spirit as I am."

Rhiannon stared up at him. "Have ye drugged me, Owein?"

Guilt flickered in his eyes, then hardened into hate. Dear Briga. She'd been gone from him for less time than it took the moon to wax. Yet in that short span, Owein had passed from lad to man.

He crouched by her side, steadying her as the walls of the hut spun wildly. " 'Tis best this way. Ye'll light the fires of Beltane. Madog and I will call Kernunnos. The foreign swine will soon be gone from the lands of the Brigantes."

She struggled to refute him, even as she felt the potion drain her resistance. "The Romans are not beasts, Owein. They are men like any others."

He eased her down on the pallet. "They will bleed and die just as well, then."

Chapter Twenty-one

Rhiannon floated as if in a dream. She wore a checkered tunic and a mantle of blue and gold fastened at her shoulder with a gold pin worked like a leaf, but she had no memory of dressing herself in such garments. A sea of bodies surrounded her, most half hidden behind the tall stones, but a few men—Madog and Owein among them—stood within. Madog's high, thin voice chanted a numbing path through her mind. Owein's low tone wove across and around his mentor's call. Ancient syllables, pulsing, urging.

Compelling.

She gripped a taper lit by the strike of iron on stone. Its flame leaped against the night, straining to break free. Two cold pyres lay within the Druid circle, great mounds of oak and fir. They wanted but the touch of her hand to send the wood into flame, but some instinct told Rhiannon to hold back. Though she couldn't remember the reason, she knew that lighting the summer fire would be a grave mistake.

But the Druid song rose, sapping her resistance until it

was as faint as a childhood memory. She stepped between the pyres and touched the taper to the tinder at the base of each. The tiny flames flickered, faded, then burst anew, snaking through the sacred wood. They lapped higher, caressing one of the white shanks that mingled with the logs and branches. Rhiannon frowned at the pale shafts, her horror rising.

Bones. Roman bones.

She watched with revulsion as flames consumed the human kindling, dancing merrily, darting into black hollows and emerging with renewed strength. The spent taper dropped from her fingers.

She was dimly aware of a man at her side. Edmyg. He wore a fur-trimmed cloak and the gold torc that marked him a king. That, too, was wrong. He was no longer her consort. He'd abandoned that right when he spilled his seed in the womb of another woman.

The flames leapt, reaching into the night sky. The throng assembled beyond the stones shifted. The chieftains approached first, offering allegiance. As they passed between the fires, she heard her own voice, accepting their troth.

Their warriors followed, then the elders, and finally the clanswomen and the children. The flames galloped to the twin peaks of the pyres and reached for each other across the heart of the circle. A sound like whipping wind drove back the night cries of the forest. The shadows of the stones flickered. Wood smoke assaulted Rhiannon's nostrils and stung her eyes.

The Druid chant quickened, Owein's young voice blending with Madog's quivering tones. The full moon, pregnant with promise, broke the edge of the hills and rode into the sky. Rhiannon felt the veil between the land of mortals and the shores of Annwyn grow gossamer-thin, as it did when death neared.

The last old woman hobbled between the fires, leaning heavily on the arm of a young lass. Madog paced behind, marking his steps with his staff. The skull perched upon it stared balefully at Rhiannon, drawing a flicker of recognition. Who had met such a gruesome fate? It was important that she remember, but she couldn't seem to snatch the answer from the fog in her brain.

Madog halted at Rhiannon's left. With Edmyg's presence crowding her on the right and the dread skull hovering above, she found she could scarcely breathe.

Only Owein hadn't yet passed between the flames. He approached now, still chanting, a low, mournful sound that seemed to be absorbed into the flames. He strode forward, halting barely more than an arm's length away from Rhiannon, at the very center of the circle. Madog's Druid sword hung in a scabbard at his side.

Owein stood as still as death for a heartbeat, then his head snapped back with such a force that Rhiannon was sure his neck had broken. He collapsed on the ground, keening, his hands tearing at his hair. A deep groan tore from his throat.

Rhiannon gave a cry and lurched toward him, only to be hauled back by Edmyg's grip. She tore at his fingers as Owein writhed at her feet. "Let me go!"

"Be still," he hissed. "He calls Kernunnos."

Rhiannon stared dumbly at Madog. When the Druid nodded, her hands began to shake.

Owein's back arched and his arms flung wide. Words long forgotten by all save those sworn to guard them poured from his lips. Their power caused Rhiannon's soul to tremble.

The wind rose, howling like a wolf, and the ground beneath her feet shook. The Roman's skull grinned as the flames consumed the bones that had once carried his flesh. The forest shrieked with a voice not of the earth.

Owein chanted louder, faster. Flames shot from the pyres to form an arch over Rhiannon's head. The face of the skull rocked toward her. Its hollow eyes, washed by flames, seemed to mark her with their gaze.

A presence touched her soul. Despairing. Desperate. Pleading. The breath squeezed from her lungs. She'd felt this soul before—where? When? It was vital that she recall. What had it asked of her?

Owein's chant rose, then fell, in cadence with the wind. His face had gone pale. Sweat dripped from his brow. His body, crouched on the ground, shook.

As if sliced by an unseen blade, the wind died. Owein's chant stopped at precisely the same instant. He lifted his head. " 'Tis finished."

Unbearable dread coiled in Rhiannon's stomach. Dark power rose, consuming the night, blanketing the stars. The forest went black, still. The clan was silent save for the muffled cries of babes at their mothers' breasts.

Those closest to the womb always knew when death was abroad.

Then, as suddenly as the wind had stopped, it returned with a vengeance in a gale so powerful Rhiannon thought the stones would fly from their ancient resting places. She clutched at her mantle as her hair worked its way from its braids and flew in wild strands into her eyes. A distant rumble sounded, then strengthened. A hundred—nay, a thousand—hooves pounded. Unearthly shrieks burst in the sky like spikes of lightning.

The skull pivoted on Madog's staff. "The Wild Hunt is upon us," the Druid cried. "Kernunnos rides at its fore. Our warriors canna fail."

Edmyg unsheathed his sword and thrust it overhead. "In the name of Rhiannon, queen of the Brigantes, death to Rome!"

The cry echoed through the crowd. "Death to Rome!"

And Rhiannon remembered.

The night was far too quiet.

The silence pricked the back of Lucius's neck like a swarm of ghost bees, driving him from his bed. He flung the shutters wide and frowned through the darkness at the torches on the battlements. He watched until he saw the night sentry pass by the first, then the second, flickering light.

Then he heard it.

Howling wind, like a pack of hounds. Or wolves. Thunder like a stampede of hooves. He leaned out over the sill and squinted up at the sky. A dark line of clouds advanced from the north, blotting the stars as it went, though the night was stiller than death.

The edge of his unease sharpened. He turned and squinted through the dim chamber at Aulus. His brother lay stretched on a cushioned bench. Asleep. His frown deepened. Did ghosts sleep? Aulus had never done so before.

He crossed the room and looked closer. Aulus's bruised face was slack. His bloodied hands were clasped across his stomach. Lucius's gut twisted. It was like looking at a dead man.

A dead man. A wild laugh escaped him, the sound of it echoing off the tiled floor and painted walls. Lucius braced one hand on the wall above Aulus and let the crazed mirth overtake him until it turned to something emptier. Tears burned his eyes. They fell, passing through Aulus to dampen the cushions beneath. His savage laughter swelled anew.

He'd gone well and truly insane. But with Rhiannon gone, he could no longer summon the energy to care.

The shutter banged against the wall. Lucius shook himself and went again to the window. A steady wind had begun to blow out of the north. The blanket of clouds swept overhead. The shriek of the wind rushed the gates.

Something was coming. A storm? Or something more?

Rhiannon's voice sounded in his memory. *Go back to Rome. You are in danger here.*

And before, on the morning after her capture. *My people will come.*

Lucius froze, the truth rising above the chaos in his mind like an eagle atop a standard. The Celts were attacking, and Rhiannon had known of it. No wonder she'd been so desperate to leave the fort.

His senses cleared, leaving only the sharp sanity that had saved his life on the battlefield more times than he cared to count. He shrugged into his armor and belted on his sword and dagger even as he strode for the door.

"Father?" Marcus stood in the passageway outside the bedchambers. "What's happening?"

"Marcus. Go back to bed."

The boy didn't move. "Are we under attack?"

Lucius drew a swift breath before answering. "Yes."

Demetrius appeared beside him. The old man's hair stuck out from his head in all directions, giving him the look of a grizzled Medusa. "It is but a storm rising."

"No ordinary storm, old man."

Marcus's eyes registered his fear. "It's the Celt forest god. Kernunnos. He rides a storm of death."

Lucius shot him an odd look. "Did Rhiannon tell you that?"

"No. It was in one of Uncle Aulus's stories."

Lucius stared at the boy, then forced himself to gather his wits. "No god attacks us, Marcus. Only men. We will defeat them." His gaze sliced through the open doorway to his bedchamber. Aulus still lay motionless on the bench.

He adjusted the straps on his helmet and returned his attention to his son. "You'll be safe here. The barbarians won't breach the fort walls." Then, to Demetrius, "Be sure the boy stays inside the residence."

He strode to the stairwell. At the bottom step, he paused and looked for Aulus. He wasn't there. Lucius was alone. No ghost, no Celtic nymph.

For the first time in six months, he faced only himself.

A downdraft blew through the courtyard, causing the night torches to flare. Lucius strode into the foyer and nudged the sleeping porter with one foot. The man opened his eyes and shot to his feet.

"My lord!"

"Rouse the household. There may be an attack."

Scant moments later, Lucius was on the battlement, looking to the north. Fierce winds buffeted his face, and the night had gone even blacker than before, if that were possible. He could make out little of the land beyond the barley fields, neither the east-west ridge to the north nor the hills beyond. The unearthly howling continued, a chill blade turning in his gut.

The night sentry seemed equally affected. The man's face was drawn, his eyes two dark pools of fear. His hands shook as they made a sign against evil.

"Sound the alert," Lucius ordered.

The soldier ran toward the gate tower. A moment later, the horn sounded the call to battle. Men spilled out of the barracks, buckling war belts about mail tunics and hefting shields as they raced to their siege posts. Footsteps punctuated by curses thudded on the battlement.

Lucius turned back to the night and fixed his gaze on the tree line at the edge of the parade grounds. There he saw it—an amorphous black form lurking against the darker mass of the forest. The first line of the attack appeared to be as many as fifty men. How many more waited among the trees? How many had circled the clearing to attack from behind?

No easy skirmish, then, but an army that had to encompass hundreds of men. Still, he'd faced worse and lived to tell of it. Vindolanda's wall might be rammed turf instead of solid stone, but the fort's defenses were strong. Even with scaling ladders, the barbarians would not find entrance easy. He wondered how the Celts would deal with the village. Would they put the civilians to the sword, or would the farmers who had sold vegetables for Lucius's table yesterday take up arms against him tonight?

The wind whipped harder as a line of bowmen took their positions on the battlement. Quartermaster Brennus appeared on the wall walk beside Lucius. Two centurions flanked him. A cluster of foot soldiers hung a few paces behind.

Brennus held a torch aloft and leaned forward to get a better view of the enemy. "Quite a horde," he murmured. "Impressive."

Lucius gave him a measured look. "The archers will thin their ranks."

"In this wind?"

Brennus lifted his torch higher, moving the flame in a circular motion, causing sparks to scatter in the gale. As if on his signal, the Celt army broke ranks and hurtled, screaming, across the parade grounds.

"Loose arrows!" Lucius shouted.

The archer beside him shifted but didn't shoot. The officer farther down the battlement refrained from relaying the order.

As if on Brennus's signal . . .

Lucius's hand flew to his sword. Too late. Hands grasped his arms from behind and twisted them behind his back. In less time than it took to utter a curse, he'd been relieved of his sword and dagger.

He glared at Brennus. "Traitorous dog."

Brennus grinned as if he'd been handed a compliment. He nodded to the soldier at his right elbow. The man stepped forward and removed Lucius's war belt, then began unfastening his armor.

Lucius bucked and twisted to no avail against the centurions who restrained him. Brennus gave a short laugh. Then, as if disenchanted with the show, he strolled to the hatch in the tower and shouted down to the guard, instructing the man to open the gates.

The creak of the hinges sounded, prompting a shout from the barbarians. Roman curses flew, followed by the clang of swords. Apparently not all the soldiers of Vindolanda had turned traitor.

Yet it seemed none of those loyal to Rome had made it

271

to the top of the wall. Rough hands, too many to fight, stripped the last of Lucius's armor from his body, leaving him clad only in his tunic. The archers, giving up their pretense of defense, crowded the narrow walkway, jostling for a view of Lucius's humiliation.

Lucius was thrown to the boards. He landed on his back, each arm and leg secured by the weight of a man sworn to obey his command. How had he missed the signs that they were not the loyal soldiers they'd seemed to be? They were Celts themselves, of Gaulish ancestry. Brennus wore the torc. Lucius had wondered at that, but hadn't bothered to reflect on its significance.

Why? Because his attention had been consumed by a wretched ghost and a woman whose beauty was surpassed only by her deceit. He would pay for his weakness with his life, for he didn't doubt that these faithless soldiers of Rome would tear him apart.

He braced for the assault. It didn't come. Instead, the crowd parted. Brennus strolled through them, fingers stroking the wolf's-head hilt of Lucius's sword.

"The mighty warrior approaches," Lucius spit out. "Tales of his prowess abound."

Brennus flushed red. "I hold your life in my hands, Aquila."

"Then kill me and be done with it."

Brennus's fingers tightened on Lucius's sword, then relaxed. "I think not, my dear commander. Much as it would give me pleasure to disembowel a Roman senator's son, I regret to inform you I promised that joy to another." He walked between Lucius's spread legs and looked down, his lips curved in a cruel smile. "However, I am loath to disappoint you entirely." He flicked his gaze to the soldiers restraining Lucius's arms. An instant later Lucius found himself on his feet, arms spread taut.

He gritted his teeth. "I'll kill you for this, Brennus." The threat sounded hollow even to his own ears.

Brennus massaged his knuckles. "Ah, Aquila, the first debt is mine. And I always repay my obligations."

The traitor's hard fist collided with Lucius's jaw, whipping his head to the side. Pain exploded in his skull. The second punch landed in his gut, bending him double. The third assault cracked a rib.

Eventually, Lucius lost count of the blows.

The wind died at midday, but it was near sunset before Rhiannon rode to Vindolanda.

She'd passed the long hours of the battle sequestered in Madog's hut with Owein for her guard. He sat by the door, not meeting her gaze, his shoulders rigid and his hand on the hilt of Madog's sword. He didn't answer when she tried to speak to him. If the lad she'd raised lived within him, he was well hidden.

Madog had stayed in the stone circle to pray. Her last glimpse of Owein's mentor showed the Druid standing between the smoldering fires, hands clasped about his staff, the skull of Lucius's brother swaying in the dying light. The shredded whisper of Aulus's soul called to her: *Tell him.* If only she had listened.

Edmyg came at midday. He stooped before the door, ignoring Owein, and barked an order at Rhiannon to rise. He'd brought Derwa, saddled and decked with flowers. He lifted her onto the pony's back but didn't relinquish the lead, even after he had swung onto his own mount. They set out on the trail, Owein following.

The walls of Vindolanda loomed high against a blazing sunset. The gates were flung wide, but the siege had not been bloodless. A pile of headless corpses lay outside the eastern gate. Their severed heads were mounted on spikes flanking the gates. Crows already picked at the eyes of one unfortunate man. Rhiannon's stomach lurched when she recognized Vetus. She quickly scanned the others but found no sign of Lucius, nor of Marcus or Demetrius.

They traversed the main avenue past the charred ruin of the fort hospital. Apparently, fear of illness had caused the Celts to torch the building. Warriors, many staggering with drink, cheered Edmyg and Rhiannon's progress and crowded behind as they passed. Edmyg steered Derwa into the gates of the fort headquarters and into the barren yard. Rhiannon felt Owein's presence at her back, but it brought no comfort.

Men filled the space. Some had scaled the columns supporting the roof of the perimeter walkway to perch on the eaves. A lone form sat higher, near the peak of the roof.

The throng on the ground parted before them, opening a path to the center of the yard where a thick stake of newly cut wood had been sunk. A man hung bound at its base.

Lucius.

His head was bowed and his hands stretched overhead, tied with rough rope to an iron spike hammered into the wood. His legs were spread and tied at the ankles to shorter stakes set several paces to the fore. The position didn't allow him to lie flat or to sit upright. He'd been beaten and stripped of all but his ragged tunic. Flies were already buzzing around the worst of his wounds. His chest heaved with the exertion of drawing air into his lungs.

He lived yet. But for how long? If Rhiannon could somehow contrive to free him, were his injuries too great to allow his escape?

Cormac and Brennus stood nearby, watching Rhiannon's advance. Her gaze tangled briefly with the dwarf's. He gave her a smug salute. His glance toward Lucius told her he'd noticed her horror before she'd carefully wiped it from her face.

Edmyg maneuvered their mounts to within a few paces of Lucius and addressed the crowd. "I give you Rhiannon, queen of the Brigantes!"

A cheer went up, but Rhiannon barely heard it. At the

sound of her name, Lucius's head had come up. He stared at her with shock, then hatred.

"You," he croaked. "You are the barbarian queen of whom my brother wrote?" He began to laugh.

Edmyg dismounted and planted his boot in the prisoner's side with a savage jab. Lucius's mad cackle ended in a grunt.

"Nay—don't hurt him further!" Rhiannon cried.

Cormac grinned. "We've barely scratched him, lass. The quartermaster sorely wanted to break his legs, but the dog will need his limbs whole to dance in Madog's circle."

Rhiannon spun on Owein. "Nay. Not that."

" 'Twill be done at dawn," her brother replied. "I will wield the sword."

Rhiannon swayed on Derwa's back and would have fallen if Edmyg hadn't caught her.

He lifted her from the pony and set her on her feet. "How pale ye are. Surely the Roman's cock wasna so skillful that ye mourn its loss?"

Rhiannon pulled from his grasp. "Release him, Edmyg. His death will bring the wrath of Rome down on our heads."

"I think not, *wife*." His lips parted in a snarl. "Did spreading your legs for him give ye so much pleasure? Perhaps I should let ye keep him as a slave, as he kept ye. I would enjoy watching you suck the marrow from his bone, I am thinking."

"Ye are a disgusting swine. Remember ye are naught but a sword in my service."

Edmyg caught her chin in his hand. "Dinna speak to me like that again, woman. I am yer king."

"Nay. I have renounced ye."

The back of Edmyg's hand struck Rhiannon's face. Rhiannon cried out in shame and rage. How dare he strike her? To her surprise, Brennus was the first to leap to her aid, lunging at Edmyg with a fierce snarl. The two warriors fell in the dirt, grappling.

Lucius groaned. Rhiannon dropped to her knees and stretched out her hand, her fingers hovering over his bruised cheek. His eyes opened, took in the sight of her, and closed again.

"Whore," he said.

Rhiannon had no answer. A fly landed on his sweat-soaked forehead. When she went to brush it away, a hand caught her wrist and hauled her to her feet.

She looked up into Owein's hard eyes. "Dinna shame yerself by touching him," he said.

"Ye don't understand."

"I understand well enough, sister. Dinna let the blood of Cartimandua show. Our people deserve better." His gaze flicked past her shoulder and turned grim. " 'Twould seem Edmyg's conceit has flung him into a boiling cauldron."

She turned. The scrapping warriors had gained their feet and were circling each other warily, swords drawn. Brennus, Rhiannon realized with a start, wielded a weapon with a hilt and crosspiece fashioned in the shape of a wolf's head—Lucius's own blade.

"The woman goes with me," Brennus said.

"Nay. She is mine."

Cormac sidled up to Rhiannon. "See what comes next." His low voice barely contained his glee.

"I delivered the garrison," Brennus said. "I was promised a throne in return."

"I promised ye nothing," Edmyg replied. "Ye'll nay be taking Rhiannon save over my dead body."

"So be it." Brennus lunged and his sword clashed with Edmyg's once, twice.

Cormac chortled. "The true battle begins. The Gaul will take it."

"Edmyg is your brother," Rhiannon said, aghast. Around her, wagers flew as the men, Brigantes and Gauls alike, moved back to make room for the dueling warriors.

"Aye, but my bet is on Brennus, his mail shirt, and his Roman sword. Edmyg has naught but pride. I've said oft enough 'twould be his downfall. I'm counting on it now."

" 'Twas you who promised Brennus the throne!"

"Aye, and the queen as well. 'Twas the bait the wolf couldna refuse. I am no fool, Rhiannon, and 'tis a wise man who seeks the sturdiest shelter in which to pass the storm."

"A storm of your own making," Rhiannon countered. "How could ye betray your own brother?"

"I was the elder brother. By rights, ye should have been mine first, along with the throne. And ye would have been if not for my stunted limbs." He paused, watching as Edmyg parried an attack from Brennus. " 'Tis a natural alliance between the Gauls and our people. We are one blood, and the Brigantes have fought alone for years with little to show for it. This fort is a boon without price and the garrison soldiers nearly double our strength. With their aid, we can hold our land."

"A fool ye be if ye think that, Cormac. The Romans will never retreat. Ye'll be fighting all your life."

"I'll gladly do that, lass, rather than bow to the likes of him." He spat at Lucius.

Owein tugged at her arm. "Rhiannon, get back. I'll nay have your blood spilled." He urged her out of the path of the combatants. She let him pull her to safety, watching in horror as Edmyg and Brennus fought for the right to her body and through it the throne. The warriors circled the post where Lucius hung. Dear Briga! If a sword went astray, Lucius could do naught but watch it come.

Brennus attacked with a wide slice inward. Edmyg caught the blade with the edge of his sword and threw it over. The opponents clashed with violent fury, grunting curses, blades clanging. Brennus gave a thrust, missing Edmyg by a mere breath. Edmyg lost his balance and fell on Lucius's outstretched leg. Rhiannon lurched forward, but Owein held her fast. Lucius's face turned gray behind his bruises as his jaw clenched against a cry.

Edmyg scrambled to his feet, narrowly avoiding a killing

blow. Brennus's blade thudded into the earth near Lucius's hip. Rhiannon slumped against Owein, shaken.

The deadly battle continued. Edmyg managed to nick the Gaul's arm with a swipe that seemed more luck than skill. Brennus swore an oath and doubled his efforts, slashing with deadly urgency, forcing Edmyg back. When Edmyg lifted his arm to make his next thrust, his enemy's blade plunged into his gut.

Rhiannon cried out. Edmyg looked down at the hilt protruding from his stomach with an expression of disbelief. Brennus twisted his sword once and withdrew. A shout rose from the crowd. Edmyg staggered and fell, his hands clutching the wound until his strength deserted him. A tremor shook his body and then he lay still, staring at the sky.

" 'Tis done, then." Cormac sounded suddenly weary.

Brennus thrust his bloody sword into its sheath. When his head rose, his gaze fixed on Rhiannon.

"Nay," she whispered.

"Who will challenge my right to be called king?" Brennus shouted.

Bryan stepped forward from a knot of Edmyg's best warriors and for one wild moment, Rhiannon thought her cousin would challenge Brennus. Her hope was dashed when the warrior placed his fist over his heart.

"I promise you my allegiance, king."

One by one the other clan chieftains came forward and pledged their fealty. Rhiannon gripped Owein's arm. "I canna go with him."

"Ye must. The hand of Kernunnos directed this contest. Refuse the god's will, and we will all fall." He gave a grim smile. "The Gaul canna be worse than Edmyg."

"I would rather die than bed him."

Owein opened his mouth to answer, then fell silent upon Brennus's approach.

The Gaul dropped on one knee before Rhiannon. "My queen. I offer you the protection of my body and my sword." He bowed his head, but the steely glint in his eye told Rhiannon his words were spoken solely to appease her kinsmen.

She looked away. It was a mistake, for she found Lucius's dark eyes upon her, filled with loathing. She held his gaze until tears blurred his image.

Brennus rose and caught her upper arm. "Come." He guided her toward the portal leading to the street. His grip was like iron, but even if she could wrench out of his grasp, where would she run? Her kinsmen had accepted this man as their king. Her only hope to avoid her fate was to contrive Lucius's escape and flee south with him.

She bit back a hysterical laugh. Even if she somehow managed to free Lucius, she could hardly expect he would risk his life to save hers. Not after she'd kept the truth of his brother's fate from him. Most likely he would tie her to a tree and leave her for the carrion eaters.

Brennus propelled her through the door of the fort commander's residence and into a small room off the foyer. How could she delay his advances? When the door thudded shut, she stiffened her spine and summoned her most regal tone.

"Unhand me."

To her surprise, Brennus complied.

"I'm in sore need of rest," she said, picking her words carefully. "You may leave me."

Brennus's mouth curved. "I've no complaint if ye take to your bed. But if ye think to delay my presence there, you're wasting precious time. I'm most eager to be wiping the memory of Aquila's cock from your body."

Chapter Twenty-two

"Did . . . did he hurt you?"

The painful throb in Owein's head quickened as he waited for Rhiannon's reply. He'd gained entrance to the chamber scant moments after Brennus's departure by threatening the Gaulish guard with a Druid curse. The man had not been able to unbolt the door fast enough.

"Nay," Rhiannon said at last. "He was called away as soon as he brought me here." She paced the room. It was crowded with dark shadows, the only illumination a shaft of dim light from the single high window. "When he returns, I'll tell him the moon flux is upon me."

"That lie willna work for long."

"I know it, brother."

He took a step toward her, then halted. "Can ye not at least give Brennus a chance? The clans need his men."

She gave a bitter laugh. "I'm ever the whore chasing power. Truly, Owein, I grow weary of it."

He went to her then, and put his arms around her. "Ye are no whore. Ye are a treasure beyond price. A queen."

"A queen, locked away? I would sooner be a hag, and free of this place."

"Our people need ye."

She threw off his embrace. "Need me? For what? The men follow their war leaders. Madog prays only to Kernunnos—he's forsaken Briga. Without the goddess to balance the god, our people will stumble and fall." She turned to him with pleading eyes. "Ye must not kill him, Owein."

Pain pounded his temple. "The Roman." The word left a foul taste in his mouth, as if he'd chewed on dung.

"Ye've taken the fort. Let him go."

"How can ye plead for your defiler, Rhiannon?"

"Lucius is no defiler."

"I saw ye crying after he took ye."

" 'Twas not joining with Lucius that made me cry. I went to his bed willingly. I love him."

His gut heaved. "I canna believe that! He took ye captive. He used ye."

"He treated me like a queen. I know ye dinna understand. How can ye when I canna understand it myself?" Her voice broke. "I canna bear Lucius's death, Owein. Free him for my sake. Let him go south to his own people. The clan has no need of his life. Not truly."

Owein gritted his teeth. " 'Tis not possible."

"That is a lie."

A spike of agony pierced his skull and the vision burst on him, so vivid he could have reached out and touched it. The ancient stones. Blood. His hand on the Druid sword.

His fingers tore at his scalp, nails rending the flesh. When the visions came upon him, he wanted nothing so much as to rip them from his mind.

He gasped for breath until the scene faded. When it did, he felt Rhiannon's hands cradling his face.

"Owein? Has it passed?"

He steadied himself with one hand on her shoulder while he blinked to clear his tears. "You bid me free the Roman. Even were I to attempt it, I wouldn't succeed. I *See* him, Rhiannon. His blood is on the stones. My hand is on the killing sword. 'Twill happen. Kernunnos has willed it."

Her hands dropped from his face. "When will ye take him to Madog?"

"In the hour before dawn," he replied.

"Father? Are you alive?"

The flood of relief that Marcus's trembling whisper brought to Lucius was so keen he was unable to answer for several seconds. His son had not been taken by the enemy. Thank the gods.

Marcus stifled a sob and crept closer. His shaking hand touched Lucius's chest. "Please be alive."

"Marcus." Lucius slitted his eyes and scanned the headquarters yard as best he could from his awkward position. The crowd had cleared at dusk. The dwarf who had posed as a slave in Lucius's house had taken the body of the Celt who had fought Brennus. The dwarf had departed, but not before he'd set a pair of Gauls as guard. Luckily the brutes had been far more interested in drinking themselves into oblivion than tending their charge. They lay snoring in the dirt.

"Where is Demetrius?" Lucius asked.

"Dead."

He fought a surge of grief. "Are you sure?"

Marcus didn't answer. Instead he produced a dagger and sawed at the rope binding Lucius's left leg. His hand was remarkably steady.

"Where did you get the blade?"

"Stole it from a drunk."

Lucius's admiration of his son rose several notches. The boy was more levelheaded than he'd given him credit for. "How did Demetrius die?" he asked softly.

Marcus's hand stilled, then began sawing again with renewed energy. "The soldiers broke down the door. Candidus and some of the other slaves fought them and were killed. The rest of the Celts joined the traitors." The boy's tone was cool, as if he recited a lesson.

Lucius kept silent. He sensed his son was close to breaking. Any sympathy he showed would nudge him over the edge.

Marcus moved to Lucius's right ankle. "Magister Demetrius and I were above stairs when the traitors entered the courtyard. He bade me get up on the roof. He met the soldiers as they gained the upper passage. They ran him through but never saw me."

Lucius flexed his legs, testing them with his full weight as Marcus stretched to cut the bonds holding his hands. Tears stung his eyes at the thought of his old teacher and friend protecting Marcus with his life. "How did you get into the headquarters?"

"I climbed back onto the roof. I saw the bastards bring you from the western gate tower. I climbed to the roof of the bathing room and jumped across the alley to the headquarters roof. I had to wait for the yard to clear before I could free you. I was so afraid that . . ." He swallowed and cut through the last of the rope. "The guards only just fell asleep," he said as if anticipating a reprimand.

Lucius rubbed the feeling back into his arms. "You're a brave one, Marcus. I'm proud to call you my son." He took the stolen dagger and crept toward the sleeping traitors who had been his guards. With ruthless efficiency, he slit the throats of the two men. He relieved the first of his war belt, sword, mail shirt, and helmet.

He strung the dead soldier up on the post as best he could with the cut ropes. With luck, he and Marcus would be long gone before the deception was noted. He stripped the second man's gear for Marcus, rejecting the sword as too heavy. The boy was tall for his age. With Fortuna's favor, he would pass without question.

He donned the first guard's mail and tested his sword. It was not as finely wrought as Lucius's own, but it would do. "Stay close," he told Marcus. "But don't crouch. Try to walk with a swagger."

He picked his way around the unconscious men sprawled in the yard, pausing at the gate to peer into the street. To the left, a rowdy cluster of soldiers played at dice near the west gate. "This way," he whispered to Marcus, moving to his right.

"But Rhiannon . . ."

Lucius's jaw clenched. "What of her?"

"I saw the quartermaster take her to the residence. We have to get her out."

"We don't. She knew of the attack. Helped plan it, most likely. She's with Brennus of her own accord."

"She's not! He nearly had to drag her to the door. He'll hurt her."

Lucius's resolve wavered, then hardened anew. Rhiannon was not some barbarian peasant girl in need of rescue. By Pollux, she was the hidden queen Aulus had written of in his history. She had fled his protection, then rallied her people to the sword. It was clear where her loyalties lay.

"We'll not endanger our escape for a barbarian woman," he told Marcus. "She's chosen her path."

"But Father, we must rescue her! She's my friend."

"No. It's not our concern."

A drunken soldier chose that moment to stumble into the road from the alley between the headquarters and the residence. He shoved past Lucius, barely sparing him a glance as he lifted his tunic and relieved himself against the wall. His need taken care of, he stumbled toward the group at the west gate.

Lucius shoved Marcus in the opposite direction. "Go."

The boy dug in his heels. "No."

"Marcus . . ."

"She doesn't want him! She wants you. You have to get her out." He darted toward the residence door. Lucius cursed and ran after him, setting his jaw against the pain that shouted from his ribs.

He caught Marcus by the scruff of the neck. "We are not going in there."

"We have to! You told me yourself that a Roman fights with honor. What honor is there in crawling out of the fort gates and leaving a helpless woman behind?"

Lucius snorted. "Rhiannon is hardly helpless. She—"

A woman's angry voice cut into the night from the high window directly above Lucius's head.

Rhiannon.

Gaius Brennus answered with a snarl. "Ye'll not deny me, woman. Remove your tunic."

Lucius's fury exploded. He looked down at Marcus. The boy's eyes had gone wide with fear. "All right," he said. "We'll save her. Keep your dagger close and follow me."

"Ye'll not deny me, woman."

Brennus had returned just as Owein was leaving. Rhiannon cursed her luck soundly. Somehow she had to get out and free Lucius. She had little time to waste before her brother located a pony on which to carry his captive to the Druid circle.

"Remove your tunic."

"I told ye, I canna lie with ye this night. 'Twill be several days at least." She dropped her chin a bit, feigning embarrassment. "The moon flux . . ."

Brennus gave her a scowl and half turned away. He unsheathed his dagger and Lucius's sword and flung the weapons onto a long stone table. His war belt clattered to the floor. Rhiannon watched with growing unease as his mail shirt followed it.

He faced her, wearing only a dirty shirt and torn *braccas,* the laces straining with his arousal. "Unclothe yourself."

"Nay," Rhiannon said, fighting the urge to step back. "I would not dishonor ye so."

He laughed. "Your concern is touching but misplaced. I've wanted ye since I saw ye in the fort hospital, and I'll have ye tonight. If your woman's flow is truly on ye, ye may service me with your mouth." His hands curled into fists.

Rhiannon didn't doubt he would use them on her. Her

gaze strayed to his dagger, lying unprotected such a short distance away. She took a step toward it, her hands lifting as she did so to the pin that fastened her cloak. The mantle fell away. Brennus's gaze raked her, leaving her feeling soiled.

She took another step, positioning herself between Brennus and the table as she twisted her fingers into her skirt and pulled the hem up over her knees, then her thighs. Swallowing her revulsion, she swept the fabric over her head.

He was on her in a heartbeat, pressing her bare buttocks against the cold granite. His arousal prodded her legs. Her fingers groped the table behind her and closed on the hilt of the dagger. When Brennus's hands moved to untie the laces on his *braccas,* she struck.

Her blade slashed across his throat, loosing a river of blood. Brennus stared at her with disbelieving eyes as his knees crumpled. Rhiannon kicked free of him and scrambled out of the path of his body. Lurching for the corner of the room, she doubled over and retched. Brennus's soul burst from his flesh in waves of pulsing rage.

When it was over, Rhiannon sprawled on the floor, gasping. A rivulet of blood made its way toward her across the tiles. She heaved herself to her feet, snatched up her tunic, and dressed swiftly. Dagger raised, she crept toward the door, praying Brennus had dismissed the guard before entering.

Her prayer went unanswered. The door opened, revealing two men in Gaulish helmets and mail. She made a desperate stab at the closer one's neck only to have her wrist caught in his unrelenting grip.

"Rhiannon. Be still. It's Lucius."

"Lucius?" She blinked up at him. "But . . . I was coming to save you!"

Lucius's gaze swept past her, taking in Brennus and the pool of blood in which he lay. "I thought to rescue you," he said. His mouth lifted, first one side, then the other, in a genuine smile. "I might have known you would need no help."

Chapter Twenty-three

Lucius watched Rhiannon greet Marcus with a glad cry. "You're safe! Thank Briga." She enfolded him in a fierce embrace.

"But Magister Demetrius . . ." He buried his face in her tunic.

Rhiannon's questioning gaze met Lucius's eyes. "Dead," he said. "But we have precious little time to mourn him. We must flee before my absence from the yard is noted."

They left the house by the front entrance, avoiding the boisterous soldiers in the courtyard. Though dawn was a few hours off, some of the men sprawled in the avenue connecting the east and west gates were already starting to stir. Since the barracks flanked the north gate, that route promised to be even more trafficked.

Lucius led them down a side alley toward the south gate, sword at the ready. His fingers gripped the wolf's head. He'd counted Aulus's gift as lost until Rhiannon had lifted it from the Egyptian table in the receiving room. She'd taken Brennus's dagger for herself, belting it in a sheath at her waist.

Lucius hadn't seen Aulus since before the Celt attack began and now, with Rhiannon nearby, he would not appear. It might be that his brother had found rest at last, but Lucius doubted it. A dread intuition whispered that when Aulus materialized again, he would be in worse agony than before.

He led his small band at a snail's pace between the granaries, only in part because of a need to avoid discovery. The bruises from Brennus's fists ached and one rib was certainly cracked. Vivid agony tore through his side with every step he took.

Marcus and Rhiannon trod softly at his back. Lucius knew that his son's store of strength, sapped by his illness and his flight over the rooftops, was nearly depleted. The boy leaned heavily on Rhiannon, but when he ventured a whisper, it was not fatigue, danger, or even Demetrius's death of which he spoke. His main concern was that Hercules had been lost. Lucius suspected the boy's numbed and grieving mind had seized upon this topic to avoid replaying the horror of the last few hours.

"He will find you," Rhiannon soothed. "He's a clever beast."

If Lucius entertained some doubts on that score, he kept them to himself. No use distressing the boy further, when they all might be dead by morning, like the two Gauls sprawled face down in the alley. The unfortunate pair had been stripped of their armor, leaving them with only torn shirts and *braccas* to cover their tangled limbs. Lucius kicked them aside to unblock the path, then paused to let the stabbing pain in his side pass.

Rhiannon shot him a glance, and though the night was dark, he did not miss the questions in her eyes. She wondered about the extent of his injuries. He steeled himself against her concern. She'd told him too many lies and owed him too many answers.

He paused at the corner of the fort workshop. The wide expanse of open air between it and the perimeter wall was useful for preventing flaming enemy arrows from firing the fort buildings, but proved a daunting barrier to a wounded man, a woman, and a boy who wished to reach the gate unnoticed. The tall doors between the south towers were ajar, affording a tantalizing glimpse of the fort village beyond. A knot of dicing soldiers hunkered nearby.

"A dog to my Venus," one of them announced in a self-satisfied tone. "The prize is mine." His opponents grumbled as they shoved their coin in his direction. Less than ten paces from the gamblers, a man was on the ground, pumping his seed into a plump woman. As Lucius watched, the soldier grunted and rolled to the side. The woman then lifted her arms to a second man. The newcomer threw down a coin and took his comrade's place between her thighs.

Marcus tugged Lucius's tunic. "How will we get past?"

"Can you walk unaided? Just until we pass the gate?"

He nodded.

Lucius cast a glance over Rhiannon. Most of the men had seen her enter the fort with the rutting bastard who had been her husband. She would be recognized when they tried to pass the gate. After a moment's thought, he paced back to the dead men and cut their shirts from their bodies.

He returned to his companions. "When the show starts, slip out the gate behind us," he told Marcus.

Rhiannon's eyes showed her confusion. "Show?"

Lucius plucked Brennus's dagger from her hand and shoved it back into the sheath at her waist. Then he threw one stolen shirt over Rhiannon's head and the other around her torso. "I hope this is disguise enough," he muttered. Gritting his teeth against the pain, he picked her up and slung her over his shoulder, one palm firmly fixed on her buttocks.

She went deathly still, whether from shock or desire he couldn't tell.

"Struggle," he told her.

The dead man's shirt muffled her voice. "Nay. You're hurt."

"We'll all be dead soon enough if you don't start screaming."

She must have guessed his plan then, because she began to twist in his arms and shriek loudly enough to wake the dead in the fort cemetery. He made a motion to Marcus and staggered toward the gate.

The gamblers looked up as he neared. "Got a reluctant one there," one of them commented.

"Aye," Lucius replied in Gaulish. "To my thinking, they're the best kind." He shut his mouth, hoping to the gods he wouldn't be forced to continue the banter. Neither his Gaulish vocabulary nor his accent would suffer much more conversation. He slapped Rhiannon's rump hard enough to make his hand sting.

"Let me go, ye brute!" Her fists pummeled his back in what Lucius suspected was genuine outrage.

"Certainly, love." He gained the gate and heaved her upright, pressing her against the wall and pinning her there with his lower body. He let one hand roam her breasts while the other lifted the hem of her tunic. Her struggles made his cock go hard. The gambling soldiers stopped their game to watch.

His lips took Rhiannon's in a savage kiss. She responded with brutal ardor, thrusting her tongue into his mouth, fingers clawing his neck. If her passion was solely for the benefit of their audience, she belonged on a theater stage.

Out of the corner of his eye, he saw Marcus slip through the gate. Abruptly Lucius released Rhiannon. Grabbing her hand, he hauled her past the tower and into the village.

Gauls and Celts crowded the center lane of the tiny settlement. Men sprawled in the road; sounds of coupling came from the huts. Afraid one of Rhiannon's kinsmen would recognize her, Lucius tugged her through the alley between two dwellings and into the barley fields beyond.

Marcus collapsed between the rows. Rhiannon flung off the soiled shirts and dropped to her knees at his side.

"I'll be all right," the boy panted. "I just need to catch my breath."

"You need herbs and a sennight's rest," Rhiannon replied.

Lucius crouched beside her. "You needn't stay. I can care for my son."

Her eyes gleamed gold in the moonlight. "Are you so eager to be rid of me, Lucius?"

Marcus grabbed her hand. "No! You must stay."

Lucius pinched the bridge of his nose. "Marcus . . ."

Gently, Rhiannon disentangled herself from the boy's embrace and rose.

"Marcus and I will travel south," Lucius said. "To Eburacum. I must inform the commander there of the mutiny." No doubt Brennus had not sent Lucius's request for reinforcements.

"Aulus's prison lies in the opposite direction," Rhiannon replied. Hugging her arms about her, she looked toward the northern hills.

He stilled. "What do you mean?"

She paused as if gathering courage. "Your brother was given to my clan as a prize."

"By Brennus."

"Yes, but at the time I didn't know who the prisoner's betrayer might have been. Aulus died on the first night of the winter moon within a circle of stones set by the Old Ones." She drew a breath. "He was slaughtered to gain the favor of Kernunnos, the Horned God."

If her words had been physical blows, they could not have fallen on Lucius more brutally. "He was sacrificed? Like a calf or a pig?" He felt ill.

"Yes," Rhiannon said. "A Druid master guides my clan. He proclaimed the blood of our enemy, offered to Kernunnos, would make our warriors invincible."

"Go on."

"Aulus died by Madog's hand. It was . . . it was not a quick death. Your brother grasped at my skirt as he took his last breath. I felt his soul fly through mine as it left his body. I've felt his touch ever since. I believe that is why he vanishes when I'm near."

Bile rose in his throat. "Then you are a witch."

"If a witch is one who merges her soul with forces beyond the physical, then yes, I am one. I often feel the passing of souls, especially of those who die in pain. But I've felt no spirit touch me as strongly as your brother's did."

"I've not seen Aulus since the attack on the fort began. Even before, he lay still as though sleeping."

"Madog called his spirit to the Druid circle before the attack to aid in your destruction."

"The youth with whom you spoke in the headquarters yard. He is the one you saved from my sword, is he not?"

"Owein. My brother. I raised him after our mother died birthing him. Madog has taught him the old ways, but I fear Owein has stumbled onto powers too strong for his flesh to contain. He suffers greatly. Madog instructed Owein to bring you to the circle at dawn, that you might meet the same fate as your brother."

"They will be sorely disappointed. I plan to be miles to the south by dawn."

"No," Rhiannon said, her tone suddenly intense. "You must go north. Aulus's skull is mounted atop Madog's staff. Until it is buried, your brother will be his slave."

Chapter Twenty-four

"I want to go with you," Marcus said.

"You'll stay here with the ponies," his father replied. "Jupiter knows I went to great trouble to steal the pair of them. I'll not have them wandering off or being taken." True enough, but Rhiannon knew Lucius was exaggerating the point as an excuse to keep his son away from the Druid circle.

"Tending the ponies is an important job," she added, trying to keep the worry out of her voice. She must not have been successful, for Marcus blinked up at her, his dark eyes brimming with fear. "What if you don't come back?"

Lucius dropped to one knee before his son and set his hands on the lad's shoulders. "I'll not lie to you, Marcus. There is a small chance I won't come back. If that happens, take the ponies and make your way south. Once you reach Roman lands, our family name will be enough to earn you passage to Rome. Your mother's uncle will welcome you."

Marcus dropped his head and nodded, tears leaking from his closed eyes.

Rhiannon gave him a fierce hug. "Stay hidden and pray."

She led the way down the steep path to the stones. They'd traveled quickly from the fort, fearful of pursuit. Surely Owein had discovered Lucius's escape by now. Had he raised an alarm? Would he guess in which direction Lucius traveled? He had little reason to expect Lucius would seek the Druid circle.

Her foreboding increased as she neared the stones. By revealing the whole truth to Lucius, she'd betrayed her clan's trust. The path she trod would end badly, no matter what came to pass within the circle. No peaceful outcome was possible—either Lucius or Madog would die. Her lover or her teacher. More blood to stain her hands.

The sky lightened, foretelling a clear dawn. Rhiannon followed a less-used trail to the stones, though she suspected such stealth would not count for much against Madog's Druid powers. He would know they were coming well before they showed themselves.

"You must keep your wits about you when you face Madog." She forced the words past her guilt.

"You told me he's an old man."

"His age is of little importance. Madog is a Druid master. He has power beyond imagining."

"He'll need every drop of it and then some to stop me."

The trail leveled out at the edge of the oak grove. Rhiannon held up one hand. "We're near." She crept forward, parting the underbrush as she went. When she was within sight of the circle, she paused. She felt Lucius's heat as he drew close behind her. She heard his sharp intake of breath as he took in the scene before them.

Madog stood in the center of the circle, his face turned away. He held his staff and its grisly trophy high. A fire burned beside him, casting flickering illumination on his long gray braids and pale cloak. A thin chant like the whistle of storm winds spiraled around him. Smoke from the fire curled into the night air, bringing a sickly sweet scent to Rhiannon's nostrils.

Lucius drew his sword from its sheath by silent degrees. "The old man will be dead before he knows he's been struck."

"Do not be so foolish as to think that he's unaware of our presence," Rhiannon whispered.

As if in response, Madog turned toward them and bowed low, tipping Aulus's head in Lucius's direction. Lucius pushed Rhiannon into the shelter of the brush. "Stay hidden." He stepped forward and passed between the stones, sword raised.

Rhiannon rose and followed. She'd set her fate when she cast her lot with Lucius. She would not cower now while he fought for his brother's soul.

"It will be my greatest pleasure to kill you," Lucius told Madog.

Madog looked at Rhiannon and laughed. "Ye have brought him to me at last, as Owein's Sight foretold. 'Tis not in the way Cormac planned, but 'twill serve."

He turned to Lucius and spoke in the Roman tongue. "She was sent to seduce you—to turn your attention from fort business so that Brennus might recruit the soldiers to our cause. She did a fine job of it, did she not? Played the innocent, I'm told, and led you to believe you were the one in pursuit."

Lucius's startled gaze met Rhiannon's. "You were ordered to bed me?"

"Yes," she said, her heart sinking. "But—"

Madog cut her off with a single syllable, spoken in the language of the Old Ones. He lifted his hand. Smoke rose and curled about him like serpent spirits. It snaked toward Lucius with unerring precision.

Lucius waved the smoldering veil away. "Your nonsense words will not stand against my blade. You will die, Druid, for what you have done to my brother."

"No. Your soul will join his in bondage. Two Romans of one blood to slave for the Brigantes."

Lucius raised his sword. Acrid smoke rose in a great wave, obscuring Madog's form. Rhiannon blinked as the curtain took on the color of the fire. When it receded, she felt Lucius's shock even before her mind registered what—who—stood before him.

Aulus. His face was bruised and bloody as it had been on the day of his death. He stood dressed in the armor of a Legionary soldier, crested helmet upon his head, curved shield in his hand, sword drawn and ready. If Rhiannon had not known he was a spirit, she would have sworn an oath that he was a living man.

Lucius went deathly still.

Madog spoke. "This slave guards my body. You must kill him if you wish to reach my side." He pounded his staff in the dirt and Aulus's blade began to glow. "I assure you, Roman, that your brother will suffer every bite of your blade as keenly as if he were alive."

"Nay," Rhiannon said, stepping to Lucius's side.

"Ye see him at last, don't ye, lass?"

Rhiannon started. " 'Twas ye who hid him from me?"

"Aye. To draw this Roman brute to ye." His gaze flicked to Lucius. "Fight him, dog. Fight and die."

The Druid's eyes rolled back in his head, giving him the look of a crazed soul escaped from Hades. His thin lips began to move, sending a shrill song into the circle. It mingled with the fading curls of smoke, strengthening, urging. Aulus lifted his blade and advanced on Lucius.

Lucius took a defensive stance as he watched the ghost's approach. Aulus was now as solid as a living man, yet his steps touched the ground without making a sound. If his ghostly heart beat, it did so in silence. Though he bore the marks of a brutal beating, he moved without regard for his wounds, a grim warrior in his prime. His weapon was a slice of light against the last hour of night.

Aulus lunged, his sword slashing with deadly precision. Lucius parried. No steel clanged, but the force of the ghost's blow jolted Lucius's arm. He gritted his teeth against the pain and blocked the next attack.

His strength was nearly gone. Would he be forced to kill his brother to get at the Druid? Lucius's logical mind argued that Aulus was already dead. But his heart saw the face of the boy who had dogged his every step in years long past, even as he looked into his opponent's grim eyes.

He feinted right, then dodged to the left, hoping to skirt Aulus and rush the Druid. The ghost materialized in his path, sword swinging in a deadly arc. Lucius leaped aside too late. The ghost sword sliced into his sword arm.

It drew blood as easily as any earthly blade.

Lucius ignored the wound and lunged again to the right. His second attempt to circumvent the apparition was no more successful than the first. The Druid song cackled, piercing his concentration.

Rhiannon's voice rang out. "Madog! Stop this, I beg ye." She flung herself at the Druid only to collide with Aulus's shield. She fell, stunned, against one of the hulking stones. She slid to the ground, clutching her elbow.

"Stay back, lass. The Roman must die. He was on the shores of Mona fifty long winters past. He killed my father, raped my mother. He will pay for their blood with his own."

" 'Twas not Lucius who committed those crimes! 'Twas before his birth."

"It matters not. He is a Roman, born to steal the freedom of any he encounters. Did he not enslave you?"

Aulus struck again, forcing Lucius's attention away from Rhiannon and the Druid. He managed to lift his sword high enough to halt a killing blow. Blood slicked his hand, making it difficult to keep his grip on the hilt. His wounded arm burned. His broken rib stabbed like a dagger in his side.

Madog flung his head back and let out the shriek of a

being not born in the land of mortals. The ghost flung himself at Lucius. Rhiannon struggled to rise, but it was as if some unseen hand held her back. Lucius was glad of that at least.

Aulus advanced, unrelenting, fighting with a level of skill he had never achieved during his life. That realization hardened Lucius's resolve against his brother. His opponent was not truly Aulus, no matter how closely the ghost resembled the brother Lucius had loved.

He would strike Madog down by killing his minion. It was the only way Lucius could hope to free his brother's soul.

He angled his blade at the ghost's heart. Aulus's eyes widened—not with anger, Lucius thought, but with relief.

"I'm sorry, brother," he said, and plunged the blade deep.

His sword sliced as if through flesh, but unlike a thrust into a man, Lucius's entire arm passed through the specter. Aulus crumpled to the ground, his mouth open in a noiseless groan.

The momentum of the thrust carried Lucius across the circle. He leapt at Madog, sweeping a stroke upward. The point of his sword plunged into the old man's throat.

Blood pulsed red like the dawn sky, splashing to the dirt, staining it black. Rhiannon gained her feet at last. Her face had gone white. Her arms were wrapped tightly around her body as if she was trying to hold herself erect. She lost the battle, gagging as she fell to her knees.

The Druid's body went slack. His gnarled fingers loosened on his staff. The twisted wood fell, sending Aulus's skull skidding across the ground. Lucius withdrew his blade from the Druid's body.

He stared at his brother's severed head, stomach heaving. He took one step then another, toward the ghastly skull. The tip of his sword sliced a line in the mud as he went.

Blackened, oiled skin—cracked in some places, curled in others—clung to white bone. Matted hair covered the scalp. Loose teeth grinned through eroded lips. Lucius stretched one shaking hand out to touch the only remnant of his brother left to him.

Footsteps thudded through the forest. "Owein! Nay!"

Lucius spun about. Rhiannon's brother was bearing down on him from across the circle, sword raised. The same crazed fury Lucius had seen in Madog's eyes illuminated the youth's face. Lucius scrambled behind one of the stones, using it as a shield while he swiftly put together a plan of attack. The youth was half-mad with fury—he wouldn't stop until one of them lay dead, of that Lucius was certain. Lucius also knew he hadn't the strength for another prolonged battle.

As he readied for a swift, deadly rush, his gaze touched on Rhiannon. Her eyes were huge and vivid with fear. They begged him not to strike a killing blow as clearly as if she'd spoken, and Lucius knew, even before he raised his sword, that he had lost the fight.

Owein and Lucius circled each other within the stones, swords raised. A mere lad against a seasoned warrior, but anger and grief fed Owein's strength, whereas Rhiannon knew that Lucius had to be near the end of his endurance. Owein struck first, swinging Madog's Druid sword in a wide, deadly arc. Lucius met the attack with the clang of steel on iron. Owein thrust again, too quickly, opening his body for a riposte.

Rhiannon's heart leaped into her throat, but Lucius kept his sword close to his body and did not pursue his opponent. Was his wounded arm failing, or did he hold back by design? Rhiannon couldn't tell.

"Owein, drop your sword!" she shouted.

"And let this dog take ye away? I'm thinking I'd rather eat dung." He gave a savage thrust that succeeded in nicking Lucius's mail shirt.

"Killing him will serve naught!"

"It will serve to rid the world of a Roman wolf. It will avenge your shame." He thrust again.

The force of Lucius's parry drove Owein back. The lad stumbled. His knee hit the ground and his sword faltered in his grasp. Lucius rose above him, both hands on the hilt of his sword, poised for a killing blow.

Rhiannon's scream lodged in her throat. In the brief span before the weapon fell, Lucius met her gaze, his expression hard, his dark eyes unreadable.

"Nay," Rhiannon whispered.

Lucius loosed the strike. At the last instant, his arms flexed, twisting his blade so the flat of it struck Owein's back as the lad gained his feet. Owein staggered under the blow, but managed to keep his balance and his grip on his sword.

The close call brought her brother new fury. He turned on Lucius, snarling, his blade flashing with the speed of a serpent. Lucius grunted as the blow struck his sword arm. His grip loosened. His weapon thudded into the dirt. He fell back against one of the stones.

Owein pointed his blade at Lucius's throat.

Rhiannon launched herself at him. "Owein, stop!" She pummeled his back, but he moved not an inch.

"Now, Roman, ye will die. I have Seen it." Owein drew his sword back, muscles tensing.

"Nay!" Rhiannon's fingers found the hilt of Brennus's dagger. She slashed at Owein, desperate to stop his killing thrust.

Her blade bit into his flesh. Owein let out a cry. Madog's Druid sword twisted and fell wide of its mark.

Blood pulsed from a gash on Owein's shoulder, soaking his tunic. It flowed over Rhiannon's hands. She dropped the dagger. A sob tore from her throat as she tried frantically to staunch the crimson flow.

Owein gazed down at her, his fury gone, his expression

bewildered. The tears of a small lad sprung into his eyes as he dropped to his knees. "Ye would kill me for him, little mama?"

Rhiannon's own tears flowed furiously as she tore a strip of linen from her hem and wound it about Owein's shoulder. "Ye idiot! Why could ye not stop!"

Owein's gaze clung to hers. "I wanted to give ye your revenge."

"Revenge? For what? For his respect? For his gentleness? For his love?"

Owein shook his head. "He enslaved ye. Used ye as a whore."

"Nay," Rhiannon said. "He set me free. I love him, Owein."

Lucius had gained his feet. She felt his presence at her back, but she didn't dare turn to meet his gaze. She'd spoken her declaration in the Celt tongue, but some instinct told her that he'd understood her words. Her fingers fumbled on the bandage's final knot.

"Can you walk?" Lucius asked Owein.

Owein scowled up at him. "Yes," he replied in Latin. He rose, shaking off Rhiannon's assistance.

"Is your village near?"

Owein nodded.

"Go home, then," said Lucius. He looked at Rhiannon, his gaze softening. "We cannot tarry here. We must be on our way south before the rest of your kin scent our trail."

Rhiannon's gaze darted first to Lucius's weary expression, then to Owein's anguished one. Her heart tore in two as a battle raged in her soul. Dear Briga. How could she choose between them?

The morning sun broke through the trees. "You mean to leave with—" Owein began, then choked on a sob.

She drew him into her arms, and he clung like a babe. She stroked his red curls as her own tears threatened. "Hush, darling, I'm here. I'll not leave you."

"Rhiannon—" Lucius began.

A rustling and heavy footfalls interrupted his words. A band of four Celt warriors burst into the circle, Rhiannon's cousin Bryan in the lead. Owein pulled himself from Rhiannon's arms and dashed the tears from his eyes with the back of his hand.

Bryan looked first at Madog's crumpled body, then at Lucius. "You will die for this, Roman." He drew his sword.

Lucius raised his weapon in response.

"Nay," said Rhiannon, placing her hand on his arm. "There will be no more fighting." She turned to face Bryan. "Ye will not harm him. I give him safe passage south."

Bryan's sword wavered. He looked at Owein, eyes questioning. "But Madog . . ."

"The hand of Kernunnos was on this contest, Bryan," said Owein. "Madog delved too deeply into the dark powers beyond death and they came to claim him." Owein met Rhiannon's gaze, eyes inscrutable. "We dare not draw the Horned God's wrath on our heads by killing the Roman."

He paced to the center of the circle and raised his uninjured hand. A single Word left his lips, a syllable of power bequeathed by the Old Ones. Bryan and the other warriors drew back as if scorched.

Owein turned his piercing blue gaze on Lucius. "Take the skull and go," he said.

Chapter Twenty-five

Lucius had but one task to complete before returning to Marcus's hiding place. He stabbed at the forest loam with a sharpened stick, gritting his teeth against the pain in his arm and ribs. The pit deepened, and still he dug.

Aulus lounged against a nearby pine, inspecting his fingernails. His bruises were gone and his chin had been shaved clean. He wore a white tunic and toga, but his face had not regained its pallor. It glowed with life and health, and if not for the rotted skull lying in the mud, Lucius might have believed his brother had risen from the grave.

The sun hung on the horizon by the time Lucius judged his labor complete. He stood silent for a long moment as the magick of the wilderness breathed its quiet spells about him. For the first time, the northern forest whispered to his heart, and he listened.

He would not leave Britannia without leaving a piece of his soul with this mysterious land and the woman he left behind.

"Perhaps the memory of her will fade," he told his brother.

Aulus looked up and raised his brows.

"We weren't fated to be together. She won't leave her brother, and I can hardly join her tribe."

Aulus pushed himself away from the tree and paced closer. He laid his hand on Lucius's shoulder, his fingers as warm and solid as a living man's. Though he didn't speak, his opinion was clear.

Lucius sighed. "You always understood more of love than I, but in this you are wrong. I cannot go after her." He covered Aulus's hand with his own. They stood unmoving while the shadows deepened and the sky darkened.

"Come," Lucius said at last. "It is time."

When he lifted his brother's skull, his vision blurred. "I'm sorry I wasn't here to defend you on that dark day."

A sad smile played about Aulus's lips, but he shook his head as if to say Lucius was a fool to question fate. He glided to the edge of the pit and looked down.

Lucius nestled Aulus's skull in the pit, weighting it with stones against the ravages of wild animals. Aulus lifted one hand in a gesture of farewell. When the first handful of dirt spattered the pit, he vanished.

Lucius stood for a long time, staring at nothing.

A tear tracked down his cheek. "Good-bye, brother," he whispered.

Rhiannon slipped out of the dun before sunset and followed the well-worn path to the sheltered glen where Briga's waters sprang from the earth. It was a place so unlike the pool in Lucius's house, but Rhiannon had felt Briga's spirit in the Roman fort as keenly as she knew it now in the forest. The Great Mother's arms embraced the entire world. Rhiannon suspected her peace flowed as easily through the streets of Rome as through the wilderness.

She imagined Lucius, garbed in a white toga, taking his father's seat in the Roman Senate. Would he think of her once he returned to his homeland? If he did, what would he remember—her love or her deceit?

The brush stirred behind her. "Rhiannon?"

Owein stood in the shadow of an elm a few paces away. Though the wound she'd inflicted had not been deep, she still shuddered when she thought of what might have happened if her blade had sliced his neck rather than his shoulder. She'd washed and rebandaged the gash upon returning to the dun this morn. In time, he would bear only a thin scar.

She waved him to her side. He came, hesitating only the briefest of instants before he bent and kissed her cheek. Rhiannon smiled up at him and lifted her hand to ruffle his red curls.

"The Roman and his son have set out on the southern trail," he said.

Rhiannon's heart cracked a little. "Ye've seen them?"

"Aye, though they did not know I watched." A solemn expression lit his blue eyes. "Go with them, little mama."

"What?"

"Go. Your spirit will travel with them in any case."

"But the clan—the tribe—needs a queen. Someone to draw them together."

Owein shook his head. "If the chieftains cannot come together in their own right, what good is a queen to draw them? Thanks to the Romans, the days when a Celt woman ruled alone are past. When the chieftains are through bickering, the strongest among them will claim ye as a prize to brace his position. Are ye willing to accept such a man?"

"Nay."

"Just so. But I am thinking with Edmyg and Kynan dead, no other will be able to hold the clans' allegiance. The Romans will come from the south. I See naught but blood and death. In the end, the conquerors will prevail and the Brigantes will be no more. There is nothing ye can do to stop it. Take what happiness ye can, Rhiannon. If 'tis with a Roman, so be it."

"But what of ye, Owein? I canna leave ye."

He lifted his head and looked through the trees with the eyes of an old man set in his young face. "I'll not be here, little mama."

"Not here? Where will ye go?"

"North to the islands beyond the mountains, where the hand of Rome will never rule. Madog once told me the stones there hold wisdom beyond a man's imagining. He abandoned that knowing in the end, but I would seek it." He sighed, his shoulders slumping. "I have the Sight, but 'tis not enough. I need the knowledge that will show me how best to use the gift Kernunnos has cursed me with."

Rhiannon took his hand. It was the hand of a man, not a lad. " 'Twill be a difficult passage," she said.

"I know it, little mama. But I am thinking 'twill be no harder than the journey ye will make."

Chapter Twenty-six

They were being followed. Lucius knew it with a certainty, but when he cocked his head to listen, he heard nothing. The twilight forest was still.

Too still.

"Draw your mount off the trail," he told Marcus.

Marcus complied, seeking shelter in a thick copse. Lucius reined in beside him and waited, sword drawn. Long seconds passed, then the underbrush rustled and a dark form streaked toward them.

"Hercules!" Marcus flung himself from his pony's back. The dog launched itself at him and the pair crashed to the ground in a tangle of human and canine limbs.

Lucius resheathed his sword. "It would seem we're to be saddled with that creature for eternity," he said with a rueful smile.

Marcus beamed up at him. "See? He *is* a clever dog, just as Rhiannon said."

"Yes," a voice behind him agreed. "I had the right of it. He led me to you."

"Rhiannon!" Marcus darted toward her, stumbling against her snow-white pony's flank and causing the beast to shy.

Rhiannon slid from the animal's back, keeping her reins firmly in hand, laughing as she scolded him. "Marcus! Has your brain slipped out of your head?" Hercules pranced about her legs.

Marcus grinned back at her, unrepentant. "No."

Rhiannon gave her head an amused shake and opened her arms in the universal gesture of motherly love. Marcus went to her, wrapping his arms about her waist fiercely. Lucius dismounted and advanced more slowly, his gut churning like a river after a storm.

Rhiannon met his gaze over Marcus's head. "Lucius?"

"Why are you here?" He had to force the words from his dry throat.

"I've . . ." She eased out of Marcus's embrace. "I thought to come with you. If you'll have me."

"What of your brother?"

Rhiannon gave a sad smile. "It was he who convinced me to follow my heart."

"And your tribe? You would leave your people without their queen?"

She shook her head, sadness showing in her eyes. "I've never truly been a queen. I've been naught but an excuse to continue the war that drains the lifeblood of my people. Whether I go or stay will make little difference. Men will still die, but at least their lives will not be lost in my name."

"Look," Marcus interjected suddenly. Lucius turned to see his son pointing at a place where sunlight splashed through a break in the forest to fall on a spray of red roses. Somehow seeds from a Roman garden had taken root in the wilderness.

Rhiannon touched the petals. " 'Tis a beautiful flower that springs from these thorns."

"It's like the witch who ate a bad boy and birthed a fair one," Marcus said.

"Yes," Rhiannon replied. "Beauty may rise from pain."

"As peace may rise from strife," Lucius said, drawing her into his arms. "For those who are willing to embrace it."

He brushed his cheek against Rhiannon's hair. "It's my dearest wish that you become my wife and Marcus's mother."

Marcus let out a whoop.

Rhiannon smiled and cupped Lucius's cheek. " 'Tis my wish as well. I love you, Lucius. Forgive me for not saying those words sooner."

"It's enough to hear them now," Lucius said, his voice thick with emotion.

"Where will we go? To Rome?"

Lucius looked down the trail. "Truly I do not know. At one time I was sure I'd take up the life my father meant me to have, though I never wanted it. But now . . ." He drew a breath. "Now I've found life is too precious to waste. I intend to live each day as it comes, even if that means I don't know what road I'll take the next morning."

"As long as I am by your side, it matters not what path I travel."

"Then let us journey together," Lucius said.

The
GRAIL KING
JOY
NASH

All who dwell in Avalon possess the powers of the Old Ones. But only some are keepers of the Light. One among them has dared to call upon the Deep Magic, conjuring up a dark storm that bodes ill for the people of Britannia....

The vision came upon him suddenly: a delicate Roman beauty materializing out of the swirling whiteness of the snow. Her appearance near his ruined Celtic village makes no sense, but when the trance leaves him, she remains, demanding that he use his Sight to help her find a stolen grail. The last thing Owein intends is to use his gifts for his enemy, yet something tells him this innocent lass has the power to heal his wounded heart.

STILL LIFE
MELANIE JACKSON

Snippets of a forgotten past are returning to Nyssa Laszlo, along with the power to project her mind. Each projection thrusts her into a glowing still life of color and time, and her every step leads deeper into undiscovered country. Things are changing, and dangerously so. She is learning who she is—whether she wants to or not. She is also learning dark things are on the rise. From the Unseelie faerie court to Abrial, the dauntless dreamwalker who pursues her, the curtain is going up on a stage Nyssa has never seen and a cast she can't imagine—and it's the final act of a play for her heart and soul.

CALL
OF THE
MOON
RONDA THOMPSON

Jason Donavon walks in darkness, seeking release from his curse. It has the power to destroy everything—to take his humanity. In a world where he no longer belongs, he feels eyes watching him. Something even more sinister than himself stalks the night.

The woman who materializes to save him from the forces of darkness holds answers to the questions he's been afraid to ask. She takes him to her world, to the wilds of the North. Yet in a place where nature rules supreme, Jason knows danger awaits. He will be forced to fight his love for a woman forbidden, and discover whether salvation will come from resisting the seductive light of the moon—or in surrendering to it.

LISA CACH

Come to Me

Samira is the lowliest creature of the Night World: a mere succubus, a winged spirit bringing dreams of passion to sleeping men. She knows every wicked wish that lurks in their hearts, and yet she has never felt the touch of a man's loving hand. Nor has she wanted to...until now.

Shattered by war and banished to a crumbling fortress, Nicolae turns to the dark arts. He plans to use Samira as a tool to find a means to oust the invader from his lands and regain all that he's lost. When she arrives on his doorstep in human form, his long-sought vengeance is lost. What happens next will change their worlds forever.